SELECTED BY

RUSKIN BOND

14 THRILLING ADVENTURE STORIES

Published by Westland Books, a division of Nasadiya Technologies Private Limited, in 2026

No. 269/2B, First Floor, 'Irai Arul', Vimalraj Street, Nethaji Nagar, Alapakkam Main Road, Maduravoyal, Chennai 600095

Westland and the Westland logo are the trademarks of Nasadiya Technologies Private Limited, or its affiliates.

ISBN: 9789371978088
10 9 8 7 6 5 4 3 2 1

Printed at Thomson Press India Private Limited

Contents

From the Editor's Desk

When I was a young boy, I was very interested in adventure stories. These stories took me through dense jungles and stormy seas, into forgotten kingdoms and strange, magical lands where I met brave heroes, sly villains, unexpected companions and ordinary people with extraordinary courage inside them. I marvelled at the authors' ability to tell a story and have readers sitting at the edge of their seats hanging onto every word.

Within the pages of the book lay adventure that at times started on a sun-soaked path meandering through the hills, with pine needles crackling under feet and the breeze whispering secrets through the deodars; or with a curious and bright-eyed boy straying just a little beyond the safe and the familiar.

So, when I first began to write, I found myself drawn strongly to adventure. And adventure became an intrinsic part of my stories. Himalayan forests breathed and listened through the tall pines and deodars, small forgotten towns hummed with hidden tales and friendships bloomed like wildflowers after rain.

This lifelong love for adventure is the inspiration behind creating this anthology. I have tried to curate some of the best short adventure stories. They have been chosen for their timeless appeal and their ability to spark the imagination. From O. Henry's tale of redemption in *A Retrieved Reformation* to Rudyard Kipling's brave mongoose in *Rikki-Tikki-Tavi* and the gripping test of survival in Richard Connell's *The Most Dangerous Game*, each story offers a journey into the unknown.

The strength of many of these stories lies in the powerful connections the authors make between different themes, experiences and the spirit of adventure.These stories remind us that the world is vast and full of wonder .

So, as you flip the pages of this collection of adventure stories, I would like you to meet magical objects, strange creatures, acts of bravery and moments of unexpected wonder. Writers like H.G. Wells, R.L. Stevenson, E. Nesbit, Guy de Maupassant and Nathaniel Hawthorne bring their unique voices to this collection, creating worlds that feel as real today as when they were first imagined.

What makes these stories last is their power to awaken something within us—a sense of curiosity, courage and possibility. They remind us that every day is one of possibilities and adventure.

As you read, I invite you to step into these worlds. Walk alongside fearless heroes, face unknown dangers and experience the thrill of the unexpected.

Enjoy the journey. Adventures await you!

Ruskin Bond
Mussoorie, India
February, 2026

1

A Retrieved Reformation

O. Henry

A guard came to the prison shoe-shop, where Jimmy Valentine was assiduously stitching uppers, and escorted him to the front office. There the warden handed Jimmy his pardon, which had been signed that morning by the governor. Jimmy took it in a tired kind of way. He had served nearly ten months of a four year sentence. He had expected to stay only about three months, at the longest. When a man with as many friends on the outside as Jimmy Valentine had is received in the 'stir' it is hardly worth while to cut his hair.

'Now, Valentine,' said the warden, 'you'll go out in the morning. Brace up, and make a man of yourself. You're not a bad fellow at heart. Stop cracking safes, and live straight.'

'Me?' said Jimmy, in surprise. 'Why, I never cracked a safe in my life.'

'Oh, no,' laughed the warden. 'Of course not. Let's see, now. How was it you happened to get sent up on that Springfield job? Was it because you wouldn't prove an alibi for fear of compromising somebody in extremely high-toned society? Or was it simply a case of a mean old jury that had it in for you? It's always one or the other with you innocent victims.'

'Me?' said Jimmy, still blankly virtuous. 'Why, warden, I never was in Springfield in my life!'

'Take him back, Cronin!' said the warden, 'and fix him up with outgoing clothes. Unlock him at seven in the morning, and let him come to the bull-pen. Better think over my advice, Valentine.'

At a quarter past seven on the next morning Jimmy stood in the warden's outer office. He had on a suit of the villainously fitting, ready-made clothes and a pair of the stiff, squeaky shoes that the state furnishes to its discharged compulsory guests.

The clerk handed him a railroad ticket and the five-dollar bill with which the law expected him to rehabilitate himself into good citizenship and prosperity. The warden gave him a cigar, and shook hands. Valentine, 9762, was chronicled on the books 'Pardoned by Governor,' and Mr James Valentine walked out into the sunshine.

Disregarding the song of the birds, the waving green trees and the smell of the flowers, Jimmy headed straight for a restaurant. There he tasted the first sweet joys of liberty in the shape of a broiled chicken and a bottle of white wine—followed by a cigar a grade better than the one the warden had given him. From there he proceeded leisurely to the depot.He tossed a quarter into the hat of a blind man sitting by the door, and boarded his train. Three hours set him down in a little town near the state line. He went to the cafe of one Mike Dolan and shook hands with Mike, who was alone behind the bar.

'Sorry we couldn't make it sooner, Jimmy, me boy,' said Mike. 'But we had that protest from Springfield to buck against, and the governor nearly balked. Feeling all right?'

'Fine,' said Jimmy. 'Got my key?'

He got his key and went upstairs, unlocking the door of a room at the rear. Everything was just as he had left it. There on the floor was still Ben Price's collar-button that had been torn from thateminent detective'sshirt-band when they had overpowered Jimmy to arrest him.

Pulling out from the wall a folding-bed, Jimmy slid back a panel in the wall anddragged out a dust-covered suit-case. He opened this andgazed fondly at the finest set of burglar's tools in the East. It was a complete set, made of specially tempered steel, the latest designs in drills, punches, braces and bits, jimmies, clamps, and augers, with two or three novelties, invented by Jimmy himself, in which he took pride. Over nine hundred dollars they had cost him to have made at—, a place where they make such things for the profession.

In half an hour Jimmy went downstairs and through the cafe. He was now dressed in tasteful and well-fitting clothes, and carried his dusted and cleaned suit-case in his hand.

'Got anything on?' asked Mike Dolan, genially.

'Me?' said Jimmy, in a puzzled tone. 'I don't understand. I'm representing the New York Amalgamated Short Snap Biscuit Cracker and Frazzled Wheat Company.'

This statement delighted Mike to such an extent that Jimmy had to take a seltzer-and-milk on the spot. He never touched 'hard' drinks.

A week after the release of Valentine, 9762, there was a neat job of safe-burglary done in Richmond, Indiana, with no clue to the author. A scant eight hundred dollars was all that was secured. Two weeks after that a patented, improved, burglar-proof safe in Logansport was opened like a cheese to the tune of fifteen hundred dollars, currency; securities and silver untouched. That began to interest the rogue-catchers. Then an old-fashioned bank-safe in Jefferson City became active and threw out of its crater an eruption of bank-notes amounting to five thousand dollars. The losses were now high enough to bring the matter up into Ben Price's class of work. By comparing notes, a remarkable similarity in the methods of the burglaries was noticed.Ben Price investigated the scenes of the robberies, and was heard to remark:

'That's Dandy Jim Valentine's autograph.He's resumed business. Look at that combination knob—jerked out as easy as pulling up a radish in wet weather. He's got the only clamps that can do it. And look how clean those tumblers were punched out! Jimmy never has to drill but one hole. Yes, I guess I want Mr Valentine.He'll do his bit next time without any short-timeor clemency foolishness.'

Ben Price knew Jimmy's habits.He had learned them while working on the Springfield case. Long jumps, quick get-aways, no confederates and a taste for good society—these ways had helped Mr Valentine to become noted as a successful dodger of retribution. It was given out that Ben Price had taken up the trail of the elusive cracksman, and other people with burglar-proof safes felt more at ease.

One afternoon Jimmy Valentineand his suit-caseclimbed out of the mail-hack in Elmore, a little town five miles off the railroad down in the black-jack country of Arkansas. Jimmy, looking like an athletic young senior just home from college, went down the board side-walk toward the hotel.

A young lady crossed the street, passed him at the corner and entered a door over which was the sign 'The Elmore Bank'. Jimmy Valentine looked into her eyes, forgot what he was,and became another man. She lowered her eyes and colored slightly. Young men of Jimmy's style and looks were scarce in Elmore.

Jimmy collared a boy that was loafing on the steps of the bank as if he were one of the stockholders, and began to ask him questions about the town, feeding him dimes at intervals. By and by the young lady came out,looking royally unconscious of the young man with the suit-case, and went her way.

'Isn't that young lady Miss Polly Simpson?' asked Jimmy, with specious guile.

'Naw,' said the boy. 'She's Annabel Adams. Her pa owns this bank. What'd you come to Elmore for? Is that a gold watch-chain? I'm going to get a bulldog. Got any more dimes?'

Jimmy went to the Planters' Hotel, registered as Ralph D. Spencer, and engaged a room. He leaned on the desk and declared his platform to the clerk. He said he had come to Elmore to look for a location to go into business. How was the shoe business, now, in the town? He had thought of the shoe business. Was there an opening?

The clerk was impressed by the clothes and manner of Jimmy. He, himself, was something of a pattern of fashion to the thinly gilded youth of Elmore, but he now perceived his shortcomings. While trying to figure out Jimmy's manner of tying hisfour-in-handhe cordially gave information.

Yes, there ought to be a good opening in the shoe line. There wasn't an exclusive shoe-store in the place. The dry-goods and general stores handled them. Business in all lines was fairly good. Hoped Mr Spencer would decide to locate in Elmore. He would find it a pleasant town to live in, and the people very sociable.

Mr Spencer thought he would stop over in the town a few days and look over the situation. No, the clerk needn't call the boy. He would carry up his suit-case, himself; it was rather heavy.

Mr Ralph Spencer, the phoenix that arose from Jimmy Valentine's ashes—ashes left by the flame of a sudden and alterative attack of love—remained in Elmore, and prospered. He opened a shoe-store and secured a good run of trade.

Socially he was also a success, and made many friends. And he accomplished the wish of his heart. He met Miss Annabel Adams, and became more and more captivated by her charms.

At the end of a year the situation of Mr Ralph Spencer was this: he had won the respect of the community, his shoe-store was flourishing and he and Annabel were engaged to be married in two weeks. Mr Adams, the typical, plodding, country banker, approved of Spencer. Annabel's pride in him almost equaled her affection. He was as much at home in the family of Mr. Adams and that of Annabel's married sister as if he were already a member.

One day Jimmy sat down in his room and wrote this letter, which he mailed to the safe address of one of his old friends in St. Louis:

> Dear Old Pal:
> I want you to be at Sullivan's place, in Little Rock, next Wednesday night, at nine o'clock. I want you to wind up some little matters for me. And, also, I want to make you a present of my kit of tools. I know you'll be glad to

get them—you couldn't duplicate the lot for a thousand dollars. Say, Billy, I've quit the old business—a year ago. I've got a nice store. I'm making an honest living, and I'm going to marry the finest girl on earth two weeks from now. It's the only life, Billy—the straight one. I wouldn't touch a dollar of another man's money now for a million. After I get married I'm going to sell out and go West, where there won't be so much danger of having old scores brought up against me. I tell you, Billy, she's an angel. She believes in me; and I wouldn't do another crooked thing for the whole world. Be sure to be at Sully's, for I must see you. I'll bring along the tools with me.

Your old friend,
Jimmy.

On the Monday night after Jimmy wrote this letter, Ben Price jogged unobtrusively into Elmore in a livery buggy. He lounged about town in his quiet way until he found out what he wanted to know. From the drug-store across the street from Spencer's shoe-store he got a good look at Ralph D. Spencer.

'Going to marry the banker's daughter are you, Jimmy?' said Ben to himself, softly. 'Well, I don't know!'

The next morning Jimmy took breakfast at the Adamses. He was going to Little Rock that day to order his wedding-suit and buy something nice for Annabel. That would be the first time he had left town since he came to Elmore. It had been more than a year now since those last professional 'jobs,' and he thought he could safely venture out.

After breakfast quite a family party went downtown together—Mr Adams, Annabel, Jimmy and Annabel's married sister with her two little girls, aged five and nine. They came by the hotel where Jimmy still boarded, and he ran up to his room and brought along his suit-case. Then they went on to the bank. There stood Jimmy's horse and buggy and Dolph Gibson, who was going to drive him over to the railroad station.

All went inside the high, carved oak railings into the banking-room—Jimmy included, for Mr Adams's future son-in-law was welcome anywhere. The clerks were pleased to be greeted by the good-looking, agreeable young man who was going to marry Miss Annabel. Jimmy set his suit-case down. Annabel, whose heart was bubbling with happiness and lively youth, put on Jimmy's hat, and picked up the suit-case. 'Wouldn't I make a nice drummer?' said Annabel.'My! Ralph, how heavy it is.Feels like it was full of gold bricks.'

'Lot of nickel-plated shoe-horns in there,' said Jimmy, coolly, 'that I'm going to return. Thought I'd save express charges by taking them up. I'm getting awfully economical.'

The Elmore Bank had just put in a new safe and vault. Mr Adams was very proud of it, and insisted on an inspection by every one. The vault was a small one, but it had a new, patented door. It fastened with three solid steel bolts thrown simultaneously with a single handle, and had a time-lock. Mr Adams beamingly explained its workings to Mr Spencer,who showed a courteous but not too intelligent interest. The two children, May and Agatha, were delighted by the shining metal and funny clock and knobs.

While they were thus engaged Ben Price sauntered in and leaned on his elbow, looking casually inside between the railings. He told the teller that he didn't want anything; he was just waiting for a man he knew.

Suddenly there was a scream or two from the women, and a commotion. Unperceived by the elders, May, the nine-year-old girl, in a spirit of play, had shut Agatha in the vault. She had then shot the bolts and turned the knob of the combination as she had seen Mr Adams do.

The old banker sprang to the handle and tugged at it for a moment. 'The door can't be opened,' he groaned. 'The clock hasn't been wound nor the combination set.'

Agatha's mother screamed again, hysterically.

'Hush!' said Mr Adams, raising his trembling hand. 'All be quite for a moment. Agatha!' he called as loudly as he could. 'Listen to me.' During the following silence they could just hearthe faint soundof the child wildly shrieking in the dark vault in a panic of terror.

'My precious darling!' wailed the mother. 'She will die of fright! Open the door! Oh, break it open! Can't you men do something?'

'There isn't a man nearer than Little Rock who can open that door,' said Mr Adams, in a shaky voice. 'My God! Spencer, what shall we do? That child—she can't stand it long in there. There isn't enough air, and, besides, she'll go into convulsions from fright.'

Agatha's mother, frantic now, beat the door of the vault with her hands. Somebody wildly suggested dynamite.

Annabel turned to Jimmy, her large eyes full of anguish, but not yet despairing. To a woman nothing seems quite impossible to the powers of the man she worships.

'Can't you do something, Ralph—try, won't you?'

He looked at her with a queer, soft smile on his lips and in his keen eyes.

'Annabel,' he said, 'give me that rose you are wearing, will you?'

Hardly believing that she heard him aright, she unpinned the bud from the bosom of her dress, and placed it in his hand. Jimmy stuffed it into his vest-pocket, threw off his coat and pulled up his shirt-sleeves. With that act Ralph D. Spencer passed away and Jimmy Valentine took his place.

'Get away from the door, all of you,' he commanded, shortly.

He set his suit-case on the table, and opened it out flat. From that time on he seemed to be unconscious of the presence of any one else. He laid out the shining, queer implements swiftly and orderly, whistling softly to himself as he always did when at work. In a deep silence and immovable, the others watched him as if under a spell.

In a minute Jimmy's pet drill was biting smoothly into the steel door. In ten minutes—breaking his own burglarious record—he threw back the bolts and opened the door.

Agatha, almost collapsed, but safe, was gathered into her mother's arms.

Jimmy Valentine put on his coat, and walked outside the railings toward the front door. As he went he thought he heard a far-away voice that he once knew call 'Ralph!' But he never hesitated.

At the doora big manstood somewhat in his way.

'Hello, Ben!' said Jimmy, still with his strange smile. 'Got around at last, have you? Well, let's go. I don't know that it makes much difference, now.'

And then Ben Price acted rather strangely.

'Guess you're mistaken, Mr Spencer,' he said. 'Don't believe I recognize you. Your buggy's waiting for you, ain't it?'

And Ben Price turned and strolled down the street.

2

The Necklace

Guy de Maupassant

The girl was one of those pretty and charming young creatures who sometimes are born, as if by a slip of fate, into a family of clerks. She had no dowry, no expectations, no way of being known, understood, loved, married by any rich and distinguished man; so she let herself be married to a little clerk of the Ministry of Public Instruction.

She dressed plainly because she could not dress well, but she was unhappy as if she had really fallen from a higher station; since with women there is neither caste nor rank, for beauty, grace and charm take the place of family and birth. Natural ingenuity, instinct for what is elegant, a supple mind are their sole hierarchy, and often make of women of the people the equals of the very greatest ladies.

Mathilde suffered ceaselessly, feeling herself born to enjoy all delicacies and all luxuries. She was distressed at the poverty of her dwelling, at the bareness of the walls, at the shabby chairs, the ugliness of the curtains. All those things, of which another woman of her rank would never even have been conscious, tortured her and made her angry. The sight of the little Breton peasant who did her humble housework aroused in her despairing regrets and bewildering dreams. She thought of silent antechambers hung with Oriental tapestry, illumined by tall bronze candelabra, and of two great footmen in knee breeches who sleep in the big armchairs, made drowsy by the oppressive heat of the stove. She thought of long reception halls hung with ancient silk, of the dainty cabinets containing priceless curiosities and of the little coquettish perfumed reception rooms made for chatting at five o'clock with intimate friends, with men famous and sought after, whom all women envy and whose attention they all desire.

When she sat down to dinner, before the round table covered with a tablecloth in use three days, opposite her husband, who uncovered the soup tureen and declared with a delighted air, 'Ah, the good soup! I don't know anything better than that,' she thought of dainty dinners, of shining silverware, of tapestry that peopled the walls with ancient personages and with strange birds flying in the midst of a fairy forest; and she thought of delicious dishes served on marvellous plates and of the whispered gallantries to which you listen with a sphinx-like smile while you are eating the pink meat of a trout or the wings of a quail.

She had no gowns, no jewels, nothing. And she loved nothing but that. She felt made for that. She would have liked so much to please, to be envied, to be charming, to be sought after.

She had a friend, a former schoolmate at the convent, who was rich, and whom she did not like to go to see any more because she felt so sad when she came home.

But one evening her husband reached home with a triumphant air and holding a large envelope in his hand.

'There,' said he, 'there is something for you.'

She tore the paper quickly and drew out a printed card which bore these words:

The Minister of Public Instruction and Madame Georges Ramponneau request the honor of M. and Madame Loisel's company at the palace of the Ministry on Monday evening, January 18th.

Instead of being delighted, as her husband had hoped, she threw the invitation on the table crossly, muttering:

'What do you wish me to do with that?'

'Why, my dear, I thought you would be glad. You never go out, and this is such a fine opportunity. I had great trouble to get it. Every one wants to go; it is very select, and they are not giving many invitations to clerks. The whole official world will be there.'

She looked at him with an irritated glance and said impatiently:

'And what do you wish me to put on my back?'

He had not thought of that. He stammered:

'Why, the gown you go to the theatre in. It looks very well to me.'

He stopped, distracted, seeing that his wife was weeping. Two great tears ran slowly from the corners of her eyes toward the corners of her mouth.

'What's the matter? What's the matter?' he answered.

By a violent effort she conquered her grief and replied in a calm voice, while she wiped her wet cheeks:

'Nothing. Only I have no gown, and, therefore, I can't go to this ball. Give your card to some colleague whose wife is better equipped than I am.'

He was in despair. He resumed:

'Come, let us see, Mathilde. How much would it cost,

a suitable gown, which you could use on other occasions—something very simple?'

She reflected several seconds, making her calculations and wondering also what sum she could ask without drawing on herself an immediate refusal and a frightened exclamation from the economical clerk.

Finally she replied hesitating:

'I don't know exactly, but I think I could manage it with four hundred francs.'

He grew a little pale, because he was laying aside just that amount to buy a gun and treat himself to a little shooting next summer on the plain of Nanterre, with several friends who went to shoot larks there of a Sunday.

But he said:

'Very well. I will give you four hundred francs. And try to have a pretty gown.'

The day of the ball drew near and Madame Loisel seemed sad, uneasy, anxious. Her frock was ready, however. Her husband said to her one evening:

'What is the matter? Come, you have seemed very queer these last three days.'

And she answered:

'It annoys me not to have a single piece of jewelry, not a single ornament, nothing to put on. I shall look poverty-stricken. I would almost rather not go at all.'

'You might wear natural flowers,' said her husband. 'They're very stylish at this time of year. For ten francs you can get two or three magnificent roses.'

She was not convinced.

'No; there's nothing more humiliating than to look poor among other women who are rich.'

'How stupid you are!' her husband cried. 'Go look up your friend, Madame Forestier, and ask her to lend you some jewels. You're intimate enough with her to do that.'

She uttered a cry of joy:

'True! I never thought of it.'

The next day she went to her friend and told her of her distress.

Madame Forestier went to a wardrobe with a mirror, took out a large jewel box, brought it back, opened it and said to Madame Loisel:

'Choose, my dear.'

She saw first some bracelets, then a pearl necklace, then a Venetian gold cross set with precious stones, of admirable workmanship. She tried on the ornaments before the mirror, hesitated and could not make up her mind to part with them, to give them back. She kept asking:

'Haven't you anymore?'

'Why, yes. Look further; I don't know what you like.'

Suddenly she discovered, in a black satin box, a superb diamond necklace, and her heart throbbed with an immoderate desire. Her hands trembled as she took it. She fastened it round her throat, outside her high-necked waist, and was lost in ecstasy at her reflection in the mirror.

Then she asked, hesitating, filled with anxious doubt:

'Will you lend me this, only this?'

'Why, yes, certainly.'

She threw her arms round her friend's neck, kissed her passionately, then fled with her treasure.

The night of the ball arrived. Madame Loisel was a great success. She was prettier than any other woman present, elegant, graceful, smiling and wild with joy. All the men looked at her, asked her name, sought to be introduced. All the attaches of the Cabinet wished to waltz with her. She was remarked by the minister himself.

She danced with rapture, with passion, intoxicated by pleasure, forgetting all in the triumph of her beauty, in the glory of her success, in a sort of cloud of happiness comprised of all this homage, admiration, these awakened desires and of that sense of triumph which is so sweet to woman's heart.

She left the ball about four o'clock in the morning. Her husband had been sleeping since midnight in a little deserted anteroom with three other gentlemen whose wives were enjoying the ball.

He threw over her shoulders the wraps he had brought, the modest wraps of common life, the poverty of which contrasted with the elegance of the ball dress. She felt this and wished to escape so as not to be remarked by the other women, who were enveloping themselves in costly furs.

Loisel held her back, saying: 'Wait a bit. You will catch cold outside. I will call a cab.'

But she did not listen to him and rapidly descended the stairs. When they reached the street they could not find a carriage and began to look for one, shouting after the cabmen passing at a distance.

They went toward the Seine in despair, shivering with cold. At last they found on the quay one of those ancient night cabs which, as though they were ashamed to show their shabbiness during the day, are never seen round Paris until after dark.

It took them to their dwelling in the Rue des Martyrs, and sadly they mounted the stairs to their flat. All was ended for her. As to him, he reflected that he must be at the ministry at ten o'clock that morning.

She removed her wraps before the glass so as to see herself once more in all her glory. But suddenly she uttered a cry. She no longer had the necklace around her neck!

'What is the matter with you?' demanded her husband, already half undressed.

She turned distractedly toward him.

'I have—I have—I've lost Madame Forestier's necklace,' she cried.

He stood up, bewildered.

'What!—how? Impossible!'

They looked among the folds of her skirt, of her cloak, in her pockets, everywhere, but did not find it.

'You're sure you had it on when you left the ball?' he asked.

'Yes, I felt it in the vestibule of the minister's house.'

'But if you had lost it in the street we should have heard it fall. It must be in the cab.'

'Yes, probably. Did you take his number?'

'No. And you—didn't you notice it?'

'No.'

They looked, thunderstruck, at each other. At last Loisel put on his clothes.

'I shall go back on foot,' said he, 'over the whole route, to see whether I can find it.'

He went out. She sat waiting on a chair in her ball dress, without strength to go to bed, overwhelmed, without any fire, without a thought.

Her husband returned about seven o'clock. He had found nothing.

He went to police headquarters, to the newspaper offices to offer a reward; he went to the cab companies—everywhere, in fact, whither he was urged by the least spark of hope.

She waited all day, in the same condition of mad fear before this terrible calamity.

Loisel returned at night with a hollow, pale face. He had discovered nothing.

'You must write to your friend,' said he, 'that you have broken the clasp of her necklace and that you are having it mended. That will give us time to turn round.'

She wrote at his dictation.

At the end of a week they had lost all hope. Loisel, who had aged five years, declared:

'We must consider how to replace that ornament.'

The next day they took the box that had contained it and went to the jeweler whose name was found within. He consulted his books.

'It was not I, madame, who sold that necklace; I must simply have furnished the case.'

Then they went from jeweler to jeweler, searching for a necklace like the other, trying to recall it, both sick with chagrin and grief.

They found, in a shop at the Palais Royal, a string of diamonds that seemed to them exactly like the one they had

lost. It was worth forty thousand francs. They could have it for thirty-six.

So they begged the jeweler not to sell it for three days yet. And they made a bargain that he should buy it back for thirty-four thousand francs, in case they should find the lost necklace before the end of February.

Loisel possessed eighteen thousand francs which his father had left him. He would borrow the rest.

He did borrow, asking a thousand francs of one, five hundred of another, five louis here, three louis there. He gave notes, took up ruinous obligations, dealt with usurers and all the race of lenders. He compromised all the rest of his life, risked signing a note without even knowing whether he could meet it; and, frightened by the trouble yet to come, by the black misery that was about to fall upon him, by the prospect of all the physical privations and moral tortures that he was to suffer, he went to get the new necklace, laying upon the jeweler's counter thirty-six thousand francs.

When Madame Loisel took back the necklace Madame Forestier said to her with a chilly manner:

'You should have returned it sooner; I might have needed it.'

She did not open the case, as her friend had so much feared. If she had detected the substitution, what would she have thought, what would she have said? Would she not have taken Madame Loisel for a thief?

Thereafter Madame Loisel knew the horrible existence of the needy. She bore her part, however, with sudden heroism. That dreadful debt must be paid. She would pay it.

They dismissed their servant; they changed their lodgings; they rented a garret under the roof.

She came to know what heavy housework meant and the odious cares of the kitchen. She washed the dishes, using her dainty fingers and rosy nails on greasy pots and pans. She washed the soiled linen, the shirts and the dishcloths, which she dried upon a line; she carried the slops down to the street every morning and carried up the water, stopping for breath at every landing. And dressed like a woman of the people, she went to the fruiterer, the grocer, the butcher, a basket on her arm, bargaining, meeting with impertinence, defending her miserable money, sou by sou.

Every month they had to meet some notes, renew others, obtain more time.

Her husband worked evenings, making up a tradesman's accounts, and late at night he often copied manuscript for five sous a page.

This life lasted ten years.

At the end of ten years they had paid everything, everything, with the rates of usury and the accumulations of the compound interest.

Madame Loisel looked old now. She had become the woman of impoverished households—strong and hard and rough. With frowsy hair, skirts askew and red hands, she talked loud while washing the floor with great swishes of water. But sometimes, when her husband was at the office, she sat down near the window and she thought of that gay evening of long ago, of that ball where she had been so beautiful and so admired.

What would have happened if she had not lost that necklace? Who knows? who knows? How strange and changeful is life! How small a thing is needed to make or ruin us!

But one Sunday, having gone to take a walk in the Champs Elysees to refresh herself after the labors of the week, she suddenly perceived a woman who was leading a child. It was Madame Forestier, still young, still beautiful, still charming.

Madame Loisel felt moved. Should she speak to her? Yes, certainly. And now that she had paid, she would tell her all about it. Why not?

She went up.

'Good-day, Jeanne.'

The other, astonished to be familiarly addressed by this plain good-wife, did not recognize her at all and stammered:

'But—madame!—I do not know—You must have mistaken.'

'No. I am Mathilde Loisel.'

Her friend uttered a cry.

'Oh, my poor Mathilde! How you are changed!'

'Yes, I have had a pretty hard life, since I last saw you, and great poverty—and that because of you!'

'Of me! How so?'

'Do you remember that diamond necklace you lent me to wear at the ministerial ball?'

'Yes. Well?'

'Well, I lost it.'

'What do you mean? You brought it back.'

'I brought you back another exactly like it. And it has taken us ten years to pay for it. You can understand that it was not easy for us, for us who had nothing. At last it is ended, and I am very glad.'

Madame Forestier had stopped.

'You say that you bought a necklace of diamonds to replace mine?'

'Yes. You never noticed it, then! They were very similar.'

And she smiled with a joy that was at once proud and ingenuous.

Madame Forestier, deeply moved, took her hands.

'Oh, my poor Mathilde! Why, my necklace was paste! It was worth at most only five hundred francs!'

3

The Magic Shop

H.G. Wells

I had seen the Magic Shop from afar several times; I had passed it once or twice, a shop window of alluring little objects, magic balls, magic hens, wonderful cones, ventriloquist dolls, the material of the basket trick, packs of cards that looked all right and all that sort of thing, but never had I thought of going in until one day, almost without warning, Gip hauled me by my finger right up to the window, and so conducted himself that there was nothing for it but to take him in. I had not thought the place was there, to tell the truth—a modest-sized frontage in Regent Street, between the picture shop and the place where the chicks run about just out of patent incubators, but there it was sure enough. I had fancied it was down nearer the Circus, or round the corner in Oxford Street, or even in Holborn; always over the way and a little inaccessible it had been, with something of the mirage in its position; but here it was now quite indisputably, and the fat end of Gip's pointing finger made a noise upon the glass.

'If I was rich,' said Gip, dabbing a finger at the Disappearing Egg, 'I'd buy myself that. And that'—which was The Crying Baby, Very Human—'and that,' which was a mystery, and called, so a neat card asserted, 'Buy One and Astonish Your Friends.'

'Anything,' said Gip, 'will disappear under one of those cones. I have read about it in a book.

'And there, dadda, is the Vanishing Halfpenny—, only they've put it this way up so's we can't see how it's done.'

Gip, dear boy, inherits his mother's breeding, and he did not propose to enter the shop or worry in any way; only, you know, quite unconsciously he lugged my finger doorward, and he made his interest clear.

'That,' he said, and pointed to the Magic Bottle.

'If you had that?' I said; at which promising inquiry he looked up with a sudden radiance.

'I could show it to Jessie,' he said, thoughtful as ever of others.

'It's less than a hundred days to your birthday, Gibbles,' I said, and laid my hand on the door-handle.

Gip made no answer, but his grip tightened on my finger, and so we came into the shop.

It was no common shop this; it was a magic shop, and all the prancing precedence Gip would have taken in the matter of mere toys was wanting. He left the burthen of the conversation to me.

It was a little, narrow shop, not very well lit, and the door-bell pinged again with a plaintive note as we closed it behind us. For a moment or so we were alone and could glance about us. There was a tiger in papier-mache on the glass case that covered the low counter—a grave, kind-eyed tiger that waggled his head in a methodical manner; there were several crystal spheres, a china hand holding magic cards, a stock of magic fish-bowls in various sizes and an immodest magic hat that shamelessly displayed its springs. On the floor were magic mirrors; one to draw you out long and thin, one to swell your head and vanish your legs, and one to make you short and fat like a draught; and while we were laughing at these the shopman, as I suppose, came in.

At any rate, there he was behind the counter—a curious, sallow, dark man, with one ear larger than the other and a chin like the toe-cap of a boot.

'What can we have the pleasure?' he said, spreading his long, magic fingers on the glass case; and so with a start we were aware of him.

'I want,' I said, 'to buy my little boy a few simple tricks.'

'Legerdemain?' he asked. 'Mechanical? Domestic?'

'Anything amusing?' said I.

'Um!' said the shopman, and scratched his head for a moment as if thinking. Then, quite distinctly, he drew from his head a glass ball. 'Something in this way?' he said, and held it out.

The action was unexpected. I had seen the trick done at entertainments endless times before—it's part of the common stock of conjurers—but I had not expected it here.

'That's good,' I said, with a laugh.

'Isn't it?' said the shopman.

Gip stretched out his disengaged hand to take this object and found merely a blank palm.

'It's in your pocket,' said the shopman, and there it was!

'How much will that be?' I asked.

'We make no charge for glass balls,' said the shopman politely. 'We get them,'—he picked one out of his elbow as he spoke—'free.' He produced another from the back of his neck, and laid it beside its predecessor on the counter. Gip regarded his glass ball sagely, then directed a look of inquiry at the two on the counter, and finally brought his round-eyed scrutiny to the shopman, who smiled.

'You may have those too,' said the shopman, 'and, if you don't mind, one from my mouth. So!'

Gip counselled me mutely for a moment, and then in a profound silence put away the four balls, resumed my reassuring finger and nerved himself for the next event.

'We get all our smaller tricks in that way,' the shopman remarked.

I laughed in the manner of one who subscribes to a jest. 'Instead of going to the wholesale shop,' I said. 'Of course, it's cheaper.'

'In a way,' the shopman said. 'Though we pay in the end. But not so heavily—as people suppose ... Our larger tricks, and our daily provisions and all the other things we want, we get out of that hat ... And you know, sir, if you'll excuse my saying it, there isn't a wholesale shop, not for Genuine Magic goods, sir. I don't know if you noticed our inscription—the Genuine Magic shop.' He drew a business-card from his cheek and handed it to me. 'Genuine,' he said, with his finger on the word, and added, 'There is absolutely no deception, sir.'

He seemed to be carrying out the joke pretty thoroughly, I thought.

He turned to Gip with a smile of remarkable affability. 'You, you know, are the Right Sort of Boy.'

I was surprised at his knowing that, because, in the interests of discipline, we keep it rather a secret even at home; but Gip received it in unflinching silence, keeping a steadfast eye on him.

'It's only the Right Sort of Boy gets through that doorway.'

And, as if by way of illustration, there came a rattling at the door, and a squeaking little voice could be faintly heard. 'Nyar! I warn 'a go in there, dadda, I warn 'a go in there. Ny-a-a-ah!' and then the accents of a down-trodden parent, urging consolations and propitiations. 'It's locked, Edward,' he said.

'But it isn't,' said I.

'It is, sir,' said the shopman, 'always—for that sort of child,' and as he spoke we had a glimpse of the other youngster, a little, white face, pallid from sweet-eating and over-sapid food, and distorted by evil passions, a ruthless little egotist, pawing at the enchanted pane. 'It's no good, sir,' said the shopman, as I moved, with my natural helpfulness, doorward, and presently the spoilt child was carried off howling.

'How do you manage that?' I said, breathing a little more freely.

'Magic!' said the shopman, with a careless wave of the hand, and behold! sparks of coloured fire flew out of his fingers and vanished into the shadows of the shop.

'You were saying,' he said, addressing himself to Gip, 'before you came in, that you would like one of our 'Buy One and Astonish your Friends' boxes?'

Gip, after a gallant effort, said 'Yes.'

'It's in your pocket.'

And leaning over the counter—he really had an extraordinarily long body—this amazing person produced the article in the customary conjurer's manner. 'Paper,' he said, and took a sheet out of the empty hat with the springs; 'string,' and behold his mouth was a string-box, from which he drew an unending thread, which when he had tied his parcel he bit off—and, it seemed to me, swallowed the ball of string. And then he lit a candle at the nose of one of the ventriloquist's dummies, stuck one of his fingers (which had become sealing-wax red) into the flame, and so sealed the parcel. 'Then there was the Disappearing Egg,' he remarked, and produced one from within my coat-breast and packed it, and also The Crying Baby, Very Human. I handed each parcel to Gip as it was ready, and he clasped them to his chest.

He said very little, but his eyes were eloquent; the clutch of his arms was eloquent. He was the playground of unspeakable emotions. These, you know, were real Magics. Then, with a start, I discovered something moving about in my hat—something soft and jumpy. I whipped it off, and a ruffled pigeon—no doubt a confederate—dropped out and ran on the counter, and went, I fancy, into a cardboard box behind the papier-mache tiger.

'Tut, tut!' said the shopman, dexterously relieving me of my headdress; 'careless bird, and—as I live—nesting!'

He shook my hat, and shook out into his extended hand two or three eggs, a large marble, a watch, about half-a-dozen of the inevitable glass balls, and then crumpled, crinkled paper, more and more and more, talking all the time of the way in which people neglect to brush their hats inside as well as out, politely, of course, but with a certain personal application. 'All sorts of things accumulate, sir … Not you, of course, in particular … Nearly every customer … Astonishing what they carry about with them …' The crumpled paper rose and billowed on the counter more and more and more, until he was nearly hidden from us, until he was altogether hidden, and still his voice went on and on. 'We none of us know what the fair semblance of a human being may conceal, sir. Are we all then no better than brushed exteriors, whited sepulchres—'

His voice stopped—exactly like when you hit a neighbour's gramophone with a well-aimed brick, the same instant silence, and the rustle of the paper stopped, and everything was still …

'Have you done with my hat?' I said, after an interval.

There was no answer.

I stared at Gip, and Gip stared at me, and there were our distortions in the magic mirrors, looking very rum, and grave and quiet …

'I think we'll go now,' I said. 'Will you tell me how much all this comes to? …

'I say,' I said, on a rather louder note, 'I want the bill; and my hat, please.'

It might have been a sniff from behind the paper pile …

'Let's look behind the counter, Gip,' I said. 'He's making fun of us.'

I led Gip round the head-wagging tiger, and what do you think there was behind the counter? No one at all! Only my hat on the floor, and a common conjurer's lop-eared white rabbit lost in meditation, and looking as stupid and crumpled as only a conjurer's rabbit can do. I resumed my hat, and the rabbit lolloped a lollop or so out of my way.

'Dadda!' said Gip, in a guilty whisper.

'What is it, Gip?' said I.

'I do like this shop, dadda.'

'So should I,' I said to myself, 'if the counter wouldn't suddenly extend itself to shut one off from the door.' But

I didn't call Gip's attention to that. 'Pussy!' he said, with a hand out to the rabbit as it came lolloping past us; 'Pussy, do Gip a magic!' and his eyes followed it as it squeezed through a door I had certainly not remarked a moment before. Then this door opened wider, and the man with one ear larger than the other appeared again. He was smiling still, but his eye met mine with something between amusement and defiance. 'You'd like to see our show-room, sir,' he said, with an innocent suavity. Gip tugged my finger forward. I glanced at the counter and met the shopman's eye again. I was beginning to think the magic just a little too genuine. 'We haven't very much time,' I said. But somehow we were inside the show-room before I could finish that.

'All goods of the same quality,' said the shopman, rubbing his flexible hands together, 'and that is the Best. Nothing in the place that isn't genuine Magic, and warranted thoroughly rum. Excuse me, sir!'

I felt him pull at something that clung to my coat-sleeve, and then I saw he held a little, wriggling red demon by the tail—the little creature bit and fought and tried to get at his hand—and in a moment he tossed it carelessly behind a counter. No doubt the thing was only an image of twisted indiarubber, but for the moment—! And his gesture was exactly that of a man who handles some petty biting bit of vermin. I glanced at Gip, but Gip was looking at a magic rocking-horse. I was glad he hadn't seen the thing. 'I say,' I said, in an undertone, and indicating Gip and the red demon with my eyes, 'you haven't many things like that about, have you?'

'None of ours! Probably brought it with you,' said the shopman—also in an undertone, and with a more dazzling smile than ever. 'Astonishing what people will carry about with them unawares!' And then to Gip, 'Do you see anything you fancy here?'

There were many things that Gip fancied there.

He turned to this astonishing tradesman with mingled confidence and respect. 'Is that a Magic Sword?' he said.

'A Magic Toy Sword. It neither bends, breaks, nor cuts the fingers. It renders the bearer invincible in battle against any one under eighteen. Half-a-crown to seven and sixpence, according to size. These panoplies on cards are for juvenile knights-errant and very useful—shield of safety, sandals of swiftness, helmet of invisibility.'

'Oh, daddy!' gasped Gip.

I tried to find out what they cost, but the shopman did not heed me. He had got Gip now; he had got him away from my finger; he had embarked upon the exposition of all his confounded stock, and nothing was going to stop him. Presently I saw with a qualm of distrust and something very like jealousy that Gip had hold of this person's finger as usually he has hold of mine. No doubt the fellow was interesting, I thought, and had an interestingly faked lot of stuff, really good faked stuff, still—

I wandered after them, saying very little, but keeping an eye on this prestidigital fellow. After all, Gip was enjoying it. And no doubt when the time came to go we should be able to go quite easily.

It was a long, rambling place, that show-room, a gallery broken up by stands and stalls and pillars, with archways leading off to other departments, in which the queerest-looking assistants loafed and stared at one, and with perplexing mirrors and curtains. So perplexing, indeed, were these that I was presently unable to make out the door by which we had come.

The shopman showed Gip magic trains that ran without steam or clockwork, just as you set the signals, and then some very, very valuable boxes of soldiers that all came alive directly you took off the lid and said—. I myself haven't a very quick ear and it was a tongue-twisting sound, but Gip—he has his mother's ear—got it in no time. 'Bravo!' said the shopman, putting the men back into the box unceremoniously and handing it to Gip. 'Now,' said the shopman, and in a moment Gip had made them all alive again.

'You'll take that box?' asked the shopman.

'We'll take that box,' said I, 'unless you charge its full value. In which case it would need a Trust Magnate—'

'Dear heart! No!' and the shopman swept the little men back again, shut the lid, waved the box in the air, and there it was, in brown paper, tied up and—with Gip's full name and address on the paper!

The shopman laughed at my amazement.

'This is the genuine magic,' he said. 'The real thing.'

'It's a little too genuine for my taste,' I said again.

After that he fell to showing Gip tricks, odd tricks, and still odder the way they were done. He explained them, he turned them inside out, and there was the dear little chap nodding his busy bit of a head in the sagest manner.

I did not attend as well as I might. 'Hey, presto!' said the Magic Shopman, and then would come the clear, small 'Hey, presto!' of the boy. But I was distracted by other things. It was being borne in upon me just how tremendously rum this place was; it was, so to speak, inundated by a sense of rumness. There was something a little rum about the fixtures even, about the ceiling, about the floor, about the casually distributed chairs. I had a queer feeling that whenever I wasn't looking at them straight they went askew, and moved about, and played a noiseless puss-in-the-corner behind my back. And the cornice had a serpentine design with masks—masks altogether too expressive for proper plaster.

Then abruptly my attention was caught by one of the odd-looking assistants. He was some way off and evidently unaware of my presence—I saw a sort of three-quarter length of him over a pile of toys and through an arch—and, you know, he was leaning against a pillar in an idle sort of way doing the most horrid things with his features! The particular horrid thing he did was with his nose. He did it just as though he was idle and wanted to amuse himself. First of all it was a short, blobby nose, and then suddenly he shot it out like a telescope, and then out it flew and became thinner and thinner until it was like a long, red, flexible whip. Like a thing in a nightmare it was! He flourished it about and flung it forth as a fly-fisher flings his line.

My instant thought was that Gip mustn't see him. I turned about, and there was Gip quite preoccupied with the shopman, and thinking no evil. They were whispering together and looking at me. Gip was standing on a little stool, and the shopman was holding a sort of big drum in his hand.

'Hide and seek, dadda!' cried Gip. 'You're He!'

And before I could do anything to prevent it, the shopman had clapped the big drum over him. I saw what was up directly. 'Take that off,' I cried, 'this instant! You'll frighten the boy. Take it off!'

The shopman with the unequal ears did so without a word, and held the big cylinder towards me to show its emptiness. And the little stool was vacant! In that instant my boy had utterly disappeared? …

You know, perhaps, that sinister something that comes like a hand out of the unseen and grips your heart about. You know it takes your common self away and leaves you tense and deliberate, neither slow nor hasty, neither angry nor afraid. So it was with me.

I came up to this grinning shopman and kicked his stool aside.

'Stop this folly!' I said. 'Where is my boy?'

'You see,' he said, still displaying the drum's interior, 'there is no deception—'

I put out my hand to grip him, and he eluded me by a dexterous movement. I snatched again, and he turned from me and pushed open a door to escape. 'Stop!' I said, and he laughed, receding. I leapt after him—into utter darkness.

Thud!

'Lor' bless my 'eart! I didn't see you coming, sir!'

I was in Regent Street, and I had collided with a decent-looking working man; and a yard away, perhaps, and looking a little perplexed with himself, was Gip. There was some sort of apology, and then Gip had turned and come to me with a bright little smile, as though for a moment he had missed me.

And he was carrying four parcels in his arm!

He secured immediate possession of my finger.

For the second I was rather at a loss. I stared round to see the door of the magic shop, and, behold, it was not there! There was no door, no shop, nothing, only the common pilaster between the shop where they sell pictures and the window with the chicks ... !

I did the only thing possible in that mental tumult; I walked straight to the kerbstone and held up my umbrella for a cab.

''Ansoms,' said Gip, in a note of culminating exultation.

I helped him in, recalled my address with an effort, and got in also. Something unusual proclaimed itself in my tail-coat pocket, and I felt and discovered a glass ball. With a petulant expression I flung it into the street.

Gip said nothing.

For a space neither of us spoke.

'Dadda!' said Gip, at last, 'that was a proper shop!'

I came round with that to the problem of just how the whole thing had seemed to him. He looked completely undamaged—so far, good; he was neither scared nor unhinged, he was simply tremendously satisfied with the afternoon's entertainment, and there in his arms were the four parcels.

Confound it! what could be in them?

'Um!' I said. 'Little boys can't go to shops like that every day.'

He received this with his usual stoicism, and for a moment I was sorry I was his father and not his mother, and so couldn't suddenly there, coram publico, in our hansom, kiss him. After all, I thought, the thing wasn't so very bad.

But it was only when we opened the parcels that I really began to be reassured. Three of them contained boxes of soldiers, quite ordinary lead soldiers, but of so good a quality as to make Gip altogether forget that originally these parcels had been Magic Tricks of the only genuine sort, and the fourth contained a kitten, a little living white kitten, in excellent health and appetite and temper.

I saw this unpacking with a sort of provisional relief. I hung about in the nursery for quite an unconscionable time …

That happened six months ago. And now I am beginning to believe it is all right. The kitten had only the magic natural to all kittens, and the soldiers seem as steady a company as any colonel could desire. And Gip—?

The intelligent parent will understand that I have to go cautiously with Gip.

But I went so far as this one day. I said, 'How would you like your soldiers to come alive, Gip, and march about by themselves?'

'Mine do,' said Gip. 'I just have to say a word I know before I open the lid.'

'Then they march about alone?'

'Oh, quite, dadda. I shouldn't like them if they didn't do that.'

I displayed no unbecoming surprise, and since then I have taken occasion to drop in upon him once or twice, unannounced, when the soldiers were about, but so far I have never discovered them performing in anything like a magical manner.

It's so difficult to tell.

There's also a question of finance. I have an incurable habit of paying bills. I have been up and down Regent Street several times, looking for that shop. I am inclined to think, indeed, that in that matter honour is satisfied, and that, since Gip's name and address are known to them, I may very well leave it to these people, whoever they may be, to send in their bill in their own time.

4

The Psammead

E. Nesbit

There were once four children who spent their summer holidays in a white house, happily situated between a sandpit and a chalkpit. One day they had the good fortune to find in the sandpit a strange creature. Its eyes were on long horns like snail's eyes, and it could move them in and out like telescopes. It had ears like a bat's ears, and its tubby body was shaped like a spider's and covered with thick soft fur—and it had hands and feet like a monkey's. It told the children—whose names were Cyril, Robert, Anthea and Jane—that it was a Psammead or sand-fairy. (Psammead is pronounced Sammy-ad.) It was old, old, old and its birthday was almost at the very beginning of everything. And it had been buried in the sand for thousands of years. But it still kept its fairylikeness, and part of this fairylikeness was its power to give people whatever they wished for. You know fairies have always been able to do this. Cyril, Robert, Anthea and Jane now found their wishes come true; but, somehow, they never could think of just the right things to wish for, and their wishes sometimes turned out very oddly indeed. In the end their unwise wishings landed them in what Robert called 'a very tight place indeed', and the Psammead consented to help them out of it in return for their promise never never to ask it to grant them any more wishes, and never to tell anyone about it, because it did not want to be bothered to give wishes to anyone ever any more. At the moment of parting Jane said politely—

'I wish we were going to see you again some day.'

And the Psammead, touched by this friendly thought, granted the wish. The book about all this is called *Five Children and It*, and it ends up in a most tiresome way by saying—

'The children did see the Psammead again, but it was not in the sandpit; it was—but I must say no more—'

The reason that nothing more could be said was that I had not then been able to find out exactly when and where the children met the Psammead again. Of course I knew they would meet it, because it was a beast of its word, and when it said a thing would happen, that thing happened without fail. How different from the people who tell us about what weather it is going to be on Thursday next, in London, the South Coast and Channel!

The summer holidays during which the Psammead had been found and the wishes given had been wonderful holidays in the country, and the children had the highest hopes of just such another holiday for the next summer. The winter holidays were beguiled by the wonderful happenings of *The Phœnix and the Carpet*, and the loss of these two treasures would have left the children in despair, but for the splendid hope of their next holiday in the country. The world, they felt, and indeed had some reason to feel, was full of wonderful things—and they were really the sort of people that wonderful things happen to. So they looked forward to the summer holiday; but when it came everything was different, and very, very horrid. Father had to go out to

Manchuria to telegraph news about the war to the tiresome paper he wrote for—the *Daily Bellower*, or something like that, was its name. And Mother, poor dear Mother, was away in Madeira, because she had been very ill. And The Lamb—I mean the baby—was with her. And Aunt Emma, who was Mother's sister, had suddenly married Uncle Reginald, who was Father's brother, and they had gone to China, which is much too far off for you to expect to be asked to spend the holidays in, however fond your aunt and uncle may be of you. So the children were left in the care of old Nurse, who lived in Fitzroy Street, near the British Museum, and though she was always very kind to them, and indeed spoiled them far more than would be good for the most grown-up of us, the four children felt perfectly wretched, and when the cab had driven off with Father and all his boxes and guns and the sheepskin, with blankets and the aluminium mess-kit inside it, the stoutest heart quailed, and the girls broke down altogether, and sobbed in each other's arms, while the boys each looked out of one of the long gloomy windows of the parlour, and tried to pretend that no boy would be such a muff as to cry.

I hope you notice that they were not cowardly enough to cry till their Father had gone; they knew he had quite enough to upset him without that. But when he was gone everyone felt as if it had been trying not to cry all its life, and that it must cry now, if it died for it. So they cried.

Tea—with shrimps and watercress—cheered them a little. The watercress was arranged in a hedge round a fat glass salt-cellar, a tasteful device they had never seen before. But it was not a cheerful meal.

After tea Anthea went up to the room that had been Father's, and when she saw how dreadfully he wasn't there, and remembered how every minute was taking him further and further from her, and nearer and nearer to the guns of the Russians, she cried a little more. Then she thought of Mother, ill and alone, and perhaps at that very moment wanting a little girl to put eau-de-cologne on her head, and make her sudden cups of tea, and she cried more than ever. And then she remembered what Mother had said, the night before she went away, about Anthea being the eldest girl, and about trying to make the others happy, and things like that. So she stopped crying, and thought instead. And when she had thought as long as she could bear she washed her face and combed her hair, and went down to the others, trying her best to look as though crying were an exercise she had never even heard of.

She found the parlour in deepest gloom, hardly relieved at all by the efforts of Robert, who, to make the time pass, was pulling Jane's hair—not hard, but just enough to tease.

'Look here,' said Anthea. 'Let's have a palaver.' This word dated from the awful day when Cyril had carelessly wished that there were Red Indians in England—and there had been. The word brought back memories of last summer holidays and everyone groaned; they thought of the white house with the beautiful tangled garden—late roses, asters, marigold, sweet mignonette and feathery asparagus—of the wilderness which someone had once meant to make into an orchard, but which was now, as Father said, 'five acres of thistles haunted by the ghosts of baby cherry-trees'. They thought of the view across the valley, where the lime-kilns looked like Aladdin's palaces in the sunshine, and they thought of their own sandpit, with its fringe of yellowy grasses and pale-stringy-stalked wild flowers, and the little holes in the cliff that were the little sand-martins' little front doors. And they thought of the free fresh air smelling of thyme and sweetbriar, and the scent of the wood-smoke from the cottages in the lane—and they looked round old Nurse's stuffy parlour, and Jane said—

'Oh, how different it all is!'

It was. Old Nurse had been in the habit of letting lodgings, till Father gave her the children to take care of. And her rooms were furnished 'for letting'. Now it is a very odd thing that no one ever seems to furnish a room 'for letting' in a bit the same way as one would furnish it for living in. This room had heavy dark red stuff curtains—the colour that blood would not make a stain on—with coarse lace curtains inside. The carpet was yellow, and violet, with bits of grey and brown oilcloth in odd places. The fireplace had shavings and tinsel in it. There was a very varnished mahogany chiffonier, or sideboard, with a lock that wouldn't act. There were hard chairs—far too many of them—with crochet antimacassars slipping off their seats, all of which sloped the wrong way. The table wore a cloth of a cruel green colour with a yellow chain-stitch pattern round it. Over the fireplace was a looking-glass that made you look much uglier than you really were, however plain you might be to begin with. Then there was a mantelboard with maroon plush and wool fringe that did not match the plush; a dreary clock like a black marble tomb—it was silent as the grave too, for it had long since forgotten how to tick. And there were painted glass vases that never had any flowers in, and a painted tambourine that no one ever played, and painted brackets with nothing on them.

> And maple-framed engravings of the Queen, The
> Houses of Parliament, the Plains of Heaven, And
> of a blunt-nosed woodman's flat return.

There were two books—last December's *Bradshaw*, and an odd volume of Plumridge's *Commentary on Thessalonians*. There were—but I cannot dwell longer on this painful picture. It was indeed, as Jane said, very different.

'Let's have a palaver,' said Anthea again.

'What about?' said Cyril, yawning.

'There's nothing to have anything about,' said Robert kicking the leg of the table miserably.

'I don't want to play,' said Jane, and her tone was grumpy.

Anthea tried very hard not to be cross. She succeeded.

'Look here,' she said, 'don't think I want to be preachy or a beast in any way, but I want to what Father calls define the situation. Do you agree?'

'Fire ahead,' said Cyril without enthusiasm.

'Well then. We all know the reason we're staying here is because Nurse couldn't leave her house on account of the poor learned gentleman on the top-floor. And there was no one else Father could entrust to take care of us—and you know it's taken a lot of money, Mother's going to Madeira to be made well.'

Jane sniffed miserably.

'Yes, I know,' said Anthea in a hurry, 'but don't let's think about how horrid it all is. I mean we can't go to things that cost a lot, but we must do something. And I know there are heaps of things you can see in London without paying for them, and I thought we'd go and see them. We are all quite old now, and we haven't got The Lamb—'

Jane sniffed harder than before.

'I mean no one can say 'No' because of him, dear pet. And I thought we must get Nurse to see how quite old we are, and let us go out by ourselves, or else we shall never have any sort of a time at all. And I vote we see everything there is, and let's begin by asking Nurse to give us some bits of bread and we'll go to St James's Park. There are ducks there, I know, we can feed them. Only we must make Nurse let us go by ourselves.'

'Hurrah for liberty!' said Robert, 'but she won't.'

'Yes she will,' said Jane unexpectedly. 'I thought about that this morning, and I asked Father, and he said yes; and what's more he told old Nurse we might, only he said we must always say where we wanted to go, and if it was right she would let us.'

'Three cheers for thoughtful Jane,' cried Cyril, now roused at last from his yawning despair. 'I say, let's go now.'

So they went, old Nurse only begging them to be careful of crossings, and to ask a policeman to assist in the more difficult cases. But they were used to crossings, for they had lived in Camden Town and knew the Kentish Town Road where the trams rush up and down like mad at all hours of the day and night, and seem as though, if anything, they would rather run over you than not.

They had promised to be home by dark, but it was July, so dark would be very late indeed, and long past bedtime.

They started to walk to St James's Park, and all their pockets were stuffed with bits of bread and the crusts of toast, to feed the ducks with. They started, I repeat, but they never got there.

Between Fitzroy Street and St James's Park there are a great many streets, and, if you go the right way you will pass a great many shops that you cannot possibly help stopping to look at. The children stopped to look at several with gold-lace and beads and pictures and jewellery and dresses, and hats, and oysters and lobsters in their windows, and their sorrow did not seem nearly so impossible to bear as it had done in the best parlour at No. 300, Fitzroy Street.

Presently, by some wonderful chance turn of Robert's (who had been voted Captain because the girls thought it would be good for him—and indeed he thought so himself—and of course Cyril couldn't vote against him because it would have looked like a mean jealousy), they came into the little interesting criss-crossy streets that held the most interesting shops of all—the shops where live things were sold. There was one shop window entirely filled with cages, and all sorts of beautiful birds in them. The children were delighted till they remembered how they had once wished for wings themselves, and had had them—and then they felt how desperately unhappy anything with wings must be if it is shut up in a cage and not allowed to fly.

'It must be fairly beastly to be a bird in a cage,' said Cyril. 'Come on!'

They went on, and Cyril tried to think out a scheme for making his fortune as a gold-digger at Klondyke, and then buying all the caged birds in the world and setting them free.

Then they came to a shop that sold cats, but the cats were in cages, and the children could not help wishing someone would buy all the cats and put them on hearthrugs, which are the proper places for cats. And there was the dog-shop, and that was not a happy thing to look at either, because all the dogs were chained or caged, and all the dogs, big and little, looked at the four children with sad wistful eyes and wagged beseeching tails as if they were trying to say, 'Buy me! buy me! buy me! and let me go for a walk with you; oh, do buy me, and buy my poor brothers too! Do! do! do!' They almost said, 'Do! do! do!' plain to the ear, as they whined; all but one big Irish terrier, and he growled when Jane patted him.

'Grrrrr,' he seemed to say, as he looked at them from the back corner of his eye—'You won't buy me. Nobody will—ever—I shall die chained up—and I don't know that I care how soon it is, either!'

I don't know that the children would have understood all this, only once they had been in a besieged castle, so they knew how hateful it is to be kept in when you want to get out.

Of course they could not buy any of the dogs. They did, indeed, ask the price of the very, very smallest, and it was sixty-five pounds—but that was because it was a Japanese toy spaniel like the Queen once had her portrait painted with, when she was only Princess of Wales. But the children thought, if the smallest was all that money, the biggest would run into thousands—so they went on.

And they did not stop at any more cat or dog or bird shops, but passed them by, and at last they came to a shop that seemed as though it only sold creatures that did not much mind where they were—such as goldfish and white mice, and sea-anemones and other aquarium beasts, and lizards and toads, and hedgehogs and tortoises, and tame rabbits and guinea-pigs. And there they stopped for a long time, and fed the guinea-pigs with bits of bread through the cage-bars, and wondered whether it would be possible to keep a sandy-coloured double-lop in the basement of the house in Fitzroy Street.

'I don't suppose old Nurse would mind very much,' said Jane. 'Rabbits are most awfully tame sometimes. I expect it would know her voice and follow her all about.'

'She'd tumble over it twenty times a day,' said Cyril; 'now a snake—'

'There aren't any snakes,' said Robert hastily, 'and besides, I never could cotton to snakes somehow—I wonder why.'

'Worms are as bad,' said Anthea, 'and eels and slugs—I think it's because we don't like things that haven't got legs.'

'Father says snakes have got legs hidden away inside of them,' said Robert.

'Yes—and he says we've got tails hidden away inside us—but it doesn't either of it come to anything really,' said Anthea. 'I hate things that haven't any legs.'

'It's worse when they have too many,' said Jane with a shudder, 'think of centipedes!'

They stood there on the pavement, a cause of some inconvenience to the passersby, and thus beguiled the time with conversation. Cyril was leaning his elbow on the top of a hutch that had seemed empty when they had inspected the whole edifice of hutches one by one, and he was trying to reawaken the interest of a hedgehog that had curled itself into a ball earlier in the interview, when a small, soft voice just below his elbow said, quietly, plainly and quite unmistakably—not in any squeak or whine that had to be translated—but in downright common English—

'Buy me—do—please buy me!'

Cyril started as though he had been pinched, and jumped a yard away from the hutch.

'Come back—oh, come back!' said the voice, rather louder but still softly; 'stoop down and pretend to be tying up your bootlace—I see it's undone, as usual.'

Cyril mechanically obeyed. He knelt on one knee on the dry, hot dusty pavement, peered into the darkness of the hutch and found himself face to face with—the Psammead!

It seemed much thinner than when he had last seen it. It was dusty and dirty, and its fur was untidy and ragged. It had hunched itself up into a miserable lump, and its long snail's eyes were drawn in quite tight so that they hardly showed at all.

'Listen,' said the Psammead, in a voice that sounded as though it would begin to cry in a minute, 'I don't think the creature who keeps this shop will ask a very high price for me. I've bitten him more than once, and I've made myself look as common as I can. He's never had a glance from my beautiful, beautiful eyes. Tell the others I'm here—but tell them to look at some of those low, common beasts while I'm talking to you. The creature inside mustn't think you care much about me, or he'll put a price upon me far, far beyond your means. I remember in the dear old days last summer you never had much money. Oh—I never thought I should be so glad to see you—I never did.' It sniffed, and shot out its long snail's eyes expressly to drop a tear well away from its fur. 'Tell the others I'm here, and then

I'll tell you exactly what to do about buying me.'

Cyril tied his bootlace into a hard knot, stood up and addressed the others in firm tones—

'Look here,' he said, 'I'm not kidding—and I appeal to your honour,' an appeal which in this family was never made in vain. 'Don't look at that hutch—look at the white rat. Now you are not to look at that hutch whatever I say.'

He stood in front of it to prevent mistakes.

'Now get yourselves ready for a great surprise. In that hutch there's an old friend of ours—don't look!—Yes; it's the Psammead, the good old Psammead! it wants us to buy it. It says you're not to look at it. Look at the white rat and count your money! On your honour don't look!'

The others responded nobly. They looked at the white rat till they quite stared him out of countenance, so that he went and sat up on his hind legs in a far corner and hid his eyes with his front paws, and pretended he was washing his face.

Cyril stooped again, busying himself with the other bootlace and listened for the Psammead's further instructions.

'Go in,' said the Psammead, 'and ask the price of lots of other things. Then say, 'What do you want for that monkey that's lost its tail—the mangy old thing in the third hutch from the end.' Oh—don't mind my feelings—call me a mangy monkey—I've tried hard enough to look like one! I don't think he'll put a high price on me—I've bitten him eleven times since I came here the day before yesterday. If he names a bigger price than you can afford, say you wish you had the money.'

'But you can't give us wishes. I've promised never to have

another wish from you,' said the bewildered Cyril.

'Don't be a silly little idiot,' said the Sand-fairy in trembling but affectionate tones, 'but find out how much money you've got between you, and do exactly what I tell you.'

Cyril, pointing a stiff and unmeaning finger at the white rat, so as to pretend that its charms alone employed his tongue, explained matters to the others, while the Psammead hunched itself, and bunched itself, and did its very best to make itself look uninteresting.

Then the four children filed into the shop.

'How much do you want for that white rat?' asked Cyril.

'Eightpence,' was the answer.

'And the guinea-pigs?'

'Eighteenpence to five bob, according to the breed.'

'And the lizards?'

'Ninepence each.'

'And toads?'

'Fourpence. Now look here,' said the greasy owner of all this caged life with a sudden ferocity which made the whole party back hurriedly on to the wainscoting of hutches with which the shop was lined. 'Lookee here. I ain't agoin' to have you a comin' in here a turnin' the whole place outer winder, an' prizing every animile in the stock just for your larks, so don't think it! If you're a buyer, be a buyer—but I never had a customer yet as wanted to buy mice, and lizards, and toads, and guineas all at once. So hout you goes.'

'Oh! wait a minute,' said the wretched Cyril, feeling how foolishly yet well-meaningly he had carried out the Psammead's instructions. 'Just tell me one thing. What do you want for the mangy old monkey in the third hutch from the end?'

The shopman only saw in this a new insult.

'Mangy young monkey yourself,' said he; 'get along with your blooming cheek. Hout you goes!'

'Oh! don't be so cross,' said Jane, losing her head altogether, 'don't you see he really does want to know that!'

'Ho! does 'e indeed,' sneered the merchant. Then he scratched his ear suspiciously, for he was a sharp business man, and he knew the ring of truth when he heard it. His hand was bandaged, and three minutes before he would have been glad to sell the 'mangy old monkey' for ten shillings. Now—

'Ho! 'E does, does 'e,' he said, 'then two pun ten's my price. He's not got his fellow that monkey ain't, nor yet his match, not this side of the equator, which he comes from. And the only one ever seen in London. Ought to be in the Zoo. Two pun ten, down on the nail, or hout you goes!'

The children looked at each other—twenty-three shillings and fivepence was all they had in the world, and it would have been merely three and fivepence, but for the sovereign which Father had given to them 'between them' at parting.

'We've only twenty-three shillings and fivepence,' said Cyril, rattling the money in his pocket.

'Twenty-three farthings and somebody's own cheek,' said the dealer, for he did not believe that Cyril had so much money.

There was a miserable pause. Then Anthea remembered, and said—

'Oh! I wish I had two pounds ten.'

'So do I, Miss, I'm sure,' said the man with bitter

politeness; 'I wish you 'ad, I'm sure!'

Anthea's hand was on the counter, something seemed to slide under it. She lifted it. There lay five bright half sovereigns.

'Why, I have got it after all,' she said; 'here's the money, now let's have the Sammy, ... the monkey I mean.'

The dealer looked hard at the money, but he made haste to put it in his pocket.

'I only hope you come by it honest,' he said, shrugging his shoulders. He scratched his ear again.

'Well!' he said, 'I suppose I must let you have it, but it's worth thribble the money, so it is—'

He slowly led the way out to the hutch—opened the door gingerly, and made a sudden fierce grab at the Psammead, which the Psammead acknowledged in one last long lingering bite.

'Here, take the brute,' said the shopman, squeezing the Psammead so tight that he nearly choked it. 'It's bit me to the marrow, it have.'

The man's eyes opened as Anthea held out her arms. 'Don't blame me if it tears your face off its bones,' he said, and the Psammead made a leap from his dirty horny hands, and Anthea caught it in hers, which were not very clean, certainly, but at any rate were soft and pink, and held it kindly and closely.

'But you can't take it home like that,' Cyril said, 'we shall have a crowd after us,' and indeed two errand boys and a policeman had already collected.

'I can't give you nothink only a paper-bag, like what we put the tortoises in,' said the man grudgingly.

So the whole party went into the shop, and the shopman's

eyes nearly came out of his head when, having given Anthea the largest paper-bag he could find, he saw her hold it open, and the Psammead carefully creep into it.

'Well!' he said, 'if that there don't beat cockfighting! But p'raps you've met the brute afore.'

'Yes,' said Cyril affably, 'he's an old friend of ours.'

'If I'd a known that,' the man rejoined, 'you shouldn't a had him under twice the money. 'Owever,' he added, as the children disappeared, 'I ain't done so bad, seeing as I only give five bob for the beast. But then there's the bites to take into account!'

The children trembling in agitation and excitement, carried home the Psammead, trembling in its paper-bag.

When they got it home, Anthea nursed it, and stroked it, and would have cried over it, if she hadn't remembered how it hated to be wet.

When it recovered enough to speak, it said—

'Get me sand; silver sand from the oil and colour shop. And get me plenty.'

They got the sand, and they put it and the Psammead in the round bath together, and it rubbed itself, and rolled itself, and shook itself and scraped itself, and scratched itself, and preened itself, till it felt clean and comfy, and then it scrabbled a hasty hole in the sand, and went to sleep in it.

The children hid the bath under the girls' bed, and had supper. Old Nurse had got them a lovely supper of bread and butter and fried onions. She was full of kind and delicate thoughts.

When Anthea woke the next morning, the Psammead was snuggling down between her shoulder and Jane's.

'You have saved my life,' it said. 'I know that man would

have thrown cold water on me sooner or later, and then I should have died. I saw him wash out a guinea-pig's hutch yesterday morning. I'm still frightfully sleepy, I think I'll go back to sand for another nap. Wake the boys and this dormouse of a Jane, and when you've had your breakfasts we'll have a talk.'

'Don't you want any breakfast?' asked Anthea.

'I daresay I shall pick a bit presently,' it said; 'but sand is all I care about—it's meat and drink to me, and coals and fire and wife and children.' With these words it clambered down by the bedclothes and scrambled back into the bath, where they heard it scratching itself out of sight.

'Well!' said Anthea, 'anyhow our holidays won't be dull now. We've found the Psammead again.'

'No,' said Jane, beginning to put on her stockings. 'We shan't be dull—but it'll be only like having a pet dog now it can't give us wishes.'

'Oh, don't be so discontented,' said Anthea. 'If it can't do anything else it can tell us about Megatheriums and things.'

5

How Fear Came

Rudyard Kipling

The stream is shrunk—the pool is dry,
And we be comrades, thou and I;
With fevered jowl and dusty flank
Each jostling each along the bank;
And by one drouthy fear made still,
Forgoing thought of quest or kill.
Now 'neath his dam the fawn may see,
The lean Pack-wolf as cowed as he,
And the tall buck, unflinching, note
The fangs that tore his father's throat.
The pools are shrunk—the streams are dry,
And we be playmates, thou and I,
Till yonder cloud—Good Hunting!—loose
The rain that breaks our Water Truce.

The Law of the Jungle—which is by far the oldest law in the world—has arranged for almost every kind of accident that may befall the Jungle People, till now its code is as perfect as time and custom can make it. You will remember that Mowgli spent a great part of his life in the Seeonee Wolf-Pack, learning the Law from Baloo, the Brown Bear; and it was Baloo who told him, when the boy grew impatient at the constant orders, that the Law was like the Giant Creeper, because it dropped across every one's back and no one could escape. 'When thou hast lived as long as I have, Little Brother, thou wilt see how all the Jungle obeys at least one Law. And that will be no pleasant sight,' said Baloo.

This talk went in at one ear and out at the other, for a boy who spends his life eating and sleeping does not worry about anything till it actually stares him in the face. But, one year, Baloo's words came true, and Mowgli saw all the Jungle working under the Law.

It began when the winter Rains failed almost entirely, and Ikki, the Porcupine, meeting Mowgli in a bamboo-thicket, told him that the wild yams were drying up. Now everybody knows that Ikki is ridiculously fastidious in his choice of food, and will eat nothing but the very best and ripest. So Mowgli laughed and said, 'What is that to me?'

'Not much now,' said Ikki, rattling his quills in a stiff, uncomfortable way, 'but later we shall see. Is there any more diving into the deep rock-pool below the Bee-Rocks, Little Brother?'

'No. The foolish water is going all away, and I do not wish to break my head,' said Mowgli, who, in those days, was quite sure that he knew as much as any five of the Jungle People put together.

'That is thy loss. A small crack might let in some wisdom.' Ikki ducked quickly to prevent Mowgli from pulling his nose-bristles, and Mowgli told Baloo what Ikki had said. Baloo looked very grave, and mumbled half to himself: 'If I were alone I would change my hunting-grounds now, before the others began to think. And yet—hunting among strangers ends in fighting; and they might hurt the Man-cub. We must wait and see how the mohwa blooms.'

That spring the mohwa tree, that Baloo was so fond of, never flowered. The greeny, cream-coloured, waxy blossoms were heat-killed before they were born, and only a few bad-smelling petals came down when he stood on his hind legs and shook the tree. Then, inch by inch, the untempered heat crept into the heart of the Jungle, turning it yellow, brown and at last black. The green growths in the sides of the ravines burned up to broken wires and curled films of dead stuff; the hidden pools sank down and caked over, keeping the last least footmark on their edges as if it had been cast in iron; the juicy-stemmed creepers fell away from the trees they clung to and died at their feet; the bamboos withered, clanking when the hot winds blew, and the moss peeled off the rocks deep in the Jungle, till they were as bare and as hot as the quivering blue boulders in the bed of the stream.

The birds and the monkey-people went north early in the year, for they knew what was coming; and the deer and the wild pig broke far away to the perished fields of the villages, dying sometimes before the eyes of men too weak to kill them. Chil, the Kite, stayed and grew fat, for there was a great deal of carrion, and evening after evening he brought the news to the beasts, too weak to force their way to fresh hunting-grounds, that the sun was killing the Jungle for three days' flight in every direction.

Mowgli, who had never known what real hunger meant, fell back on stale honey, three years old, scraped out of deserted rock-hives—honey black as a sloe, and dusty with dried sugar. He hunted, too, for deep-boring grubs under the bark of the trees, and robbed the wasps of their new broods. All the game in the jungle was no more than skin and bone, and Bagheera could kill thrice in a night, and hardly get a full meal. But the want of water was the worst, for though the Jungle People drink seldom they must drink deep.

And the heat went on and on, and sucked up all the moisture, till at last the main channel of the Waingunga was the only stream that carried a trickle of water between its dead banks; and when Hathi, the wild elephant, who lives for a hundred years and more, saw a long, lean blue ridge of rock show dry in the very centre of the stream, he knew that he was looking at the Peace Rock, and then and there he lifted up his trunk and proclaimed the Water Truce, as his father before him had proclaimed it fifty years ago. The deer, wild pig and buffalo took up the cry hoarsely; and Chil, the Kite, flew in great circles far and wide, whistling and shrieking the warning.

By the Law of the Jungle it is death to kill at the drinking-places when once the Water Truce has been declared. The reason of this is that drinking comes before eating. Every one in the Jungle can scramble along somehow when only game is scarce; but water is water, and when there is but one source of supply, all hunting stops while the Jungle People go there for their needs. In good seasons, when water was plentiful, those who came down to drink at the Waingunga—or anywhere else, for that matter—did so at the risk of their lives, and that risk made no small part of the fascination of the night's doings. To move down so cunningly that never a leaf stirred; to wade knee-deep in the

roaring shallows that drown all noise from behind; to drink, looking backward over one shoulder, every muscle ready for the first desperate bound of keen terror; to roll on the sandy margin, and return, wet-muzzled and well plumped out, to the admiring herd, was a thing that all tall-antlered young bucks took a delight in, precisely because they knew that at any moment Bagheera or Shere Khan might leap upon them and bear them down. But now all that life-and-death fun was ended, and the Jungle People came up, starved and weary, to the shrunken river,—tiger, bear, deer, buffalo, and pig, all together,—drank the fouled waters, and hung above them, too exhausted to move off.

The deer and the pig had tramped all day in search of something better than dried bark and withered leaves. The buffaloes had found no wallows to be cool in, and no green crops to steal. The snakes had left the Jungle and come down to the river in the hope of finding a stray frog. They curled round wet stones, and never offered to strike when the nose of a rooting pig dislodged them. The river-turtles had long ago been killed by Bagheera, cleverest of hunters, and the fish had buried themselves deep in the dry mud. Only the Peace Rock lay across the shallows like a long snake, and the little tired ripples hissed as they dried on its hot side.

It was here that Mowgli came nightly for the cool and the companionship. The most hungry of his enemies would hardly have cared for the boy then, His naked hide made him seem more lean and wretched than any of his fellows. His hair was bleached to tow colour by the sun; his ribs stood out like the ribs of a basket, and the lumps on his knees and elbows, where he was used to track on all fours, gave his shrunken limbs the look of knotted grass-stems. But his eye, under his matted forelock, was cool and quiet, for Bagheera was his adviser in this time of trouble, and told him to go quietly, hunt slowly and never, on any account, to lose his temper.

'It is an evil time,' said the Black Panther, one furnace-hot evening, 'but it will go if we can live till the end. Is thy stomach full, Man-cub?'

'There is stuff in my stomach, but I get no good of it. Think you, Bagheera, the Rains have forgotten us and will never come again?'

'Not I! We shall see the mohwa in blossom yet, and the little fawns all fat with new grass. Come down to the Peace Rock and hear the news. On my back, Little Brother.'

'This is no time to carry weight. I can still stand alone, but—indeed we be no fatted bullocks, we two.'

Bagheera looked along his ragged, dusty flank and whispered. 'Last night I killed a bullock under the yoke. So low was I brought that I think I should not have dared to spring if he had been loose. Wou!'

Mowgli laughed. 'Yes, we be great hunters now,' said he. 'I am very bold—to eat grubs,' and the two came down together through the crackling undergrowth to the river-bank and the lace-work of shoals that ran out from it in every direction.

'The water cannot live long,' said Baloo, joining them. 'Look across. Yonder are trails like the roads of Man.'

On the level plain of the farther bank the stiff jungle-grass had died standing, and, dying, had mummied. The beaten tracks of the deer and the pig, all heading toward the river, had striped that colourless plain with dusty gullies driven through the ten-foot grass, and, early as it was, each long avenue was full of first-comers hastening to the water. You could hear the does and fawns coughing in the snuff-like dust.

Up-stream, at the bend of the sluggish pool round the Peace Rock, and Warden of the Water Truce, stood Hathi, the wild elephant, with his sons, gaunt and gray in the moonlight, rocking to and fro—always rocking. Below him a little were the vanguard of the deer; below these, again, the pig and the wild buffalo; and on the opposite bank, where the tall trees came down to the water's edge, was the place set apart for the Eaters of Flesh—the tiger, the wolves, the panther, the bear and the others.

'We are under one Law, indeed,' said Bagheera, wading into the water and looking across at the lines of clicking horns and starting eyes where the deer and the pig pushed each other to and fro. 'Good hunting, all you of my blood,' he added, lying own at full length, one flank thrust out of the shallows; and then, between his teeth, 'But for that which is the Law it would be very good hunting.'

The quick-spread ears of the deer caught the last sentence, and a frightened whisper ran along the ranks. 'The Truce! Remember the Truce!'

'Peace there, peace!' gurgled Hathi, the wild elephant. 'The Truce holds, Bagheera. This is no time to talk of hunting.'

'Who should know better than I?' Bagheera answered, rolling his yellow eyes up-stream. 'I am an eater of turtles—a fisher of frogs. Ngaayah! Would I could get good from chewing branches!'

'We wish so, very greatly,' bleated a young fawn, who had only been born that spring, and did not at all like it. Wretched as the Jungle People were, even Hathi could not help chuckling; while Mowgli, lying on his elbows in the warm water, laughed aloud, and beat up the scum with his feet.

'Well spoken, little bud-horn,' Bagheera purred. 'When the Truce ends that shall be remembered in thy favour,' and he looked keenly through the darkness to make sure of recognising the fawn again.

Gradually the talking spread up and down the drinking-places. One could hear the scuffling, snorting pig asking for more room; the buffaloes grunting among themselves as they lurched out across the sand-bars and the deer telling pitiful stories of their long foot-sore wanderings in quest of food. Now and again they asked some question of the Eaters of Flesh across the river, but all the news was bad, and the roaring hot wind of the Jungle came and went between the rocks and the rattling branches, and scattered twigs, and dust on the water.

'The men-folk, too, they die beside their ploughs,' said a young sambhur. 'I passed three between sunset and night. They lay still, and their Bullocks with them. We also shall lie still in a little.'

'The river has fallen since last night,' said Baloo. 'O Hathi, hast thou ever seen the like of this drought?'

'It will pass, it will pass,' said Hathi, squirting water along his back and sides.

'We have one here that cannot endure long,' said Baloo; and he looked toward the boy he loved.

'I?' said Mowgli indignantly, sitting up in the water. 'I have no long fur to cover my bones, but—but if thy hide were taken off, Baloo—'

Hathi shook all over at the idea, and Baloo said severely:

'Man-cub, that is not seemly to tell a Teacher of the Law. Never have I been seen without my hide.'

'Nay, I meant no harm, Baloo; but only that thou art, as it were, like the cocoanut in the husk, and I am the same cocoanut all naked. Now that brown husk of thine—' Mowgli was sitting cross-legged, and explaining things with his forefinger in his usual way, when Bagheera put out a paddy paw and pulled him over backward into the water.

'Worse and worse,' said the Black Panther, as the boy rose spluttering. 'First Baloo is to be skinned, and now he is a cocoanut. Be careful that he does not do what the ripe cocoanuts do.'

'And what is that?' said Mowgli, off his guard for the minute, though that is one of the oldest catches in the Jungle.

'Break thy head,' said Bagheera quietly, pulling him under again.

'It is not good to make a jest of thy teacher,' said the bear, when Mowgli had been ducked for the third time.

'Not good! What would ye have? That naked thing running to and fro makes a monkey-jest of those who have once been good hunters, and pulls the best of us by the whiskers for sport.' This was Shere Khan, the Lame Tiger, limping down to the water. He waited a little to enjoy the sensation he made among the deer on the opposite to lap, growling: 'The jungle has become a whelping-ground for naked cubs now. Look at me, Man-cub!'

Mowgli looked—stared, rather—as insolently as he knew how, and in a minute Shere Khan turned away uneasily. 'Man-cub this, and Man-cub that,' he rumbled, going on with his drink, 'the cub is neither man nor cub, or he would have been afraid. Next season I shall have to beg his leave for a drink. Augrh!'

'That may come, too,' said Bagheera, looking him steadily between the eyes. 'That may come, too—Faugh, Shere Khan!—what new shame hast thou brought here?'

The Lame Tiger had dipped his chin and jowl in the water, and dark, oily streaks were floating from it down-stream.

'Man!' said Shere Khan coolly, 'I killed an hour since.' He went on purring and growling to himself.

The line of beasts shook and wavered to and fro, and a whisper went up that grew to a cry. 'Man! Man! He has killed Man!' Then all looked towards Hathi, the wild elephant, but he seemed not to hear. Hathi never does anything till the time comes, and that is one of the reasons why he lives so long.

'At such a season as this to kill Man! Was no other game afoot?' said Bagheera scornfully, drawing himself out of the tainted water, and shaking each paw, cat-fashion, as he did so.

'I killed for choice—not for food.' The horrified whisper began again, and Hathi's watchful little white eye cocked itself in Shere Khan's direction. 'For choice,' Shere Khan drawled. 'Now come I to drink and make me clean again. Is there any to forbid?'

Bagheera's back began to curve like a bamboo in a high wind, but Hathi lifted up his trunk and spoke quietly.

'Thy kill was from choice?' he asked; and when Hathi asks a question it is best to answer.

'Even so. It was my right and my Night. Thou knowest, O Hathi.' Shere Khan spoke almost courteously.

'Yes, I know,' Hathi answered; and, after a little silence, 'Hast thou drunk thy fill?'

'For to-night, yes.'

'Go, then. The river is to drink, and not to defile. None but the Lame Tiger would so have boasted of his right at this season when—when we suffer together—Man and Jungle People alike. Clean or unclean, get to thy lair, Shere Khan!'

The last words rang out like silver trumpets, and Hathi's three sons rolled forward half a pace, though there was no need. Shere Khan slunk away, not daring to growl, for he knew—what every one else knows—that when the last comes to the last, Hathi is the Master of the Jungle.

'What is this right Shere Khan speaks of?' Mowgli whispered in Bagheera's ear. 'To kill Man is always, shameful. The Law says so. And yet Hathi says—'

'Ask him. I do not know, Little Brother. Right or no right, if Hathi had not spoken I would have taught that lame butcher his lesson. To come to the Peace Rock fresh from a kill of Man—and to boast of it—is a jackal's trick. Besides, he tainted the good water.'

Mowgli waited for a minute to pick up his courage, because no one cared to address Hathi directly, and then he cried: 'What is Shere Khan's right, O Hathi?' Both banks echoed his words, for all the People of the Jungle are intensely curious, and they had just seen something that none except Baloo, who looked very thoughtful, seemed to understand.

'It is an old tale,' said Hathi; 'a tale older than the Jungle. Keep silence along the banks and I will tell that tale.'

There was a minute or two of pushing a shouldering among the pigs and the buffalo, and then the leaders of the herds grunted, one after another, 'We wait,' and Hathi strode forward, till he was nearly knee-deep in the pool by the Peace Rock. Lean and wrinkled and yellow-tusked though he was, he looked what the Jungle knew him to be—their master.

'Ye know, children,' he began, 'that of all things ye most fear Man;' and there was a mutter of agreement.

'This tale touches thee, Little Brother,' said Bagheera to Mowgli.

'I? I am of the Pack—a hunter of the Free People.' Mowgli answered. 'What have I to do with Man?'

'And ye do not know why ye fear Man?' Hathi went on. 'This is the reason. In the beginning of the Jungle, and none know when that was, we of the Jungle walked together, having no fear of one another. In those days there was no drought, and leaves and flowers and fruit grew on the same tree, and we ate nothing at all except leaves and flowers and grass and fruit and bark.'

'I am glad I was not born in those days,' said Bagheera. 'Bark is only good to sharpen claws.'

'And the Lord of the Jungle was Tha, the First of the Elephants. He drew the Jungle out of deep waters with his trunk; and where he made furrows in the ground with his tusks, there the rivers ran; and where he struck with his foot, there rose ponds of good water; and when he blew through his trunk,—thus,—the trees fell. That was the manner in which the Jungle was made by Tha; and so the tale was told to me.'

'It has not lost fat in the telling,' Bagheera whispered, and Mowgli laughed behind his hand.

'In those days there was no corn or melons or pepper or sugar-cane, nor were there any little huts such as ye have all seen; and the Jungle People knew nothing of Man, but lived in the Jungle together, making one people. But presently they began to dispute over their food, though there was grazing enough for all. They were lazy. Each wished to eat where he lay, as sometimes we can do now when the spring rains are good. Tha, the First of the Elephants, was busy making new jungles and leading the rivers in their beds. He could not walk in all places; therefore he made the First of the Tigers the master and the judge of the Jungle, to whom the Jungle People should bring their disputes. In those days the First of the Tigers ate fruit and grass with the others. He was as large as I am, and he was very beautiful, in colour all over like the blossom of the yellow creeper. There was never stripe nor bar upon his hide in those good days when this the Jungle was new. All the Jungle People came before him without fear, and his word was the Law of all the Jungle. We were then, remember ye, one people.

'Yet upon a night there was a dispute between two bucks—a grazing-quarrel such as ye now settle with the horns and the fore-feet—and it is said that as the two spoke together before the First of the First of the Tigers lying among the flowers, a buck pushed him with his horns, and the First of the Tigers forgot that he was the master and judge of the Jungle, and, leaping upon that buck, broke his neck.

'Till that night never one of us had died, and the First of the Tigers, seeing what he had done, and being made foolish by the scent of the blood, ran away into the marshes of the North, and we of the Jungle, left without a judge, fell to fighting among ourselves; and Tha heard the noise of it and came back. Then some of us said this and some of us said that, but he saw the dead buck among the flowers, and asked who had killed, and we of the Jungle would not tell because the smell of the blood made us foolish. We ran to and fro in circles, capering and crying out and shaking our heads. Then Tha gave an order to the trees that hang low, and to the trailing creepers of the Jungle, that they should mark the killer of the buck so that he should know him again, and he said, "Who will now be master of the Jungle People?" Then up leaped the Gray Ape who lives in the branches, and said, "I will now be master of the Jungle."

'At this Tha laughed, and said, "So be it," and went away very angry.

'Children, ye know the Gray Ape. He was then as he is now. At the first he made a wise face for himself, but in a little while he began to scratch and to leap up and down, and when Tha came back he found the Gray Ape hanging, head down, from a bough, mocking those who stood below; and they mocked him again. And so there was no Law in the Jungle—only foolish talk and senseless words.

'Then Tha called us all together and said: "The first of your masters has brought Death into the Jungle, and the second Shame. Now it is time there was a Law, and a Law that ye must not break. Now ye shall know Fear, and when ye have found him ye shall know that he is your master, and the rest shall follow." Then we of the jungle said, "What is Fear?" And Tha said, "Seek till ye find."

So we went up and down the Jungle seeking for Fear, and presently the buffaloes—'

'Ugh!' said Mysa, the leader of the buffaloes, from their sand-bank.

'Yes, Mysa, it was the buffaloes. They came back with the news that in a cave in the Jungle sat Fear, and that he had no hair, and went upon his hind legs. Then we of the Jungle followed the herd till we came to that cave, and Fear stood at the mouth of it, and he was, as the buffaloes had said, hairless, and he walked upon his hinder legs. When he saw us he cried out, and his voice filled us with the fear that we have now of that voice when we hear it, and we ran away, tramping upon and tearing each other because we were afraid. That night, so it was told to me, we of the Jungle did not lie down together as used to be our custom, but each tribe drew off by itself—the pig with the pig, the deer with the deer; horn to horn, hoof to hoof,—like keeping to like, and so lay shaking in the Jungle.

'Only the First of the Tigers was not with us, for he was still hidden in the marshes of the North, and when word was brought to him of the Thing we had seen in the cave, he said. "I will go to this Thing and break his neck." So he ran all the night till he came to the cave; but the trees and the creepers on his path, remembering the order that Tha had given, let down their branches and marked him as he ran, drawing their fingers across his back, his flank, his forehead, and his jowl. Wherever they touched him there was a mark and a stripe upon his yellow hide. AND THOSE STRIPES DO THIS CHILDREN WEAR TO THIS DAY! When he came to the cave,

Fear, the Hairless One, put out his hand and called him "The Striped One that comes by night," and the First of the Tigers was afraid of the Hairless One, and ran back to the swamps howling.'

Mowgli chuckled quietly here, his chin in the water.

'So loud did he howl that Tha heard him and said, "What is the sorrow?" And the First of the Tigers, lifting up his muzzle to the new-made sky, which is now so old, said: "Give me back my power, O Tha. I am made ashamed before all the Jungle, and I have run away from a Hairless One, and he has called me a shameful name." "And why?" said Tha. "Because I am smeared with the mud of the marshes," said the First of the Tigers. "Swim, then, and roll on the wet grass, and if it be mud it will wash away," said Tha; and the First of the Tigers swam, and rolled and rolled upon the grass, till the Jungle ran round and round before his eyes, but not one little bar upon all his hide was changed, and Tha, watching him, laughed. Then the First of the Tigers said: "What have I done that this comes to me?" Tha said, "Thou hast killed the buck, and thou hast let Death loose in the Jungle, and with Death has come Fear, so that the people of the Jungle are afraid one of the other, as thou art afraid of the Hairless One." The First of the Tigers said, "They will never fear me, for I knew them since the beginning." Tha said, "Go and see." And the First of the Tigers ran to and fro, calling aloud to the deer and the pig and the sambhur and the porcupine and all the Jungle Peoples, and they all ran away from him who had been their judge, because they were afraid.

'Then the First of the Tigers came back, and his pride was broken in him, and, beating his head upon the ground, he tore up the earth with all his feet and said: "Remember that I was once the Master of the Jungle. Do not forget me, O Tha! Let my children remember that I was once without shame or fear!" And Tha said: "This much I will do, because thou and I together saw the Jungle made. For one night in each year it shall be as it was before the buck was killed—for thee and for thy children. In that one night, if ye meet the Hairless One—and his name is Man—ye shall not be afraid of him, but he shall be afraid of you, as though ye were judges of the Jungle and masters of all things. Show him mercy in that night of his fear, for thou hast known what Fear is."

'Then the First of the Tigers answered, "I am content"; but when next he drank he saw the black stripes upon his flank and his side, and he remembered the name that the Hairless One had given him, and he was angry. For a year he lived in the marshes waiting till Tha should keep his promise. And upon a night when the jackal of the Moon (the Evening Star) stood clear of the Jungle, he felt that his Night was upon him, and he went to that cave to meet the Hairless One. Then it happened as Tha promised, for the Hairless One fell down before him and lay along the ground, and the First of the Tigers struck him and broke his back, for he thought that there was but one such Thing in the Jungle, and that he had killed Fear. Then, nosing above the kill, he heard Tha coming down from the woods of the North, and presently the voice of the First of the Elephants, which is the voice that we hear now—'

The thunder was rolling up and down the dry, scarred hills, but it brought no rain—only heat—lightning that flickered along the ridges—and Hathi went on: 'That was the voice he heard, and it said: "Is this thy mercy?" The First of the Tigers licked his lips and said: "What matter? I have killed Fear." And Tha said: "O blind and foolish! Thou hast untied the feet of Death, and he will follow thy trail till thou diest. Thou hast taught Man to kill!"

'The First of the Tigers, standing stiffly to his kill, said "He is as the buck was. There is no Fear. Now I will judge the Jungle Peoples once more."

'And Tha said: "Never again shall the Jungle Peoples come to thee. They shall never cross thy trail, nor sleep near thee, nor follow after thee, nor browse by thy lair. Only Fear shall follow thee, and with a blow that thou canst not see he shall bid thee wait his pleasure. He shall make the ground to open under thy feet, and the creeper to twist about thy neck, and the tree-trunks to grow together about thee higher than thou canst leap, and at the last he shall take thy hide to wrap his cubs when they are cold. Thou hast shown him no mercy, and none will he show thee."

'The First of the Tigers was very bold, for his Night was still on him, and he said: "The Promise of Tha is the Promise of Tha. He will not take away my Night?" And Tha said: "The one Night is thine, as I have said, but there is a price to pay. Thou hast taught Man to kill, and he is no slow learner."

'The First of the Tigers said: "He is here under my foot, and his back is broken. Let the Jungle know I have killed Fear."

'Then Tha laughed, and said: "Thou hast killed one of many, but thou thyself shalt tell the Jungle—for thy Night is ended."

'So the day came; and from the mouth of the cave went out another Hairless One, and he saw the kill in the path, and the First of the Tigers above it, and he took a pointed stick—'

'They throw a thing that cuts now,' said Ikki, rustling down the bank; for Ikki was considered uncommonly good eating by the Gonds—they called him Ho-Igoo—and he knew something of the wicked little Gondee axe that whirls across a clearing like a dragon-fly.

'It was a pointed stick, such as they put in the foot of a pit-trap,' said Hathi, 'and throwing it, he struck the First of the Tigers deep in the flank. Thus it happened as Tha said, for the First of the Tigers ran howling up and down the Jungle till he tore out the stick, and all the Jungle knew that the Hairless One could strike from far off, and they feared more than before. So it came about that the First of the Tigers taught the Hairless One to kill—and ye know what harm that has since done to all our peoples—through the noose, and the pitfall, and the hidden trap, and the flying stick and the stinging fly that comes out of white smoke (Hathi meant the rifle), and the Red Flower that drives us into the open. Yet for one night in the year the Hairless One fears the Tiger, as Tha promised, and never has the Tiger given him cause to be less afraid. Where he finds him, there he kills him, remembering how the First of the Tigers was made ashamed. For the rest, Fear walks up and down the Jungle by day and by night.'

'Ahi! Aoo!' said the deer, thinking of what it all meant to them.

'And only when there is one great Fear over all, as there is now, can we of the Jungle lay aside our little fears, and meet together in one place as we do now.'

'For one night only does Man fear the Tiger?' said Mowgli.

'For one night only,' said Hathi.

'But I—but we—but all the Jungle knows that Shere Khan kills Man twice and thrice in a moon.'

'Even so. Then he springs from behind and turns his head aside as he strikes, for he is full of fear. If Man looked at him he would run. But on his one Night he goes openly down to the village. He walks between the houses and thrusts his head into the doorway, and the men fall on their faces, and there he does his kill. One kill in that Night.'

'Oh!' said Mowgli to himself, rolling over in the water. 'Now I see why it was Shere Khan bade me look at him! He got no good of it, for he could not hold his eyes steady, and—and I certainly did not fall down at his feet. But then I am not a man, being of the Free People.'

'Umm!' said Bagheera deep in his furry throat. 'Does the Tiger know his Night?'

'Never till the Jackal of the Moon stands clear of the evening mist. Sometimes it falls in the dry summer and sometimes in the wet rains—this one Night of the Tiger. But for the First of the Tigers, this would never have been, nor would any of us have known fear.'

The deer grunted sorrowfully and Bagheera's lips curled in a wicked smile. 'Do men know this—tale?' said he.

'None know it except the tigers, and we, the elephants—the children of Tha. Now ye by the pools have heard it, and I have spoken.'

Hathi dipped his trunk into the water as a sign that he did not wish to talk.

'But—but—but,' said Mowgli, turning to Baloo, 'why did not the First of the Tigers continue to eat grass and leaves and trees? He did but break the buck's neck. He did not EAT. What led him to the hot meat?'

'The trees and the creepers marked him, Little Brother, and made him the striped thing that we see. Never again would he eat their fruit; but from that day he revenged himself upon the deer, and the others, the Eaters of Grass,' said Baloo.

'Then thou knowest the tale. Heh? Why have I never heard?'

'Because the Jungle is full of such tales. If I made a beginning there would never be an end to them. Let go my ear, Little Brother.'

6

Mrs Packletide's Tiger

Saki (H.H. Munro)

It was Mrs Packletide's pleasure and intention that she should shoot a tiger. Not that the lust to kill had suddenly descended on her, or that she felt that she would leave India safer and more wholesome than she had found it, with one fraction less of wild beast per million of inhabitants. The compelling motive for her sudden deviation towards the footsteps of Nimrod was the fact that Loona Bimberton had recently been carried eleven miles in an aeroplane by an Algerian aviator, and talked of nothing else; only a personally procured tiger-skin and a heavy harvest of press photographs could successfully counter that sort of thing. Mrs Packletide had already arranged in her mind the lunch she would give at her house in Curzon Street, ostensibly in Loona Bimberton's honour, with a tiger-skin rug occupying most of the foreground and all of the conversation. She had also already designed in her mind the tiger-claw brooch that she was going to give Loona Bimberton on her next birthday. In a world that is supposed to be chiefly swayed by hunger and by love Mrs Packletide was an exception; her movements and motives were largely governed by dislike of Loona Bimberton.

Circumstances proved propitious. Mrs Packletide had offered a thousand rupees for the opportunity of shooting a tiger without overmuch risk or exertion, and it so happened that a neighbouring village could boast of being the favoured rendezvous of an animal of respectable antecedents, which had been driven by the increasing infirmities of age to abandon game-killing and confine its appetite to the smaller domestic animals. The prospect of earning the thousand rupees had stimulated the sporting and commercial instinct of the villagers; children were posted night and day on the outskirts of the local jungle to head the tiger back in the unlikely event of his attempting to roam away to fresh hunting-grounds, and the cheaper kinds of goats were left about with elaborate carelessness to keep him satisfied with his present quarters. The one great anxiety was lest he should die of old age before the date appointed for the memsahib's shoot. Mothers carrying their babies home through the jungle after the day's work in the fields hushed their singing lest they might curtail the restful sleep of the venerable herd-robber.

The great night duly arrived, moonlit and cloudless. A platform had been constructed in a comfortable and conveniently placed tree, and thereon crouched Mrs Packletide and her paid companion, Miss Mebbin. A goat, gifted with a particularly persistent bleat, such as even a partially deaf tiger might be reasonably expected to hear on a still night, was tethered at the correct distance. With an accurately sighted rifle and a thumb-nail pack of patience cards the sportswoman awaited the coming of the quarry.

'I suppose we are in some danger?' said Miss Mebbin.

She was not actually nervous about the wild beast, but she had a morbid dread of performing an atom more service than she had been paid for.

'Nonsense,' said Mrs Packletide; 'it's a very old tiger. It couldn't spring up here even if it wanted to.'

'If it's an old tiger I think you ought to get it cheaper. A thousand rupees is a lot of money.'

Louisa Mebbin adopted a protective elder-sister attitude towards money in general, irrespective of nationality or denomination. Her energetic intervention had saved many a rouble from dissipating itself in tips in some Moscow hotel, and francs and centimes clung to her instinctively under circumstances which would have driven them headlong from less sympathetic hands. Her speculations as to the market depreciation of tiger remnants were cut short by the appearance on the scene of the animal itself. As soon as it caught sight of the tethered goat it lay flat on the earth, seemingly less from a desire to take advantage of all available cover than for the purpose of snatching a short rest before commencing the grand attack.

'I believe it's ill,' said Louisa Mebbin, loudly in Hindustani, for the benefit of the village headman, who was in ambush in a neighbouring tree.

'Hush!' said Mrs Packletide, and at that moment the tiger commenced ambling towards his victim.

'Now, now!' urged Miss Mebbin with some excitement; 'if he doesn't touch the goat we needn't pay for it.' (The bait was an extra.)

The rifle flashed out with a loud report, and the great tawny beast sprang to one side and then rolled over in the stillness of death. In a moment a crowd of excited natives had swarmed on to the scene, and their shouting speedily carried the glad news to the village, where a thumping of

tom-toms took up the chorus of triumph. And their triumph and rejoicing found a ready echo in the heart of Mrs Packletide; already that luncheon-party in Curzon Street seemed immeasurably nearer.

It was Louisa Mebbin who drew attention to the fact that the goat was in death-throes from a mortal bullet-wound, while no trace of the rifle's deadly work could be found on the tiger. Evidently the wrong animal had been hit, and the beast of prey had succumbed to heartfailure, caused by the sudden report of the rifle, accelerated by senile decay. Mrs Packletide was pardonably annoyed at the discovery; but, at any rate, she was the possessor of a dead tiger, and the villagers, anxious for their thousand rupees, gladly connived at the fiction that she had shot the beast. And Miss Mebbin was a paid companion. Therefore did Mrs Packletide face the cameras with a light heart, and her pictured fame reached from the pages of the Texas Weekly Snapshot to the illustrated Monday supplement of the Novoe Vremya. As for Loona Bimberton, she refused to look at an illustrated paper for weeks, and her letter of thanks for the gift of a tiger-claw brooch was a model of repressed emotions. The luncheon-party she declined; there are limits beyond which repressed emotions become dangerous.

From Curzon Street the tiger-skin rug travelled down to the Manor House, and was duly inspected and admired by the county, and it seemed a fitting and appropriate thing when Mrs Packletide went to the County Costume Ball in the character of Diana.

'How amused everyone would be if they knew what really happened,' said Louisa Mebbin a few days after the ball.

'What do you mean?' asked Mrs Packletide quickly.

'How you shot the goat and frightened the tiger to death,' said Miss Mebbin with her disagreeably pleasant laugh.

'No one would believe it,' said Mrs Packletide, her face changing colour as rapidly as though it were going through a book of patterns before post-time.

'Loona Bimberton would,' said Miss Mebbin. Mrs Packletide's face settled on an unbecoming shade of greenish white.

'You surely wouldn't give me away?' she asked.

'I've seen a week-end cottage near Dorking that I should rather like to buy,' said Miss Mebbin with seeming irrelevance. 'Six hundred and eighty, freehold. Quite a bargain, only I don't happen to have the money.'

Louisa Mebbin's pretty week-end cottage, christened by her 'Les Fauves' and gay in summer-time with its garden borders of tiger-lilies, is the wonder and admiration of her friends.

'It is a marvel how Louisa manages to do it,' is the general verdict.

Mrs Packletide indulges in no more big-game shooting.

'The incidental expenses are so heavy,' she confides to inquiring friends.

7

The Bottle Imp

R.L. Stevenson

There was a man of the Island of Hawaii, whom I shall call Keawe; for the truth is, he still lives, and his name must be kept secret. This man was poor, brave, and active; he could read and write like a schoolmaster, and was a first-rate mariner besides. At length it came into Keawe's mind to have a sight of the great world, and he shipped on a vessel bound to San Francisco.

This is a fine town, with a fine harbour, and rich people uncountable. One day Keawe walked upon a hill covered with palaces, admiring the houses, when he came to one smaller than the rest, but finished and beautified like a toy. As he wondered at it, he saw an elderly man looking out through the window, with a bald head, black beard, and a face heavy with sorrow.

All of a sudden the man beckoned Keawe to enter.

'This is a fine house of mine,' said the man, sighing. 'Would you not care to view the chambers?'

He led Keawe all over it, and there was nothing that was not perfect of its kind.

'How comes it, then,' asked Keawe, 'that you should be sighing?'

'There is no reason,' said the man, 'why you should not have such a house yourself. You have some money, I suppose?'

'I have fifty dollars,' said Keawe.

'It shall be yours for fifty dollars,' replied the man. 'Not the house—but the bottle.'

He took from a lockfast place a round-bellied bottle with a long neck. The glass was white like milk, with changing rainbow colours, and within something moved obscurely, like a shadow and a fire.

'This bottle,' said the man, 'contains an imp. All that you desire—love, fame, money, houses—are yours at the word uttered. Napoleon had this bottle, and Captain Cook had it. But if a man die before he sells it, he must burn in hell forever.'

'That is a drawback,' said Keawe. 'I would not meddle with the thing.'

'All you have to do,' said the man, 'is to use it in moderation, and sell it on. But it must be sold for less than you paid for it, or it returns to you.'

To prove his tale, the man bade Keawe buy the bottle and wish his money back. Keawe did so, and found his pocket heavy again.

'That is a wonderful bottle,' said Keawe.

'And now,' said the man, 'the devil go with you for me.'

Keawe tried to return the bottle, but the man refused it. When Keawe left the house, he tested the bottle further. He could not break it, nor draw its cork; and when he sold it for more than he had paid, it returned to him again.

Then he went aboard his ship, where he told the story to his mate, Lopaka. They agreed to take the bottle back to Hawaii.

On landing, Keawe learned that his uncle and cousin were dead, and that he had inherited land and money. Lopaka wondered if this were the doing of the bottle.

They consulted a lawyer and an architect, and found that all fell out exactly as Keawe had imagined in his mind. A great house was built for him on the Kona coast, furnished beyond his dreams.

When Keawe saw it, he said, 'It is better than I dreamed, and I am sick with satisfaction.'

Lopaka then desired one proof more. Keawe called on the imp, and the imp showed itself, swift as a lizard. Lopaka bought the bottle and departed that night.

Keawe lived in great happiness in the Bright House, until one evening he met a young woman bathing by the shore. Her name was Kokua. He loved her at once, and she loved him.

They were soon married. But on the night of his great joy, Keawe saw upon his flesh a mark of sickness, and knew he was stricken with the Chinese Evil. In despair, he remembered the bottle.

Keawe remembered the bottle, and though his blood ran cold at the thought of it, he saw no other hope to cure his sickness or to wed Kokua. He resolved to find it again, and set out at once to Honolulu to seek Lopaka.

But Lopaka had sailed away in a schooner of his own, and could not be found. Keawe went from one rich man to another, tracing the bottle by the signs it left behind—new houses, fine clothes and faces glad with sudden fortune. At last he came to a young Haole in Beritania Street, pale as death, with black rings about his eyes.

'I am come to buy the bottle,' said Keawe.

At the word the young man reeled and clutched the wall.

'The price,' he gasped, 'the price! You do not know the price?'

'It is for that I am asking you,' replied Keawe.

'Two cents,' said the man.

At this Keawe's heart sank; for if the bottle were sold for one cent, it could never be sold again. The buyer would be lost forever.

'For God's sake buy it!' cried the young man. 'I was mad when I bought it. I had embezzled money, and must have gone to jail.'

'Poor creature,' said Keawe. 'You risked your soul to escape disgrace. Give me the bottle.'

He paid the cent, clasped the bottle, and wished himself cured. When he stripped before a glass, his flesh was whole like an infant's. But at the same moment terror seized him, for he knew he was now bound to the bottle for ever.

He returned to Hawaii and was wedded to Kokua. When they were together, Keawe's heart was at peace; but when alone, he saw in his mind the flames of hell. Kokua was all cheer and song, but Keawe grew silent and oppressed.

At length Kokua perceived his misery, and pressed him to tell the truth. He told her all.

'You have done this for me?' she cried. 'Then what do I care! I shall save you, or perish in your company.'

She remembered that in France there were coins smaller than a cent, and urged that they sail to the French islands. There, perhaps, the bottle might yet be sold.

They travelled to Tahiti and lived in great show, using the bottle to appear rich. But when they tried to sell it,

people shrank from them as from persons who had dealings with the devil. Fear and despair fell upon them.

One night Kokua woke and found Keawe gone. She discovered him lying beneath the banana trees, moaning in his despair.

Then Kokua resolved upon a dreadful sacrifice.

She dressed herself, took the small coins they had prepared, and went out alone into the night. She met an old poor man and told him the whole tale.

'Buy the bottle from my husband,' she said, 'and sell it to me. Thus he shall be saved.'

The old man trembled, but consented.

When he returned with the bottle, Kokua took it from him, knowing that her soul was lost. She returned home, and Keawe slept peacefully, ignorant of her deed.

In the morning Keawe rejoiced, believing himself saved, and spoke lightly of the man who now held the bottle. Kokua said little, but her heart was breaking.

That evening Keawe, led astray by drink and evil counsel, suspected his wife. He returned secretly and saw Kokua weeping over the bottle. Then he understood all.

'My wife has given her soul for mine,' he said. 'Now I must give mine for hers.'

He enlisted a brutal sailor, gave him two centimes, and sent him to buy the bottle from Kokua. The sailor bought it gladly—but when Keawe offered to buy it back for one cent, the man refused.

'This is my bottle now,' cried the sailor. 'I reckon I'm going to hell anyway.'

So the bottle passed out of their lives.

Keawe ran home to Kokua, and great was their joy. From that day forth they lived in peace in the Bright House, and were troubled no more by the bottle or its imp.

Keawe and Kokua lived happily together, and no shadow of the bottle lay any longer upon their days. The house stood fair upon the mountain-side, and its balconies were bright with song. And if at times Keawe remembered the bottle and the dreadful peril from which he had escaped, he gave thanks to God for the love that had redeemed him.

As for Kokua, she was honoured in the land for her courage and devotion; and the story of her sacrifice was long remembered among the islands.

And the bottle—if it still wanders from hand to hand in the world—may God preserve all honest men from its temptation.

8

The Empire of the Ants

H.G. Wells

When Captain Gerilleau received instructions to take his new gunboat, the *Benjamin Constant*, to Badama on the Batemo arm of the Guaramadema and there assist the inhabitants against a plague of ants, he suspected the authorities of mockery. His promotion had been romantic and irregular, the affections of a prominent Brazilian lady and the captain's liquid eyes had played a part in the process, and the Diario and O Futuro had been lamentably disrespectful in their comments. He felt he was to give further occasion for disrespect.

He was a Creole, his conceptions of etiquette and discipline were pure-blooded Portuguese, and it was only to Holroyd, the Lancashire engineer, who had come over with the boat, and as an exercise in the use of English—his 'th' sounds were very uncertain—that he opened his heart.

'It is in effect,' he said, 'to make me absurd! What can a man do against ants? Dey come, dey go.'

'They say,' said Holroyd, 'that these don't go. That chap you said was a Sambo—'

'Zambo—it is a sort of mixture of blood.'

'Sambo. He said the people are going!'

The captain smoked fretfully for a time. 'Dese tings 'ave to happen,' he said at last. 'What is it? Plagues of ants and suchlike as God wills. Dere was a plague in Trinidad—the like ants that carry leaves. Orl der oranges-trees, all der mangoes! What does it matter? Sometimes ant armies come into your houses—fighting ants; a different sort. You go and they clean the house. Then you come back again;—the house is clean, like new! No cockroaches, no fleas, no jiggers in the floor.'

'That Sambo chap,' said Holroyd, 'says these are a different sort of ant.'

The captain shrugged his shoulders, fumed and gave his attention to a cigarette.

Afterwards he reopened the subject. 'My dear 'Olroyd, what am I to do about dese infernal ants?'

The captain reflected. 'It is ridiculous,' he said. In the afternoon he went ashore in full uniform; jars and boxes returned to the ship, followed by the captain. On deck that evening, Holroyd smoked and marvelled at Brazil. Six days up the Amazon, the horizon looked like the sea, save for a scrub-tufted sand-bank. The water ran like a sluice, thick with dirt, crocodiles and fallen trees. The town of Alemquer seemed lost in this wilderness. Fresh from England's drained landscapes, Holroyd discovered the insignificance of man. For days they had steamed through unfrequented channels where humans were as rare as butterflies. He perceived that man held but a precarious grip upon this land.

He understood this more as they neared the Batemo with his commander, who ruled one big gun but was forbidden to waste ammunition. Holroyd was learning Spanish, but remained at a basic level; the stoker's English was poor, and the second-in-command, da Cunha, spoke a French Holroyd could not follow. Their talk was limited to polite remarks about the weather. The air was hot steam, smelling of decay, where alligators and insects seemed to wonder what man was doing in such a climate. Clothing was intolerable yet necessary against the sun and mosquitoes; the deck was blinding, and the cabin suffocating. Captain Gerilleau, Holroyd's sole distraction, became a bore, recounting his past loves daily. Sometimes they shot at alligators or stopped at small settlements to drink and dance. These were mere breaks in the long passage up the streaming river where the engines throbbed and alcohol held court.

But Gerilleau learned things about the ants, more things and more, at this stopping-place and that, and became interested in his mission.

'Dey are a new sort of ant,' he said. 'We have got to be—what do you call it?—Entomologie? Big. Five centimetres! Some bigger! It is ridiculous. We are like monkeys—sent to pick insects ... But dey are eating up the country.'

He burst out indignantly. 'Suppose—suddenly, there are complications with Europe. Here am I—soon we shall be above the Rio Negro—and my gun, useless!'

He nursed his knee and mused.

'Dose people who were dere at de dancing place, dey 'ave come down. Dey 'ave lost all they got. De ants come to deir house one afternoon. Everyone run out. You know when de ants come one must—every one runs out and they go over the house. If you stayed they'd eat you. See? Well, presently dey go back; dey say, "The ants 'ave gone ..." De ants 'aven't gone. Dey try to go in—de son, 'e gose in. De ants fight.'

'Swarm over him?'

'Bite 'im. Presently he comes out again—screaming and running. He runs past them to river. See? He get into de water and drowns de ants—yes.' Gerilleau paused, brought his liquid eyes close to Holroyd's face, tapped Holroyd's knee with his knuckle. 'That night he dies, just as if he was stung by snake.'

'Poisoned—by the ants?'

'Who knows?' Gerilleau shrugged his shoulders. 'Perhaps they bit him badly ... When I joined dis service I joined to fight men. Dese things, dese ants, dey come and go. It is no business for men.'

After that he talked frequently of ants to Holroyd, and whenever they chanced to drift against any speck of humanity in that waste of water and sunshine and distant trees, Holroyd's improving knowledge of the language enabled him to recognise the ascendant word Sauba, more and more completely dominating the whole.

He perceived the ants were becoming interesting, and the nearer he drew to them the more interesting they became. Gerilleau abandoned his old themes almost suddenly, and the Portuguese lieutenant became a conversational figure; he knew something about the leaf-cutting ant, and expanded his knowledge. Gerilleau sometimes rendered what he had to tell to Holroyd. He told of the little workers that swarm and fight, and the big workers that command and rule, and how these latter always crawled to the neck and how their bites drew blood. He told how they cut leaves and made fungus beds, and how their nests in Caracas are sometimes a hundred yards across. Two days the three men spent disputing whether ants have eyes. The discussion grew dangerously heated on the second afternoon, and Holroyd saved the situation by going ashore in a boat to catch ants and see. He captured various specimens and returned and some had eyes and some hadn't. Also, they argued, do ants bite or sting?

'Dese ants,' said Gerilleau, after collecting information at a rancho, 'have big eyes. They don't run about blind—not as most ants do. No! Dey get in corners and watch what you do.'

'And they sting?' asked Holroyd.

'Yes. Dey sting. Dere is poison in the sting.' He meditated. 'I do not see what men can do against ants. Dey come and go.'

'But these don't go.'

Past Tamandu, eighty miles of unpeopled coast led to the Batemo confluence. The forest drew close. As snags increased, the *Benjamin Constant* moored under dark trees. A rare coolness allowed Holroyd and Gerilleau to smoke late into the night. Gerilleau, preoccupied by ants, eventually lay on deck. Before sleeping, he asked despairingly, 'What can one do with ants? ... De whole thing is absurd.' Holroyd remained, scratching bites and meditating.

Watching the sleeping commander, Holroyd felt the immense scale of the land. Beyond the gunboat's lone light lay the mysterious, murmuring forest. In England, he viewed land as man's domain—fenced, drained and secure. Even maps claimed the earth with vibrant colours. He had assumed global industry and order were inevitable, but now he doubted.

The invincible forest made man seem a precarious intruder. Amidst the struggle of giant trees and creepers, animals dwelt securely while humans fought for a bare foothold against weeds and fever. Ruined walls along the river marked where man had been driven back. Jaguars were the true masters here.

Who held the real power? Holroyd realised a few miles of forest contained more ants than the world had men. If humans rose from barbarism to civilization, what prevented ants from evolving? They possessed language and intelligence. He wondered what would happen if ants began to store knowledge, use weapons and sustain organised war.

Things came back to him that Gerilleau had gathered about these ants they were approaching. They used a poison like the poison of snakes. They obeyed greater leaders even as the leaf-cutting ants do. They were carnivorous, and where they came they stayed …

The forest was very still. The water lapped incessantly against the side. About the lantern overhead there eddied a noiseless whirl of phantom moths.

Gerilleau stirred in the darkness and sighed. 'What can one do?' he murmured, and turned over and was still again.

Holroyd was roused from meditations that were becoming sinister by the hum of a mosquito.

2.

The next morning Holroyd learned they were within forty kilometers of Badama, and his interest in the banks intensified. He came up whenever an opportunity offered to examine his surroundings. He could see no signs of human occupation whatever, save for a weedy ruin of a house and green-stained facade of the long-deserted monastery at Moju, with a forest tree growing out of a vacant window space, and great creepers netted across its vacant portals. Several flights of strange yellow butterflies with semi-transparent wings crossed the river that morning, and many alighted on the monitor and were killed by men. It was towards afternoon that they came upon the derelict cuberta.

She did not at first appear to be derelict; both her sails were set and hanging slack in the afternoon calm, and there was the figure of a man sitting on the fore planking beside the shipped sweeps. Another man appeared to be sleeping face downwards on the sort of longitudinal bridge, these big canoes have in the waist. But it was presently apparent, from the sway of her rudder and the way she drifted into the course of the gunboat, that something was out of order with her. Gerilleau surveyed her through a field-glass, and became interested in queer darkness of the face of the sitting man, a red-faced man he seemed, without a nose—crouching he was rather than sitting, and the longer the captain looked the less he liked to look at him, and the less able he was to take his glasses away.

But he did so at last, and went a little way to call up Holroyd. Then he went back to hail the cuberta. He hailed her again, and so she drove past him. Santa Rosa stood out clearly as her name.

As she came by and into the wake of the monitor, she pitched a little, and suddenly the figure of the crouching man collapsed as though all it's joints had given way. His hat fell off, his head was not nice to look at, and his body flopped lax and rolled out of sight behind the bulwarks.

'Caramba!' cried Gerilleau, and resorted to Holroyd forthwith.

Holroyd was halfway up the companion. 'Did you see dat?' said the captain.

'Dead!' said Holroyd. 'Yes. You'd better send a boat aboard. There's something wrong.'

'Did you—by any chance—see his face?'

'What was it like?'

'It was—ugh—! I have no words.' And the captain suddenly turned his back on Holroyd and became a active and strident commander.

The gunboat came about, steamed parallel to the erratic course of the canoe, and dropped the boat with Lieutenant da Cunha and three sailors to board her. Then the curiosity of the captain made him draw up almost alongside as the lieutenant got aboard, so that the whole of the Santa Rosa deck and hold, was visible to Holroyd.

He saw now clearly that the sole crew of the vessel was these two dead men, and though he could not see their faces, he saw by their outstretched hands, which were all of ragged flesh, that they had been subjected to some strange exceptional process of decay. For a moment his attention, concentrated on these two enigmatical bundles of dirty cloths and laxly flung limbs, and then his eyes went forward to discover the open hold piled high with trunks and cases, and aft, to where the little cabin gaped inexplicably empty. Then he became aware that the planks of the middle decking were dotted with moving black specks.

His attention was riveted by these specks. They were all walking in directions radiating from the fallen man in a

manner—the image came unsought to his mind—like the crowd dispersing from a bull-fight.

He became aware of Gerilleau beside him. 'Capo,' he said, 'have you your glasses? Can you focus as closely as those planks there?'

Gerilleau made an effort, grunted, and handed him the glasses.

There followed a moment of scrutiny. 'It's ants,' said the Englishman, and handed the focused field-glasses back to Gerilleau.

His impression of them was of a crowd of large black ants, very like ordinary ants except for size, and for the fact some of the larger of them bore a sort of clothing of grey. But at the time his inspection was too brief for particulars. The head of Lieutenant da Cunha appeared over the side of the cuberta, and a brief colloquy ensued.

'You must go aboard,' said Gerilleau.

The lieutenant objected that the boat was full of ants.

'You have your boots,' said Gerilleau.

The lieutenant changed the subject. 'How did these men die?' he asked.

Captain Gerilleau embarked upon speculation that Holroyd could not follow, and the two men disputed with a certain vehemence. Holroyd took up the field-glass and resumed his scrutiny, first of ants and then of the dead man amidships.

He has described these ants to me very particularly.

He says they were as large as any ants he has ever seen, black and moving with a steady deliberation very different from the mechanical fussiness of the common ant. About one in twenty was much larger than it's fellows, and with an exceptionally large head. These reminded him at once of the master workers who are said to rule over the leaf-cutter ants; like them they seemed to be directing and co-ordinating the general movements. They tilted their bodies back in a manner altogether singular, as if they made some use of the fore feet. And he had a curious fancy, that he was too far off to verify, that most of these ants of both kinds were wearing accoutrements, had things strapped about their bodies by bright white bands like white metal threads ...

He put down the glasses abruptly, realising that the question of discipline between the captain and his subordinate had become acute.

'It is your duty,' said the captain, 'to go aboard. It is my instructions.'

The lieutenant seemed on the verge of refusing. The head of one of the mulatto sailors appeared beside him.

'I believe these men were killed by ants,' said Holroyd abruptly in English.

The captain burst into rage. He made no answer to Holroyd. 'I have commanded you to go aboard,' he screamed to his subordinate in Portuguese. 'If you do not go aboard forthwith it is mutiny—rank mutiny. Mutiny and cowardice! Where is the courage that should animate us? I will have you in irons, I will have you shot like a dog.' He began a torrent of abuse and curses, he danced to and fro. He shook his fists, he behaved as if beside himself with rage, and the lieutenant, white and still, stood looking at him. The crew appeared forward, with amazed faces.

Suddenly, in a pause of this outbreak, the lieutenant came to some heroic decision, saluted, drew himself together and clambered upon the deck of the cuberta.

'Ah!' said Gerilleau, and his mouth shut like a trap. Holroyd saw the ants retreating before da Cunha's boots. The Portuguese walked slowly to the fallen man, stooped down, hesitated, clutched his coat and turned him over. A black swarm of ants rushed out of the clothes, and da Cunha stepped back very quickly and trod two or three times on the deck.

Holroyd put up the glasses. He saw the scattered ants about the invader's feet, and doing what he had never seen ants doing before. They had nothing of the blind movements of the common ant; they were looking at him—as a rallying crowd of men might look at some gigantic monster that had dispersed it.

'How did he die?' the captain shouted.

Holroyd understood the Portuguese to say the body was too much eaten to tell.

'What is there forward?' asked Gerilleau.

The lieutenant walked a few paces, and began his answer in Portuguese. He stopped abruptly and beat off something from his leg. He made some peculiar steps as if he was trying to stamp on something invisible, and went quickly towards the side. Then he controlled himself, turned about, walked deliberately forward to the hold, clambered up to the fore decking, from which the sweeps are worked, stooped for a time over the second man, groaned audibly, and made his way back and aft to the cabin; moving very rigidly. He turned and began a conversation with his captain, cold and respectful in tone on either side, contrasting vividly with the wrath and insult of a few moments before. Holroyd gathered only fragments of it's purport.

He reverted to the field-glass, and was surprised to find the ants had vanished from all exposed surfaces of the deck. He turned towards the shadow beneath the decking, and it seemed to him they were full of watching eyes.

The cuberta, it was agreed, was derelict, but too full of ants to put men aboard to sit and sleep: it must be towed. The lieutenant went forward to take in and adjust the cable, and the men in the boat stood up to be ready to help him. Holroyd's glasses searched the canoe.

He became more and more impressed by the fact that a great if minute and furtive activity was going on. He perceived that a number of gigantic ants—they seemed nearly a couple of inches in length—carrying oddly-shaped burthens for which he could imagine no use—were moving in rushes from one point of obscurity to another. They did not move in columns across the exposed places, but in open, spaced-out lines, oddly suggestive of the rushes of modern infantry advancing under fire. A number were taking cover under the dead man's clothes, and a perfect swarm was gathering along the side over which da Cunha must presently go.

He did not see them actually rush for the lieutenant as he returned, but he has no doubt they did make a concerted rush. Suddenly the lieutenant was shouting and cursing and beating at his legs. 'I'm stung!' he shouted, with a face of hate and accusation towards Gerilleau.

Then he vanished over the side, dropped into his boat, and plunged at once into the water. Holroyd heard the splash.

The three men in the boat pulled him out and brought him aboard, and that night he died.

3.

Holroyd and the captain came out of the cabin in which the swollen and contorted body of the lieutenant lay, and stood together at the stern of the monitor, staring at the sinister vessel they trailed behind them. It was a close, dark night that had only phantom flickers of sheet lightning to illuminate it. The cuberta, a vague black triangle, rocked about in the steamer's wake, her sails bobbing and flapping, and the black smoke from the funnels, spark-lit ever and again, streamed over her swaying masts.

Gerilleau's mind was inclined to run on the unkind things the lieutenant had said in the heat of his last fever.

'He says I murdered 'im,' he protested. 'It is simply absurd. Someone 'ad to go aboard. Are we to run away from these confounded ants whenever they show up?'

Holroyd said nothing. He was thinking of a disciplined rush of little black shapes across bare sunlit planking.

'It was his place to go,' harped Gerilleau. 'He died in the execution of his duty. What has he to complain of? Murdered! ... But the poor fellow was—what is it—? Demented. He was not in his right mind. The poison swelled him ... U'm.'

They came to a long silence.

'We will sink that canoe—burn it.'

'And then?'

The inquiry irritated Gerilleau. His shoulders went up,

his hands flew out at right angles from his body. 'What is one to do?' he said, his voice going up to an angry squeak.

'Anyhow,' he broke out vindictively, 'every ant in dat cuberta—! I will burn dem alive!'

Holroyd was not moved to conversation. A distant ululation of howling monkeys filled the sultry night with foreboding sounds, and as the gunboat drew near the black mysterious banks this was reinforced by a depressing clamour of frogs.

'What is one to do?' the captain repeated after a vast interval, and suddenly becoming active and savage and blasphemous, decided to burn the Santa Rosa without further delay. Everyone aboard was pleased by that idea, everyone helped with zest; they pulled in the cable, cut it, and dropped the boat and fired her with tow and kerosene, and soon the cuberta was crackling and flaring merrily amidst the immensities of the tropical night. Holroyd watched the mounting yellow flare against the blackness, and the livid flashes of sheet lightning that came and went above the forest summits, throwing them into momentary silhouette, and his stoker stood behind him watching also.

The stoker was stirred to the depths of his linguistics. 'Sauba go pop, pop,' he said. 'Wahaw!' and laughed richly.

But Holroyd was thinking that these little creatures on the decked canoe had also eyes and brains.

The whole thing impressed him as incredibly foolish and wrong, but—what was one to do? This question came back enormously reinforced on the morrow, when at last the gunboat reached Badama.

This place, with its leaf-thatch-covered houses and sheds, its creeper-invaded sugar-mill, its little jetty of timber and canes, was very still in the morning heat, and showed never a sign of living men. Whatever ants there were at that distance were too small to see.

'All the people have gone,' said Gerilleau, 'but we will do one thing anyhow. We will 'oot and vissel.'

So Holroyd hooted and whistled.

Then the captain fell into a doubting fit of the worst kind. 'Dere is one thing we can do,' he said presently.

'What's that?' said Holroyd.

''Oot and vissel again.'

So they did.

The captain walked his deck and gesticulated to himself. He seemed to have many things on his mind. Fragments of speeches came from his lips. He appeared to be addressing some imaginary public tribunal either in Spanish or Portuguese. Holroyd's improving ear detected something about ammunition. He came out of these preoccupations suddenly into English. 'My dear 'Olroyd!' he cried, and broke off with 'But what can one do?'

They took the boat and field-glasses, and went close in to examine the place. They made out a number of big ants, whose still postures had a certain effect of watching them, dotted about the edge of the rude embarkation jetty. Gerilleau tried ineffectual pistol shots at these. Holroyd thinks he distinguished curious earthworks running between the nearer houses, that may have been the work of insect conquerors of those human habitations. The explorers pulled past the jetty, and became aware of a human skeleton wearing a loin cloth, and very bright and clean and shining, lying beyond. They came to a pause regarding this …

'I 'ave all dose lives to consider,' said Gerilleau suddenly.

Holroyd turned and stared at the captain, realising slowly that he referred to the unappetising mixture of races that constituted his crew.

'To send a landing party—it is impossible—impossible. They will be poisoned, they will swell, they will swell up and abuse me and die. It is totally impossible … If we land, I must land alone, alone in thick boots and with my life in my hand. Perhaps I should live. Or again—I might not land. I do not know. I do not know.'

Holroyd thought he did, but he said nothing.

'De whole thing,' said Gerilleau suddenly, ''as been got up to make me ridiculous. De whole thing!'

They paddled about and regarded the clean white skeleton from various points of view, and then they returned to the gunboat. Then Gerilleau's indecisions became terrible. Steam was got up, and in the afternoon the monitor went on up the river with an air of going to ask somebody something, and by sunset came back again, and anchored. A thunderstorm gathered and broke furiously, and then the night became beautifully cool and quiet and everyone slept on deck. Except Gerilleau, who tossed about and muttered. In the dawn he awakened Holroyd.

'Lord!' said Holroyd, 'what now?'

'I have decided,' said the captain.

'What—to land?' said Holroyd, sitting up brightly.

'No!' said the captain, and was for a time very reserved. 'I have decided,' he repeated, and Holroyd manifested symptoms of impatience.

'Well—yes,' said the captain. 'I shall fire de big gun!'

And he did! Heaven knows what the ants thought of it, but he did. He fired it twice with great sternness and ceremony. All the crew had wadding in their ears, and there was effect of going into action about the whole affair, and first hit and wrecked the old sugar-mill, and then they smashed the abandoned store behind the jetty. And then Gerilleau experienced the inevitable reaction.

'It is no good,' he said to Holroyd; 'no good at all. No sort of bally good. We must go back—for instructions. Dere will be de devil of a row about dis ammunition—oh! De devil of a row! You don't know, 'Olroyd ...'

He stood regarding the world in infinite perplexity for a space.

'But what else was there to do?' he cried.

In the afternoon the monitor started down stream again, and in the evening a landing party took the body of the lieutenant and buried it on the bank upon which the new ants have so far not appeared ...

4.

I heard this fragmentary story from Holroyd three weeks ago. The ants have invaded his mind; he returned to England to 'excite people' before it is too late. He claims they threaten British Guiana, a thousand miles away, and urges the Colonial Office to act. He declaims passionately: 'These are intelligent ants. Just think what that means!'

They are undeniably a serious pest. The Brazilian Government rightly offers a five-hundred-pound prize for their extirpation. Since appearing beyond Badama three years ago, they have conquered extraordinarily. They occupy sixty miles of the Batemo River's south bank, driving men out, seizing settlements and capturing a ship. They have even bridged the Capuarana arm, pushing towards the Amazon.

They possess better social organisation than any known ant species, acting as a single nation rather than dispersed societies. Their immediate threat, however, lies in their intelligent use of poison. Akin to snake venom, they likely manufacture it, with larger ants carrying needle-like crystals into battle against men.

Detailed information remains scarce; few eyewitnesses besides Holroyd survive. Extraordinary legends of their prowess circulate the Upper Amazon, growing with their steady advance. These creatures are credited with using implements, fire, metals, staggering engineering feats and a communication method analogous to books. Their progressive settlement guarantees the flight or slaughter of every human they encounter. Multiplying rapidly, Holroyd is firmly convinced they will ultimately dispossess man across tropical South America.

And why should they stop at tropical South America?

Well, there they are, anyhow. By 1911 or thereabouts, if they go on as they are going, they ought to strike the Capuarana Extension Railway, and force themselves upon the attention of the European capitalist.

By 1920 they will be halfway down the Amazon. I fix 1950 or '60 at least for the discovery of Europe.

9

The Tailor of Gloucester

Beatrix Potter

In the time of swords and periwigs and full-skirted coats with flowered lappets—when gentlemen wore ruffles, and gold-laced waistcoats of paduasoy and taffeta—there lived a tailor in Gloucester.

He sat in the window of a little shop in Westgate Street, cross-legged on a table, from morning till dark.

All day long while the light lasted he sewed and snippeted, piecing out his satin and pompadour, and lutestring; stuffs had strange names, and were very expensive in the days of the Tailor of Gloucester.

But although he sewed fine silk for his neighbours, he himself was very, very poor—a little old man in spectacles, with a pinched face, old crooked fingers and a suit of thread-bare clothes.

He cut his coats without waste, according to his embroidered cloth; they were very small ends and snippets that lay about upon the table—'Too narrow breadths for nought—except waistcoats for mice,' said the tailor.

One bitter cold day near Christmastime the tailor began to make a coat—a coat of cherry-coloured corded silk embroidered with pansies and roses, and a cream coloured satin waistcoat—trimmed with gauze and green worsted chenille—for the Mayor of Gloucester.

The tailor worked and worked, and he talked to himself. He measured the silk, and turned it round and round, and trimmed it into shape with his shears; the table was all littered with cherry-coloured snippets.

'No breadth at all, and cut on the cross; it is no breadth at all; tippets for mice and ribbons for mobs! for mice!' said the Tailor of Gloucester.

When the snow-flakes came down against the small leaded window-panes and shut out the light, the tailor had done his day's work; all the silk and satin lay cut out upon the table.

There were twelve pieces for the coat and four pieces for the waistcoat; and there were pocket flaps and cuffs, and buttons all in order. For the lining of the coat there was fine yellow taffeta; and for the button-holes of the waistcoat, there was cherry-coloured twist. And everything was ready to sew together in the morning, all measured and sufficient—except that there was wanting just one single skein of cherry-coloured twisted silk.

The tailor came out of his shop at dark, for he did not sleep there at nights; he fastened the window and locked the door, and took away the key. No one lived there at night but little brown mice, and they run in and out without any keys!

For behind the wooden wainscots of all the old houses in Gloucester, there are little mouse staircases and secret trap-doors; and the mice run from house to house through those long narrow passages; they can run all over the town without going into the streets.

But the tailor came out of his shop, and shuffled home through the snow. He lived quite nearby in College Court, next the doorway to College Green; and although it was not a big house, the tailor was so poor he only rented the kitchen.

He lived alone with his cat; it was called Simpkin.

Now all day long while the tailor was out at work, Simpkin kept house by himself; and he also was fond of the mice, though he gave them no satin for coats!

'Miaw?' said the cat when the tailor opened the door. 'Miaw?'

The tailor replied—'Simpkin, we shall make our fortune, but I am worn to a ravelling. Take this groat (which is our last fourpence) and Simpkin, take a china pipkin; buy a penn'orth of bread, a penn'orth of milk and a penn'orth of sausages. And oh, Simpkin, with the last penny of our fourpence buy me one penn'orth of cherry-coloured silk. But do not lose the last penny of the fourpence, Simpkin, or I am undone and worn to a thread-paper, for I have NO MORE TWIST.'

Then Simpkin again said, 'Miaw?' and took the groat and the pipkin, and went out into the dark.

The tailor was very tired and beginning to be ill. He sat down by the hearth and talked to himself about that wonderful coat.

'I shall make my fortune—to be cut bias—the Mayor of Gloucester is to be married on Christmas Day in the morning, and he hath ordered a coat and an embroidered waistcoat—to be lined with yellow taffeta—and the taffeta sufficeth; there is no more left over in snippets than will serve to make tippets for mice—'

Then the tailor started; for suddenly, interrupting him, from the dresser at the other side of the kitchen came a number of little noises—

Tip tap, tip tap, tip tap tip!

'Now what can that be?' said the Tailor of Gloucester, jumping up from his chair. The dresser was covered with crockery and pipkins, willow pattern plates and tea-cups and mugs.

The tailor crossed the kitchen, and stood quite still beside the dresser, listening, and peering through his spectacles. Again from under a tea-cup, came those funny little noises—

Tip tap, tip tap, tip tap tip!

'This is very peculiar,' said the Tailor of Gloucester; and he lifted up the tea-cup which was upside down.

Out stepped a little live lady mouse, and made a curtsey to the tailor! Then she hopped away down off the dresser, and under the wainscot.

The tailor sat down again by the fire, warming his poor cold hands, and mumbling to himself—

'The waistcoat is cut out from peach-coloured satin—tambour stitch and rose-buds in beautiful floss silk. Was I wise to entrust my last fourpence to Simpkin? One-and-twenty button-holes of cherry-coloured twist!'

But all at once, from the dresser, there came other little noises:

Tip tap, tip tap, tip tap tip!

'This is passing extraordinary!' said the Tailor of Gloucester, and turned over another tea-cup, which was upside down.

Out stepped a little gentleman mouse, and made a bow to the tailor!

And then from all over the dresser came a chorus of little tappings, all sounding together, and answering one another, like watch-beetles in an old worm-eaten window-shutter—

Tip tap, tip tap, tip tap tip!

And out from under tea-cups and from under bowls and basins, stepped other and more little mice who hopped away down off the dresser and under the wainscot.

The tailor sat down, close over the fire, lamenting—'One-and-twenty button-holes of cherry-coloured silk! To be finished by noon of Saturday: and this is Tuesday evening. Was it right to let loose those mice, undoubtedly the property of Simpkin? Alack, I am undone, for I have no more twist!'

The little mice came out again, and listened to the tailor; they took notice of the pattern of that wonderful coat. They whispered to one another about the taffeta lining, and about little mouse tippets.

And then all at once they all ran away together down the passage behind the wainscot, squeaking and calling to one another, as they ran from house to house; and not one mouse was left in the tailor's kitchen when Simpkin came back with the pipkin of milk!

Simpkin opened the door and bounced in, with an angry 'G-r-r-miaw!' like a cat that is vexed: for he hated the snow, and there was snow in his ears, and snow in his collar at the back of his neck. He put down the loaf and the sausages upon the dresser, and sniffed.

'Simpkin,' said the tailor, 'where is my twist?'

But Simpkin set down the pipkin of milk upon the dresser, and looked suspiciously at the tea-cups. He wanted his supper of little fat mouse!

'Simpkin,' said the tailor, 'where is my TWIST?'

But Simpkin hid a little parcel privately in the tea-pot, and spit and growled at the tailor; and if Simpkin had been able to talk, he would have asked: 'Where is my MOUSE?'

'Alack, I am undone!' said the Tailor of Gloucester, and went sadly to bed.

All that night long Simpkin hunted and searched through the kitchen, peeping into cupboards and under the wainscot, and into the tea-pot where he had hidden that twist; but still he found never a mouse!

Whenever the tailor muttered and talked in his sleep, Simpkin said 'Miaw-ger-r-w-s-s-ch!' and made strange horrid noises, as cats do at night.

For the poor old tailor was very ill with a fever, tossing and turning in his four-post bed; and still in his dreams he mumbled—'No more twist! no more twist!'

All that day he was ill, and the next day, and the next; and what should become of the cherry-coloured coat? In the tailor's shop in Westgate Street the embroidered silk and satin lay cut out upon the table—one-and-twenty button-holes—and who should come to sew them, when the window was barred, and the door was fast locked?

But that does not hinder the little brown mice; they run in and out without any keys through all the old houses in Gloucester!

Out of doors the market folks went trudging through the snow to buy their geese and turkeys, and to bake their Christmas pies; but there would be no Christmas dinner for Simpkin and the poor old Tailor of Gloucester.

The tailor lay ill for three days and nights; and then it was Christmas Eve, and very late at night. The moon climbed up over the roofs and chimneys, and looked down over the gateway into College Court. There were no lights in the windows, nor any sound in the houses; all the city of Gloucester was fast asleep under the snow.

And still Simpkin wanted his mice, and he mewed as he stood beside the four-post bed.

But it is in the old story that all the beasts can talk, in the night between Christmas Eve and Christmas Day in the morning (though there are very few folk that can hear them, or know what it is that they say).

When the Cathedral clock struck twelve there was an answer—like an echo of the chimes—and Simpkin heard it, and came out of the tailor's door, and wandered about in the snow.

From all the roofs and gables and old wooden houses in Gloucester came a thousand merry voices singing the old Christmas rhymes—all the old songs that ever I heard of, and some that I don't know, like Whittington's bells.

First and loudest the cocks cried out: 'Dame, get up, and bake your pies!'

'Oh, dilly, dilly, dilly!' sighed Simpkin.

And now in a garret there were lights and sounds of dancing, and cats came from over the way.

'Hey, diddle, diddle, the cat and the fiddle! All the cats in Gloucester—except me,' said Simpkin.

Under the wooden eaves the starlings and sparrows sang of Christmas pies; the jack-daws woke up in the Cathedral tower; and although it was the middle of the night the throstles and robins sang; the air was quite full of little twittering tunes.

But it was all rather provoking to poor hungry Simpkin!

Particularly he was vexed with some little shrill voices from behind a wooden lattice. I think that they were bats, because they always have very small voices—especially in a black frost, when they talk in their sleep, like the Tailor of Gloucester.

They said something mysterious that sounded like—

'Buz, quoth the blue fly, hum, quoth the bee,
Buz and hum they cry, and so do we!'

and Simpkin went away shaking his ears as if he had a bee in his bonnet.

From the tailor's shop in Westgate came a glow of light; and when Simpkin crept up to peep in at the window it was full of candles. There was a snippeting of scissors, and snappeting of thread; and little mouse voices sang loudly and gaily—

'Four-and-twenty tailors
Went to catch a snail,
The best man amongst them
Durst not touch her tail,
She put out her horns
Like a little kyloe cow,
Run, tailors, run! or she'll have you all e'en now!'

Then without a pause the little mouse voices went on again—

'Sieve my lady's oatmeal,
Grind my lady's flour,
Put it in a chestnut,
Let it stand an hour—'

'Mew! Mew!' interrupted Simpkin, and he scratched at

the door. But the key was under the tailor's pillow, he could not get in.

The little mice only laughed, and tried another tune—

'Three little mice sat down to spin,
Pussy passed by and she peeped in.
What are you at, my fine little men?
Making coats for gentlemen.
Shall I come in and cut off your threads?
Oh, no, Miss Pussy, you'd bite off our heads!'

'Mew! Mew!' cried Simpkin. 'Hey diddle dinketty?' answered the little mice—

'Hey diddle dinketty, poppetty pet!
The merchants of London they wear scarlet;
Silk in the collar, and gold in the hem,
So merrily march the merchantmen!'

They clicked their thimbles to mark the time, but none of the songs pleased Simpkin; he sniffed and mewed at the door of the shop.

'And then I bought
A pipkin and a popkin,
A slipkin and a slopkin,
All for one farthing—
and upon the kitchen dresser!' added the rude little mice.

'Mew! scratch! scratch!' scuffled Simpkin on the window-sill; while the little mice inside sprang to their feet, and all began to shout at once in little twittering voices: 'No more twist! No more twist!' And they barred up the window shutters and shut out Simpkin.

But still through the nicks in the shutters he could hear the click of thimbles, and little mouse voices singing—

'No more twist! No more twist!'

Simpkin came away from the shop and went home, considering in his mind. He found the poor old tailor without fever, sleeping peacefully.

Then Simpkin went on tip-toe and took a little parcel of silk out of the tea-pot, and looked at it in the moonlight; and he felt quite ashamed of his badness compared with those good little mice!

When the tailor awoke in the morning, the first thing which he saw upon the patchwork quilt, was a skein of cherry-coloured twisted silk, and beside his bed stood the repentant Simpkin!

'Alack, I am worn to a ravelling,' said the Tailor of Gloucester, 'but I have my twist!'

The sun was shining on the snow when the tailor got up and dressed, and came out into the street with Simpkin running before him.

The starlings whistled on the chimney stacks, and the throstles and robins sang—but they sang their own little noises, not the words they had sung in the night.

'Alack,' said the tailor, 'I have my twist; but no more strength—nor time—than will serve to make me one single button-hole; for this is Christmas Day in the Morning! The Mayor of Gloucester shall be married by noon—and where is his cherry-coloured coat?'

He unlocked the door of the little shop in Westgate Street, and Simpkin ran in, like a cat that expects something.

But there was no one there! Not even one little brown mouse!

The boards were swept clean; the little ends of thread and the little silk snippets were all tidied away, and gone from off the floor.

But upon the table—oh joy! the tailor gave a shout—there, where he had left plain cuttings of silk—there lay the most beautifullest coat and embroidered satin waistcoat that ever were worn by a Mayor of Gloucester.

There were roses and pansies upon the facings of the coat; and the waistcoat was worked with poppies and corn-flowers.

Everything was finished except just one single cherry-coloured button-hole, and where that button-hole was wanting there was pinned a scrap of paper with these words—in little teeny weeny writing—

NO MORE TWIST

And from then began the luck of the Tailor of Gloucester; he grew quite stout, and he grew quite rich.

He made the most wonderful waistcoats for all the rich merchants of Gloucester, and for all the fine gentlemen of the country round.

Never were seen such ruffles, or such embroidered cuffs and lappets! But his button-holes were the greatest triumph of it all.

The stitches of those button-holes were so neat—so neat—I wonder how they could be stitched by an old man in spectacles, with crooked old fingers, and a tailor's thimble.

The stitches of those button-holes were so small—so small—they looked as if they had been made by little mice!

10

Rikki-Tikki-Tavi

Rudyard Kipling

At the hole where he went in
Red-Eye called to Wrinkle-Skin.
Hear what little Red-Eye saith:
'Nag, come up and dance with death!'
Eye to eye and head to head,
(Keep the measure, Nag.)
This shall end when one is dead;
(At thy pleasure, Nag.)
Turn for turn and twist for twist-
(Run and hide thee, Nag.)
Hah! The hooded Death has missed!
(Woe betide thee, Nag!)

This is the story of the great war that Rikki-tikki-tavi fought single-handed, through the bath-rooms of the big bungalow in Segowlee cantonment. Darzee, the Tailorbird, helped him, and Chuchundra, the muskrat, who never comes out into the middle of the floor, but always creeps round by the wall, gave him advice, but Rikki-tikki did the real fighting.

He was a mongoose, rather like a little cat in his fur and his tail, but quite like a weasel in his head and his habits. His eyes and the end of his restless nose were pink. He could scratch himself anywhere he pleased with any leg, front or back, that he chose to use. He could fluff up his tail till it looked like a bottle brush, and his war cry as he scuttled through the long grass was: 'Rikk-tikk-tikki-tikki-tchk!'

One day, a high summer flood washed him out of the burrow where he lived with his father and mother, and carried him, kicking and clucking, down a roadside ditch. He found a little wisp of grass floating there, and clung to it till he lost his senses. When he revived, he was lying in the hot sun on the middle of a garden path, very draggled indeed, and a small boy was saying, 'Here's a dead mongoose. Let's have a funeral.'

'No,' said his mother, 'let's take him in and dry him. Perhaps he isn't really dead.'

They took him into the house, and a big man picked him up between his finger and thumb and said he was not dead but half choked. So they wrapped him in cotton wool, and warmed him over a little fire, and he opened his eyes and sneezed.

'Now,' said the big man (he was an Englishman who had just moved into the bungalow), 'don't frighten him, and we'll see what he'll do.'

It is the hardest thing in the world to frighten a mongoose, because he is eaten up from nose to tail with curiosity. The motto of all the mongoose family is 'Run and find out,' and Rikki-tikki was a true mongoose. He looked at the cotton wool, decided that it was not good to eat, ran all round the table, sat up and put his fur in order, scratched himself, and jumped on the small boy's shoulder.

Rikki-tikki looked down between the boy's collar and neck

'Don't be frightened, Teddy,' said his father. 'That's his way of making friends.'

'Ouch! He's tickling under my chin,' said Teddy.

Rikki-tikki looked down between the boy's collar and neck, snuffed at his ear, and climbed down to the floor, where he sat rubbing his nose.

'Good gracious,' said Teddy's mother, 'and that's a wild creature! I suppose he's so tame because we've been kind to him.'

'All mongooses are like that,' said her husband. 'If Teddy doesn't pick him up by the tail, or try to put him in a cage, he'll run in and out of the house all day long. Let's give him something to eat.'

They gave him a little piece of raw meat. Rikki-tikki liked it immensely, and when it was finished he went out into the veranda and sat in the sunshine and fluffed up his fur to make it dry to the roots. Then he felt better.

He put his nose into the ink

'There are more things to find out about in this house,' he said to himself, 'than all my family could find out in all their lives. I shall certainly stay and find out.'

He spent the day roaming the house, nearly drowning in the bath, sniffing ink, and burning his nose on the big man's cigar. At nightfall, he joined Teddy in bed but proved a restless companion, investigating every nocturnal noise. When Teddy's parents checked on the boy, Rikki-tikki was awake on the pillow. 'I don't like that,' said Teddy's mother. 'He may bite the child.' 'He'll do no such thing,' said the father. 'Teddy's safer with that little beast than if he had a bloodhound to watch him. If a snake came into the nursery now—'

Rikki-tikki was awake on the pillow.

But Teddy's mother wouldn't think of anything so awful.

Rikki-tikki came to breakfast on the verandah, eating banana and boiled egg. He sat on their laps, following his mother's advice on becoming a house mongoose.

He finished his meal on Teddy's shoulder.

Then he explored the large, half-cultivated garden of roses, fruit trees and high grass. Rikki-tikki licked his lips. 'This is a splendid hunting-ground,' he said. His tail grew bottle-brushy as he scuttled about, sniffing until he heard sorrowful voices in a thorn-bush.

It was Darzee, the Tailor-bird, and his wife. They had made a beautiful nest by pulling two big leaves together and stitching them up the edges with fibers, and had filled the hollow with cotton and downy fluff. The nest swayed to and fro, as they sat on the rim and cried.

'We are very miserable,' said Darzee.

'What is the matter?' asked Rikki-tikki.

'We are very miserable,' said Darzee. 'One of our babies fell out of the nest yesterday and Nag ate him.'

'H'm!' said Rikki-tikki, 'that is very sad—but I am a stranger here. Who is Nag?'

Darzee and his wife only cowered down in the nest without answering, for from the thick grass at the foot of the bush there came a low hiss—a horrid cold sound that made Rikki-tikki jump back two clear feet. Then inch by inch out of the grass rose up the head and spread hood of Nag, the big black cobra, and he was five feet long from tongue to tail. When he had lifted one-third of himself clear of the ground, he stayed balancing to and fro exactly as a dandelion tuft balances in the wind, and he looked at Rikki-tikki with the wicked snake's eyes that never change their expression, whatever the snake may be thinking of.

'Who is Nag?' said he. 'I am Nag. The great God Brahm put his mark upon all our people, when the first cobra spread his hood to keep the sun off Brahm as he slept. Look, and be afraid!'

Nag spread his hood, displaying his spectacle-mark. Rikki-tikki was briefly afraid, but a mongoose's business is fighting snakes. Nag knew this and was secretly afraid. 'Well,' said Rikki-tikki, his tail fluffing up, 'marks or no marks, do you think it is right for you to eat fledglings out of a nest?' Nag watched the grass behind the mongoose, hoping to catch him off guard. 'Let us talk,' he said. 'You eat eggs. Why should not I eat birds?'

'Behind you! Look behind you!' sang Darzee. Rikki-tikki jumped as high as he could, and Nagaina—Nag's wicked wife—whizzed beneath him. He came down across her back and bit her, but fearing the return stroke, he jumped clear, leaving her torn and angry. 'Wicked, wicked Darzee!' said Nag, lashing towards the nest, but it was safely out of reach. Rikki-tikki's eyes grew red with anger; he sat back and chattered with rage. Nag and Nagaina disappeared into the grass. Unwilling to fight two snakes at once, Rikki-tikki trotted to the gravel path to think.

Old natural history books claim a bitten mongoose eats a curing herb. That is untrue; victory is purely a matter of quickness. Escaping a blow from behind gave the young

Rikki-tikki confidence, and when Teddy came running down the path, he was ready to be petted.

But just as Teddy was stooping, something wriggled a little in the dust, and a tiny voice said: 'Be careful. I am Death!' It was Karait, the dusty brown snakeling that lies for choice on the dusty earth; and his bite is as dangerous as the cobra's. But he is so small that nobody thinks of him, and so he does the more harm to people.

Rikki-tikki's eyes grew red again, and he danced up to Karait with the peculiar rocking, swaying motion that he had inherited from his family. It looks very funny, but it is so perfectly balanced a gait that you can fly off from it at any angle you please, and in dealing with snakes this is an advantage. If Rikki-tikki had only known, he was doing a much more dangerous thing than fighting Nag, for Karait is so small, and can turn so quickly, that unless Rikki bit him close to the back of the head, he would get the return stroke in his eye or his lip. But Rikki did not know. His eyes were all red, and he rocked back and forth, looking for a good place to hold. Karait struck out. Rikki jumped sideways and tried to run in, but the wicked little dusty gray head lashed within a fraction of his shoulder, and he had to jump over the body, and the head followed his heels close.

Teddy shouted, 'Oh, look here! Our mongoose is killing a snake.' His mother screamed, and his father ran out with a stick. By then, Karait had lunged too far. Rikki-tikki sprang, bit high on the snake's back, and rolled away. The bite paralysed Karait. Rikki-tikki almost ate him but remembered that a full meal makes a slow mongoose; to keep his quickness, he must stay thin.

He took a dust bath while Teddy's father beat the dead Karait. 'What is the use of that?' thought Rikki-tikki. 'I have settled it all.' Teddy's mother hugged him, crying he had saved Teddy, and his father called him a providence. Amused by the fuss, Rikki-tikki thoroughly enjoyed himself.

At dinner, he could have stuffed himself with treats, but he remembered Nag and Nagaina. Though he enjoyed being petted, his eyes occasionally reddened, and he would emit his war cry of 'Rikktikk-tikki-tikki-tchk!'

In the dark he ran up against Chuchundra, the musk-rat.

Teddy took him to bed to sleep under his chin. Once Teddy slept, Rikki-tikki began his nightly patrol. Creeping by the wall, he met Chuchundra. The broken-hearted beast whimpered all night, trying to find the courage to run into the middle of the room, but never did.

'Don't kill me,' said Chuchundra, almost weeping. 'Rikki-tikki, don't kill me!'

'Do you think a snake-killer kills musk-rats?' said Rikki-tikki scornfully.

'Those who kill snakes get killed by snakes,' said Chuchundra, more sorrowfully than ever. 'And how am I to be sure that Nag won't mistake me for you some dark night?'

'There's not the least danger,' said Rikki-tikki. 'But Nag is in the garden, and I know you don't go there.'

'My cousin Chua, the rat, told me—' said Chuchundra, and then he stopped.

'Told you what?'

'H'sh! Nag is everywhere, Rikki-tikki. You should have talked to Chua in the garden.'

'I didn't—so you must tell me. Quick, Chuchundra, or I'll bite you!'

Chuchundra sat down and cried till the tears rolled off his whiskers. 'I am a very poor man,' he sobbed. 'I never had spirit enough to run out into the middle of the room. H'sh! I mustn't tell you anything. Can't you hear, Rikki-tikki?'

Rikki-tikki listened. The house was as still as still, but he thought he could just catch the faintest scratch-scratch in the world—a noise as faint as that of a wasp walking on a window-pane—the dry scratch of a snake's scales on brick-work.

'That's Nag or Nagaina,' he said to himself, 'and he is crawling into the bath-room sluice. You're right, Chuchundra; I should have talked to Chua.'

He stole into Teddy's bathroom, found nothing, then into Teddy's mother's. By the bath's sluice, he heard Nag and Nagaina whispering outside in the moonlight.

'When the house is emptied of people,' said Nagaina, 'he will have to go away, and the garden will be ours again. Go in quietly; the big man who killed Karait is the first to bite. Then tell me, and we will hunt Rikki-tikki together.'

'But are you sure there is anything to be gained by killing the people?' said Nag.

'Everything. Without people, did we have a mongoose? If the bungalow is empty, we are king and queen. When our eggs hatch tomorrow, our children will need room and quiet.'

'I had not thought of that,' said Nag. 'I will go, but we need not hunt Rikki-tikki afterwards. I will kill the big man, his wife and the child, and come away quietly. Then the bungalow will be empty, and Rikki-tikki will go.'

Rikki-tikki tingled with rage. Nag's head came through the sluice, followed by five feet of cold body. Despite his anger, Rikki-tikki was frightened by the cobra's size. Nag coiled, raised his head and investigated the dark bathroom, his eyes glittering.

'If I kill him here, Nagaina will know; if I fight him on the open floor, the odds are in his favour. What am I to do?' said Rikki-tikki.

Nag drank from the biggest water-jar. 'That is good,' said the snake. 'When Karait was killed, the big man had a stick. When he comes to bathe in the morning, he will not have one. Nagaina—do you hear me?—I shall wait here in the cool till daytime.'

With no answer from outside, Rikki-tikki knew Nagaina had gone. Nag coiled around the base of the water jar. Rikki-tikki stayed still as death. After an hour, he moved slowly towards the sleeping snake, wondering where to get a good hold. 'If I don't break his back at the first jump,' said Rikki, 'he can still fight.' The neck was too thick, and a bite near the tail would only make Nag savage.

'It must be the head'' he said at last; 'the head above the hood. And, when I am once there, I must not let go.'

Then Rikki-tikki was battered to and fro as a rat is shaken by a dog.

Then he jumped. The head was lying a little clear of the water jar, under the curve of it; and, as his teeth met, Rikki braced his back against the bulge of the red earthenware to hold down the head. This gave him just one second's purchase, and he made the most of it. Then he was battered to and fro as a rat is shaken by a dog—to and fro on the floor, up and down and around in great circles, but his eyes were red and he held on as the body cart-whipped over the floor, upsetting the tin dipper and the soap dish and the flesh brush, and banged against the tin side of the bath. As he held he closed his jaws tighter and tighter, for he made sure he would be banged to death, and, for the honor of his family, he preferred to be found with his teeth locked. He was dizzy, aching, and felt shaken to pieces when something went off like a thunderclap just behind him. A hot wind knocked him senseless and red fire singed his fur. The big man had been wakened by the noise, and had fired both barrels of a shotgun into Nag just behind the hood.

Rikki-tikki held on with his eyes shut, for now he was quite sure he was dead. But the head did not move, and the big man picked him up and said, 'It's the mongoose again, Alice. The little chap has saved our lives now.'

Then Teddy's mother came in with a very white face, and saw what was left of Nag, and Rikki-tikki dragged himself to Teddy's bedroom and spent half the rest of the night shaking himself tenderly to find out whether he really was broken into forty pieces, as he fancied.

When morning came he was very stiff, but well pleased with his doings. 'Now I have Nagaina to settle with, and she will be worse than five Nags, and there's no knowing when the eggs she spoke of will hatch. Goodness! I must go and see Darzee,' he said.

Without waiting for breakfast, Rikki-tikki ran to the thornbush where Darzee was singing a song of triumph at the top of his voice. The news of Nag's death was all over the garden, for the sweeper had thrown the body on the rubbish-heap.

'Oh, you stupid tuft of feathers!' said Rikki-tikki angrily. 'Is this the time to sing?'

'Nag is dead—is dead—is dead!' sang Darzee. 'The valiant Rikki-tikki caught him by the head and held fast. The big man brought the bang-stick, and Nag fell in two pieces! He will never eat my babies again.'

'All that's true enough. But where's Nagaina?' said Rikki-tikki, looking carefully round him.

'Nagaina came to the bathroom sluice and called for Nag,' Darzee went on, 'and Nag came out on the end of a stick—the sweeper picked him up on the end of a stick and threw him upon the rubbish heap. Let us sing about the great, the red-eyed Rikki-tikki!' And Darzee filled his throat and sang.

'If I could get up to your nest, I'd roll your babies out!' said Rikki-tikki. 'You don't know when to do the right thing at the right time. You're safe enough in your nest there, but it's war for me down here. Stop singing a minute, Darzee.'

'For the great, the beautiful Rikki-tikki's sake I will stop,' said Darzee. 'What is it, O Killer of the terrible Nag?'

'Where is Nagaina, for the third time?'

'On the rubbish heap by the stables, mourning for Nag. Great is Rikki-tikki with the white teeth.'

'Bother my white teeth! Have you ever heard where she keeps her eggs?'

'In the melon bed, on the end nearest the wall, where the sun strikes nearly all day. She hid them there weeks ago.'

'And you never thought it worth while to tell me? The end nearest the wall, you said?'

'Rikki-tikki, you are not going to eat her eggs?'

Darzee's wife pretends to have a broken wing

'Not eat exactly; no. Darzee, if you have a grain of sense you will fly off to the stables and pretend that your wing is broken, and let Nagaina chase you away to this bush. I must get to the melon-bed, and if I went there now she'd see me.'

Darzee was a feather-brained little fellow who could never hold more than one idea at a time in his head. And just because he knew that Nagaina's children were born in eggs like his own, he didn't think at first that it was fair to kill them. But his wife was a sensible bird, and she knew that cobra's eggs meant young cobras later on. So she flew off from the nest, and left Darzee to keep the babies warm, and continue his song about the death of Nag. Darzee was very like a man in some ways.

She fluttered in front of Nagaina by the rubbish heap and cried out, 'Oh, my wing is broken! The boy in the house threw a stone at me and broke it.' Then she fluttered more desperately than ever.

Nagaina lifted up her head and hissed, 'You warned Rikki-tikki when I would have killed him. Indeed and truly, you've chosen a bad place to be lame in.' And she moved toward Darzee's wife, slipping along over the dust.

'The boy broke it with a stone!' shrieked Darzee's wife.

'Well! It may be some consolation to you when you're dead to know that I shall settle accounts with the boy. My husband lies on the rubbish heap this morning, but before night the boy in the house will lie very still. What is the use of running away? I am sure to catch you. Little fool, look at me!'

Darzee's wife knew better than to do that, for a bird who looks at a snake's eyes gets so frightened that she cannot move. Darzee's wife fluttered on, piping sorrowfully, and never leaving the ground, and Nagaina quickened her pace.

Rikki-tikki heard them going up the path from the stables, and he raced for the end of the melon patch near the wall. There, in the warm litter above the melons, very cunningly hidden, he found twenty-five eggs, about the size of a bantam's eggs, but with whitish skin instead of shell.

'I was not a day too soon,' he said, for he could see the baby cobras curled up inside the skin, and he knew that the minute they were hatched they could each kill a man or a mongoose. He bit off the tops of the eggs as fast as he could, taking care to crush the young cobras, and turned over the litter from time to time to see whether he had missed any. At last there were only three eggs left, and Rikki-tikki began to chuckle to himself, when he heard Darzee's wife screaming:

'Rikki-tikki, I led Nagaina toward the house, and she has gone into the veranda, and—oh, come quickly—she means killing!'

Rikki-tikki smashed two eggs, and tumbled backward down the melon-bed with the third egg in his mouth, and scuttled to the veranda as hard as he could put foot to the ground. Teddy and his mother and father were there at early breakfast, but Rikki-tikki saw that they were not eating anything. They sat stone-still, and their faces were white. Nagaina was coiled up on the matting by Teddy's chair, within easy striking distance of Teddy's bare leg, and she was swaying to and fro, singing a song of triumph.

'Son of the big man that killed Nag,' she hissed, 'stay still. I am not ready yet. Wait a little. Keep very still, all you three! If you move I strike, and if you do not move I strike. Oh, foolish people, who killed my Nag!'

Teddy's eyes were fixed on his father, and all his father could do was to whisper, 'Sit still, Teddy. You mustn't move. Teddy, keep still.'

Then Rikki-tikki came up and cried, 'Turn round, Nagaina. Turn and fight!'

'All in good time,' said she, without moving her eyes. 'I will settle my account with you presently. Look at your friends, Rikki-tikki. They are still and white. They are afraid. They dare not move, and if you come a step nearer I strike.'

'Look at your eggs,' said Rikki-tikki, 'in the melon bed near the wall. Go and look, Nagaina!'

The big snake turned half around, and saw the egg on the veranda. 'Ah-h! Give it to me,' she said.

Rikki-tikki put his paws one on each side of the egg, and his eyes were blood-red. 'What price for a snake's egg? For a young cobra? For a young king cobra? For the last—the very last of the brood? The ants are eating all the others down by the melon bed.'

Nagaina spun clear round, forgetting everything for the sake of the one egg. Rikki-tikki saw Teddy's father shoot out a big hand, catch Teddy by the shoulder, and drag him across the little table with the tea-cups, safe and out of reach of Nagaina.

'Tricked! Tricked! Tricked! Rikk-tck-tck!' chuckled Rikki-tikki. 'The boy is safe, and it was I—I—I that caught Nag by the hood last night in the bathroom.' Then he began to jump up and down, all four feet together, his head close to the floor. 'He threw me to and fro, but he could not shake me off. He was dead before the big man blew him in two. I did it! Rikki-tikki-tck-tck! Come then, Nagaina. Come and fight with me. You shall not be a widow long.'

Nagaina saw that she had lost her chance of killing Teddy, and the egg lay between Rikki-tikki's paws. 'Give me the egg, Rikki-tikki. Give me the last of my eggs, and I will go away and never come back,' she said, lowering her hood.

'Yes, you will go away, and you will never come back. For you will go to the rubbish heap with Nag. Fight, widow! The big man has gone for his gun! Fight!'

Nagaina flew down the path, with Rikki-tikki behind her.

Rikki-tikki was bounding all round Nagaina, keeping just out of reach of her stroke, his little eyes like hot coals. Nagaina gathered herself together and flung out at him. Rikki-tikki jumped up and backward. Again and again and again she struck, and each time her head came with a whack on the matting of the veranda and she gathered herself together like a watch spring. Then Rikki-tikki danced in a circle to get behind her, and Nagaina spun round to keep her head to his head, so that the rustle of her tail on the matting sounded like dry leaves blown along by the wind.

He had forgotten the egg. It still lay on the veranda, and Nagaina came nearer and nearer to it, till at last, while Rikki-tikki was drawing breath, she caught it in her mouth, turned to the veranda steps, and flew like an arrow down the path, with Rikki-tikki behind her. When the cobra runs for her life, she goes like a whip-lash flicked across a horse's neck.

Rikki-tikki knew that he must catch her, or all the trouble would begin again. She headed straight for the long grass by the thorn-bush, and as he was running Rikki-tikki heard Darzee still singing his foolish little song of triumph. But Darzee's wife was wiser. She flew off her nest as Nagaina came along, and flapped her wings about Nagaina's head. If Darzee had helped they might have turned her, but Nagaina only lowered her hood and went on. Still, the instant's delay brought Rikki-tikki up to her, and as she plunged into the rat-hole where she and Nag used to live, his little white teeth were clenched on her tail, and he went down with her—and very few mongooses, however wise and old they may be, care to follow a cobra into its hole. It was dark in the hole; and Rikki-tikki never knew when it might open out and give Nagaina room to turn and strike at him. He held on savagely, and stuck out his feet to act as brakes on the dark slope of the hot, moist earth.

Then the grass by the mouth of the hole stopped waving, and Darzee said, 'It is all over with Rikki-tikki! We must sing his death song. Valiant Rikki-tikki is dead! For Nagaina will surely kill him underground.'

So he sang a very mournful song that he made up on the spur of the minute, and just as he got to the most touching part, the grass quivered again, and Rikki-tikki, covered with dirt, dragged himself out of the hole leg by leg, licking his whiskers. Darzee stopped with a little shout. Rikki-tikki shook some of the dust out of his fur and sneezed. 'It is all over,' he said. 'The widow will never come out again.' And the red ants that live between the grass stems heard him, and began to troop down one after another to see if he had spoken the truth.

Rikki-tikki curled himself up in the grass and slept where he was—slept and slept till it was late in the afternoon, for he had done a hard day's work.

'Now,' he said, when he awoke, 'I will go back to the house. Tell the Coppersmith, Darzee, and he will tell the garden that Nagaina is dead.'

It is all over.

The Coppersmith is a bird who makes a noise exactly like the beating of a little hammer on a copper pot; and the reason he is always making it is because he is the town crier to every Indian garden, and tells all the news to everybody who cares to listen. As Rikki-tikki went up the path, he heard his 'attention' notes like a tiny dinner gong, and then the steady 'Ding-dong-tock! Nag is dead—dong! Nagaina is dead! Ding-dong-tock!' That set all the birds in the garden singing, and the frogs croaking, for Nag and Nagaina used to eat frogs as well as little birds.

When Rikki got to the house, Teddy and Teddy's mother (she looked very white still, for she had been fainting) and Teddy's father came out and almost cried over him; and that night he ate all that was given him till he could eat no more, and went to bed on Teddy's shoulder, where Teddy's mother saw him when she came to look late at night.

'He saved our lives and Teddy's life,' she said to her husband. 'Just think, he saved all our lives.'

Rikki-tikki woke up with a jump, for the mongooses are light sleepers.

'Oh, it's you,' said he. 'What are you bothering for? All the cobras are dead. And if they weren't, I'm here.'

Rikki-tikki had a right to be proud of himself. But he did not grow too proud, and he kept that garden as a mongoose should keep it, with tooth and jump and spring and bite, till never a cobra dared show its head inside the walls.

Darzee's Chant
(Sung in honor of Rikki-tikki-tavi)

Singer and tailor am I—
Doubled the joys that I know—
Proud of my lilt to the sky,
Proud of the house that I sew.
Over and under, so weave I my music—so weave
I the house that I sew.
Sing to your fledglings again,
Mother, oh lift up your head!
Evil that plagued us is slain,
Death in the garden lies dead.
Terror that hid in the roses is impotent—flung on the dung-hill and dead!
Who has delivered us, who?
Tell me his nest and his name.
Rikki, the valiant, the true,
Tikki, with eyeballs of flame—
Rikk-tikki-tikki, the ivory-fanged,
the hunter with eyeballs of flame!
Give him the Thanks of the Birds, Bowing with tail feathers spread,
Praise him with nightingale words—
Nay, I will praise him instead.
Hear! I will sing you the praise of the bottle-tailed Rikki, with eyeballs of red!

(Here Rikki-tikki interrupted, and the rest of the song is lost.)

11

The Most Dangerous Game

Richard Connell

'Off there to the right—somewhere—is a large island,' said Whitney. 'It's rather a mystery—'

'What island is it?' Rainsford asked.

'The old charts call it "Ship-Trap Island,"' Whitney replied. 'A suggestive name, isn't it? Sailors have a curious dread of the place. I don't know why. Some superstition—'

'Can't see it,' remarked Rainsford, trying to peer through the dank tropical night that was palpable as it pressed its thick warm blackness in upon the yacht.

'You've good eyes,' said Whitney, with a laugh, 'and I've seen you pick off a moose moving in the brown fall bush at four hundred yards, but even you can't see four miles or so through a moonless Caribbean night.'

'Nor four yards,' admitted Rainsford. 'Ugh! It's like moist black velvet.'

'It will be light enough in Rio,' promised Whitney. 'We should make it in a few days. I hope the jaguar guns have come from Purdey's. We should have some good hunting up the Amazon. Great sport, hunting.'

'The best sport in the world,' agreed Rainsford.

'For the hunter,' amended Whitney. 'Not for the jaguar.'

'Don't talk rot, Whitney,' said Rainsford. 'You're a big-game hunter, not a philosopher. Who cares how a jaguar feels?'

'Perhaps the jaguar does,' observed Whitney.

'Bah! They've no understanding.'

'Even so, I rather think they understand one thing—fear. The fear of pain and the fear of death.'

'Nonsense,' laughed Rainsford. 'This hot weather is making you soft, Whitney. Be a realist. The world is made up of two classes—the hunters and the huntees. Luckily, you and I are hunters. Do you think we've passed that island yet?'

'I can't tell in the dark. I hope so.'

'Why?' asked Rainsford.

'The place has a reputation—a bad one.'

'Cannibals?' suggested Rainsford.

'Hardly. Even cannibals wouldn't live in such a God-forsaken place. But it's gotten into sailor lore, somehow. Didn't you notice that the crew's nerves seemed a bit jumpy to-day?'

'They were a bit strange, now you mention it. Even Captain Nielsen—'

'Yes, even that tough-minded old Swede, who'd go up to the devil himself and ask him for a light. Those fishy blue eyes held a look I never saw there before. All I could get out of him was: 'This place has an evil name among sea-faring men, sir.' Then he said to me, very gravely: 'Don't you feel anything?'—as if the air about us was actually poisonous. Now, you mustn't laugh when I tell you this—I did feel something like a sudden chill.

'There was no breeze. The sea was as flat as a plate-glass window. We were drawing near the island then. What I felt was a—a mental chill; a sort of sudden dread.'

'Pure imagination,' said Rainsford. 'One superstitious sailor can taint the whole ship's company with his fear.'

'Maybe. But sometimes I think sailors have an extra sense that tells them when they are in danger. Sometimes I think evil is a tangible thing—with wave lengths, just as sound and light have. An evil place can, so to speak, broadcast vibrations of evil. Anyhow, I'm glad we're getting out of this zone. Well, I think I'll turn in now, Rainsford.'

'I'm not sleepy,' said Rainsford. 'I'm going to smoke another pipe up on the after deck.'

'Good-night, then, Rainsford. See you at breakfast.'

'Right. Good-night, Whitney.'

The only sounds were the yacht's throbbing engine and the propeller's wash.

Reclining in a steamer chair, Rainsford puffed his favourite briar, feeling drowsy. 'It's so dark,' he thought, 'that I could sleep without closing my eyes; the night would be my eyelids ...'

An abrupt sound startled him. Off to the right, he heard someone fire a gun three times.

Mystified, Rainsford sprang to the rail. He leaped up to balance on it for a better view. His pipe struck a rope and fell; lunging for it, he lost his balance and fell into the warm Caribbean Sea.

He surfaced, gagging on salt water. He swam desperately after the receding yacht but soon stopped, regaining his coolheadedness. Realising the slender chance of being heard, he wrestled off his clothes and shouted, but the yacht's lights soon vanished.

Remembering the shots, Rainsford swam doggedly to the right, using slow strokes to conserve strength. He fought the sea until he felt he could only manage a hundred more strokes.

Suddenly, he heard the high, screaming sound of an animal in terror.

Unconcerned with what animal made it, he swam toward the noise with fresh vitality until a crisp, staccato sound cut it short.

'Pistol shot,' muttered Rainsford, swimming on.

Ten minutes of effort brought the sound of the sea breaking on a rocky shore. He nearly hit the rocks before seeing them. With his remaining strength, he dragged himself from the water and forced himself upward. He reached a flat place at the top, bordered by dense jungle. Unconcerned by potential perils, he flung himself down at the jungle edge and slept.

When he woke, the sun showed it was late afternoon. Sleep had given him new vigour, but he was sharply hungry. He looked about.

'Where there are pistol shots, there are men. Where there are men, there is food,' he thought. But what kind of men lived in such a forbidding place? An unbroken jungle fringed the shore.

Seeing no trail, Rainsford floundered along the shore. Not far from where he landed, he stopped.

A large, wounded animal had thrashed in the underbrush; weeds were crushed and one patch was stained crimson. Rainsford picked up a small, glittering object nearby. It was an empty cartridge.

'A twenty-two,' he remarked. 'That's odd. It must have been a fairly large animal, too. The hunter had his nerve with him to tackle it with a light gun. It's clear that the brute put up a fight. I suppose the first three shots I heard was when the hunter flushed his quarry and wounded it. The last shot was when he trailed it here and finished it.'

He examined the ground and found the prints of hunting boots pointing along the cliff. He hurried in that direction as night began to settle.

Darkness was falling when Rainsford sighted lights around a bend in the coast. He initially thought it was a village, but soon saw all the lights belonged to one enormous building. It was a palatial château set on a high bluff, surrounded on three sides by steep cliffs.

'Mirage,' thought Rainsford. But it was nó mirage. He opened the tall iron gate and climbed the stone steps to a massive door with a gargoyle knocker.

He lifted the stiff knocker and let it fall with a booming loudness. He heard steps within, but the door remained closed.

Rainsford knocked again. The door opened suddenly, pouring out glaring light. Inside stood a gigantic, black-bearded man pointing a long-barrelled revolver straight at Rainsford's heart.

Out of the snarl of beard two small eyes regarded Rainsford.

'Don't be alarmed,' said Rainsford, with a smile which he hoped was disarming. 'I'm no robber. I fell off a yacht. My name is Sanger Rainsford of New York City.'

The giant's menacing look did not change, and his revolver remained rigid. He gave no sign of hearing Rainsford. He wore a black uniform trimmed with grey astrakhan.

'I'm Sanger Rainsford of New York,' Rainsford began again. 'I fell off a yacht. I am hungry.'

The man cocked his revolver, then suddenly clicked his heels and saluted. An erect, slender man in evening clothes descended the broad marble steps and held out his hand.

In a cultivated, accented voice, he said: 'It is a very great pleasure and honour to welcome Mr Sanger Rainsford, the celebrated hunter, to my home.'

Automatically, Rainsford shook his hand.

'I've read your book about hunting snow leopards in Tibet,' the man explained. 'I am General Zaroff.'

Rainsford found the singularly handsome general almost bizarre. He was an aristocratic man past middle age, with vivid white hair contrasting his bright black eyes and pointed moustache. Turning to the giant, the general made a sign. The giant holstered his pistol, saluted, and withdrew.

'Ivan is an incredibly strong fellow,' remarked the general, 'but he has the misfortune to be deaf and dumb. A simple fellow, but, I'm afraid, like all his race, a bit of a savage.'

'Is he Russian?'

'He is a Cossack,' said the general, smiling to show pointed teeth. 'So am I.'

'Come,' he said. 'We can talk later. Now you want clothes, food, rest. You shall have them. This is a most restful spot.'

Ivan reappeared, and the general gave him a soundless order.

'Follow Ivan, if you please, Mr Rainsford,' said the general. 'I was about to dine. I'll wait for you. You'll find my clothes will fit you.'

Rainsford followed the silent giant to a huge bedroom with a massive canopied bed. Ivan laid out an evening suit, tailored by a high-end London firm.

Ivan led him to a remarkable, medieval-style dining room. The baronial hall featured oaken panels, a high ceiling, and a vast table. Perfect, large mounted animal heads covered the walls. The general sat alone at the great table.

'You'll have a cocktail, Mr Rainsford,' he suggested. The cocktail was surpassingly good, and, Rainsford noted, the table appointments were of the finest—the linen, the crystal, the silver, the china.

They were eating borsch, the rich red soup with whipped cream so dear to Russian palates. Half apologetically General Zaroff said: 'We do our best to preserve the amenities of civilization here. Please forgive any lapses. We are well off the beaten track, you know. Do you think the champagne has suffered from its long ocean trip?'

'Not in the least,' declared Rainsford. He was finding the general a most thoughtful and affable host, a true cosmopolite. But there was one small trait of the general's that made Rainsford uncomfortable. Whenever he looked up from his plate he found the general studying him, appraising him narrowly.

'Perhaps,' said General Zaroff, 'you were surprised that I recognized your name. You see, I read all books on hunting published in English, French and Russian. I have but one passion in my life, Mr Rainsford, and it is the hunt.'

'You have some wonderful heads here,' said Rainsford as he ate a particularly well-cooked filet mignon. 'That Cape buffalo is the largest I ever saw.'

'Oh, that fellow. Yes, he was a monster.'

'Did he charge you?'

'Hurled me against a tree,' said the general. 'Fractured my skull. But I got the brute.'

'I've always thought,' said Rainsford, 'that the Cape buffalo is the most dangerous of all big game.'

For a moment the general did not reply; he was smiling his curious red-lipped smile. Then he said slowly: 'No. You are wrong, sir. The Cape buffalo is not the most dangerous big game.' He sipped his wine. 'Here in my preserve on this island,' he said, in the same slow tone, 'I hunt more dangerous game.'

Rainsford expressed his surprise. 'Is there big game on this island?'

The general nodded. 'The biggest.'

'Really?'

'Oh, it isn't here naturally, of course. I have to stock the island.'

'What have you imported, General?' Rainsford asked. 'Tigers?'

The general smiled. 'No,' he said. 'Hunting tigers ceased to interest me some years ago. I exhausted their possibilities, you see. No thrill left in tigers, no real danger. I live for danger, Mr Rainsford.'

The general took from his pocket a gold cigarette case and offered his guest a long black cigarette with a silver tip; it was perfumed and gave off a smell like incense.

'We will have some capital hunting, you and I,' said the general. 'I shall be most glad to have your society.'

'But what game—' began Rainsford.

'I'll tell you,' said the general. 'You will be amused, I know. I think I may say, in all modesty, that I have done a rare thing. I have invented a new sensation. May I pour you another glass of port, Mr Rainsford?'

'Thank you, General.'

The general filled both glasses. 'God makes some men poets, kings, or beggars. Me He made a hunter. My father encouraged this, complimenting my marksmanship when I shot his prize turkeys at age five. I killed my first bear at ten. Despite commanding Cossack cavalry, my real interest remained hunting. I have hunted every kind of game in every land.' The general puffed his cigarette.

'After leaving Russia, my American investments allowed me to continue hunting globally. After a Cape buffalo laid me up for six months, I hunted Amazonian jaguars. They weren't cunning enough.' The Cossack sighed. 'They were no match for a hunter with a rifle. One night, a terrible thought struck me: hunting was beginning to bore me. And hunting had been my life.'

'Yes, that's so,' said Rainsford.

The general smiled. 'I had no wish to go to pieces. Having an analytical mind, I enjoy the problems of the chase.'

'No doubt, General Zaroff.'

'So, I asked myself why the hunt no longer fascinated me. Perhaps you can guess the answer.'

'What was it?'

'Simply this: hunting had ceased to be a sporting proposition. It had become too easy. There is no greater bore than perfection.'

The general lit a fresh cigarette.

'No animal had a chance against me. Instinct is no match for reason. Realising this was a tragic moment.'

Rainsford leaned across the table, absorbed.

'An inspiration came to me,' the general went on.

'And that was?'

The general smiled successfully. 'I had to invent a new animal to hunt,' he said.

'A new animal? You're joking.'

'Not at all. I found one. So I bought this island and built this house. The island is perfect—jungles, hills, swamps—'

'But the animal, General Zaroff?'

'Oh,' said the general, 'it supplies the most exciting hunting in the world. I never grow bored now, for I have a quarry with which I can match my wits.'

Rainsford's bewilderment showed in his face.

'I wanted the ideal animal to hunt,' explained the general. 'So I said: 'What are the attributes of an ideal quarry?' And the answer was, of course: 'It must have courage, cunning and above all, it must be able to reason.'

'But no animal can reason,' objected Rainsford.

'My dear fellow,' said the general, 'there is one that can.'

'But you can't mean—' gasped Rainsford.

'And why not?'

'I can't believe you are serious, General Zaroff. This is a grisly joke.'

'Why should I not be serious? I am speaking of hunting.'

'Hunting? Good God, General Zaroff, what you speak of is murder.'

The general laughed with entire good nature. He regarded Rainsford quizzically. 'I refuse to believe that so modern and civilized a young man as you seem to be harbours romantic ideas about the value of human life. Surely your experiences in the war—'

'Did not make me condone cold-blooded murder,' finished Rainsford, stiffly.

Laughter shook the general. 'How droll! One does not expect an educated American to have such a naïve point of view. I wager you'll forget your notions when we hunt. You've a genuine thrill in store.'

'Thank you, I'm a hunter, not a murderer.'

'Dear me,' said the general. 'That unpleasant word again. I will show you your scruples are ill-founded.'

'Yes?'

'Life is for the strong, to be taken by the strong. The weak exist for the strong's pleasure. I am strong. Why should I not hunt? I hunt the scum of the earth. A thoroughbred hound is worth more than a score of them.'

'But they are men,' said Rainsford.

'Precisely,' said the general. 'That is why I use them. They can reason. They are dangerous.'

'Where do you get them?'

The general winked. 'This island is called Ship Trap. Sometimes the sea sends them. Sometimes, I help Providence. Come to the window.'

Rainsford looked toward the sea. 'Watch!' the general said, pressing a button. Flashing lights appeared far out.

The general chuckled. 'They indicate a false channel. Giant rocks crouch there to crush a ship as easily as I crush this nut.' He ground a walnut under his heel.

'Oh, yes,' he added. 'I have electricity. We try to be civilised here.'

'Civilised? And you shoot down men?'

Anger briefly crossed the general's eyes. 'What a righteous young man! I do not do that. That would be barbarous. I treat visitors with consideration. They receive food and exercise. You shall see tomorrow.'

'What do you mean?'

'We'll visit my cellar training school,' the general smiled. 'I have a dozen pupils from a wrecked Spanish bark. An inferior lot, accustomed to decks, not jungles.'

Ivan brought Turkish coffee. Rainsford held his tongue.

'It's a game,' the general continued. 'I give a man food, a knife and a three-hour start. I follow with a small-calibre pistol. If my quarry eludes me for three days, he wins. If I find him'—he smiled—'he loses.'

'Suppose he refuses to be hunted?'

'Oh,' said the general, 'I give him his option, of course. He need not play that game if he doesn't wish to. If he does not wish to hunt, I turn him over to Ivan. Ivan once had the honour of serving as official knouter to the Great White Tsar, and he has his own ideas of sport. Invariably, Mr Rainsford, invariably they choose the hunt.'

'And if they win?'

The smile on the general's face widened. 'To date I have not lost,' he said.

Then he added, hastily: 'I don't wish you to think me a braggart, Mr Rainsford. Many of them afford only the most elementary sort of problem. Occasionally I strike a tartar. One almost did win. I eventually had to use the dogs.'

'The dogs?'

'This way, please. I'll show you.'

The general steered Rainsford to a window. In the courtyard below, a dozen huge black shapes moved, their eyes glittering greenly.

'A rather good lot,' observed the general. 'They are let out at seven every night. If anyone should try to get in or out, something regrettable would occur.' He hummed a song.

'And now,' said the general, 'I want to show you my new collection of heads. Will you come to the library?'

'I hope,' said Rainsford, 'you will excuse me tonight. I'm not feeling well.'

'Ah, indeed?' the general inquired. 'That's natural after your swim. You need sleep. To-morrow you'll feel like a new man. Then we'll hunt, eh? I've one promising prospect—'

Rainsford hurried from the room.

'Sorry you can't go to-night,' called the general. 'I expect fair sport—a strong black. He looks resourceful. Good-night, Mr Rainsford.'

Despite his exhaustion, Rainsford could not sleep. Hearing stealthy steps outside, he tried his door, but it was locked. He looked out his high window into the dark courtyard. By moonlight, he saw the black hounds looking up expectantly. Rainsford returned to bed. He finally dozed when, near morning, he heard the faint report of a pistol in the jungle.

General Zaroff appeared at luncheon, dressed in tweeds. He asked after Rainsford's health.

'As for me,' sighed the general, 'I do not feel well. I am worried. Last night I detected traces of my old complaint.'

To Rainsford's glance the general said: 'Ennui. Boredom.'

The general explained: 'The hunting was not good last night. The fellow lost his head and made a straight trail. Sailors have dull brains and do excessively stupid things in the woods. It's annoying. Will you have another glass of Chablis?'

'General,' said Rainsford firmly, 'I wish to leave this island at once.'

The general seemed hurt. 'But, my dear fellow, you've only just come. You've had no hunting—'

'I wish to go to-day,' said Rainsford. The general studied him, then his face brightened.

He filled Rainsford's glass.

'Tonight,' said the general, 'we will hunt—you and I.'

Rainsford shook his head. 'No, General. I will not hunt.'

The general shrugged and ate a grape. 'As you wish. The choice rests entirely with you. But may I suggest you will find my idea of sport more diverting than Ivan's?'

He nodded towards the corner where the scowling giant stood with crossed arms.

'You don't mean—' cried Rainsford.

'My dear fellow,' said the general, 'have I not told you I always mean what I say about hunting? This is really an inspiration. I drink to a foeman worthy of my steel—at last.'

The general raised his glass, but Rainsford sat staring at him.

'You'll find this game worth playing,' the general said, enthusiastically. 'Your brain against mine. Your woodcraft against mine. Your strength and stamina against mine. Outdoor chess! And the stake is not without value, eh?'

'And if I win—' began Rainsford, huskily.

'I'll cheerfully acknowledge myself defeated if I do not find you by midnight of the third day,' said General Zaroff. 'My sloop will place you on the mainland near a town.'

The general read what Rainsford was thinking.

'Oh, you can trust me,' said the Cossack. 'I will give you my word as a gentleman and a sportsman. Of course, you, in turn, must agree to say nothing of your visit here.'

'I'll agree to nothing of the kind,' said Rainsford.

'Oh,' said the general, 'in that case— But why discuss that now? Three days hence we can discuss it over a bottle of Veuve Cliquot, unless—'

The general sipped his wine.

A businesslike air animated him. 'Ivan,' he said, 'will supply clothes, food, and a knife. Wear moccasins; they leave a poorer trail. Avoid the quicksand in Death Swamp; it claimed one foolish fellow and my finest hound, Lazarus. Excuse me; I take a siesta. You'll want to start. I shall follow at dusk. Au revoir.' He bowed and left.

Ivan entered carrying clothes, food, a knife and a cocked revolver.

Rainsford fought through the bush for two hours. 'I must keep my nerve,' he said.

Initially panicked, his only thought had been flight. Now, taking stock, he realised running straight was futile; the sea framed his prison.

'I'll give him a trail,' he muttered, striking into the wilderness. He executed intricate loops, doubling back like a fox. Night found him leg-weary on a wooded ridge. Too exhausted to continue, he decided to play the cat.

Leaving no marks, he climbed a large tree to rest. This brought confidence; surely Zaroff could not trace that complicated trail in the dark.

A sleepless night crawled by. At dawn, a startled bird focussed his attention. Someone was slowly following his exact winding path. He flattened himself and watched.

It was General Zaroff. He advanced, eyes fixed on the ground, then dropped to his knees beneath the tree.

Rainsford wanted to pounce, but saw the general's small automatic pistol.

Zaroff shook his head, stood and lit a black cigarette.

Rainsford held his breath as the general's eyes travelled up the trunk. He froze. The hunter's eyes stopped before reaching the branch. Zaroff smiled, blew a smoke ring, turned and carelessly walked away.

Air burst from Rainsford's lungs. He felt sick; the general could follow an extremely difficult trail at night. Only by chance had the Cossack missed him.

A second thought brought cold horror. Why had the general smiled and turned back? The truth was evident.

The general was playing with him, saving him for another day. The Cossack was the cat; Rainsford was the mouse. He knew true terror.

'I will not lose my nerve. I will not.'

He slid down and struck off into the woods. Three hundred yards away, he stopped by a huge dead tree leaning on a living one. He drew his knife and worked with all his energy.

The job finished, he hid behind a log a hundred feet away. He did not wait long. The cat was coming.

Following the trail came General Zaroff. Nothing escaped his searching eyes. So intent was the Cossack that his foot touched the protruding bough trigger before he saw it. Sensing danger, he leapt back. The dead tree crashed down, striking the general a glancing blow on the shoulder. He staggered but stood, retaining his revolver. Rubbing his shoulder, he laughed mockingly.

'Rainsford,' called the general, 'if you are within sound of my voice, let me congratulate you. Not many men know how to make a Malay man-catcher. Luckily for me I, too, have hunted in Malacca. You are proving interesting, Mr Rainsford. I am going now to have my wound dressed. But I shall be back. I shall be back.'

When the general left, Rainsford resumed his desperate flight. Dusk fell, then darkness. The ground grew softer, vegetation denser. His foot sank into the ooze, the muck sucking viciously until he tore it loose.

He knew where he was. Death Swamp and its quicksand.

Gripping his nerves, the soft earth gave him an idea. Stepping back from the quicksand, he began to dig.

He had dug trenches in France, but that was placid compared to this. When the pit was above his shoulders, he climbed out, sharpened saplings into stakes, and planted them pointing up at the bottom. He wove a rough carpet of weeds to cover the pit, then crouched behind a charred stump.

He heard padded footsteps and smelt the general's cigarette. The general was approaching swiftly, no longer feeling his way.

Crouching, Rainsford could see neither the general nor the pit. Suddenly, branches crackled and a sharp scream indicated the stakes had found their mark. Rainsford leapt up, then cowered. Three feet from the pit stood a man with a torch.

'You've done well, Rainsford,' the general called. 'Your Burmese tiger pit has claimed one of my best dogs. I think I'll see what you can do against my whole pack. I'm going home for a rest. Thank you for an amusing evening.'

At daybreak, Rainsford awoke to a faint, terrifying sound: the baying of hounds.

Waiting was suicide; fleeing postponed the inevitable. Tightening his belt, he gambled on a wild idea and hurried from the swamp.

As the baying drew nearer, Rainsford climbed a tree. Down a watercourse, he spotted General Zaroff. Ahead of him surged the giant Ivan, holding the pack on a leash.

His mind worked frantically, recalling a trick from Uganda. Sliding down, he fastened his knife to a springy sapling, tied it back with grapevine, and ran for his life. The hounds howled, hitting the fresh scent.

Rainsford knew how a hunted animal feels.

He stopped for breath. The baying abruptly ceased; they must have reached the knife.

Climbing a tree to look back, his hope died. General Zaroff was still standing, but Ivan was not. The springing knife had not wholly failed.

Rainsford tumbled to the ground as the pack resumed their cry.

'Nerve, nerve, nerve!' he panted. He forced himself toward a blue gap between the trees. It was the shore.

Across a cove sat the grey château. Twenty feet below, the sea rumbled. Hearing the hounds, Rainsford leapt far out into the water.

Reaching the shore, the Cossack stopped and regarded the water. He shrugged, sat down, drank from a silver flask, lit a cigarette and hummed a bit from 'Madama Butterfly.'

General Zaroff had an exceedingly good dinner in his panelled hall. Two annoyances marred his enjoyment: replacing Ivan, and his escaped quarry. Convinced the American hadn't played the game, he read Marcus Aurelius to soothe himself. At ten, he locked himself in his bedroom. He looked down at the moonlit courtyard, called to the hounds, 'Better luck another time,' and switched on the light.

A man stepped from the bed curtains.

'Rainsford!' screamed the general. 'How in God's name did you get here?'

'Swam,' said Rainsford. 'I found it quicker than walking through the jungle.'

The general smiled. 'I congratulate you,' he said. 'You have won the game.'

Rainsford did not smile. 'I am still a beast at bay,' he said. 'Get ready, General Zaroff.'

The general bowed deeply. 'I see,' he said. 'Splendid! One of us is to furnish a repast for the hounds. The other will sleep in this excellent bed. On guard, Rainsford … '

He had never slept in a better bed, Rainsford decided.

12

The Golden Touch

Nathaniel Hawthorne

At noon, our juvenile party assembled in a dell, through the depths of which ran a little brook. The dell was narrow, and its steep sides, from the margin of the stream upward, were thickly set with trees, chiefly walnuts and chestnuts, among which grew a few oaks and maples. In the summer time, the shade of so many clustering branches, meeting and intermingling across the rivulet, was deep enough to produce a noontide twilight. Hence came the name of Shadow Brook. But now, ever since autumn had crept into this secluded place, all the dark verdure was changed to gold, so that it really kindled up the dell, instead of shading it. The bright yellow leaves, even had it been a cloudy day, would have seemed to keep the sunlight among them; and enough of them had fallen to strew all the bed and margin of the brook with sunlight, too. Thus the shady nook, where summer had cooled herself, was now the sunniest spot anywhere to be found.

The little brook ran along over its pathway of gold, here pausing to form a pool, in which minnows were darting to and fro; and then it hurried onward at a swifter pace, as if in haste to reach the lake; and, forgetting to look whither it went, it tumbled over the root of a tree, which stretched quite across its current. You would have laughed to hear how noisily it babbled about this accident. And even after it had run onward, the brook still kept talking to itself, as if it were in a maze. It was wonder-smitten, I suppose, at finding its dark dell so illuminated, and at hearing the prattle and merriment of so many children. So it stole away as quickly as it could, and hid itself in the lake.

In the dell of Shadow Brook, Eustace Bright and his little friends had eaten their dinner. They had brought plenty of good things from Tanglewood, in their baskets, and had spread them out on the stumps of trees, and on mossy trunks, and had feasted merrily, and made a very nice dinner indeed. After it was over, nobody felt like stirring.

'We will rest ourselves here,' said several of the children, 'while Cousin Eustace tells us another of his pretty stories.'

Cousin Eustace had earned a rest after an active morning climbing nut-trees and showering the children—Dandelion, Clover, Cowslip and Buttercup—with walnuts. He flung himself onto the leaves.

But children show no mercy for weariness; they always demand a story.

'Cousin Eustace,' said Cowslip, 'that was a very nice story of the Gorgon's Head. Do you think you could tell us another as good?'

'Yes, child,' said Eustace, pulling his cap over his eyes. 'I can tell you a dozen, as good or better, if I choose.'

'O Primrose and Periwinkle, do you hear what he says?' cried Cowslip. 'Cousin Eustace is going to tell us a dozen better stories than that about the Gorgon's Head!'

'I did not promise you even one, you foolish little Cowslip!' said Eustace. 'However, I suppose you must have it. This is the consequence of having earned a reputation! I wish I were a great deal duller than I am, or that I had never shown half the bright qualities with which nature has endowed me; and then I might have my nap out, in peace and comfort!'

But Eustace enjoyed telling stories as much as they loved hearing them.

This spontaneous play of intellect differs greatly from the trained diligence of mature years.

Eustace Bright began his story, inspired by the autumn leaves turning to gold above him.

Once upon a time lived King Midas, a very rich man. He had a little daughter I choose to call Marygold.

King Midas loved gold more than anything, except perhaps Marygold. Yet, the more he loved her, the more he sought wealth, believing a massive pile of coin was the best inheritance. He devoted all his time to this purpose, even wishing golden sunsets were real gold for his strongbox.

When Marygold brought him buttercups, he would say, 'Poh, poh, child! If these flowers were as golden as they look, they would be worth the plucking!'

Before his obsession, Midas loved flowers and planted a magnificent rose garden. Now, he only calculated their worth if the petals were solid gold. Similarly, his former love of music was replaced by the chink of coins.

Midas grew so unreasonable he could scarcely bear touching anything but gold. He spent hours daily in a dark underground dungeon where he kept his wealth. Locking the door, he would bring his gold into the single sunbeam entering the room. He valued the light only because it made his treasure shine. He sifted his gold, examined his reflection in a golden cup, and whispered, 'O Midas, rich King Midas, what a happy man art thou!' But his reflected face seemed to grin, mocking his foolish behaviour.

Midas called himself a happy man, but felt that he was not yet quite so happy as he might be. The very tip-top of enjoyment would never be reached, unless the whole world were to become his treasure-room, and be filled with yellow metal which should be all his own.

In King Midas's time, wonderful things happened. But I must go on with my story.

Midas was in his treasure-room when a shadow fell over his gold. He looked up to see a cheerful young man in the sunbeam. Midas fancied the stranger's smile radiated a golden light, casting a brighter gleam upon the piled-up treasures than the sun itself.

Knowing the door was locked, Midas concluded his visitor was supernatural. Midas had met such beings before and, seeing the stranger's good-humoured aspect, suspected no mischief. He assumed the stranger came to do him a favour—likely to multiply his treasure.

The stranger surveyed the room. 'You are a wealthy man, friend Midas!' he observed. 'I doubt whether any other four walls contain so much gold.'

'I have done pretty well,' answered Midas, discontentedly. 'But it is a trifle. If one lived a thousand years, he might grow rich!'

'What!' exclaimed the stranger. 'Then you are not satisfied?'

Midas shook his head.

'And pray what would satisfy you?' asked the stranger. 'I should be glad to know.'

Midas meditated. He sensed this stranger could grant his utmost wishes. He imagined golden mountains, but none seemed big enough. Finally, a brilliant idea occurred to him. He looked the stranger in the face.

'Well, Midas,' observed his visitor. 'Tell me your wish.'

'I am weary of collecting my treasures with so much trouble,' replied Midas. 'I wish everything I touch to be changed to gold!'

The stranger's smile grew so broad it seemed to fill the room like sunlight.

'The Golden Touch!' he exclaimed. 'But are you quite sure that this will satisfy you?'

'How could it fail?' said Midas.

'And will you never regret it?'

'What could induce me?' asked Midas. 'I ask nothing else to render me perfectly happy.'

'Be it as you wish, then,' replied the stranger, waving farewell. 'To-morrow, at sunrise, you will find yourself gifted with the Golden Touch.'

The stranger became exceedingly bright, forcing Midas to close his eyes.

On opening them, he beheld only the sunbeam and his hoarded gold.

Day had hardly broken when Midas awoke. Stretching out of bed, he touched nearby objects to test the stranger's promise. He laid his finger on a chair but was grievously disappointed to perceive it remained wood. He feared he had only dreamed of the lustrous stranger.

All this while, it was only the gray of the morning, with but a streak of brightness along the edge of the sky, where Midas could not see it. He lay in a very disconsolate mood, regretting the downfall of his hopes, and kept growing sadder and sadder, until the earliest sunbeam shone through the window, and gilded the ceiling over his head. It seemed to Midas that this bright yellow sunbeam was reflected in rather a singular way on the white covering of the bed. Looking more closely, what was his astonishment and delight, when he found that this linen fabric had been transmuted to what seemed a woven texture of the purest and brightest gold! The Golden Touch had come to him with the first sunbeam!

Midas started up in a joyful frenzy, touching everything in his way. He turned a bed-post into a fluted pillar, a window-curtain tassel into a solid mass and a book into unreadable golden plates. He dressed in a flexible, though heavy, gold cloth suit. He drew out a handkerchief Marygold had hemmed, which also became gold. This last transformation vexed him; he preferred his little daughter's handiwork as it was.

Dismissing the trifle, Midas put on his spectacles. To his perplexity, he could not see; the crystals had turned to opaque yellow metal. It struck him as inconvenient that, despite his wealth, he could never again own serviceable spectacles.

'It is no great matter,' he philosophised. 'The Golden Touch is worth the sacrifice of a pair of spectacles. Marygold will soon be old enough to read to me.'

Exalted by his fortune, Midas went downstairs, turning the balustrade and door-latch to burnished gold. He emerged into the garden among beautiful, fragrant roses. Midas indefatigably exercised his magic touch until every flower, bud and even the worms within, were gold. His work completed, he returned to the palace for breakfast.

His morning meal consisted of hot cakes, trout, potatoes, eggs and coffee, with a bowl of bread and milk for Marygold.

Marygold had not yet appeared. Midas loved his daughter and eagerly awaited her. Soon, he heard her crying bitterly in the passageway—a rare occurrence for the cheerful girl. Hoping to lift her spirits with a surprise, he touched her china bowl, transmuting it to gleaming gold.

Marygold opened the door, sobbing into her apron.

'How now, my little lady!' cried Midas. 'Pray what is the matter with you this bright morning?'

Still crying, Marygold held out one of the roses Midas had just transmuted.

'Beautiful!' exclaimed her father. 'And what is there in this magnificent golden rose to make you cry?'

'Ah, dear father!' answered the child through her sobs. 'It is the ugliest flower that ever grew! I ran to gather roses for you, but they are all blighted and spoilt! They have grown quite yellow and have no fragrance! What can have been the matter with them?'

'Poh, my dear little girl,—pray don't cry about it!' said Midas, who was ashamed to confess that he himself had wrought the change which so greatly afflicted her. 'Sit down and eat your bread and milk! You will find it easy enough to exchange a golden rose like that (which will last hundreds of years) for an ordinary one which would wither in a day.'

'I don't care for such roses as this!' cried Marygold, tossing it contemptuously away. 'It has no smell, and the hard petals prick my nose!'

Marygold sat down, too occupied with her grief over the roses to notice her transmuted bowl and its lost painted figures. Midas, meanwhile, poured coffee from a newly golden pot. He tried to eat a trout, but it had become an elaborate golden imitation.

'I don't quite see,' he thought, 'how I am to get any breakfast!'

He broke a hot cake, but it immediately assumed the heavy, yellow hue of solid gold. In despair, he tried a boiled egg, which underwent a similar change.

'Well, this is a quandary!' he thought, looking enviously at Marygold eating her bread and milk. 'Such a costly breakfast before me, and nothing that can be eaten!'

Hoping to outpace the magic, Midas snatched a hot potato and crammed it into his mouth. But the Golden Touch was too nimble. His mouth filled with solid, burning metal. He roared aloud, jumping and stamping about the room in pain and fright.

'Father, dear father!' cried Marygold. 'Pray what is the matter? Have you burnt your mouth?'

'Ah, dear child,' groaned Midas. 'I don't know what is to become of your poor father!'

It was a pitiable case. The richest breakfast was absolutely worthless. The poorest labourer was better off than King Midas, whose delicate food was now worth its weight in gold. He was already excessively hungry; how many days could he survive this rich fare?

These reflections so troubled wise King Midas, that he began to doubt whether, after all, riches are the one desirable thing in the world, or even the most desirable. But this was only a passing thought. So fascinated was Midas with the glitter of the yellow metal, that he would still have refused to give up the Golden Touch for so paltry a consideration as a breakfast. Just imagine what a price for one meal's victuals! It would have been the same as paying millions and millions of money (and as many millions more as would take forever to reckon up) for some fried trout, an egg, a potato, a hot cake, and a cup of coffee!

'It would be quite too dear,' thought Midas.

Nevertheless, so great was his hunger, and the perplexity of his situation, that he again groaned aloud, and very grievously too. Our pretty Marygold could endure it no longer. She sat, a moment, gazing at her father, and trying, with all the might of her little wits, to find out what was the matter with him. Then, with a sweet and sorrowful impulse to comfort him, she started from her chair, and, running to Midas, threw her arms affectionately about his knees. He bent down and kissed her. He felt that his little daughter's love was worth a thousand times more than he had gained by the Golden Touch.

'My precious, precious Marygold!' cried he.

But Marygold made no answer.

Alas, what had he done? How fatal was the gift which the stranger bestowed! The moment the lips of Midas touched Marygold's forehead, a change had taken place. Her sweet, rosy face, so full of affection as it had been, assumed a glittering yellow color, with yellow tear-drops congealing on her cheeks. Her beautiful brown ringlets took the same tint. Her soft and tender little form grew hard and inflexible within her father's encircling arms. Oh, terrible misfortune!

The victim of his insatiable desire for wealth, little Marygold was a human child no longer, but a golden statue!

Yes, there she was, with the questioning look of love, grief and pity hardened into her face. The perfect resemblance deepened the father's agony. He had often said she was worth her weight in gold, and now the phrase was literally true. He finally understood that a loving heart exceeded the value of all piled-up wealth.

Midas wept, wishing he were the poorest man in the world if it might bring the faintest rose-colour back to his child's face.

Amidst his despair, Midas beheld the stranger from the treasure-room standing near the door. The stranger's smile still shed a yellow lustre across the transmuted room.

'Well, friend Midas,' said the stranger, 'pray how do you succeed with the Golden Touch?'

Midas shook his head.

'I am very miserable,' said he.

'Very miserable, indeed!' exclaimed the stranger. 'Have I not faithfully kept my promise? Have you not everything your heart desired?'

'Gold is not everything,' answered Midas. 'I have lost all my heart really cared for.'

'Ah! So you have made a discovery?' observed the stranger. 'Which is worth more: the Golden Touch, or a cup of clear cold water?'

'O blessed water!' exclaimed Midas. 'It will never moisten my parched throat again!'

'The Golden Touch,' continued the stranger, 'or a crust of bread?'

'A piece of bread,' answered Midas, 'is worth all the gold on earth!'

'The Golden Touch,' asked the stranger, 'or your own little Marygold, warm, soft, and loving as she was an hour ago?'

'Oh my child, my dear child!' cried poor Midas, wringing his hands. 'I would not have given that one dimple in her chin for the power of changing this whole earth into a solid lump of gold!'

'You are wiser than you were, King Midas!' said the stranger. 'Your heart has not been entirely changed to gold. Tell me, do you sincerely desire to rid yourself of this Golden Touch?'

'It is hateful to me!' replied Midas.

A fly settled on his nose and fell to the floor, having become gold. Midas shuddered.

'Go, then,' said the stranger, 'and plunge into the river at the bottom of your garden. Take a vase of the water and sprinkle it over any object you desire to change back. If you do this in earnestness, it may repair the mischief your avarice occasioned.'

King Midas bowed low; when he lifted his head, the stranger had vanished.

Midas snatched a great earthen pitcher—which instantly turned to gold—and hastened to the river, leaving a trail of yellow foliage behind him. On reaching the brink, he plunged headlong into the water, shoes and all.

'Poof! poof! poof!' snorted King Midas, emerging. 'This is a refreshing bath, and I think it must have washed away the Golden Touch. Now for filling my pitcher!'

As he dipped the pitcher, it gladdened his heart to see it change back into an honest earthen vessel. A cold, heavy weight left his bosom; his transmuting heart had softened back into flesh. He touched a violet on the bank and was overjoyed to find it retained its purple hue. The curse of the Golden Touch was removed.

King Midas hastened back to the palace; and, I suppose, the servants knew not what to make of it when they saw their royal master so carefully bringing home an earthen pitcher of water. But that water, which was to undo all the mischief that his folly had wrought, was more precious to Midas than an ocean of molten gold could have been. The first thing he did, as you need hardly be told, was to sprinkle it by handfuls over the golden figure of little Marygold.

No sooner did it fall on her than you would have laughed to see how the rosy color came back to the dear child's cheek! and how she began to sneeze and sputter!—and how astonished she was to find herself dripping wet, and her father still throwing more water over her!

'Pray do not, dear father!' cried she. 'See how you have wet my nice frock, which I put on only this morning!'

For Marygold did not know that she had been a little golden statue; nor could she remember anything that had happened since the moment when she ran with outstretched arms to comfort poor King Midas.

Her father did not think it necessary to tell his beloved child how very foolish he had been, but contented himself with showing how much wiser he had now grown. For this purpose, he led little Marygold into the garden, where he sprinkled all the remainder of the water over the rose-bushes, and with such good effect that above five thousand roses recovered their beautiful bloom. There were two circumstances, however, which, as long as he lived, used to put King Midas in mind of the Golden Touch. One was, that the sands of the river sparkled like gold; the other, that little Marygold's hair had now a golden tinge, which he had never observed in it before she had been transmuted by the effect of his kiss. This change of hue was really an improvement, and made Marygold's hair richer than in her babyhood.

When King Midas had grown quite an old man, and used to trot Marygold's children on his knee, he was fond of telling them this marvellous story, pretty much as I have now told it to you. And then would he stroke their glossy ringlets, and tell them that their hair, likewise, had a rich shade of gold, which they had inherited from their mother.

'And to tell you the truth, my precious little folks,' quoth King Midas, diligently trotting the children all the while, 'ever since that morning, I have hated the very sight of all other gold, save this!'

'Well, children,' inquired Eustace, who was very fond of eliciting a definite opinion from his auditors, 'did you ever, in all your lives, listen to a better story than this of 'The Golden Touch'?'

'Why, as to the story of King Midas,' said saucy Primrose, 'it was a famous one thousands of years before Mr Eustace Bright came into the world, and will continue to be so as long after he quits it. But some people have what we may call "The Leaden Touch", and make everything dull and heavy that they lay their fingers upon.'

'You are a smart child, Primrose, to be not yet in your teens,' said Eustace, taken rather aback by the piquancy of her criticism. 'But you well know, in your naughty little heart, that I have burnished the old gold of Midas all over anew, and have made it shine as it never shone before. And then that figure of Marygold! Do you perceive no nice workmanship in that? And how finely I have brought out and deepened the moral! What say you, Sweet Fern, Dandelion, Clover, Periwinkle? Would any of you, after hearing this story, be so foolish as to desire the faculty of changing things to gold?'

'I should like,' said Periwinkle, a girl of ten, 'to have the power of turning everything to gold with my right forefinger; but, with my left forefinger, I should want the power of changing it back again, if the first change did not please me. And I know what I would do, this very afternoon!'

'Pray tell me,' said Eustace.

'Why,' answered Periwinkle, 'I would touch every one of these golden leaves on the trees with my left forefinger, and make them all green again; so that we might have the summer back at once, with no ugly winter in the meantime.'

'O Periwinkle!' cried Eustace Bright, 'there you are wrong, and would do a great deal of mischief. Were I Midas, I would make nothing else but just such golden days as these over and over again, all the year throughout. My best thoughts always come a little too late. Why did not I tell you how old King Midas came to America, and changed the dusky autumn, such as it is in other countries, into the burnished beauty which it here puts on? He gilded the leaves of the great volume of Nature.'

'Cousin Eustace,' said Sweet Fern, a good little boy, who was always making particular inquiries about the precise height of giants and the littleness of fairies, 'how big was Marygold, and how much did she weigh after she was turned to gold?'

'She was about as tall as you are,' replied Eustace, 'and, as gold is very heavy, she weighed at least two thousand pounds, and might have been coined into thirty or forty thousand gold dollars. I wish Primrose were worth half as much. Come, little people, let us clamber out of the dell, and look about us.'

They did so. The sun was now an hour or two beyond its noontide mark, and filled the great hollow of the valley with its western radiance, so that it seemed to be brimming with mellow light, and to spill it over the surrounding hill-sides, like golden wine out of a bowl. It was such a day that you could not help saying of it, 'There never was such a day before!' although yesterday was just such a day, and to-morrow will be just such another. Ah, but there are very few of them in a twelvemonth's circle! It is a remarkable peculiarity of these October days, that each of them seems to occupy a great deal of space, although the sun rises rather tardily at that season of the year, and goes to bed, as little children ought, at sober six o'clock, or even earlier. We cannot, therefore, call the days long; but they appear, somehow or other, to make up for their shortness by their breadth; and when the cool night comes, we are conscious of having enjoyed a big armful of life, since morning.

'Come, children, come!' cried Eustace Bright. 'More nuts, more nuts, more nuts! Fill all your baskets; and, at

Christmas time, I will crack them for you, and tell you beautiful stories!'

So away they went; all of them in excellent spirits, except little Dandelion, who, I am sorry to tell you, had been sitting on a chestnut-bur, and was stuck as full as a pincushion of its prickles. Dear me, how uncomfortably he must have felt!

13

The Aunt and Amabel

E. Nesbit

It is not pleasant to be a fish out of water. To be a cat in water is not what any one would desire. To be in a temper is uncomfortable. And no one can fully taste the joys of life if he is in a Little Lord Fauntleroy suit. But by far the most uncomfortable thing to be in is disgrace, sometimes amusingly called Coventry by the people who are not in it.

We have all been there. It is a place where the heart sinks and aches, where familiar faces are clouded and changed, where any remark that one may tremblingly make is received with stony silence or with the assurance that nobody wants to talk to such a naughty child. If you are only in disgrace, and not in solitary confinement, you will creep about a house that is like the one you have had such jolly times in, and yet as unlike it as a bad dream is to a June morning. You will long to speak to people, and be afraid to speak. You will wonder whether there is anything you can do that will change things at all. You have said you are sorry, and that has changed nothing. You will wonder whether you are to stay for ever in this desolate place, outside all hope and love and fun and happiness. And though it has happened before, and has always, in the end, come to an end, you can never be quite sure that this time it is not going to last for ever.

'It is going to last for ever,' said Amabel, who was eight. 'What shall I do? Oh whatever shall I do?'

What she had done ought to have formed the subject of her meditations. And she had done what had seemed to her all the time, and in fact still seemed, a self-sacrificing and noble act. She was staying with an aunt—measles or a new baby, or the painters in the house, I forget which, the cause of her banishment. And the aunt, who was really a great-aunt and quite old enough to know better, had been grumbling about her head gardener to a lady who called in blue spectacles and a beady bonnet with violet flowers in it.

'He hardly lets me have a plant for the table,' said the aunt, 'and that border in front of the breakfast-room window—it's just bare earth—and I expressly ordered chrysanthemums to be planted there. He thinks of nothing but his greenhouse.'

The beady-violet-blue-glassed lady snorted, and said she didn't know what we were coming to, and she would have just half a cup, please, with not quite so much milk, thank you very much.

Now what would you have done? Minded your own business most likely, and not got into trouble at all. Not so Amabel. Enthusiastically anxious to do something which should make the great-aunt see what a thoughtful, unselfish, little girl she really was (the aunt's opinion of her being at present quite otherwise), she got up very early in the morning and took the cutting-out scissors from the work-room table drawer and stole, 'like an errand of mercy,' she told herself, to the greenhouse where she busily snipped off every single flower she could find. MacFarlane was at his breakfast. Then with the points of the cutting-out scissors she made nice deep little holes in the flower-bed where the chrysanthemums ought to have been, and struck the flowers in—chrysanthemums, geraniums, primulas, orchids and carnations. It would be a lovely surprise for Auntie.

Then the aunt came down to breakfast and saw the lovely surprise. Amabel's world turned upside down and inside out suddenly and surprisingly, and there she was, in Coventry, and not even the housemaid would speak to her. Her great-uncle, whom she passed in the hall on her way to her own room, did indeed, as he smoothed his hat, murmur, 'Sent to Coventry, eh? Never mind, it'll soon be over,' and went off to the City banging the front door behind him.

He meant well, but he did not understand.

Amabel understood, or she thought she did, and knew in her miserable heart that she was sent to Coventry for the last time, and that this time she would stay there.

'I don't care,' she said quite untruly. 'I'll never try to be kind to any one again.' And that wasn't true either. She was to spend the whole day alone in the best bedroom, the one with the four-post bed and the red curtains and the large wardrobe with a looking-glass in it that you could see yourself in to the very ends of your strap-shoes.

The first thing Amabel did was to look at herself in the glass. She was still sniffing and sobbing, and her eyes were swimming in tears, another one rolled down her nose as she looked—that was very interesting. Another rolled down, and that was the last, because as soon as you get interested in watching your tears they stop.

Next she looked out of the window, and saw the decorated flower-bed, just as she had left it, very bright and beautiful.

'Well, it does look nice,' she said. 'I don't care what they say.'

Then she looked round the room for something to read; there was nothing. The old-fashioned best bedrooms never did have anything. Only on the large dressing-table, on the left-hand side of the oval swing-glass, was one book covered in red velvet, and on it, very twistily embroidered in yellow silk and mixed up with misleading leaves and squiggles were the letters, A.B.C.

'Perhaps it's a picture alphabet,' said Mabel, and was quite pleased, though of course she was much too old to care for alphabets. Only when one is very unhappy and very dull, anything is better than nothing. She opened the book.

'Why, it's only a time-table!' she said. 'I suppose it's for people when they want to go away, and Auntie puts it here in case they suddenly make up their minds to go, and feel that they can't wait another minute. I feel like that, only it's no good, and I expect other people do too.'

She had learned how to use the dictionary, and this seemed to go the same way. She looked up the names of all the places she knew.—Brighton where she had once spent a month, Rugby where her brother was at school, and Home, which was Amberley—and she saw the times when the trains left for these places, and wished she could go by those trains.

And once more she looked round the best bedroom which was her prison, and thought of the Bastille, and wished she had a toad to tame, like the poor Viscount, or a flower to watch growing, like Picciola, and she was very sorry for herself, and very angry with her aunt, and very grieved at the conduct of her parents—she had expected better things from them—and now they had left her in this dreadful place where no one loved her, and no one understood her.

There seemed to be no place for toads or flowers in the best room, it was carpeted all over even in its least noticeable corners. It had everything a best room ought to have—and everything was of dark shining mahogany. The toilet-table had a set of red and gold glass things—a tray, candlesticks, a ring-stand, many little pots with lids, and two bottles with stoppers. When the stoppers were taken out they smelt very strange, something like very old scent, and something like cold cream also very old, and something like going to the dentist's.

I do not know whether the scent of those bottles had anything to do with what happened. It certainly was a very extraordinary scent. Quite different from any perfume that I smell nowadays, but I remember that when I was a little girl I smelt it quite often. But then there are no best rooms now such as there used to be. The best rooms now are gay with chintz and mirrors, and there are always flowers and books, and little tables to put your teacup on, and sofas, and armchairs. And they smell of varnish and new furniture.

When Amabel had sniffed at both bottles and looked in all the pots, which were quite clean and empty except for a pearl button and two pins in one of them, she took up the A.B.C. again to look for Whitby, where her godmother lived. And it was then that she saw the extraordinary name 'Whereyouwantogoto.' This was odd—but the name of the station from which it started was still more extraordinary, for it was not Euston or Cannon Street or Marylebone.

The name of the station was 'Bigwardrobeinspareroom.' And below this name, really quite unusual for a station, Amabel read in small letters:

'Single fares strictly forbidden. Return tickets No Class Nuppence. Trains leave Bigwardrobeinspareroom all the time.'

And under that in still smaller letters—

'You had better go now.'

What would you have done? Rubbed your eyes and thought you were dreaming? Well, if you had, nothing more would have happened. Nothing ever does when you behave like that. Amabel was wiser. She went straight to the Big Wardrobe and turned its glass handle.

'I expect it's only shelves and people's best hats,' she said. But she only said it. People often say what they don't mean, so that if things turn out as they don't expect, they can say 'I told you so,' but this is most dishonest to one's self, and being dishonest to one's self is almost worse than being dishonest to other people. Amabel would never have done it if she had been herself. But she was out of herself with anger and unhappiness.

Of course it wasn't hats. It was, most amazingly, a crystal cave, very oddly shaped like a railway station. It seemed to be lighted by stars, which is, of course, unusual in a booking office, and over the station clock was a full moon. The clock had no figures, only 'Now' in shining letters all round it, twelve times, and the 'Nows' touched, so the clock was bound to be always right. How different from the clock you go to school by!

A porter in white satin hurried forward to take Amabel's luggage. Her luggage was the A.B.C. which she still held in her hand.

'Lots of time, Miss,' he said, grinning in a most friendly way, 'I am glad you're going. You will enjoy yourself! What a nice little girl you are!'

This was cheering. Amabel smiled.

At the pigeon-hole that tickets come out of, another person, also in white satin, was ready with a mother-of-pearl ticket, round, like a card counter.

'Here you are, Miss,' he said with the kindest smile, 'price nothing, and refreshments free all the way. It's a pleasure,' he added, 'to issue a ticket to a nice little lady like you.' The train was entirely of crystal, too, and the cushions were of white satin. There were little buttons such as you have for electric bells, and on them 'Whatyouwantoeat,' 'Whatyouwantodrink,' 'Whatyouwantoread,' in silver letters.

Amabel pressed all the buttons at once, and instantly felt obliged to blink. The blink over, she saw on the cushion by her side a silver tray with vanilla ice, boiled chicken and white sauce, almonds (blanched), peppermint creams, and mashed potatoes and a long glass of lemonade—beside the tray was a book. It was Mrs Ewing's Bad-tempered Family, and it was bound in white vellum.

There is nothing more luxurious than eating while you read—unless it be reading while you eat. Amabel did both: they are not the same thing, as you will see if you think the matter over.

And just as the last thrill of the last spoonful of ice died away, and the last full stop of the Bad-tempered Family met Amabel's eye, the train stopped, and hundreds of railway officials in white velvet shouted, 'Whereyouwantogoto! Get out!'

A velvety porter, who was somehow like a silkworm as well as like a wedding handkerchief sachet, opened the door.

'Now!' he said, 'come on out, Miss Amabel, unless you want to go to Whereyoudon'twantogoto.'

She hurried out, on to an ivory platform.

'Not on the ivory, if you please,' said the porter, 'the white Axminster carpet—it's laid down expressly for you.'

Amabel walked along it and saw ahead of her a crowd, all in white.

'What's all that?' she asked the friendly porter.

'It's the Mayor, dear Miss Amabel,' he said, 'with your address.'

'My address is The Old Cottage, Amberley,' she said, 'at least it used to be'—and found herself face to face with the Mayor. He was very like Uncle George, but he bowed low to her, which was not Uncle George's habit, and said:

'Welcome, dear little Amabel. Please accept this admiring address from the Mayor and burgesses and apprentices and all the rest of it, of Whereyouwantogoto.'

The address was in silver letters, on white silk, and it said:

'Welcome, dear Amabel. We know you meant to please your aunt. It was very clever of you to think of putting the greenhouse flowers in the bare flower-bed. You couldn't be expected to know that you ought to ask leave before you touch other people's things.'

'Oh, but,' said Amabel quite confused. 'I did . . .'

But the band struck up, and drowned her words. The instruments of the band were all of silver, and the bandsmen's clothes of white leather. The tune they played was 'Cheero!'

Then Amabel found that she was taking part in a procession, hand in hand with the Mayor, and the band playing like mad all the time. The Mayor was dressed entirely in cloth of silver, and as they went along he kept saying, close to her ear.

'You have our sympathy, you have our sympathy,' till she felt quite giddy.

There was a flower show—all the flowers were white. There was a concert—all the tunes were old ones. There was a play called Put yourself in her place. And there was a banquet, with Amabel in the place of honour.

They drank her health in white wine whey, and then through the Crystal Hall of a thousand gleaming pillars, where thousands of guests, all in white, were met to do honour to Amabel, the shout went up—'Speech, speech!'

I cannot explain to you what had been going on in Amabel's mind. Perhaps you know. Whatever it was it began like a very tiny butterfly in a box, that could not keep quiet, but fluttered, and fluttered and fluttered. And when the Mayor rose and said:

'Dear Amabel, you whom we all love and understand; dear Amabel, you who were so unjustly punished for trying to give pleasure to an unresponsive aunt; poor, ill-used, ill-treated, innocent Amabel; blameless, suffering Amabel, we await your words,' that fluttering, tiresome butterfly-thing inside her seemed suddenly to swell to the size and strength of a fluttering albatross, and Amabel got up from her seat of honour on the throne of ivory and silver and pearl, and said, choking a little, and extremely red about the ears—

'Ladies and gentlemen, I don't want to make a speech, I just want to say, "Thank you", and to say—to say—to say ...'

She stopped, and all the white crowd cheered.

'To say,' she went on as the cheers died down, 'that I wasn't blameless, and innocent, and all those nice things. I ought to have thought. And they were Auntie's flowers. But I did want to please her. It's all so mixed. Oh, I wish Auntie was here!'

And instantly Auntie was there, very tall and quite nice-looking, in a white velvet dress and an ermine cloak.

'Speech,' cried the crowd. 'Speech from Auntie!'

Auntie stood on the step of the throne beside Amabel, and said:

'I think, perhaps, I was hasty. And I think Amabel meant to please me. But all the flowers that were meant for the winter ... well—I was annoyed. I'm sorry.'

'Oh, Auntie, so am I—so am I,' cried Amabel, and the two began to hug each other on the ivory step, while the crowd cheered like mad, and the band struck up that well-known air, 'If you only understood!'

'Oh, Auntie,' said Amabel among hugs, 'This is such a lovely place, come and see everything, we may, mayn't we?' she asked the Mayor.

'The place is yours,' he said, 'and now you can see many things that you couldn't see before. We are The People who Understand. And now you are one of Us. And your aunt is another.'

I must not tell you all that they saw because these things are secrets only known to The People who Understand, and perhaps you do not yet belong to that happy nation. And if you do, you will know without my telling you.

And when it grew late, and the stars were drawn down, somehow, to hang among the trees, Amabel fell asleep in her aunt's arms beside a white foaming fountain on a marble terrace, where white peacocks came to drink.

She awoke on the big bed in the spare room, but her aunt's arms were still round her.

'Amabel,' she was saying, 'Amabel!'

'Oh, Auntie,' said Amabel sleepily, 'I am so sorry. It was stupid of me. And I did mean to please you.'

'It was stupid of you,' said the aunt, 'but I am sure you meant to please me. Come down to supper.' And Amabel has a confused recollection of her aunt's saying that she was sorry, adding, 'Poor little Amabel.'

If the aunt really did say it, it was fine of her. And Amabel is quite sure that she did say it.

Amabel and her great-aunt are now the best of friends. But neither of them has ever spoken to the other of the beautiful city called 'Whereyouwantogoto.' Amabel is too shy to be the first to mention it, and no doubt the aunt has her own reasons for not broaching the subject.

But of course they both know that they have been there together, and it is easy to get on with people when you and they alike belong to the Peoplewhounderstand.

If you look in the A.B.C. that your people have you will not find 'Whereyouwantogoto.' It is only in the red velvet bound copy that Amabel found in her aunt's best bedroom.

14

The Flying Trunk

Hans Christian Andersen

There was once upon a time a merchant so rich that he could have paved the whole street, and almost all of a little alley besides, with silver money. But he didn't do that, for he knew of another use for his money: if he paid a penny out, he got a dollar back: that's the sort of merchant he was, and then he died.

His son got all this money, and he lived a merry life: he went to the fancy ball every night, he made paper kites out of banknotes, and played ducks and drakes in the lake with sovereigns instead of stones. That was the way to make the money go, and go it did. At last he had nothing left but fourpence, and no clothes but a pair of slippers and an old dressing-gown. His friends didn't care about him any more, for they couldn't walk about the streets with him; but one of them, who was good-natured, sent him an old trunk and said, 'Pack up'. Well, that was all very well, but he hadn't got anything to pack up; so he got into the trunk himself.

It was a funny trunk, that. The moment you pressed on the lock of it, it could fly. And so it did: whizz! It flew up with him through the chimney, and high up above the clouds, far and far away. The bottom of it gave a crack every now and then, and he was very much afraid it would go to pieces, for then he would have made a pretty jump, preserve us all! And at last he got to Turkey. He hid the trunk in a wood under dead leaves and went into the town, which he could perfectly well do, for all the Turks went about in dressing-gowns and slippers like him. He met a nurse with a baby. 'Look here, you Turkey nurse,' said he, 'what's that great big palace close by the town with the windows set so high up?'

'That's the King's daughter's,' she said. 'It's been foretold of her that she will be unlucky in a lover, and therefore nobody is allowed to visit her without the King and Queen are there.' 'Thanks,' said the merchant's son: and he went into the wood, got into his trunk, and flew up on to the roof and crept in at the window to the Princess.

She was lying on the sofa asleep, and she was so pretty that the merchant's son couldn't help kissing her. She woke up and was terribly startled; but he explained that he was the Turkish God who had come down to her through the sky; and that pleased her very much. So they sat side by side, and he told her stories about her eyes. They were the most lovely dark lakes, and her thoughts floated in them like mermaids: and he told her about her forehead: it was a snow mountain with the most splendid halls and images in it; and he told about the Stork, how it brings the dear little babies. Ah, those were beautiful stories! And thereupon he proposed to the Princess, and she said yes at once.

'But you must come here on Saturday,' she said, 'the King and Queen are coming to tea with me then. They will be very proud that I am marrying the Turkish God: but be sure you have a really beautiful story ready, for my parents are particularly fond of stories. My mother likes them to be moral and genteel, and my father likes them amusing, so that he can laugh.'

'Yes, I shall bring no wedding gift but a story,' said he, and they parted; but the Princess gave him a sword set with gold coins, and for these he had plenty of use.

He flew off and bought a new dressing-gown and then stayed out in the wood and made up a story. It had to be ready by Saturday, which is not so easy, I can tell you. At last he was ready, and it was Saturday.

The King, the Queen, and all the court were waiting at tea at the Princess's. He was most kindly received.

'Now will you tell us a story?' said the Queen. 'One that has a deep meaning and is instructive?'

'But let there be something one can laugh at,' said the King.

'Very well,' said he and began; and now we must listen carefully.

'Once upon a time there was a bundle of matches which were extremely proud of being of high degree. Their family tree, that is, the great pine tree of which each of them was a chip, had been a large old tree in the forest. The matches now lay on the dresser between a fire-box and an old iron pot, and to them they told the story of their youth. "Yes," they said, "when we were on the green bough we did indeed flourish like the green bay tree. Every morning and evening we had diamond tea (that was the dew), all day we had the sunshine (if the sun shone) and all the little birds were obliged to tell us stories. We could easily see, too, that we were rich, for the trees with leaves were clad only in summer, while our family could afford green clothes both in summer and winter. But then came the woodcutters; in other words, the great Revolution—and our family was split in pieces. The head of the house obtained a situation as mainmast on a magnificent vessel which could sail the whole world round if it pleased, the other branches went elsewhere, and we are now commissioned to kindle light for the common people: that's why we distinguished folk are come here to the kitchen."

'"Yes, it has been otherwise with me," said the iron pot beside which the matches lay. "From the moment I came out into the world I have been scoured and set to boil many a time. I minister to solid needs, and properly speaking am the first person in the house. My one pleasure is, as it might be after dinner, to lie cleansed and neat on the dresser, and carry on a reasonable conversation with my colleagues: but with the exception of the water bucket, which every now and then goes down to the yard, we live entirely indoors; our only news bringer is the market basket, but it talks very unrestfully about the government and the people; lately indeed, there was an elderly pot which in its alarm at this fell down and broke itself to pieces. That basket is of a turbulent disposition, I must say."

'"Now you're talking too much," said the fire-box, and the steel knocked on the flint till the sparks came: "Ought we not to have a gay evening?" "Yes, let us speak of who is most distinguished," said the matches. "No, I don't care for talking about myself," said the cooking pot, "let us have an evening conversation. I will begin. I will tell of things that everyone has experienced; there is opportunity for all to imagine it, and that is pleasant."

'"Near the eastern sea, among the beech woods of Denmark."—"That is a delightful commencement," said all the plates; "it will, I am sure, be a story I shall enjoy." "Yes, there it was that I passed my early years in a quiet family. The furniture was polished, the floor was washed, clean curtains were put up once a fortnight." "Now, how interesting you make your story," said the broom. "One can tell at once that it is a lady speaking: something so maidenly runs through it all."

'"Indeed, yes, one does feel that," said the water bucket, and out of pure pleasure it gave a little hop, and "plop" sounded on the floor.

'The pot went on with its story, and the end was every bit as good as the beginning. All the plates rattled with pleasure, and the broom got some green parsley out of the dust-hole and crowned the pot with it, for it knew this would annoy the rest, and, it reflected, "if I crown her to-day, she will crown me to-morrow."

'"I shall now dance," said the tongs, and dance it did. Yes, heaven be good to us, how it did kick up in the air with its leg! The old chair cushion away in the corner split with looking at it. "Can I be crowned?" said the tongs, and crowned it was.

'"Mere rabble, after all, these people," thought the matches.

'The tea urn was now asked to sing; but it had a cold, it said; it could only sing when on the boil. But this was merely standoffishness; it wouldn't sing unless it was set on the table and the family were there.

'Over in the window lay an old quill pen which the maid used to write with; there was nothing remarkable about it except that it had been dipped too deep in the inkstand, but of this it was quite proud. "If the tea urn won't sing," it said, "it can let it alone. Outside, there's a nightingale hung up in a cage; it can sing. It hasn't to be sure been trained at all, but we won't say anything unkind about that to-night."

'"I think it extremely improper", said the tea kettle, which was the kitchen singer-in-chief and half-sister to the tea urn, "that a foreign bird like that should be listened to. Is it patriotic? I leave it to the market basket."

'"I", said the market basket, "am merely annoyed. I am more intensely annoyed than can be imagined. Is this a fitting manner of spending the evening? Would it not be far better to set the house to rights? Everyone would then fall into his right place, and I should lead the whole dance. We should then have a very different state of things." "Yes, let's make a real row," they all cried out together. At that moment the door opened. It was the maid. They all stopped; no one made a sound; but there wasn't a single pot that wasn't conscious of what it could do and how distinguished it was. "If only I had chosen," they thought, "it would have been a gay evening indeed."

'The maid picked up the matches and struck them. Gracious! How they did sputter and burst into flame! "Now," thought they, "everybody can see we are the quality: what a flash we make! What a light!" And with that they burnt out.'

'That was a beautiful story,' said the Queen. 'I seemed to be really in the kitchen with the matches. Yes, now thou shalt have our daughter.'

'Certainly,' said the King, 'thou shalt marry our daughter on Monday.' (They said 'thou' to him now, since he was to be one of the family.)

So the wedding was fixed, and on the evening before the whole town was illuminated. Buns and tarts were thrown to be scrambled for. The street-boys stood on tiptce and shouted 'Hurrah!' and whistled on their fingers. It was a most brilliant affair.

'Well, I must see about doing something too,' thought the merchant's son: so he bought rockets and throw-downs and every imaginable kind of firework, and put it all in his trunk and flew up in the air with it.

Whizz, how they all went off and how they popped! It made all the Turks jump in the air till their slippers flew about their ears; never before had they seen such sights in the heavens. They could see now that it really was the Turkish God who was to marry the Princess.

As soon as the merchant's son was back in the wood with his trunk he thought: 'I'll go into the town and try to hear how the thing went,' and very natural too that he should want to hear.

Well, well, what stories the people did tell! Every single one he asked had seen it his own way, but all of them had found it charming.

'I saw the Turkish God himself,' said one. 'He had eyes like bright stars and a beard like foaming water.' 'He was flying in a mantle of fire,' said another, 'and lovely little angels were peeping out from the folds of it.' Indeed, he heard a number of charming things said, and the next day he was to be married.

He went back to the wood to get into his trunk—but where was it? The trunk was burnt. A spark from the fireworks had remained in it, had set it alight, and the trunk was in ashes. Never again could he fly, never again visit his bride. She stayed on the roof the whole day, waiting. She's waiting still. He is wandering the world over, telling stories. But they aren't so gay now as the one he told about the matches.

MOUNTAIN

Other book in this series

FINANCE COMMISSION AND CENTRE-STATE FINANCIAL RELATIONS

Finance Commission and Centre-State Financial Relations

by
G. Thimmaiah and Hemlata Rao
Institute for Social and Economic Change, Bangalore-72

ASHISH PUBLISHING HOUSE
8/81, PUNJABI BAGH
NEW DELHI-110026

Published by

S.B. Nangia
for Ashish Publishing House
8/81, Punjabi Bagh
New Delhi-110026
Tele : 500581,5410924

2021

Printed at:

Dhawan Printing Works
A-26, Mayapuri Phase I
New Delhi-110064

Preface

The debate on Centre-State relations has acquired multi-dimensions particularly in the wake of non-Congress (I) governments coming into power in several States. The framers of the Indian Constitution visualised that constitutionally provided Finance Commission will be able to minimise the Centre-State conflicts relating to the financial issues. But the Finance Commission, due to time and data constraints, could not fulfil the expectations of the framers of the Constitution. Further they have gone on assessing the financial needs of the State Governments on the basis of an out-moded methodology. What is worse, Central Government has been making in-roads into the Financial powers of State Governments. These two factors have given rise to misunderstanding between the Central and the State Governments. It was hoped that the Eighth Finance Commission at least will make a beginning in minimising such misunderstandings. But even the Eighth Finance Commission has disappointed the States.

As soon as the Eighth Finance Commission was appointed, the issues pertaining to the way the Commission would function and formulate its recommendations were debated. We actively participated in this debate and we also submitted individual as well as joint memoranda to the Eighth Finance Commission and gave evidence before the Commission. Subsequently, after the Eighth Finance Commission submitted its disappointing report, we evaluated the recommendations from the point of view of maintaining financial stability of the State Governments. In this book we have brought together all our ideas which we presented to the Eighth Finance Commission and also our critical views on the recommendations of the Eighth Finance Commission. We hope that this book will be of some help in understanding the issues involved in the Centre-State financial relations in India.

We wish to acknowledge the assistance rendered by Mr. P. Thippaiah in the collection of data and preparation of Tables and to Mr. P. Shankar for typing several drafts of the manuscript.

G THIMMAIAH, HEMLATA RAO

ISEC
Bangalore 560 072

Contents

List of Tables

CHAPTER I

Introduction

It is common knowledge that in all federations some degree of vertical fiscal federal imbalance arises. It is a normal feature of most of the federations that horizontal federal fiscal imbalance[1] is inevitable mainly because of diversity in economic structure and the levels of economic development of different constituent units which determine on the one hand varying degree of fiscal capacity and on the other hand the revenue needs. The combined operation of these two factors creates horizontal federal fiscal imbalance. This coupled with the vertical federal fiscal imbalance, increases the need for federal fiscal assistance to the constituent States of any federation.

In vertical federal fiscal imbalance, the fiscal needs of all the State Governments taken together are considered *vis-a-vis* that of the federal government. In view of the fact that the sources of revenue and items of public expenditure are generally allocated to the federal and State Governments on the basis of conflicting principles, they invariably leave more and highly elastic sources

1. See for more rigorous analysis of these concepts, G. Thimmaiah, "Vertical Inter-governmental Financial Imbalance : A Restatement". *Finanzarchiv*, Vol. 33, No. 3, 1976.

of revenue with the federal government and more expanding items of expenditure with the State Governments.

Under these circumstances vertical federal fiscal imbalance is bound to arise. To illustrate this point, it may be reasonably presumed that some kind of comparative cost advantage principle is used for allotting sources of revenue which have a national base and whose cost of collection would enjoy economies of scale would automatically go to the federal government. Therefore, guided by this principle most of the elastic sources of revenue would be justified and tend to be allotted to the federal government. On the expenditure side, the tastes and preferences of different groups of citizens in a federation vary from place to place. Consequently one national government cannot supply certain essential public services to suit such variety of tastes and preferences. Efficient supply of these services requires lower Level government like the State Government to render these services. As a result, decentralisation of these functions becomes a necessary condition for achieving efficiency in rendering these services. Therefore, the gap between the sources of revenue and expenditure of State Governments is required to be filled by the federal government under certain obligatory and discretionary conditions by transferring a portion of its revenue to the State Governments.

At the disaggregate level of different State Governments, though all the State Governments would face vertical federal fiscal imbalance, different State Governments face it in different degrees because of their varying revenue potential and expenditure needs. Horizontal federal imbalance adds to the vertical federal fiscal imbalance and magnifies the fiscal needs of different State Governments. Therefore, the gap between revenues and expenditures of State Governments is required to be filled by the financial transfers from the federal government.

In most of the federations these federal fiscal imbalances are recognised in advance and some constitutional provisions are made with a view to guiding federal government for transferring a portion of its revenue to the State Governments. However, the nature and type of such arrangements differ from federation to federation. For instance, in India specific fiscal provisions are made for such financial transfers under Articles 270, 272, 275 and 282. Besides a unique feature of the Indian Constitution is that it provides for a constitutional commission—Finance Commission—under Article 280 to examine the specific fiscal needs of State Governments and to determine the nature and extent of financial transfers from the Centre to different States.[2] Thus, it would be evident from the foregoing observations, that the main objective of federal fiscal transfers is to reduce vertical as well as horizontal federal fiscal imbalances.

2. See for details G. Thimmaiah, *A Critique of the Finance Commission*, Wheeler & Co., Allahabad, 1981.

CHAPTER IJ

Vertical Federal Fiscal Imbalance in India

Federal-State financial relations are a perennial source of controversy in all federations. The controversy is even greater in India where we have a constitutional body like the Finance Commission as also an extra-constitutional body, the Planning Commission, which recommend financial transfers from the Centre to the States. The Eighth Finance Commission is deliberating on the financial needs of the State Governments for their non-plan current expenditures purpose. A National Commission has also been appointed to suggest measures to establish a more healthy relations between the Centre and the States. In recent years the issue of financial transfers from the Centre to the States has been politicised by the non-Congress (I) ruled States by mounting a joint attack against the Centre. The main motive appears to be to dislodge it from its dominant financial position by demanding a rearrangement of the financial powers between the Centre and States in such a way as to free them from their increasing dependence on the Centre. In this current debate on Centre-State financial relations, the most important problems which figure prominently are the magnitude of the financial transfers from the Centre to the States and the manner in which they are distributed among the States.

Article 246 of the Constitution demarcates the sphere of responsibilities of the Centre and the States in terms of their legislative jurisdiction as laid down in the Seventh Schedule. While the Centre has been entrusted with a few major responsibilities like defence, external affairs, industrial development, etc., the States have to shoulder major responsibility for most of the developmental and welfare functions like irrigation, power, agriculture, education, health and social welfare, in addition to law and order.

As far as the division of sources of revenue is concerned, the Central Government enjoys a comfortable position with many elastic sources of revenue like union excise duties, customs duties, and corporate tax which have national tax base. In contrast, the States are given inadequate and less elastic sources of revenue like land revenue. A possible exception is sales tax. But its scope has been gradually reduced by the Central Government by making many inroads into its coverage like centralisation of sales tax on inter-State trade, taking over the power of fixing the rates of sales tax on declared goods and services, and gradual extension of additional union excise duties to more commodities. What is more, some of the sources of revenue like land taxation and State excise duties are entangled in political constraints making it difficult for the State Governments to raise more revenue. Under these circumstances, vertical federal fiscal imbalance invariably arises and consequently, the State Governments have to depend to a large extent on the Centre for financial assistance to meet their growing expenditure needs. The growing financial dependency and the nature of financial dependency are important problems which deserve our attention here.

It may be observed from Table 2.1 that from the period of Second Five-Year Plan there has been growing centralisation of revenues raised by both the levels of Governments in the country. A cursory look at Table 2.1 reveals that until 1979-80, the States shared less than 30% of the total revenues raised by both the Centre and the States and less than 17% of the total capital receipts, while the Centre shared about 70% of the aggregate revenue receipts and about 83% of the capital receipts. On the other hand, compared with the revenue at its command, the Centre assumed relatively less responsibility in the total public expenditure of the country. While the States had to shoulder responsibility for about 50% of the aggregate revenue expenditure as against less than 20% of the share in revenue receipts, and 38% of the capital expenditure as against 17% of the capital receipts. Consequently the Centre cornered more revenue receipts than its responsibility in the total expenditure. The position seems to have changed since 1979-80 and States appear to be in better position. This is a welcome trend. However, it does not imply that the magnitude of dependency of the States has become insignificant.

It is not only the magnitude of vertical federal fiscal imbalance which deserves our attention but also the trend in the vertical federal fiscal imbalance which requires serious attention.

It may be observed from Table 2.1 that over the period under study, there has been an increase in the centralisation of revenues. The percentage share of the States in total revenue receipts declined from 38.97% to 32.06% and the percentage share of States in the aggregate revenues also declined from 29.28% during the Second Plan period to 27.35% during the Fifth Plan period. There has been very little change in the expenditure responsibilities of the Centre and the States. The declining share of States in the total revenues confirms increasing centralisation of revenues in the country. Thus, the magnitude of vertical federal fiscal imbalance has been increasing in India though it is showing a declining trend in recent years. This is evident from Table 2.2.

The magnitude of vertical federal fiscal imbalance has been higher on capital account mainly because of additional expenditure burden imposed on the State Governments on account of planning. Most of the development projects which require capital funds have to be implemented in the State sector. This has necessitated increasing financial dependence of the States on the Centre. Increasing financial dependence of the States on the Central Government is clearly reflected in Table 2.3 which presents data relating to percentage share of expenditure financed by States' own revenues.

TABLE 2.1

Percentage Share of States in the Total Revenue and Expenditure of the Centre and States

Plan Period	*Percentage share of States in the total revenues of Centre and States*			*Percentage share of States in the total expenditure of the Centre and States*		
	Revenue Receipts %	*Capital receipts* %	*Aggregate revenues* %	*Revenue expenditure* %	*Capital expenditure* %	*Aggregate expenditure* %
Second Plan	38.97	15.51	29.28	54.07	35.77	45.34
Third Plan	30.52	13.46	23.27	48.51	35.38	42.30
Three Annual Plans	30.32	13.91	23.27	49.01	35.66	43.18
Fourth Plan	30.65	15.71	24.94	51.84	38.18	46.31
Fifth Plan	32.06	16.09	27.35	49.17	38.49	45.06

Source : Compiled from various sources of R.B.I. Bulletins

TABLE 2.2

Magnitude of Vertical Federal Fiscal Imbalance in India

Plan Period	*Magnitude of vertical federal fiscal imbalance on*		
	Revenue Account %	*Capital Account* %	*Aggregate* %
Second Plan	15.10	20.26	16.06
Third Plan	17.99	21.92	19.03
Three Annual Plans	18.69	21.75	19.81
Fourth Plan	21.19	22.47	21.38
Fifth Plan	17.11	21.80	17.71
Sixth Plan	—	—	—

Source : Compiled from various issues of R.B.I. Bulletin.

TABLE 2.3

Financial Dependence of the State Governments on the Central Government

Plan Period	*Central Assistance as percentage of States' total revenue*	*States' own revenues as percentage of total revenues of the States*	*States' own revenues as percentage of total expenditure of the States*
First Plan	37.64	62.23	62.02
Second Plan	39.87	59.98	59.75
Third Plan	46.15	54.09	54.37
Three Annual Plans	46.10	53.55	53.14
Fourth Plan	47.51	52.33	52.14
Fifth Plan	42.06	58.54	59.39
1979-80	36.45	59.71	67.36
Sixth Plan 1980-84	33.88	61.43	65.15

Note : Due to adjustments made in R.B.I. Bulletins, columns (2) and (3) show marginal differences in the percentage share.

It may be observed from Table 2.3 that the States' own revenues, (both capital and revenue), could finance less than 60% of their total expenditure. The Central assistance accounted for about 40% of the total revenues to finance the remaining 40% of the States Governments' expenditure. It may be observed that it is not only the magnitude of Central assistance which influences the State Governments' expenditure level, but also the trends in Central assistance. This needs to be closely examined. As is evident from Table 2.3 the percentage share of Central assistance is gradually increasing over the period under study. During the First Plan period the Central assistance accounted for 37.64% and by the end of Fourth Plan period it increased to 47.51% and even during the Fifth Plan period, the Central assistance was as high as 42.06%. Along with such increase in the percentage share of Central assistance, there has been a corresponding decline in the contribution of States' own revenues to finance States total expenditure. This, in the context of increasing additional resource mobilisation by the States in the recent years, would imply that while their capacity to raise their own revenues has reached a plateau, their expenditure needs are increasing faster owing to the increasing demand for developmental and welfare expenditures from the people consequent on political awakening. Whether this trend is healthy or not is a value judgment. If the federal fiscal transfers are made on an objective basis by taking into account the true fiscal needs of the States and through assured sources, the States may have little apprehension. But if they are of discretionary nature influenced by the whims and fancics of the ruling party at the Centre, it will result in distrust and conflict. If the State Governments feel uncertain about the amount of resources they are going to get from the Centre and the manner in which they will be assisted under these circumstances, it will result in an unhealthy trend in federal fiscal set-up.

The manner in which federal fiscal transfers are made in India can be observed from Table 2.4. It may be noted that federal fiscal transfers are made through three channels *viz.*, on the recommendations of Finance Commission, Planning Commission and through various Central Ministries. Finance Commission is a statutory body and hence the financial transfers made on the recommendations of the Finance Commission are more assured than the transfers made through other two channels. Out of the remaining two, the financial assistance provided on the recommendations of the Planning Commission is more assured than the purely discretionary transfers made at the discretion of various Central Ministries. It may be observed from Table 2.4 that until the end of Fourth Five-Year Plan, the financial transfer made on the recommendations of the Finance Commission constituted only about one-third of the total federal financial transfers, while those made on the recommendations of the Planning Commission and other discretionary transfers constituted the remaining two-thirds. However, during the Fifth Plan period the share of the Finance Commission transfers increased from 35.90% to 44.17%. Despite this increase, the discretionary transfers made on the recommendations of the Planning Commission and by various Central Ministries continued to constitute more than 55% of the total federal financial transfers. Up to the beginning of the Fifth Plan period, financial transfers made through various Central Ministries accounted for about 33% and then they were reduced to 14.14% during the Fifth Plan period. This is a healthy trend, provided it is maintained in the coming years too. Nevertheless, when viewed in the light of the total federal financial transfers, a large part of them still flows to the States at the discretion of the Central Government.

Even out of the financial transfers made on the recommendations of the Finance Commission only a small portion is assured, while the bulk of it is through less assured sources. Finance Commissions recommend transfer of financial resources through divisible taxes and duties and grants-in-aid. The divisible taxes and duties are of two types : obligatory and discretionary. While a share in net yield from income-tax, other than corporation tax is obligatory the share of the net yield from union excise duties is shared at the discretion of the Centre. It may be observed from Table 2.4 that over the period under study, the States received more financial assistance through the share in the net yield from union excise duties which was about

18.60% of the total transfers during the First Plan period which increased to 44.58% during the Fifth Plan period. During the same period the relative position of the States' share in the net yield from income-tax declined from 80.81% to 39.31%. This has been due to the narrowing down of the divisible pool of income-tax owing to (*a*) exclusion of the yield from corporate income-tax from the divisible pool, (*b*) raising of exemption limit of individual income-tax which has resulted in loss of revenue, (*c*) reduction of income-tax rates on certain slabs, (*d*) liberal concessions offered to savings under various provisions of the Act, and (5) large scale evasion of income-tax by the self-employed and others.

Further it may be observed that the relative position of grants-in-aid under Article 275 though increased in the First and Second Plan periods, has stabilised around 25%. The percentage share increased from 12.08% during the First Plan period, 21.79% during the Second Plan period and further to 24.61% during the Fifth Plan period. Grants-in-aid are given to only those States that are adjudged to be in need of assistance even after receiving a share in the divisible pool of Central taxes. Therefore all States are not eligible to receive grants-in-aid. This would indicate that grants-in-aid are less assured sources of revenue in the States and hence increase the financial dependence of the poorer States on the Centre. In fact, out of the total federal financial transfers only about 13%, which constitute a share in the yield from income-tax, is assured to the States, while the remaining 87% of the total federal financial transfers is neither certain nor assured and hence would indicate an unhealthy dependence of the States on the Centre. Apart from the share in income-tax, the States have a statutory claim on taxes levied under Article 269 of the Constitution. However, as is evident from Table 2.4, the States received meagre amount from estate duty and other taxes which were levied under Article 269. In the later years the tax on railway fare and freight was converted into grants-in-aid in lieu of the tax which made it a stagnating source of federal financial transfer. Thus the share from these was negligible right from the beginning and over the years their importance has further gone down. Their share in the total federal financial transfers declined from 1.50% during the Second Plan period to 0.33% during the Fifth Plan period. This clearly shows that the States are getting gradually less and less proportion of Central assistance through assured sources.

TABLE 2.4

Composition of Federal Financial Transfers in India

Plan Periods	*Share in Divisible Taxes and Duties*			*Agreed and Assigned Shares*				
	Income-tax	*Union excise duties*	*Total (1+2)*	*Additional excise duty*	*Estate duty*	*Other taxes or grants in lieu*	*Total agreed and assigned taxes (4+5+6)*	*Total transfers through tax shares (3+7)*
	1	*2*	*3*	*4*	*5*	*6*	*7*	*8*
I. 1st Plan period								
1. Total share (Rs. crores)	278	64	342	—	2	—	2	344
2. Percentage to sub-group total	81.29	18.71	100	—	100	—	100	—
3. Percentage to group total	80.81	18.61	99.41	—	0.58	—	0.58	100
4. Percentage to FC total	62.19	14.32	76.51	—	0.45	—	0.45	76.96
5. Percentage to total federal finance transfers	19.43	4.17	23.89	—	0.14	—	0.14	24.04
II. 2nd Plan Period								
1. Total share (Rs. crores)	375	153	528	128	12	43	183	711

(contd.)

Table 2.4 (*Contd.*)

	1	*2*	*3*	*4*	*5*	*6*	*7*	*8*
2. Percentage to sub-group total	71.82	28.98	100	69.95	6.55	23.50	100	—
3. Percentage to group total	52.74	21.52	74.26	18.00	1.69	6.05	25.74	100
4. Percentage to FC transfers	40.85	16.67	57.51	13.94	1.31	4.68	19.93	77.45
5. Percentage to total federal finance transfers	13.07	5.33	18.41	4.46	0.42	1.50	6.38	24.79
III. 3rd Plan Period								
1. Total share (Rs. crores)	555	398	953	217	26	63	306	1259
2. Percentage to sub-group total	58.24	41.76	100	70.92	8.50	20.58	100	—
3. Percentage to group total	44.08	31.61	75.69	17.69	2.07	5.00	24.31	100
4. Percentage to FC transfers	34.91	25.03	59.93	13.65	1.64	3.96	19.24	79.18
5. Percentage to total federal finance transfers	9.91	7.11	17.01	3.88	0.46	1.13	5.46	20.48
IV. Three Annual Plans								
1. Total share (Rs. crores)	507	628	1135	129	18	48	195	1330
2. Percentage to sub group total	44.67	55.33	100	66.15	9.23	24.62	100	—
3. Percentage to group total	38.12	47.22	85.33	9.70	1.35	3.61	14.66	100
4. Percentage to FC transfers	28.45	35.24	63.69	7.24	1.02	2.69	10.94	74.63

5. Percentage to total federal financial transfers	9.48	11.74	21.22	2.41	0.34	0.90	3.64	24.87
V. 4th Plan period								
1. Share in crores	21.38	1850	3988	535	39	85	659	4647
2. Percentage to sub-group	53.61	46.39	100	81.18	5.92	12.90	100	—
3. Percentage to group	46.01	39.81	85.81	11.51	0.84	1.33	14.18	100
4. Percentage to FC transfers	39.44	34.13	73.56	9.86	0.72	1.57	12.16	85.72
5. Percentage to total federal financial transfers	14.16	12.25	26.40	3.54	0.26	0.56	4.36	30.77
VI. 5th Plan Period								
1. Total share (Rs. crores)	3310	3717	7027	1262	48	83	1393	8420
2. Percentage to sub-group	47.10	52.90	100	90.60	3.45	5.96	100	—
3. Percentage to group	39.31	44.14	83.45	14.99	0.57	0.99	16.54	100.00
4. Percentage to FC transfers	29.64	33.28	62.92	11.30	0.43	0.74	12.47	75.39
5. Percentage to total federal financial transfers	13.09	13.14	27.79	4.99	0.19	0.33	5.50	33.30
VII. 6th Plan Period								
1. Total share (Rs. crores)	—	—	—		—	—	—	—
2. Percentage to sub-group	—	—	—	—	—	—	—	—
3. Percentage to group	—	—	—	—	—	—	—	—
4. Percentage to FC transfers	—	—	—	—	—	—	—	—
5. Percentage to total federal financial transfers	—	—	—	—	—	—	—	—

(Contd.)

Table 2.4—(*Contd.*)

	Grants			*Total*	*Assistance for State plans and centrally sponsored schemes*						*Total*
	Article 275	*Other Grants grants*	*Total grants (9+10)*	*Finance Common. trans-fers*	*Plan grants (7+11)*	*Plan loans*	*Total*	*Central Centrally sponsored schemes Grants*	*Loans*	*Total*	*Planning Trans-fers*
	9	*10*	*11*	*12*	*13*	*14*	*15*	*16*	*17*	*18*	*19*
I 1st. Plan Period											
1. Total share (Rs. crores)	54	49	103	447	—	—	350	—	—	530	880
2. Percentage to sub-group total	52.43	47.57	100	—	—	—	100	—	—	100	
3. Percentage to group total	—	—	—	—	—	—	39.77	—	—	60.23	100
4. Percentage to FC total	12.08	10.96	23.04	100	—	—	—	—	—	—	—
5. Percentage to total federal fiscal transfers	3.77	3.42	720	31.24	—	—	24.46	—	—	37.04	61.49
II. 2nd Plan Period											
1. Total share (Rs. crores)	200	7	207	918	254	804	1058	—	—	—	1058
2. Percentage to sub-group total	96.62	3.38	100	—	—	—	—	—	—	—	—
3. Percentage to group total	—	—	—	—	24.00	75.99	100	—	—	—	100
4. Percentage to FC transfers	21.79	0.76	22.55	100	—	—	—	—	—	—	—

5. Percentage to total federal financial transfers	6.79	0.24	7.22	32.01	8.86	28.03	36.88	—	—	—	36.88
III. 3rd Plan Period											
1. Total share (Rs. crores)	331	—	331	1590	—	—	2515	175	48	223	2738
2. Percentage to sub-group total	100	—	100	—	—	—	100	78.48	21.52	100	—
3. Percentage to group total	—	—	—	—	—	—	91.86	6.39	1.75	8.14	100
4. Percentage to FC transfers	20.81	—	20.81	100	—	—	—	—	—	—	—
5. Percentage to total federal financial transfers	5.91	—	5.91	28.39	—	—	44.91	3.13	.86	3.88	48.89
IV. Three Annual Plans											
1. Total share (Rs. crores)	452	—	452	1782	—	—	1767	—	—	150	1917
2. Percentag to sub-group total	100.00	—	100	—	—	—	100	—	—	100	100
3. Percentage to group total	—	—	—	—	—	—	92.17	—	—	3.23	100
4. Percentage to FC transfers	25.36	—	25.36	100	—	—	—	—	—	—	—
5. Percentage to total federal financial transfers	8.45	—	8.45	33.33	—	—	33.04	—	—	2.80	35.8

(Contd.)

Table 2.4—(*Contd.*)

	9	*10*	*11*	*12*	*13*	*14*	*15*	*16*	*17*	*18*	*19*
V. 5th Plan Period											
1. Total share (Rs. crores	774	—	774	5421	1077	2458	35.35	969	227	1196	4731
2. Percentage to sub-group total	100	—	100	—	30.46	69.54	100	81.02	18.98	100	—
3. Percentage to group total	—	—	—	—	22.76	51.96	74.7	20.48	4.80	25.28	100
4. Percentage to FC transfers	14.28	—	14.28	100	—	—	—	—	—	—	—
5. Percentage to total federal financial transfers	5.13	—	5.13	35.90	7.13	16.28	23.41	6.42	1.50	7.92	31.33
VI. 6th Plan Period											
1. Total share (Rs. crores)	2748	—	2748	11168	2814	4943	7757	1958	638	2596	1035
2. Percentage to sub-group total	100	—	100	—	36.28	63.72	100	75.58	24.58	100	—
3. Percentage to group total	24.61	—	24.61	100	27.18	47.74	74.26	18.91	6.16	25.07	100
3. Percentage to FC transfers	—	—	—	—	—	—	—	—	—	—	—
5. Percentage to total federal fiscal tranfers	24.61	—	10.86	44.17	11.13	19.55	30.68	7.74	2.52	10.27	40.95

(Contd.)

Table 2.4 (*Contd.*)

Plan Periods	*Other discretionary Assistance*			*Total federal fiscal financial transfers*
	Grands	*Loans*	*Total*	
	20	*21*	*22*	*23*
I. 1st Plan period				
1. Total share (Rs. crores)	—	—	104	1431
2. Percentage to group total	—	—	100	—
3. Percentage to FC/PL transfers	—	—	—	—
4. Percentage total federal financial transfers	—	—	7.26	100
II. 2nd Plan period				
1. Total share (Rs. crores)	—	—	892	2868
2. Percentage to FC/PC transfers	—	—	100	—
3. Percentage to PC/FC transfers	—	—	—	—
4. Percentage to total federal financial transfers	—	—	31.10	100
III 3rd Plan period				
1. Total share (Rs. crores)	—	—	1272	5600
2. Percentage to group total	—	—	100	—
3. Percentage to FC/PC transfers	—	—	—	—
3. Percentnge to total federal financial transfers	—	—	22.71	100

(Contd.)

Table 2.4—(*Contd.*)

	20	*21*	*22*	*23*
IV. Three Annual Plans				
1. Total share (Rs. crores)	—	—	1648	5347
2. Percentage to Group total	—	—	—	—
3. Percentage to FC/PC transfers	—	—	100	—
4. Pereentege to total federal financial transfers	—	—	30.82	100
V. 4th Plan Period				
1. Total share (Rs. crores)	926	4023	4949	15101
2. Percentnge to group total	18.71	81.29	100	—
3. Percentage to FC/PC total transfers	—	—	—	—
4. Percentage to total federa financial transfers	6.13	26.64	32,77	100
VI. 5th Plan Period				
1. Total share (Rs. crores)	532	3229	3761	25282
2. Percentage to group total	14.14	85.85	100	—
3. Percentage to FC/PC transfers	—	—	—	—
4. Percentage to total federal financial transfers	2.10	12.77	14.88	100

VII. 6th Plan Period				
1. Total share (Rs. crores)	—	—	—	—
2. Percentage to group total	—	—	—	—
3. Percentage to FC/PC transfer	—	—	—	—
4. Percentage to total federal financial transfers	—	—	—	—

CHAPTER III

Federal Fiscal Equity in india

3.1 Background

Fiscal federalism refers to the constitutional structure which divides the powers to raise revenue and to spend it between the Central and State Governments and also the system of periodic financial transfers from the federal government to the State Governments to reduce vertical as well as horizontal federal fiscal imbalances. It is believed that if the federal fiscal imbalances tend to operate discriminately between States, and the expected hopes and aspirations which initiated the formation of a federation fail to materialise, instability sets in. Instability of a federation manifests itself in economic instability of its constituent States and the consequent dissatisfaction or even frustration with the operation of fiscal federalism. If these symptoms of instability are not recognised early and corrective measures are not taken, the federation may eventually break down.

The conditions for the stability of a federation are the following :

1. The policy of reducing wide inter-State economic disparities which exist not only at the time of the formation of federation but also which result from the operation of federal policies after the formation of the federation should be accepted unanimously by all the federating States.

2. Such a policy should be unanimously entrusted to the federal government.

3. The federal government should try to achieve this policy within a reasonable period of time say over a decade or two.

The federal government is, therefore, expected to use federal financial transfers to minimise wide inter-State as well as inter-personal inequalities of income with a view to maintaining stability of the federation.

First, the federal government should use the federal financial transfers to off-set unequal impact of its own taxation as well as expenditure policies on the budgets of the constituent States. Otherwise discriminatory impact of taxation and expenditure policies on the budgets of the poorer States may frustrate them and create the problem of instability of a federation.

Secondly, the federal government should use federal financial transfers to off-set adverse impact of inter-State spillovers of expenditure benefits and tax costs of the State Governments. If such spillovers are unequal between States, inter-State fiscal imbalances result and they may give rise to inter-State conflicts and instability of a federation. Such imbalances should be minimised by the federal government through appropriate federal financial transfers.

Thirdly, the federal financial transfers should be used to ensure a minimum level of essential public services to all the citizens all over the federation. Such provision may not be possible in all States because of varying fiscal capacity and fiscal needs of different States. Therefore, federal financial transfer should be linked to the fiscal needs of the State Governments for ensuring minimum level of essential public services.

Finally, with a view to reducing inter-State economic disparities, the federal government will have to use federal financial transfers in such a way as to generate economic activities in poorer States. This, in other words, means the federal government will have to interfere in the process and pattern of development of the constituent States with a view to reducing wide inter-State economic disparities.

Against this background an attempt is made in this Chapter to indicate the inter-State economic disparities and to examine the equity in the distribution of federal financial transfers made on the recommendations of the Finance Commission among individual States.

3.2 Inter-State Economic Disparities

Before we go to examine the distribution of federal financial transfers among individual States, it would be appropriate to make a brief reference to the existing inter-State economic disparities. Though several indicators have been used to measure the relative backwardness of different States, they do not indicate any common pattern in the level of development of different States. The widely accepted summary indicator, *i.e.*, per capita State domestic product at constant prices, would, no doubt, indicate the overall level of development of different States. But in view of its average entity, it hides the distributional aspect of development.[1] In order to overcome this deficiency, percentage of people below poverty line is often suggested as an indicator of backwardness. Even in regard to this there is a controversy relating to its reliability and magnitude of absolute poverty. We have examined the association between percentage of people below poverty line and per capita SDP at constant prices. It has been observed that there is no clear-cut pattern of association between the level of per capita SDP and percentage of people below poverty line, the level of per capita SDP and PQLI and between percentage of people below poverty line and PQLI.[2] This incompatibility may be partly explained by unreliability of the estimates of absolute poverty in States like

1. It should be also mentioned in this context that both biased and unbiased methodological deffciencies are evident in the estimates of State domestic product in India.
2. Sec for details G. Thimmaiah, "Inter-State Disparities in the Allocation of Financial Assistance by the Centre", *Vishleshan*, Dec. 1982.

Kerala and Rajasthan and of per capital. SDP of States like Maharashtra and Assam. However, there seems to be close association between composite index of development and per capita SDP.[3] After examining all these indicators and relying mainly on the basis of composite index and per capita SDP, we have identified relatively developed, middle level and less developed States.

Accordingly, we have grouped Punjab, Haryana, Gujarat, and Maharashtra as relatively developed States; Andhra Pradesh, Karnataka, Kerala, Tamil Nadu and West Bengal as middle level States and Assam and all the north eastern States, Bihar, Orissa, Rajasthan, Madhya Pradesh and Jammu and Kashmir as relatively less developed States in the Indian Union. This sort of categorisation indicates only very broad trend as it is very difficult to make a categorical distinction between various States based on all relevant indicators of backwardness. Further, we have not gone into intra-State economic disparities which are as prominent as inter-States economic disparities in States like Uttar Pradesh, Andhra Pradesh, Madhya Pradesh, etc. However, for the purpose of making federal financial transfers legal, economic and administrative units are the States. Therefore, the above-mentioned grouping of States is only intended to capture the phenomenon of relative economic backwardness for the purpose of examining the distribution of federal financial transfers made on the recommendations of the Finance Commissions.

It may be observed from the above grouping that Tamil Nadu and West Bengal which were considered as relatively developed States during the sixties have come down to middle level status, whereas Kerala, Karnataka and Andhra Pradesh which were considered as less developed States have moved up to middle level status. The less developed States have continued to be so even after 32 years of planning.

3.3 Equity in Finance Commissions' Transfers

The federal financial transfers made on the recommenda-

3. See for details Hemlata Rao, "Inter-State Disparities in India", (Mimeo), ISEC, 1983.

tions of the Finance Commissions may be characterised as statutory transfers. This is because, under Article 280 the recommendations of the Finance Commissions, once accepted, are binding on the part of the Central Government. It should be mentioned, however, that there are certain discretionary components, such as share in the net yield from union excise duties, in the recommendations of the Finance Commissions. Even so, once the recommendations of the Finance Commissions on such shares are accepted it is legally binding on the Central Government to transfer them to the State Governments except in a period of financial emergency. This legal status of the Finance Commissions' transfers gives some guarantee and certainty for the State Governments in regard to the flow of financial resources from the Central Government. They can fairly anticipate the expected annual financial flows while determining the size of their budgets and also some of their development programmes.

There is another merit in the financial transfers made on the recommendations of Finance Commissions. The Finance Commissions recommend tax shares as well as grants-in-aid. Of late the proportion of tax shares has been increasing and that of grants-in-aid has been going down in the total amount of financial resources recommended by the Finance Commissions. This is evident from Table 2.1. This trend has one advantage for the State Governments in that the tax shares which are fixed in percentage terms tend to increase the actual amount of revenue received by the State Governments in view of the buoyancy of the yield of the taxes whose yield is shared. As compared to this, the grants-in-aid are fixed amounts which cannot be varied for five years. Therefore, the tax shares which are elastic and which are becoming prominent in the Finance Commissions' transfers have been giving required buoyancy for the State Governments' total financial resources. Furthermore, the tax shares are mostly in the form of unconditional grants which leave the State Governments free to utilise them according to their own budget priorities. This is so even in the case of statutory grants under Article 275. But the conditional grants which have been introduced under the recommendations of the Sixth and Seventh Finance Commissions to upgrade the standard of administrative and other essential public services are not allowed to be diverted for other purposes. In a way this combination of freedom to use a major portion of the financial resources according to the priorities of different State Governments combined with some earmarking of a small portion of the resources transferred by the Centre under the recommendations of the Finance Commissions tends to achieve the desired allocative efficiency in the distribution of federal financial transfers.

But most part of the resources transferred under the recommendations of the Finance Commissions are intended to meet the non-plan recurring expenditure of the State Governments which includes mostly the 'police state' and a few 'merit goods' functions. No doubt, in the past 10 to 15 years the Finance Commissions have been leaving non-plan surpluses with the State Governments for utilisation for plan purposes. These surpluses become unconditional grants for plan purpose which distort the allocative efficiency. By and large, the recommendations of the Finance Commissions are not intended to promote development activities though they go to improve the infrastructure support for development programmes. This limitation has to be borne in mind, while examining the role of Finance Commissions' transfers in reducing inter-State disparities in economic development.

Table 3.2 presents the extent of aggregate financial transfers made by the Central Government to the States on the recommendations of the past Finance Commissions. The ranks indicate very obvious pattern. There is a broad indication that relatively developed and middle level States have received higher absolute amounts as well as percentage shares. Even in per capita terms the middle level and relatively developed States have received higher amounts. Among the less developed States only Uttar Pradesh and Jammu and Kashmir have received higher per capita amounts. It may be observed that less developed States like Assam, Rajasthan and Orissa have not received as much as the other less developed States let alone relatively developed and middle level States.

These observations are only based on the comparison of

TABLE 3.1

Indicators of Levels of Backwardness of Different States in India

State	*Percentage of people below poverty line (61-62)*	*RANK*	*Per capita SDP (Average for the years 1961-62—1965-66) (Rs.)*	*RANK*	*Per capita SDP (Average for the years 1966-67—1970-71) (Rs.)*	*RANK*	*PQLI Index (1970-71)*	*RANK*	*Percentage of the people below poverty line (1977-78)*	*RANK*	*Per-capita SDP (Average for the years 1973-74 to 1977-78) (Rs.)*	*RANK*
1. Andhra Pradesh	60.13	3	291	7	289	14	43	6	42.10	10	324	15
2. Assam	35.52	9	265	9	538	2	37	9	51.10	5	554	7
3. Bihar	32.33	12	221	14	241	16	—	—	57.49	3	408	13
4. Gujarat	34.60	10	389	5	471	3	40	7	39.04	11	778	2
5. Haryana	—	—	319	6	393	6	—	—	24.84	15	460	12
6. J & K	28.00	13	263	11	260	15	—	—	34.06	12	335	14
7. Kerala	89.82	1	260	12	338	9	70	1	48.34	7.5	560	6
8. Madhya Pradesh	38.71	8	246	14.5	293	11	37	9	47.71	9	466	10
9. Maharastra	59.61	4	401	1	416	5	49	3	57.75	2	489	8
10. Karnataka	47.16	5	204	10	358	8	48	4	48.34	7.5	694	4
11. Orissa	39.73	7	246	14.5	300	10	37	9	66.40	1	461	11
12. Punjab	33.04	11	378	4	557	1	50	2	15.13	15	1138	1
13. Rajasthan	17.57	15	285	8	292	12.5	33	11	33.76	13	301	16
14. Tamil Nadu	62.99	2	326	5	381	7	46	5	52.12	4	596	5

15. U. P.	27.89	14	250	13	292	12.5	25	12	50.09	6	470	9
16. Wes Bengal	46.31	6	395	2	456	4	—	—	32.54	14	749	3
ALL INDIA	38.71		319		390		40		46.11		655	

Notes : (1) Per captia state domestic product (SDP) figures are at constant prices, (2) *PQLI*-Physical Quality of Life Index, *ED*=Quick Estimates, *P*=Provisional, *Pr*=Preliminary.

Source : (1) SDP data are taken from RBI Bulletins. Apr. 78, and Sept. 1981 (2) Percentage of people below poverty-line are taken from VM Dandekar and Nilakanth ; Rath—*Poverty in India* for the year 1961-62 and from *Sixth Five-Year Plan*, 1984-85. Government of India, for the year 1977-78.

TABLE 3.2

Devolution of Financial Resources from the Centre to the States on the Recommendation of the Finance Commission

States	Second Finance Commission[a] [1957-1958 to 1961-62 (5 years)]						Third Finance Commission[a] [1962-63 to 1965-66 (4 years)]					
	Total Assistance (Rs. Crs)	RANK	Per cent to total	RANK	Per-capita (Rs.)	RANK	Total Assistance (Rs. Crs)	RANK	Per-cent to total	RANK	Per-capita (Rs.)	RANK
	1	2	3	4	5	6	7	8	9	10	11	12
1. Andhra Pradesh	90.05	5	8.5	5	26.48	8	122.12	3	9.3	2	33.94	8
2. Assam	45.36	12	4.3	12	42.17	3	58.57	14	4.5	13.5	49.33	3
3. Bihar	95.32	4	9.0	4	22.00	13	102.63	4	7.8	4	22.09	14
4. Gujarat	35.79	14	3.4	14	18.94	15	85.18	9	6.4	9	41.28	4
5. Haryana	—		—		—		—		—		—	
6. Himachal Pradesh	—		—		—		—		—		—	
7. Jammu & Kashmir	24.57	15	2.3	15	71.76	1	21.75	15	1.6	15	61.08	1
8. Kerala	37.91	13	3.6	13	24.31	10	68.45	12	5.2	12	40.49	5
9. Madhya Pradesh	71.54	8	6.8	8	24.18	11	86.81	8	6.6	8	26.82	13
10. Tamil Nadu	72.88	7	6.9	7	22.68	12	91.75	7	6.9	7	27.24	11
11. Maharashtra	108.85	2	10.4	2	30.12	6	119.52	2	9.1	3	30.22	9
12. Manipur	—		—		—		—		—		—	
13. Meghalaya	—		—		—		—		—		—	
14. Karnataka	73.46	6	7.0	6	33.49	4	81.23	10	6.1	10	34.44	7

15. Nagaland	—		—		—		0.68	16	0.5	16	18.23	16
16. Orissa	47.25	11	4.5	10.5	28.84	7	101.20	5	7.7	5	57.67	2
17. Punjab	51.92	9	4.9	9	51.13	2	58.99	13	4.5	13.5	29.05	10
18. Rajasthan	48.02	10	4.5	10.5	26.47	9	70.21	11	5.3	11	34.83	9
19. Tripura	—		—		—		—		—		—	
20. Uttar Pradesh	141.69	1	13.5	1	20.49	14	147.95	1	11.2	1	20.06	15
21. West Bengal	108.36	3	9.8	3	32.55	5	93.72	6	7.1	6	26.83	12
22. Sikkim	—		—		—		—		—		—	
TOTAL	1048.97		100.0		26.74		1310.76		100.0		30.39	

Table 3.2 (*Contd.*)

State	Fourth Finance Commission [1966-67 to 1970-71 (4-Yrs)]						Fifth Finance Commission [1969-70 to 1973-74 (5-Years)]					
	Total Asssistance (Rs. Crs)	*RANK*	*Per-cent to total*	*RANK*	*Per-capita (Rs.)*	*RANK*	*Total Assistance (Rs. Crs)*	*RANK*	*Per-cent to total*	*RANK*	*Per-cent (Rs.)*	*RANK*
	13	*14*	*15*	*16*	*17*	*18*	*19*	*20*	*21*	*22*	*23*	*24*
1. Andhra Pradesh	234.18	3	8.1	3	65.00	8	339.26	5	7.5	5	77.99	8
2. Assam	144.96	11	5.0	11	122.09	4	195.21	11	4.5	11.5	130.51	3
3. Bihar	197.46	7	6.8	7.5	42.51	16	407.38	2	9.5	2	72.79	10
4. Gujarat	121.55	13	4.2	13	58.91	11	182.75	13	4.2	13	68.45	13
5. Haryana	—		—		—		59.61	17	1.3	17	59.39	17
6. Himachal Pradesh	—		—		—		—		—		—	
7. Jammu & Kashmir	66.10	14	2.2	14	185.62	2	106.84	14	2.5	14	231.42	2
8. Kerala	188.61	9	6.5	9	111.58	5	193.43	12	4.5	11.5	98.61	5
9. Madhya Pradesh	162.08	10	5.6	10	50.05	14	274.02	7	6.4	7	65.78	16
10. Tamil Nadu	207.37	6	7.1	6	61.56	10	295.11	6	6.8	6	71.63	11
11. Maharashtra	260.38	2	9.0	2	65.83	7	383.66	3	8.9	3	76.10	9
12. Manipur	—		—		—		—		—		—	
13. Meghalaya	—		—		—		—		—		—	
14. Karnataka	215.42	5	7.4	5	91.33	6	197.42	10	4.6	10	67.38	14
15. Nagaland	58.46	15	2.0	15.5	2164.08	1	80.72	16	1.8	16	1562.98	1
16. Orissa	231.85	4	8.0	4	132.12	3	250.68	8	5.0	2	114.23	4

17. Punjab	57.51*	16	2.0	15.5	28.32	15	89.16	15	2.8	15	65.80	15
18. Rajasthan	130.41	12	4.5	12	64.70	9	221.65	9	5.1	9	66.02	6
19. Tripura	—		—		—		—		—		—	
20. Uttar Pradesh	373.02	1	12.9	1	50.58	13	620.12	1	14.5	1	70.20	21
21. West Bengal	197.41	8	6.8	7.5	56.52	12	369.26	4	8.6	4	83.33	7
22. Sikkim	—		—		—		—		—		—	
TOTAL	2865.86		100.0		65.68		4263.30	—	100.0		79.76	—

(*Contd.*

Table 3.2 (*Contd.*)

States	*Sixth Finance Commission]1974-75 to 1978-79 (5 Years]*						*Seventh Finance Commissiona [1979-80 to 1983-84 (5 Years]*					
	Total Assis-tance (Rs. Crs)	*RANK*	*Per-cent to total*	*RANK*	*Per-capita (Rs.)*	*RANK*	*Total Assis-tance (Rs. Crs)*	*RANK*	*Per-cent to total*	*RANK*	*Per Capita (Rs.)*	*RANK*
	25	*26*	*27*	*28*	*29*	*30*	*31*	*32*	*33*	*34*	*35*	*36*
1. Andhra Pradesh	776.01	4	8.08	4	162.69	12	1522.49	6	7.30	6	294.54	15
2. Assam	439.62	11	4.57	11	248.09	7	518.65	13	2.49	13	251.77	21
3. Bihar	844.72	2	8.79	2	134.98	4	2212.87	2	10.67	2	322.34	10
4. Gujarat	368.64	13	3.83	13	122.96	16	963.87	10	4.62	10	289.80	16
5. Haryana	120.66	20	1.26	20	107.16	21	308.57	17	1.48	17	245-48	22
6. Himachal Pradesh	204.06	15	2.12	15	526.65	5	325.07	16	1.56	10	764.87	6
7. Jammu & Kashmir	232.28	14	2.42	14	436.62	6	376.89	15	1.81	15	625.02	—
8. Kerala	479 97	10	5.00	10	200.99	9	770.84	12	3.70	12	295.04	14
9. Madhya Pradesh	543.57	8	5.66	8	113.39	20	1597.46	5	7.66	4.5	298.87	13
10. Tamil Nadu	538.57	9	5.60	9	121.11	17	1503.60	7	7.21	7	316.81	11
11. Maharashtra	711.53	5	7.40	5	127.06	15	1714.06	4	8.23	3	280.44	18
12. Manipur	128.01	19	1.33	19	1007.95	2	194.03	20	0.93	20	1311.01	3
13. Meghalaya	87.52	21	0.91	21	748.03	3	134.15	21	0.64	21	1008.65	3
14. Karnataka	383.64	12	3.99	12	117.72	18	1005 00	8	4.82	8	280.57	17
15. Nagaland	135.67	17	1.41	17	2188.23	1	240.59	18	1.16	18	3341.53	1
16. Orissa	577.32	6	6.01	6	234.40	8	984.45	9	4.72	9	361.80	8

17. Punjab	168.97	16	1.76	16	114.09	19	419.53	14	2.01	14	259.93	20
18. Rajasthan	563.92	7	5.87	7	189.49	10	902.81	11	4.33	11	267.58	19
19. Tripura	132.19	18	1.38	18	718.42	4	199.84	19	0.96	19	942.64	5
20. Uttar Pradesh	1349.05	1	14.05	1	138.96	13	3344.74	1	15.91	1	314.56	12
21. West Bengal	822.93	3	8.56	3	162.73	11	1957.11	3	7.66	4.5	347.50	9
22. Sikkim	—		—		—		36.85	22	0.18	22	1474.00	2
TOTAL	9608.85		100.0		158.71		20842.97		100.0		312.64	

Notes : (1) For estimating the per capita figures, 1957 estimated population figures have been used for Second F. C. 1961 population for the Third and 1971 population figures for the Fourth and Fifth Finance Commissions.

(2) Per capita figures are estimated by using mid-year population for 1974-78 and for 1979-83.

(3) *The share of composite Punjab has been allocated on population basis between Punjab, Haryana and Union Territories.

(4) *Excludes Rs. 64 crores towards State duty the details of which are not available.

Sources :

(1)[a] *Report of the Fifth Finance Commission* pp. 210 to 211.

(2) (+) *Reserve Bank of India Bulletins*, Sept 1969, pp 1429 to 1453.

(3) (a) *Centre-State Financial Relations*, Certain Relevant Data.

(*Contd.*)

TABLE 3.2 (*Contd.*)

States	Eighth Finance Commission (1984-89) 5 years					
	Total Assistance (Rs. crores)	*Rank*	*Per cent total*	*Rank*	*Per capita (Rs.)*	*Rank*
1. Andhra Pradesh	2896.52	5	7.34	5	540.90	14
2. Assam	1607.48	11	4.07	10	807.90	8
3. Bihar	4220.47	2	10.70	2	603.66	11
4. Gujarat	1489.05	12	3.77	12	436.85	19
5. Haryana	439.22	20	1.11	19	339.88	22
6. Himachal Pradesh	774.37	15	1.96	15	1808.92	7
7. Jammu & Kashmir	1119.69	14	2.84	14	1870.08	6
8. Karnataka	1727.97	9	4.38	9	465.31	18
9. Kerala	1288.25	13	3.27	13	506.11	16
10. Madhya Pradesh	2957.68	4	7.50	4	566.83	12
11. Maharashtra	2635.42	6	6.68	6	419.75	20
12. Manipur	469.05	19	1.19	18	3300.95	3
13. Meghalaya	381.86	21	0.97	21	2858.62	4
14. Nagaland	527.42	18	1.34	20	6806.03	1
15. Orissa	1909.66	8	4.84	8	724.17	9
16. Punjab	646.15	16	1.64	16	384.86	21

17. Rajasthan	1676.17	10	4.25	11	489.22	17
18. Sikkim	104.45	22	0.25	22	3301.35	2
19. Tamil Nadu	2464.94	7	6.25	7	509.20	15
20. Tripura	561.18	17	1.42	17	2733.38	5
21. Uttar Pradesh	6105.03	1	15.47	1	550.68	13
22. West Bengal	3449.98	3	8.74	3	632.08	10
TOTAL	39452.01		100.00			

Sources: Report of the Eighth Finance Commission 1984, p. 96

Note : Per capita figures are calculated by using 1981 census final population figures.

TABLE 3.3

Rank Correlation Between Federal Financial Transfers made on the Recommendations of the Finance Commission and Indicators of Relative Backwardness

Indicators of relative backwardness	*Finance Commission' Transfers*						
	2nd F.C.	*3rd F.C.*	*4th F.C.*	*5th F.C.*	*6th F.C.*	*7th F.C.*	*8th F.C.*
Per capita SDP at constant prices	0.08	0.14	0.09	—0.44	—0.14	0.01	—
Poverty	0.03	—0.36	—0.12	—0.18	—0.44	—0.55	
PQLI	—0.03	—0.29	—0.05	—0.28	—0.44	—0.26	

Notes : (*a*) For purpose of estimating rank correlation, per capita SDP, percentage of people below poverty line and PQLI are ranked in descending order.

(*b*) These indicators of backwardness and federal financial transfers are first converted into average per capita figures for the relevant periods covered by the recommendation of the respective Finance Commissions and Five-Year Plans.

(*c*) F.C.=Finance Commission.

ranks. A more reliable estimate of the distribution of federal financial transfers made on the recommendations of the Finance Commission may be obtained by finding out rank correlation between financial transfers and level of development as reflected by the indicators of backwardness. It may be observed from Table 3.3 that most of the rank correlation coefficients are negative thereby implying presence of some degree of equity. However, the values of these coefficients are not statistically significant. This would imply that the degree of equity has been very low. In other words, Finance Commissions' fiscal transfers have not been in favour of *all* the needy or less developed States.

The main reason for this inequity in the distribution of federal fiscal transfers has been the defective methodology[4] adopted by the past Finance Commissions, which has come to be known as the "gap filling" approach. This is discussed in Chapter IV.

4. A detailed analysis of the defects of the methodology of the past Finance Commissions has been made in G. Thimmaiah, *A Critique of the Finance Commission*, Wheeler & Co., Allahabad, 1981, and in Hemlata Rao, *Centre-State Financial Relations*, Allied Publishers, New Delhi, 1981.

CHAPTER IV

Fiscal Needs Approach

4.1 Weaknesses of 'Gap Filling' Approach

In India the Finance Commissions have been following the 'gap filling' approach which was earlier used by Otto Niemeyer. The Finance Commissions used to ask the State Governments to submit forecasts of their revenues and expenditures over the ensuing five years taking into account their probable growth. Such forecasts of each State were adjusted by the Finance Commissions so as to make them comparable and used to work out the gross deficits on the non-plan current accounts of the State Government budgets excluding the share from the divisible pool of Central taxes. These gaps were treated as the budgetary needs of the State Governments. After devolution of divisible pool of Central taxes. These gaps were treated as the budgetary needs of the State Governments. After devolution of divisible pool of Central taxes, these gaps were treated as the budgetary needs of the State Governments. If some States still experienced deficits in their non-plan current budgets even after devolution of divisible taxes and duties, they were considered to be in need of grants-in-aid. Thus, the estimated non-plan current account budgetary gaps based on mere growth rates of revenues and expenditures were treated as the fiscal needs of the State Governments. Tax shares of different States were determined entirely on different set of criteria. Grants-in-aid were recommended to only those States which experienced non-plan revenues gaps even after receiving their tax shares. The Finance Commissions could not reduce the shares of those States which experienced non-plan revenue surpluses after receiving tax shares. This was a situation in which the criteria, which were independent of estimated non-plan budgetary gaps, used for distributing tax shares provided growing amounts of unconditional grants to relatively better-off States whereas relatively poorer States were left with only 'gap-filling' fixed amounts of grants-in-aid. This anomaly originated from the methodology of the Finance Commissions.

The past seven Finance Commissions never tried to estimate the relative true fiscal needs of the State Governments and recommend federal financial transfers accordingly. The First Finance Commission made a reference to the budgetary needs of the States while recommending only grants-in-aid and treated tax efforts and standard of social services as independent criteria instead of their being integral parts of estimating fiscal needs of the States. However, the Commission recommended special grants for the promotion of primary education in eight educationally backward States. Though these recommendations were accepted by the Central Government, they did not form integral part of the Commission's approach to federal financial transfers. The Second Finance Commission, no doubt, made a reference to the fiscal needs of the States in the following way: "We endorse the principles of fiscal need and interpret fiscal need comprehensively by taking into account the impact of the completion of the First Five Year Plan and the needs of the Second.[1] And the Commission tried to adjust various items of expenditure and also took into consideration the additional tax efforts made by the States during the period of the First Five Year Plan while arriving at their budgetary needs. But the Commission did not try to equalise any essential public and/or social services through grants-in-aid on the ground that that job was entrusted to the Planning Commission and the National Development Council. The latter Commissions did not even bother to take into account either tax efforts or special expenditure needs of the States while recommending grants-in-aid. No doubt, the Third Finance Commission recommended special grants

1. *Report of the Sixth Finance Commission*, New Delhi, 1957, p. 24.

for improving road communications in some backward States. But it was not a part of its overall approach, consistent with the functioning of the Planning Commission and hence those recommendations were not accepted by the Central Government. The Fifth Finance Commission mentioned broad fiscal needs of the States but did not estimate them for purposes of recommending even the grants-in-aid. The Sixth Finance Commission openly declared that "in indicating our general approach to leading issues of current fiscal relations between the Union and the States, we feel that it would be more purposeful if we confine ourselves to delineating certain directions in which, in our judgment new initiatives need to be attempted without of course disturbing too violently the delicate framework that has been painstakingly evolved in the last 25 years.[2]

Thus, the estimated non-plan budgetary gap was equated with the fiscal need of a State invariably by all the past Finance Commissions. This method of measuring fiscal needs is based on the assumption that the gap between estimated revenue and expenditure represent the fiscal need of a State. It is open to dispute, because, the fiscal need of a State refers to its financial need dictated by economic factors levels of development, disparities in the fiscal potential and levels of essential public services. Even if we assume that the budgetary gaps do indicate some sort of fiscal need, their use has been very much limited to the distribution of grants-in-aid only. In order to achieve the objectives of equity and incentive, first and foremost thing is to estimate fiscal needs in a more comprehensive and objective manner.

However, it has been argued that it is not enough to transfer financial resources in a federation to meet the fiscal needs of State Governments. It is emphasized that it is also necessary to reduce the imbalance in the levels of development and also to provide incentives for efficient management of the economy and finances by the State Governments. In other words, federal financial transfers are expected to achieve three objectives namely : (*a*) meeting the fiscal needs of the States,

2. *Report of Sixth Finance Commission*, New Delhi, 1973, p. 5.

(*b*) reducing inter-State economic imbalances, and (*c*) providing incentives for efficient management of the finances.

While reducing economic imbalances is, no doubt, a laudable objective, we should realise that it is a long term objective which requires huge investment funds. Similarly, while the efficiency should be rewarded, it should not be allowed to create economic imbalances in long-run. Efficiency objective can be achieved by objectively estimating the fiscal needs of the State Governments. Therefore, federal financial transfers should pay more attention to the fiscal needs of the State Governments, and try to achieve reduction of economic imbalances in the long-run. This long-run objective is intended to maintain national unity which is crucial for holding the federal structure together. Reduction of inter-State economic disparities in the context of a developing federal economy means much more than merely helping the economically backward States. In a developing economy inter-State economic disparities hide intra-State economic disparities. For instance, even in economically better-off States like Gujarat, Haryana, Maharashtra and Punjab there are several districts and talukas which are much more backward than their counterparts in backward States. What is more, the economic base of some of the so-called better-off States like Maharashtra and West Bengal is concentrated in their capital cities of Bombay and Calcutta respectively, leaving other parts as backward as the so-called backward States. If the economic status of these States is considered separately excluding these metropolitan cities, they will get classified as economically backward States. But these so-called better-off States are forced with additional burden of providing tolerable level of civic amenities to the urban areas which are the mainstay of their economic and fiscal bases. Thus, even a part of the objective of reducing economic disparities gets integrated into the short term fiscal needs of the States. On all count, meeting the fiscal needs becomes an overriding objective of federal financial transfers. But in the long-run economic disparities will have to be reduced through proper planning and development policies.

For this purpose, in India we have two Commissions to examine independently these two issues and recommend appropriate financial transfers. The Finance Commission is supposed, (both in letter and spirit of the Constitution). to examine the fiscal needs of the State Governments and to recommend the required federal financial assistance. The Planning Commission has been constituted to determine the potentials for development in different States and formulate appropriate plans and projects and recommend financial assistance for such long-term plans and projects. Thus, the organisational set-up for the purpose of recommending federal financial transfers is logically fitted into the short-term and long-term objectives of federal financial transfers in India.

We are concerned here with suggesting a methodology for determining the fiscal needs of the State Governments in order to recommend federal financial assistance to meet the short-term fiscal needs of the State Governments.

4.2 An Outline of Fiscal Needs Approach

To begin with the Finance Commission should assess the budgetary position of the Central Government, including its revenue efforts, expenditure needs and estimate the probable surplus revenue which it can spare for transfer to the State Governments annually over the next five years. since, the Finance Commission is a constitutional body and is appointed by the President (which also reports to the President), this procedure will not undermine the constitutional status of the Central Government. In fact, the State Governments will be more co-operative in Centre-State relations if this procedure is followed. After estimating the revenue surplus of the Central Government, the Finance Commission should estimate the fiscal need of each State.

The fiscal needs approach has got two sides : (*a*) revenue side; and (*b*) expenditure side. On the revenue side, the Finance Commission will have to examine the revenue potential of individual State Governments on the basis of the existing sources of revenue allotted to them. This include both tax and non-tax revenues. It is not enough to examine to overall revenue potential and revenue efforts. It is necessary to evaluate the revenue effort under each and every source of revenue allotted to the State Governments. Otherwise, the State Governments may tend to over-exploit the source which is easy and let go other sources which are politically difficult. This has happened in most of the States. For instance, sales tax has been over exploited making frequent changes in rates, but agricultural income-tax has not even been uniformly levied. The Finance Commission should determine an objective norm up to which the State Governments are expected to tap each of their sources of revenue.

Here one may think of three alternatives; (*a*) all States average; (*b*) average of the highest performance States; and (*c*) independently determined norm. In the case of the first method the norm will be lower, and in the case of the second it will be higher. It may be advisable to take the first type of norm for estimating the revenue potential and efforts and the third type of norm for estimating expenditure needs. Because, many States will lose financial assistance if the first or second type of norm is adopted for estimating the expenditure needs. Though the third type of norm is difficult to estimate, it is necessary to make a beginning.

For the purpose of estimating the revenue potential and the expenditure needs of the State Governments the Finance Commission may adopt either direct approach or indirect approach or combination of both depending upon the availability of the required data. Under the direct approach the Finance Commission may use the Representative Tax System approach to measure the revenue potential and revenue efforts of the States. The Commission will have to estimate the potential revenue base of each source of revenue. For this purpose, it will have to determine the probable standard rate at which the potential revenue base can be taxed in all the States and apply that standard rate to the actual existing revenue base in each of the States. The actual revenue as compared with the resulting revenue by applying standard rate to the actually existing base would give the revenue efforts. If it is less than 100 per cent, to that extent the estimated fiscal need of the concerned State on the revenue side may be reduced. Though such a step will result in an unequal distribution of revenues, this is necessary to ensure that the State Governments' revenue needs are met by the Central Government only after making sure that they have tapped their own sources to the hilt. Therefore, it would be better to reduce the fiscal need on the revenue side if the actual revenue is less than the potential revenue. This will ensure proper revenue efforts on the part of such State Governments. However, there is no need to reward those States whose revenue efforts exceed their potential as it would encourage excessive fiscal burden on the citizens.

While estimating the revenue potential of the State Governments, in the field of financial returns from their public undertakings the Finance Commission will have to take a more realistic view of the extent of revenue which the State Governments can raise from their public undertakings. In the past the Finance Commissions assumed positive rates of return even from State Government owned public utility undertakings like Electricity Boards and Road Transport Corporations. The Finance Commissions also expected the State Governments to generate commercial rate of return from irrigation projects. We consider that these assumptions are unrealistic in the Indian context. Because they are based on the questionable premise, that every public utility should become profit making enterprise to generate public savings for investment in other sectors. This premise has remained only a normative objective because, it treats pubic utilities on par with competitive productive enterprises in the private sector. It is necessary to remember that public utilities are partial monopolies. This position calls for State Governments' control over their pricing policies. Besides the State Governments have to exercise control over their recruitment and personnel policies and also function as a model employer, in view of certain social obligations cast on the Government in India. Further, economic infra-structure projects like rural electrification and irrigation projects have wider social implications. Rural electrification and irrigation projects serve much broad social objectives than merely supplying inputs are competitive prices.

Therefore, for the purpose of estimating the revenue potential of State Governments in the field of financial returns from their undertakings, the Finance Commission may divide the State Government undertakings into three categories :

(*a*) Production and financial oriented commercial undertakings which produce competitive products and services, (*b*) public utility undertakings, and (*c*) socio-economic infrastructure projects.

The Finance Commission should expect the first category of State Government undertakings to earn rate of return equivalent to at least the prevailing market rate of interest. In the case of second category, that is public utilities, the Commission should apply no-profit-no-loss criterion. Losses incurred by the public utilities should be treated as wasteful expenditure and the estimated fiscal need of the concerned States should be reduced to that extent. Such penalty has become necessary to discourage total disregard for efficiency.

In the case of irrigation projects (other than projective works), they should be expected to earn direct revenue to meet the interest cost on capital invested and maintenance cost. These norms are more realistic than the norms assumed by past Finance Commissions.

On the expenditure side, there are many steps to be followed for determining the expenditure needs of the States. In the first step, the Finance Commission will have to list the functions which are expected to be performed by the State Governments in a federation. Traditionally the governments in all democracies were supposed to perform certain basic 'police State' functions like general administration, police, courts, jails and the like. While these functions are still basic even today, they are not enough to justify a democratic welfare government. Hence, there is demand for adding some time more functions like adequate provisions for elementary education and primary health facilities which are in the nature of "merit goods". The listing of such functions is, no doubt, arbitrary as it involves value judgment. But in all civilised societies these functions are considered necessary in order to justify democratic government. One may argue that functions like health and education are in the nature of development functions. It may be true. But we will argue here that these functions, though fall under development category, have to go to be looked after by the Finance Commission for the purpose of equalising these essential services in a vast and desparate country like India. In other words, while the "police State" functions will have to be rendered to all citizens on equal measure, the adequacy of "merit goods" may be assessed by the Finance Commission to make sure of their adequate supply to all citizens in the country.

After listing these functions, in the next step the Commission will have to categorise them for the purpose of including in the estimation of expenditure side of the fiscal needs. For this purpose, the Commission will have to classify the fiscal needs of the State Governments on the expenditure side into: (*a*) general fiscal needs; and (*b*) specify fiscal needs. The Commission may include in the general fiscal needs the essential basic services which are included under "police State" functions like general administration, police, courts, jails, etc. In the first step, the Finance Commission will have to allow for the growth of these expenditure items over the next five years. The earlier Commissions allowed unrealistically low rates. We would suggest an average normal growth rate of 10 per cent plus 5 per cent for inflation indexing thus making the total average growth rate of 15 per cent per annum. This is more realistic in the light of the actual growth rates experienced by the State Governments in the recent past. It may be argued that in this context that if uniform growth rates of expenditure are allowed for all States, those States which have already reached higher levels of these expenditures will benefit more than those States which have maintained lower levels either for want of adequate funds or for minimising non-development expenditure or for both. However, these differences in the base year levels will be reduced when the inter-State disparities in these expenditures are equalised with reference to an objectively determined normative level. Those States whose per capita levels of these items of expenditure are above normative level will not get any assistance on account of this component of the expenditure side of the fiscal needs.

In the next step, the Commission will have to include in the specific fiscal needs: (*a*) financial requirements for maintaining capital assets such as roads, bridges, public buildings, tanks, canals etc., (*b*) financial requirements for upgrading the "merit goods" services like primary and secondary education, primary health facilities to a standard level, and (*c*) for improving urban civic services like urban sanitation, etc.

The cost of maintaining capital assets will have to be realistically estimated taking into account the actual conditions prevailing in each State. The standard level of expenditure required for this should be added to the specific fiscal need of the States. In the past the Finance Commissions used to include this part of the expenditure in their normal growth of expenditure thus making it a part of their general fiscal needs. But such procedure did not ensure proper maintenance of capital assets. Hence, the Finance Commission should make it a part of specific fiscal needs.

In the case of "merit goods", a standard level of expenditure, either per capita or the cost of rendering a normative standard level of real services, will have to be determined and the actual level existing in each State should be assessed. The difference between these two will have to be converted into the fiscal needs of different States on their expenditure side. If the actual level is less than the standard level, the additional funds required will have to be added to the specific fiscal needs and if the actual level is more than the standard level no adjustment need be made on this specific expenditure side of the fiscal needs.

Finally, there is need for taking into account the expenditure needs of the State Governments for enabling the civic bodies to improve urban civic services which have deteriorated partly on account of meagre resources at the disposal of urban local bodies and partly on account of the State Government's diversion of funds to rural development. The Finance Commission, in addition to including State Governments financial transfers to local bodies in their expenditure forecastes, should determine the additional assistance required for improving urban roads and sanitation. This need has been long neglected. It is high time the Commission recognised this specific fiscal need. The method suggested for equalising "merit goods" may be used for determining the specific fiscal needs under civic services also.

One may argue in this context that in the case of those States which are already providing merit goods services above the normative level, the cess amount should be deducted from their estimated fiscal needs. This is not necessary because if a State has decided to provide above the normative level services it should be free to do so but without the assistance from the Central Government for such higher level of services. This is in keeping with the philosophy of democratic decentralisation. Such better performance should not invite financial penalty nor should it be financially rewarded. The demand for providing incentive to such States cannot be justified while distributing limited resources.

The above outlined direct approach to estimate the expenditure needs of the States is laborious, time consuming and requires countrywide network of data banks. This does not mean that it is not a practicable or feasible approach. In fact a federal country should be well-equipped with State level research cells specifically working on these aspects using a common methodology all over the country like the one used for estimating the State income. But this approach may be beyond the capacity of individual scholers and small organisations. This may be so even for quinquinnial body like the Finance Commission. However, if the Finance Commission is made a standing body it will be in a position to estimate these fiscal needs by using the direct approach which is more reliable.

If the Finance Commission is faced with time and data constraints, it may use indirect approach. It may estimate the revenue potential either on the basis of income or stochastic method. To estimate the fiscal need on the expenditure side the

Commission will have to take some general determinants like population, area and the assessment of sectoral and composite levels of development of general and specific services identified above, based on various quantifiable indicators on levels of these services. But all these indicators and proxy variables are only near approximations and do not provide the true magnitude of revenue potential and expenditure needs. Therefore, in the case of revenue potential it is possible to use the Representative Tax System approach for most of the revenue sources and only in a few cases stochastic and/or income method may be used. Similarly for estimating the expenditure needs, in most of the cases the direct unit-cost method may be used and wherever such method is not possible, proxy variables may be used to estimate the expenditure needs in specific areas.

Thus under our suggested fiscal needs approach, there are three components: (*i*) revenue need of each State on account of inadequate revenue (raising) capacity; (*ii*) general expenditure need in the field of 'police State' functions; (*iii*) specific expenditure needs for (*a*) maintaining capital assets, (*b*) equalising "merit goods"; and (*c*) improving urban civic services. The sum of the fiscal needs on the revenue side and general and specific expenditure needs on the non-plan current expenditure side should be totalled. This totalled amount in the case of each State is the true fiscal need of each State. This fiscal need will have to be met by the Central Government through financial transfers in the form of tax shares and grants. Before distributing the divisible pool of Central taxes, it is necessary to transfer first the net yield from assigned taxes under Article 269 and rented tax, *i.e.*, additional Union excise duties.

CHAPTER V

Assigned and Rented Taxes

5.1 Background

The Constitution of India has made detailed allocation of revenue sources between the Central and State Governments. Some sources of revenue are entirely assigned to the Central and some others entirely to the State Governments. For example, customs duties, wealth-tax, gift-tax and corporation tax are exclusively assigned to the Central Government, and State excise, taxation of agriculture and sales tax are assigned to the State Governments. Some sources of revenue are made divisible such as individual income-tax under Article 270, and some are made to be levied, and collected by the Centre but the net yield should be transferred to the States. These are the seven taxes enumerated under Article 269. Besides these, the additional union excise duties have been levied by the Central Government in place of the State Governments' sales-tax under a tax rental arrangement. The net yield from these duties has to be transferred to the State Governments.

5.2 Rented Tax

While income-tax under Article 270 is a divisible source, the taxes levied under Article 269 have to be assigned to the States. More or less the same position is obtained in the case of additional union excise duties also. Because of this constitutional status, the Central Government has to transfer the net yield from these taxes whether the State Governments require the revenue or not. Therefore, before finally determining the fiscal needs, it would be better if the net yield from the additional excise duties and the revenue due from the taxes under Article 269 are first allocated to the State Governments on the basis of the derivation principle. Hitherto the past Finance Commissions distributed the net yield from additional union excise duties on the basis of population and sales tax collection of different States. These criteria would look irrelevant if we consider the fact that the additional Union excise duties are rented taxes. The net yield from the rented taxes should be distributed on the basis of origin of collection. Though it may be difficult to keep account of the yield from the additional union excise duties on the basis of the State-wise origin, of collection, the practice of introducing an element of equity into the distribution of the net yield from additional excise duties is wrong as these duties are not meant for achieving redistributive objective. Every State should get the revenue which it could have raised had it levied sales tax on these commodities. The best way of ensuring this would be to distribute the net yield on the basis of the statewise consumption of these commodities. If it is not possible to get reliable state-wise data on consumption of these commodities, the next best alternative would be to distribute the net yield from additional Union excise duties in proportion to the yield from the sales tax of each to the total yield from sales tax of all the States. This criterion takes into account consumption of these commodities and also changes in the tax rates, etc. We have presented in Table 5.1 the comparative picture relating to the relative shares of different States in the additional Union excise duties.

In addition to this, it is necessary that the Finance Commission should determine the net yield from additional Union excise duties on the basis of the overall incidence of 10.8 per cent of the value of clearance of these commodities as agreed to by the Central Government earlier. Though the Central Government agreed to convert specific duties into *ad valorem* duties except on unmanufactured tobacco, and to reach the ratio of 2 : 1 between the yields of the basic and special duties on the one hand and additional excise duties on the other hand, it has been noticed that the Central Government has not fulfilled these terms of agreement. Therefore, the Finance Commission should estimate probable yield from additional Union excise duties if all the three conditions has been fulfilled and recommended to the Central Government to transfer so estimated hypothetical yield rather than the actual net yield from additional Union excise duties in proportion to the sales tax yield of each State. This would act as a penalty on the Central Government for the non-fulfilment of the terms of agreement.

5.3 Assigned Taxes under Article 269

Under Article 269 seven taxes are expected to be levied by the Central Government and the net yield from these should be transferred to the States. They include:

(*a*) Duties in respect of succession to property other than agricultural lands;

(*b*) Estate duty in respect of property other than agricultural land;

(*c*) Terminal tax on goods and passengers carried by railway, sea or air;

(*d*) Tax on railway fares and frieghts;

(*e*) Taxes other than plan duties of transaction in stock exchanges and future markets;

(*f*) Taxes on the sale of purchase or newspapers on advertisements published therein;

(*g*) Taxes on the sale or purchase of goods other than the newspapers where such sale or purchase takes place in the case of inter-State trade and commerce.

Of these taxes, item No. 7 has been levied in the form of

Central sales tax and the State Governments are allowed to collect and appropriate the revenues. Item No. 3 was levied up to 1955 but later on it was discontinued on the ground of administrative complications and a lump sum amount has been distributed in the form of grant in lieu of taxes on railway fares and frieghts.

Until 1985, estate duty was levied and the amount was distributed to the State Governments on the basis of the origin of collection in the case of immovable property and on the basis of population in the case of movable property.

The Fifth Finance Commission was asked to examine the scope for increasing the revenue under these taxes. But the Fifth Finance Commission recommended that in view of the estate duty which was already operating along with gift-tax and wealth-tax, there was no need to levy another tax on the succession to property as it would amount to double taxation on wealth or property. In regard to the tax on sale or purchase of newspapers and on advertisements published therein, the Fifth Finance Commission felt that newspapers were an effective medium of public communication and it was necessary to encourage newspaper reading habit in a democracy. Therefore, they opined that the time had not yet come to levy a tax on newspapers and advertisements published therein.

Since then the situation has changed substantially. Today there is a strong case for succession duty in view of the abolition of estate duty. Besides, there is also a case for taxing goods and passengers carried by railway, sea and air at the point of terminals. The Central Government has partially pre-empted this tax by leaving airport tax on passengers travelling abroad. Therefore, the State Governments have a right to expect this source being tapped for their purpose. Considering the class of passengers who normally travel by air, there is a definite case for levying a terminal tax on air passengers for the benefit of the State Governments. Similarly there is a case for taxing at least first class railway passengers who enjoy certain special privileges and benefits at all railway stations in India.

Newspaper reading is no longer the only means of conveying news to the public. The newspapers, particularly some of those published by large industrial houses, are making profit by publishing advertisements. The revenue from advertisement is estimated to constitute between 50% to 70% of the total revenue of these newspapers. Besides these, newspapers have been allotting too much of imported newsprint for advertisements rather than for news and therefore, they cannot claim to serve the public purpose in the name of publishing newspapers. In view of this, it is necessary that the newspapers should be made to pay some proportion of their revenue for the benefit of the State Governments. In order to encourage small newspapers which serve the local needs, (and particularly the regional language newspapers which cater to the needs of the rural people), which have circulation of 25,000 per day may be exempted from this tax. A graduated tax based on the extent of circulation, may be levied on the sale as well as on the tariff charged for advertisement in these newspapers. The resistance to these taxes by newspaper lobby will be minimised if small newspapers are exempted.

Though there is a talk about the depressed state of stock exchange and share market in the country, the 1984 events in the Bombay share market have revealed the speculative tendency which still rules the so-called centres of capitalistic enterprise. Therefore, it is necessary to levy transaction tax or a tax on the transfer of stocks and shares all over the India. This will also provide a necessary information on the ownership of assets for the purpose of taxing of wealth and gifts which are otherwise evaded.

The present position of the tax on railway fare and freight is unsatisfactory. Many State Governments have voiced their dissatisfaction in the past and the previous Finance Commissions have not bothered to make satisfactory recommendations on this. The grant-in-lieu of this tax which was increased from Rs. 12.5 crores ot Rs. 16.5 crores in 1966 has not been enhanced since then and as a result the amount has stagnated. The argument that railways have to charge concessional freights to movement of cssential goods like foodgrains, raw materials and concessional fares to urban commuters and hence cannot afford to enhance the grant, seem to be unwarranted. The State Governments have to provide free education, health and drinking water to rural areas and hence need more money than the railway. The Railway Convention Committee seem to have ignored the demand of the State Governments for enhancing the amount of grant. This is a constitutional issue which will give rise to Centre-State dispute, if the State Governments decide to politicise the issue. Therefore, the Eighth Finance Commission should make a firm recommendation for the reimposition of the tax on railway fare and freights. In the alternative the grant may be increased to not less than Rs. 50 crores, or to the level which will be equivalent to the amount if the originally fixed Rs. 12.5 crores were to increase by the same rate at which the revenue from railway fares and freights has increased since 1966.

We would like to present here our views on a related term of reference, that is the scope for raising the rates of taxes under Article 260, which relate to the stamp duties and excise duty on medicinal preparations. Stamp duties here refer to judicial stamp duties. In the light of the present debate going on the desirability of making legal aid freely accessible to the masses, it will be unwise to recommend revision of judicial stamp duties. Similarly in an inflationary situation with protected market, the drug prices have gone up and if duties of excise on medicinal preparations are increased, the drug prices will further go up. Therefore, there is no justifiable cases for increasing the rates of judicial stamp duties and excise duties on medicinal preparations. However, there is scope for upward revision of excise duties on toilet preparation as they come under the category of luxury commodities. Therefore, the Finance Commission should recommend increase in the rates of excise duties on articles used in toilet preparations.

TABLE 5.1

Comparative Shares of States in the Net Yield from Additional Excise Duties

States	*Share in the additional Union Excise Duties under Sixth Finance Commission recommendation*	*Share in the sale tax yield (Average of 5 yrs covered by Sixth Finance Commission)*	*Difference between the two [Loss (−) gains (+)] percentage*	*Share in the Additional excise duties under Seventh Finance Commission recommendation*	*Share in the sale tax yield (Average of 4 Yrs covered by Seventh Finance Commission)*	*Difference between the two [Loss (−)] gain (+) percentage*
1. Andhra Pradesh	8.39	7.94	− 0.45	7.09	8.46	+ 1.37
2. Assam	2.47	1.10	− 1.37	2.33	0.93	− 1.40
3. Bihar	9.36	5.52	− 3.84	5.12	5.12	—
4. Gujarat	5.91	8.27	+ 2.36	6.92	8.36	+ 1.44
5. Haryana	1.94	2.05	+ 0.11	2.75	2.09	− 6.66
6. Himachal Pradesh	0.59	00.33	− 0.26	0.78	0.42	− 0.36
7. Jammu & Kashmir	0.73	0.41	− 0.32	0.77	0.49	− 0.28
8. Karnataka	5.62	6.56	+ 0.94	5.69	6.82	+ 1.13
9. Kerala	5.58	6.18	+ 0.60	3.94	6.32	+ 2.38
10. Madhya Pradesh	6.98	5.66	− 1.32	6.29	5.05	+ 1.24
11. Maharashtra	11.65	17.09	+ 5.44	14.70	17.33	+ 2.63
12. Manipur	0.17	0.07	− 0.10	0.17	—	—
13. Meghalaya	0.17	0.05	− 0.12	0.12	0.05	− 0.07
14. Nagaland	0.08	0.05	− 0.03	0.09	0.04	− 0.05
15. Orissa	3.59	1.82	− 1.77	3.03	1.91	− 1.12

16. Punjab	2.68	4.02	+ 1.34	4.92	4.10	− 0.82
17. Rajasthan	4.17	4.46	+ 0.29	4.49	4.70	+ 0.21
18. Sikkim	−	0.02	−	0.05	0.02	− 0.03
19. Tamil Nadu	7.27	10.65	+ 3.38	7.29	11.90	+ 4.61
20. Tripura	0.25	0.07	− 0.18	0.23	0.07	− 0.16
21. Uttar Pradesh	16.10	10.49	− 5.61	12.76	8.79	− 3.97
22. West Bengal	8.30	7.19	− 1.11	8.11	7.83	− 1.78
TOTAL	100.00	100.00		98.34	100.00	

CHAPTER VI

Shared Taxes

6.1 Introduction

After distributing the net yield from assigned taxes among the States, the Finance Commission will have to determine: (*a*) the composition of the divisible pool of Central taxes, (*b*) the size of the divisible pool of Central taxes, and (*c*) the share of each State in this divisible pool. However, from the point of view of meeting the true fiscal needs of the State Governments, what is important is the size of the divisible pool and not the composition of the divisible pool. This is because once the fiscal needs of the State Governments, what is important is the size of the divisible pool and not the composition of the divisible pool. This is because once the fiscal needs of the State Governments are determined, it does not matter how and from what source the financial assistance is transferred to the State Governments to meet the fiscal needs. What matters is the extent of revenue required as indicated by the estimated fiscal needs of the State Governments.

In the past the Finance Commissions used to determine individual tax shares independently of each other and also distribute them on the basis of certain criteria and then used to find out the gap, if any, left in the non-plan budgetary position of the State Governments, after distributing the tax shares. Consequently some of the better-off States used to experience huge non-plan budgetary surpluses. In order to avoid this embarrassing situation of transferring Central Government funds to the better-off States, without establishing the need for such surplus transfers, we have suggested in the earlier Chapter the fiscal needs approach which objectively establishes the total amount of financial assistance required by different State Governments. Therefore, the size of the divisible pool should be equivalent to the sum total of fiscal needs of all the States on revenue side, general expenditure needs and specific expenditure needs on the expenditure side. As such, the fiscal needs approach will pre-empt the State Governments' demand for increasing the size of the divisible pool.

Once the size of the divisible pool is determined on the basis of the total fiscal needs of the States, the next task of the Finance Commission will be to recommend for the inclusion of a share in the net yield from individual income-tax, and the entire net yielded from estate duty and wealth on non-agricultural property. Besides, under the agreement entered into with the State Governments the Central Government will have to transfer the net yield from additional Union excise duties. Further the Commission will have to include the grants-in-aid in lieu of tax on railway fare. The Finance Commission has also been asked to examine the scope for levying tax under Article 269 and transferring it to the State Governments. Because of these constitutional requirements, the Finance Commission should first determine the shares in the taxes which are compulsorily divisible and which are compulsorily assigned to the States. We propose to discuss the relevant issue relating to these tax shares in this Chapter.

6.2 Income-tax Shares

Of all these tax shares, sharing of the net yield from income-tax is obligatory on the part of the Central Government and it is also obligatory that every State should receive some portion of this tax share. In the past the State Governments have been making demand for including the tax on corporate income into the divisible pool of income-tax. This demand has been mainly based on the assumption that the financial needs of the State Governments are increasing and the yield from individual income-tax is inadequate to meet their financial needs. Besides, the increase in the yield from corporate income-tax has been more than that from individual income-tax. This is evident from Table 8.1.

TABLE 8. 1

Growth of Yield from Income-tax, Surcharge and Corporate Income-Tax in India.

(*Rs. in Crores*)

Years	*Yield from income-tax*	*Yield from Surcharge*	*Yield from corporate income-tax*
1952-53	137.1	6.1	43.8
1960-61	163.0	5.7	110.7
1965-66	264.8	7.1	304.8
1970-71	453.9	19.3	370.5
1975-76	1155.9	58.5	861.7
1978-79	996.0	144.0	1420.0
1981-82(RE)	1000.0	152.0	1962.0

But the restrictive terms of reference prevented the Finance Commissions from recommending its inclusion in the divisible pool. Instead, the earlier Finance Commissions increased the States' share in the net yield from Union excise duties. Particularly the Seventh Finance Commission doubled the States' share in the net yield from Union excise duties. But even after receiving such increased share in the net yield from Union excise duties, many States Governments are still demanding the inclusion of the net yield from the corporate income-tax into the divisible pool.

As we have already argued earlier, the major issue is not how much net yield from individual or corporate income-tax should be shared with the State Governments. The main question is how much total financial assistance is required by the State Governments for meeting their true fiscal needs. We have established a reasonably strong needs of the States, it is equally important to examine the increased responsibilities of and hence the budgetary strain on the Central Government also.

Further, the State Governments have also been demanding the inclusion of surcharges in the divisible pool of income-tax. Such a view makes a reference to the situation in which surcharge has become a permanent feature of income-tax instead of being a temporary measure. That is surcharge on income-tax was intended to be used in times of abnormal financial needs of the Central Government, and since it has become a permanent feature, the net yield from that also should be shared. It is further argued that corporate income-tax has been taken out of the divisible pool, inclusion of the net yield from surcharge would compensate the loss. Yet another suggestion advanced by the State Governments is to discontinue the levy of surcharge on income-tax and increase the rates of income-tax correspondingly without imposing any burden on the tax payers. This will increase the size of the divisible pools.

It should be remembered here that the surcharge on income-tax comes under Article 271 and the Constitution itself does not expect the Central Government to share the net yield from this source. Furthermore, this surcharge may be treated as an off setting device to enable the Central Government to make good the loss of revenue from income-tax as a result of substantial transfer to the State Governments. Therefore, both in intent and practice the net yield from surcharge should be retained by the Central Government in view of the changed financial position of the Central Government itself. Though surcharge has become a permanent feature of our income-tax structure, constitutionally Central Government has the exclusive right on its proceeds.

In the event of not making the net yield from surcharges divisible, a suggestion is made to the effect that the present share of the States in the net yield from income-tax may be increased say from 85% to 95%. There is a point of view, however, against this kind of near total transfer of the net yield from income-tax. This tax pointed out by Sixth Finance Commission which maintained that if 95% of yield is made to be transferred to the divisible pool, the Central Government will have no incentive to exploit that source of revenue to increase the yield from it. This is a naive argument because the Central Government has been levying estate duty and wealth-tax, whose yield has been transferred to the State Governments. Similarly there are many taxes in the hands of the State Governments which are entirely levied and collected and the revenue is transferred to the local bodies as in the case of land revenue, entertainment tax, etc. Even so the Central Government will be retaining 5% of the net yield from income-tax plus the entire yield from surcharge. These proceeds are large enough to provide the required incentive to the Central Government to exploit income-tax to the hilt. Keeping all these aspects in view, we have to examine the advisability of making the net yield from corporate income-tax also divisible. We would like to examine the issue in a much broader perspective.

The yield from income-tax on individuals has not been increasing as fast as the yield from the corporate income-tax. Further, the recent enhancement of the exemption limit for income-tax and reduction of rates of tax on the first slab have narrowed down the size of the share of the States in the divisible pool of income-tax. Furthermore, various concessions offered under various sections of the Income-tax Act, such as for approved savings, etc., have also reduced the States' share in the net yield from income-tax. Therefore, we suggest the following alternatives for the consideration of the Finance Commission to resolve the problem:

(*a*) The first alternative is that it would be better to bring back the net yield from corporate income-tax into the divisible pool and make it divisible along with the net yield from individual income-tax. This would satisfy both the spirit and letter of the Constitution and also the long standing demand of the State Governments. Mere inclusion of the net yield from corporate income-tax in the divisible pool will not reduce the revenue available for the Central Government under our fiscal needs approach, because ultimately it is the objectively assessed fiscal needs which determine the extent of financial transfers from the Central Government to the States. However, if the Finance Commission also decides to use the same old outmoded methodology, inclusion of the net yield from corporate income-tax may harm the financial interests of the Central Government. But the thrust of our argument in this memorandum is against the continuation of the present methodology and to adopt the fiscal needs approach outlined in an earlier Chapter. If such an approach is adopted, the financial interests of both the Central and State Governments will be protected even if the net yield from corporate income-tax is included in the divisible pool.

(*b*) The second alternative would be to amend the Constitution and bring in the net yield from corporate income-tax under Article 270, make the net yield from it divisible and exclude the net yield from income-tax on individuals from the divisible pool. This alternative of substituting corporate income-tax in place of income-tax on individuals in the divisible pool is also suggested within the framework of our suggested fiscal needs approach. Under both these suggested alternatives the Central Government may retain the net yield from surcharge.

6.3 Inter Se Distribution

In regard to distribution of the States' share of the net yield from income-tax among the State Governments, hitherto population and collection criteria have been used by the past Finance Commissions. Collection basis has been opposed by economists as well as backward States whereas it has been staunchly defended and even increased weightage has been demanded by States like Maharashtra and Gujarat. On the face of it, the argument in favour of using origin of collection and distributing a part of the net yield from income-tax on the basis of this criteria is rather weak. Several arguments for and against this particular basis have been advanced in the literature. Therefore, there is no need to repeat them. Our main contention is that the origin of collection will neutralise the redistributive effect of fiscal needs approach which we have already recommended earlier. Therefore, in order to make the federal financial transfers to the State Governments equitable under the recommendations of the Finance Commission, it is necessary to scrap the origin of collection basis.

In regard to the population criterion, it has been found that it has no relation to the fiscal needs of different State Governments, nor is it associated with the level of backwardness of different States.[1] Therefore, we would argue that even the general population criterion should also be dropped altogether. Instead the entire 95% of net yield from income-tax on individuals or corporate income-tax may be distributed in proportion to the estimated fiscal needs of different States. Alternatively, this share of the divisible pool may be added to the overall divisible pool of resources which the Central Government can spare for the States. Then the entire amount of divisible pool may be distributed among the State Governments on the basis of the estimated fiscal needs. If the Finance Commission is not in a position to estimate fiscal needs realistically in view of the time and data constraints, it would be better to distribute the entire share on the basis of population criterion. However, the thrust of our main argument is that the Commission should make sincere efforts to estimate the fiscal needs of the State Governments and recommend financial transfers to fill these fiscal needs, by treating the sum total of all divisible tax shares as one pool.

As far as the net yield from estate duty and wealth-tax on non-agricultural property is concerned, the criterion used by the Seventh Finance Commission seem to be in order and almost all the State Governments have accepted them as realistic. Our suggested fiscal needs approach requires that the net yield from these assigned taxes should be distributed on the basis of origin of collection. Since the Central Government has not been able to keep accounts to suit this criterion, the proxy variables used for distributing the net yield from these assigned taxes are fair enough.

The grant in lieu of tax on railway fares comes under Article 269. Here the State Governments have a right to expect the Central Government to levy the tax and hand over the net yield to the concerned States. But because of the difficulty faced in administering this tax, the Railway Convention Committee recommended it to be abolished and be substituted by lump sum grant. Even this grant has not increased substantially *pari passu* with the increase in railway fares. The State Government's point of view has been ignored repeatedly by the Railway Board and Railway Convention Committee. This shows their gross disregard to the financial interests of the State Governments. The State

Governments' demand is to reimpose the tax and leave the administrative problems created by such reimposition of the tax to the Railway Board is justified. Otherwise, the Finance Commission should increase the grant in lieu of this tax to Rs. 30 crores per year and distribute it in proportion to the original shares of the State Governments in the net yield from the tax on railway fares. This amount is determined on the basis of the extent of increase in the total railway receipts between 1966-67 and 1982-83.

The major source of tax share for the State Governments has been the net yield from the Union excise duties. Constitutionally it comes under Article 272 which is a permissive provision. Because of the past decision to transfer a share in the yield from this tax, the State Governments have taken it as an obligatory tax share. It should be mentioned here that in the light of a constitutional controversy between the Central and the State Governments for the right to levy tax, the Central Government need not have given a share from this as it is similar to sales tax. But taking into account the financial needs of the State Governments, the earlier Finance Commissions made a beginning in a small way to give a share in the net yield from this source to the State Governments. The Seventh Finance Commission unfortunately increased this to as much as 40% which resulted in giving unconditional grants to the State Governments without their need being established on their non-plan current account. Though the resulting revenue surpluses were supposed to be taken into account by the Planning Commission while determining the Central assistance for State plan, in effect, most of the State Governments have not bothered to use it entirely for plan purpose. The point is that the estimated non-plan budgetary gaps of the State Governments, before the devolution of tax shares, were unrealistic. Because the growth rate of non-plan expenditure was assumed at 7% which is just 50% of the actual growth rate. Even so huge surpluses would not have been experienced by 15 States if the non-plan revenue expenditures of all the State Governments were assumed to grow at the rate of 10% per annum. In other words the share in the net yield from excise duties need not have been increased by much. Probably this awkward problem would not have arisen if the Seventh Finance

Commission had recommended to increase the States' share marginally from the earlier 20% to 25%.

The main thrust of our submission is that the Finance Commission should estimate the net fiscal needs of the State Governments, then estimate the surplus of revenue which the Central Government can spare and recommend the transfer of that surplus first under obligatory tax shares. Then the remaining amount may be recommended to be transferred from the Union excise duties. It may be difficult to match the estimated fiscal needs of the States with the estimated revenue surplus which the Central Government can spare, when they are estimated independently. The Finance Commission may estimate the fiscal needs of the States first, and proceed on to the estimation of revenue surplus and use its best judgment to reconcile both, depending upon the relevance and importance of different items of fiscal needs and bare minimum surplus which the Central Government can spare for transfer to the State Governments. Such a methodology will avoid unnecessary waste of energy and time in searching for criteria to be used for *inter se* distribution of the divisible pool of tax shares.

It should be mentioned here that the grant in-lieu-of tax on railway fare, the net yield from all taxes levied under Article 269 and the net yield from additional Union excise duties should be distributed first, as they are State sources of revenue. It would be better to estimate the net fiscal needs of the State Governments after distributing the net yield (or grant) from these assigned and rented sources. In addition to these, the Central Government may first distribute the net yield from the income-tax or corporate tax under Article 270. After distributing all these tax shares, it should determine the extent of revenue required still to fill the gaps in the fiscal needs of the State and accordingly determine the exact share of the net yield from Union excise duties to be distributed among the States. A part of this share will have to be provided in the form of earmarked grant under Article 275 for the purpose of maintaining capital assets and for improving urban civic services.

CHAPTER VII

Financial Assistance for Relief and Rehabilitation Works

7.1 Introduction

We have presented our views in the previous Chapter on the major terms of reference referred to the Eighth Finance Commission, particularly the methodology of the Finance Commission. In this Chapter we should like to present our views on other aspects referred to the Eighth Finance Commission as also those which are relevant to the working of the Finance Commission.

We have already suggested earlier that unconditional grants should be made for upgrading the essential public services. We have also suggested conditional grants for maintaining capital assets and for upgrading urban essential civic services. Therefore there is no need for considering grants-in-aid separately though it has been referred to the Finance Commission. It has been referred separately because the Finance Commission did not bother about it for long. Since the task of equalisation of essential public services is an integral part of the fiscal needs approach, and if the Eighth Finance Commission uses fiscal needs approach, there is no need to recommend earmarked grants separately for that purpose. Earmarked conditional grants are required for improving the maintenance of capital assets and essential civic services.

7.2 Financial Burden of Natural Calamities

The Eighth Finance Commission was asked to "Review the policy and arrangements in regard to the financing of relief expenditure by the States affected by natural calamities and suggested such modifications as it considers appropriate, in the existing arrangements, having regard among other considerations, to the need for avoidance of wasteful expenditure."

The impact of natural calamities like droughts, famines, cyclones and floods is intensely felt in a predominantly agrarian country like India. The geographical vastness, diversity in climate and other natural factors expose different parts of the country to one or the other natural calamity. As a matter of fact, it has become so common that when floods ravage some parts of the country drought occurs in other parts at the same time. Cyclones have become regular features in coastal State and floods damage standing crops almost every year in the gangetic unforeseen expenditure for providing quick relief like supply of food, shelter, some clothing and medical aid and also on preventive works against such occurrences in future. In drought affected areas similar unforeseen expenditure is imposed on the State Governments for supplying foodgrains, provision for drinking water and fodder for cattle, and for the creation of employment opportunities. Such calamities also generally dislocate the State Governments' finances. As the State Governments are nearer to the people affected by such calamities they are forced by 'political circumstances' to relief measures. It may be mentioned here that such problem is faced by the State Governments in almost all federations and almost all federal governments have been assisting the State Governments to enable them to provide relief.

7.3 Recommendations of Earlier Commissions

In India the Second Finance Commission for the first time recognised the financial problem posed by the natural calamities. It suggested making regular provisions in the expenditure forecasts of the State Governments to meet this type of expenditure.

Accordingly, while estimating the committed expenditure of the State Governments, the Second Finance Commission provided a 'margin' for enabling the State Governments to set apart annually from their own revenues sizeable sums to be accumulated in the fund for meeting such expenditures. The Second and the Third Finance Commissions prescribed such annual amounts on the basis of the average annual expenditure of the preceding 10 years and suggested to the State Governments to transfer the amounts to special fund every year. The balance of the funds were suggested to be invested in readily marketable assets which would be drawn upon when needed. The Fourth Finance Commission followed the previous Commission's approach and assessed the relief need on the basis of average performance over a decade.

During the years 1966-67 and 1967-68 large part of the country suffered from severe drought conditions and hence there was an abnormal amount of expenditure on relief works. The Fifth Finance Commission, therefore, reassessed the amounts likely to be required for this item on the basis of the average expenditure for the nine years 1957-58 to 1965-66 and increased it by 25 per cent in each case. The provision allowed by the Fourth Finance Commission was, however, retained, if it was higher than the figures worked out on this basis.

The Fifth Finance Commission while continuing the practice of making a separate annual provision for expenditure under 'Famine Relief' considered that the excess of such provision over the actual expenditure on famine relief in each year should be transferred to a separate famine relief fund which may be drawn upon in other years for meeting expenditure required in excess of the provision allowed by them. Further they suggested that the amount of appropriations to the 'Famine Relief Fund' should be invested in easily realisable securities. The Fifth Finance Commission noted that the earlier suggestions were not implemented by the State Governments. In order to make their suggestions effective, the Fifth Finance Commission further suggested that in determining Central assistance to be given under this scheme of assistance to be given to States for expenditure on relief measures, the accumulated provision for the entire period from 1969-70 and not merely the annual provision relating to the year in which the natural calamity occurs, should be taken into account. The Commission thought it more appropriate if the 75% assistance to those States, whose finances would also have been adversely affected on the receipt side, was given wholly in the form of grants and only the amount required for State loans to others may be covered by Central loans. The remaining burden of famine relief expenditure was recommended to be met by the State Government itself, as it would be the primary authority for deciding the level of famine expenditure. In order to meet temporary difficulties, the Commission suggested to the Central Government to give ways and means assistance.

The Sixth Finance Commission was specially asked to look into the matter in detail and to examine the feasibility of establishing a National Fund to which the Central and State Governments may contribute a percentage of their revenue receipts. The Sixth Finance Commission observed the increasing trend of relief expenditure and the Central assistance given for this purpose. There was a sharp increase in expenditure on relief particularly since 1966-67. As against the annual average of expenditure of 13.41 crores during the period of the Third Plan, expenditure under "64 Famine Relief" in State budgets rose to an average of Rs. 81.01 crores during the period of the three annual plans. This rising trend gathered unprecedented during the period of the Fourth Five-Year Plan. The expenditure which stood at Rs. 151.87 crores in 1969-70 rose to an all time peak of Rs. 818 crores in 1972-73. Central assistance to the States for financing such expenditure also registered an equally disturbing increase. In fact Central assistance to some States for drought relief far exceeded the assistance for their plans. In the light of the massive expenditure undertaken by many State Governments, the provisions made by Finance Commissions in their awards for Famine Relief lost their significance.

Therefore, in 1966 it was decided, as a policy measure, to depute a team of officers of the Central Government to make an on-the-spot assessment of the situation created by a natural calamity and to recommend ceilings of expenditure to be incurred on relief measures and loans for rehabilitation, repairs to public properties damaged in cyclones, floods or earthquakes. Of the various types of expenditure on natural calamities, expenditure on relief measure alone was shareable by the Central Government to the extent of 75% in excess of the margin provided for by the Finance Commission, 50% as loan and 25% as grants. Of the remaining 25% of the relief expenditure, the expenditure on loans to third parties and on repairs was expected to be met by the State Governments themselves. If the ways and means position was difficult, the State Governments could obtain loan assistance from the Centre. In 1972, the concept and the scope of relief assistance as embodied in the policy enunciated in 1966 was significantly altered. In particular, the practice of imposing ceilings was given up towards the middle of 1972. Since then relief expenditure has reached alarming proportions.

The Sixth Finance Commission felt that this alarmingly increased magnitude of expenditure on relief works was not entirely due to the increasing severity of the natural calamities, and opined that there had been a good deal of avoidable waste in the expenditure incurred in the name of drought relief. However, after examining the issue of financing relief expenditure, the Commission felt that some States had real constraints of resources for development programmes in the plan and had to resort to larger Central assistance for purposes of drought relief. But, the Commission realised that the distribution of assistance for drought relief outside the framework of Central assistance for plans, nullifies the formula for distribution of Central assistance evolved by the NDC. Therefore, the Commission felt that the present system of assistance for natural calamities introduced serious distortions in the scheme of allocation of Central funds among the States which is injurious to the federal fiscal set-up. The Commission rightly opined that all rationality and objectivity in the scheme of federal fiscal transfers adopted by the Finance and Planning Commissions are lost when large *ad hoc* assistance are given for the relief purposes. In view of this the Sixth Finance Commission recommended that whatever amount of assistance for relief purposes are given they should be adjusted against the ceilings of Central assistance for the plan.

The Commission further observed that the Central teams entrusted with the task of assessing the requirements of relief are constituted at short notice and have to complete their assessment of the situation within a short period. Due to lack of time at their disposal they have to work on the data supplied by the State, and the Central team has no effective means to check these data and thus their findings by and large tend to be of an impressionistic nature. There is also no satisfactory arrangement anywhere in the Central Government to keep close and critical watch on the implementation of the recommendations of the Central team.

However, the Sixth Finance Commission did not favour the idea of establishing a National Fund. It recommended that instead of incurring large scale expenditure on relief on an *ad hoc* basis on schemes of dubious value, provision should be made on much larger scale for development of drought and flood prone areas in the Fifth Five-Year Plan both in State and Central sectors. It also recommended that the provision of reasonable margin in the forecasts of State expenditure should be considered as a legitimate charge on the revenue accounts of the States. The most scientific basis for determination of the margin would be to assess the proneness of different areas in the States to occurrence of droughts or cyclones or other natural calamities with reference to meteorological and other data. But for practical purposes, the Commission like its predecessors, relied upon the past performance of the State and determined the provisions needed by the States for providing subsidy and other relief on the basis of the average expenditure over the period from 1956-57 to 1971-72.

Following the report of the Sixth Finance Commission the Central Government gave up its relief assistance policy to 1966 and adopted the procedure recommended by that to be adjusted within the ceiling of Central assistance for the States plan. Further, as envisaged by the Commission, under the new policy, a Central team is deputed to the natural calamity hit area for a on-the-spot assessment. The report of the team is considered by a high level committee headed by a member of Planning Commission and for purposes of advance plan assistance are placed before the Union Finance Minister for approval before the allocations are finalised.

The Seventh Finance Commission after reviewing then existed policy, took into consideration certain relevant factors before suggesting changes in the scheme of Central assistance for State Governments for undertaking relief expenditure. The first consideration was to place the States in such a position that they can maintain financial equilibrium. Secondly, the Commission considered the point of reducing or minimising any tendency for wasteful expenditure on the part of the States. From this point of view, the Commission felt that States should bear a significant share of the relief expenditure burden. Thirdly, the burden of non-plan expenditure which does not create any new assets, cannot be properly taken care of in the present scheme of Central assistance. A fourth aspect was that the Central Government did not find it possible to adjust advance plan assistance given after 1976-77 against plan ceilings of the States concerned. Keeping these points in view, the Commission thought it fit to suggest some modifications in the then existing policy of relief expenditure. The Sixth Finance Commission took 9 year average annual expenditure for each State from 1969-70 to 1977-78 and enhanced it by 15%, on consideration that the averages are somewhat depressed on account of the price levels before they rose steeply in the middle of seventies.

The Commission made a distinction between expenditure for drought relief and expenditure for providing relief to the people affected by floods and cyclones. The Commission felt that the first type of expenditure could be integrated with States, annual plan outlay. The Commission suggested that for expenditure in excess of the 'margin' provided in any year as estimated by the Central team, the State Governments should make a contribution from their plans for providing employment mostly to mitigate the effects of drought. The extent to which the State Governments should contribute from their plan outlay in this manner should be assessed by the Central team and approved by a high level Committee headed by a member of the Planning Commission. But the contribution should not exceed about 5% of the Annual Plan outlay. The Plan outlay thus to be taken as a contribution from the State Government should be treated as an addition to the plan outlay in that year and covered by advance plan assistance from the Central Government. The adjustment of the advance plan assistance against the ceiling of the Central assistance for the annual plans of the States was to be adjusted within five years following the end of the drought. If the expenditure required, as assessed by the Central teams and the high level committee, cannot be adequately met by the State Government even after the State plan contribution is taken into account, the extra expenditure should be taken as an indication of the special severity of the calamity which should justify the Central Government assisting the State to the full extent of the extra expenditure. This assistance should be made available fifty per cent in the form of grant and fifty per cent in loans. The Commission felt that the loan burden would curb the wasteful expenditure on the part of the States.

In regard to expenditure on relief, repairs and restorations of public works following floods, cyclones, etc. , the Commission felt that the Central assistance should be made available as a non-plant grant, not adjustable against the plan outlay of a State or against the Central assistance for plan. The Central Government should provide assistance to the extent of 75% of the total estimated expenditure in excess of the margin in loans and the remaining 25% should be borne by the State Government, which would discourage wasteful expenditure. Where a calamity is of rare severity, it may be necessary for the Central Government to extend assistance to the State Government concerned even beyond the above suggested scheme. These recommendations were accepted by the Central Government.

7.4 Our Suggestions

We feel that it would be unwise to give plan assistance as an advance assistance to the State Government to undertake drought relief works, because Government assistance to poor people is highly politicised in the rural areas so much so that the affected people are made to believe by the political leaders that the entire assistance is free without expecting any work from them to create or improve community assets. Therefore, there is need for modification in the scheme of assistance to the State for undertaking relief works.

In the first instance it would be better to allow higher level of expenditure on drought and natural calamities in the State Governments' budgets so that a part of this need will be built into the normal non-plan expenditure of the State Governments. Such normal growth of expenditure has been estimated by the past Finance Commissions on the basis of the average of the preceding eight to ten years. Such trend fails to take into account the impact of inflation. Therefore, it would be better to add a growth element to such average estimated expenditure. The growth element may be uniform for all the States to prevent uncontrolled increase of such expenditure.

Over and above such estimated normal growth of expenditure which is foreseen, if any unprecedented natural calamity occurs then it is the bounden duty of the Central Government to help such States with outright grants. The usual objection to this suggestion is that if grants are given for providing relief to the people affected by natural calamities, the State Governments headed by unscrupulous politicians may misuse the money. Even if this apprehension is real, the victims of natural calamities should not be punished because of corrupt government and administration. The Indian electorate are becoming vigilant and effective in punishing the corrupt politicians. The long-term solution to corruption is such eternal vigilance. Therefore, it would be wrong on the part of Central Government to provide Central assistance for normal periodic droughts. Such normal droughts will have to be looked after by the State Governments with their normal revenue. But unprecedented natural calamities like total failure of rains resulting in famine condition, earthquake, floods and cyclones should invite Central assistance in the form of outright grants. It would be unwise to provide loan assistance with a view to preventing misuse and write-off such loans after a lapse of time.

It may be recalled in this context that the Sixth Finance Commission was asked to suggest a National Relief Fund for assisting such States which would be affected by natural calamities, to which both the Central and the State Governments should contribute from their own normal revenues. The Sixth Finance Commission ruled out the case for such relief fund and instead, suggested that the States should prepare special plans for such areas and integrate them into their Five-Year Plans. It is probably because of this opinion of the Sixth Finance Commission that there is no mention of National Relief Fund in the terms of reference of the Eighth Finance Commission.

It is clear from the past experience that development planning has not solved the problem of natural calamities in any way and it would be pious hope to expect a special plan to prevent natural calamities whose severity cannot be predicted. Therefore, the case for assisting the State in the task of undertaking adequate and timely relief works is still stronger notwithstanding its absence in the terms of reference of the Eighth Finance Commission. It would be ideal if the State Governments transfer their earmarked revenue expenditure to their Famine Relief Funds to which the Central Government should make equal matching contribution annually. It is quite possible that if the State Governments are asked to contribute to the 'Famine Relief Fund' whatever revenue expenditure they used to allocate for relief works, they may not allocate much in order to reduce their own contributions. Therefore, it would be desirable to make it binding on each State to contribute annually an amount determined by the Finance Commission for the period covered by its recommendations. This amount along with the matching contribution from the Central Government should be credited to the respective States' Famine Relief Funds. This amount should not be allowed to be diverted or to lapse if a State does not require relief works in a particular year. The total amount should be invested in the interest bearing Government of India securities which should be encashable whenever the drought relief work becomes essential. This will reduce unforeseen and unbearable financial burden on the State Governments as also on the Central Government.

Thus, the expenditure on drought relief may be made to be met from 'Famine Relief Fund' by making annual matching contributions by both the State and Central Governments. This will prevent the State Governments from politicising Central Government's inability to help the States in times of periodic droughts.

Expenditure necessitated by other devastating natural calamities like floods and cyclones should be entirely assisted by earmarked grants from the Central Government.

CHAPTER VIII

Non-Plan Capital Gaps

8.1 Background

The Eighth Finance Commission was asked to "make an assessment of the non-plan capital gap of the States on a uniform and comparable basis for the five years ending with 1988-89, and "In the light of such an assessment, the Commission may undertake a general review of the States' debt position with particular reference to the Central loans advanced to them and likely to be outstanding as at the end of 1983-84 and suggest appropriate measures to deal with the non-plan capital gap, having regard *inter alia* to the overall non-plan gap of the States, their relative position, and the purposes for which the loans have been utilised and the requirements of the Centre."

This term of reference was referred to the Sixth and Seventh Finance Commission also. However, the Sixth Finance Commission also was asked to suggest changes in the terms of repayment of the Central loans, whereas the Seventh Finance Commission was asked to suggest appropriate measures to deal with the non-plan capital gap of the States.

The estimation of non-plan capital gap of the States is purely an empirical exercise based on the State Governments' forecastes of their non-plan capital expenditures. However, the Sixth and the Seventh Finance Commissions excluded certain items of non-plan capital expenditure of the State Governments while estimating their non-plan gaps. For instance the Sixth and Seventh Finance Commissions did not include the entire capital expenditure incurred on the construction of non-residential buildings and the committed expenditure on account of the implementation of land reforms. Many State Governments have complained that such exclusion is arbitrary. Therefore, the eighth Finance Commission should seriously examine this complaint and give justifications wherever necessary for making adjustments in the States forecasts of non-plan capital expenditure.

The problem of Central loans to the State Governments has become an important issue in the debate on Centre-State relations. Hence any suggestions to reduce the non-plan capital gap of the States should take into account the mounting burden of Central loans on the States. The problem of increasing State Governments' indebtedness to the Central Government had come up for examination before the earlier Commissions also. For instance, the Second Finance Commission was asked to examine the modifications if any, in the rates of interest and the terms of repayment of the loans made to the various States by the Government of India between the 15th day of August, 1947 and the 31st day of March, 1956." The Commission recommended consolidation of the various Central loans into a few categories with reduced interest rates. The recommendation was not accepted by the Central Government in to though certain modifications in terms of repayment and interest rates were made by the Central Government resulting in saving of Rs. 5 crores for the States. The Fourth Finance Commission was asked to estimate the extent of assistance required by the States owing to "further expenditure likely to devolve upon those States for the servicing of their debt," and to examine the desirability of "creation of a fund out of the excess, if any, over a limit to be specified by the Commission, of the net proceeds of estate duty on property other than agricultural land accruing to a State in any financial year, for the repayment of the States' debt to the Central Government." However, the Commission considered that the States' share of estate duty was not sufficient for the intended purpose and hence recommended that an expert body may be appointed to study the whole problem of inter-governmental borrowing and to recommend suitable remedies. The Central Government is yet to act on this recommendation. In the meanwhile, the States' debt has gone on increasing in its magnitude. The Fifth Finance Commission was asked to examine only States' unauthorised overdrafts and to suggest remedies to reduce them. The Commission did its job in a rather cut and dried fashion. But the problem of States' debt and their indebtedness to the Central Government has come up for investigation once again, say for the fifth time, before the Finance Commission. Central loans have been made to the States under the plan assistance scheme. Under this scheme, most of the States get 70 per cent of Central assistance in the form of loans and the remaining 30 per cent in the form of outright grants. In this way the States have been dragged into a vicious circle of Central loans, which create interest and repayment charges on these loans, and then the need for more loans from the Centre to meet these interest and repayment charges. Unless this is ended, the States' finances will go from the present bad position to a much worse position.

The Sixth Finance Commission was asked for the first time to estimate the non-plan capital gap in the States' budgets during the period of the Fifth Five Year Plan and suggest measures to reduce such gaps by making appropriate modifications in the terms of Central loans to the States. The Commission recommended: (a) consolidation of some loans into uniform types, (b) extension of the period of repayment of some loans, (c) moratorium on the repayment of some loans, and (d) writing-off of some loans. All these recommendations of the Commission were accepted by the Central Government.

The measures recommended by the Sixth Finance Commission to provide relief to the States from the mounting burden of Central loans were well conceived. However, the Commission did not recommend substantial debt cancellation on the ground it would reduce the pool of resources available with the Central Government for providing further assistance to the States. But this cannot be justification for burdening the poorer States with loans even for relief works of unproductive nature though the Commission rightly recommended writing off of certain loans made to the States to undertake activities which were mainly of national character. Therefore, there is need for reducing not merely the non-plan capital gaps in the States' budgets but also the burden of Central loans on the States.

The Seventh Finance Commission also supported the Sixth Finance Commission approach, though with cautionary note, regarding the plea of the States to write-off the outstanding loans. The Commission felt that "writing off of loans, except on a carefully selective basis, could well discourage conscious efforts on the part of the State Governments for mobilising tax and other resources to meet their requirements."

In regard to the small savings loan, the Commission recommended to consolidate the outstanding amount against each State into one loan as on 1st April 1979 and to convert such outstanding loans in perpetuity, in respect of which the States need not make any repayment of principal with effect from 1979-80. The States were, however, required to pay the interest at prevailing rate.

In regard to Central loans applied to unproductive purposes amounting to Rs. 942.42 crores excluding the loans for rehabilitation purposes.

Further, with regard to loans for semi-productive purposes, the Seventh Finance Commission recommended that such outstanding loans may be repaid in 30 years from 1979-80 and the balance of outstanding loans for productive uses may be repaid over a period of 15 years from 1979-80. The Commission recommended charging of a preferential rate of interest at 4.75% and 5% respectively for productive loans.

The recommendations of the Seventh Finance Commission relating to the conversion of small savings loans into perpetual loans and writing off of certain loans resulted in total reduction of States' debt burden to the extent of Rs. 30.76 crores.

8.2 Our suggested Short-term Measures

Any attempt to suggest solutions to the problem of burden of Central loans on the States should have both short-term and long-term perspectives. This is essential because any realistic solution should go to minimise the immediate financial burden of Central loans on the States, as otherwise they will not help much in solving their immediate financial problems. At the same time these short-term solutions should not become *ad hoc* measures as in the case of the recommendations of the Finance Commissions, which, after temporarily easing the financial stringency, will perpetuate the basic problem in the long-run. Thus while the short-term solutions are required for reducing the immediate strains on the States' finances, they should be linked with long-term solutions which will, in course of time, reduce the economic as well as financial burdens[1] of Central loans on the States.

An important short-term policy measure should be debt adjustment in the form of writing off of certain loans made for socially as well as financially unproductive purposes such as drought relief and rehabilitation, (including outstanding principal as well as interest payment on them), and interest payments due on loans provided for certain socially productive but financially non-productive purposes like expansion of health and education facilities and construction of rural roads. Similar solution was suggested by Neimeyer as far back as 1936 and was accepted by the then Central Government to reduce the financial burden on the then provinces. He highlighted the core of this method of providing federal fiscal assistance to the then provinces in a federation in the following way:

> "Where financial assistance is to be given by a creditor to an existing debtor, elementary commonsense suggests that the shortest and simplest method of adjustment is by reducing the claim of the creditor on the debtor."

1. For details on these concepts see G. Thimmaiah, *Burden of Union Loans on the States*, Sterling Publishers, New Delhi, 1977.

Thus, loans are granted by the national government in a federation to the constituent States for the purpose of undertaking specific programmes and in rare cases for normal budgetary needs. The States which do not find normal budgetary funds including public loans at reasonable terms, are encouraged to undertake them by providing loans on reasonable terms. But when the payment of interest and/or repayment of principal becomes due or even earlier, the national government may reduce or write-off the payment of interest and/or the repayment of principal, if it finds that some or all the State Governments are financially week *for reasons beyond their control.*

This form of debt adjustment has been used to provide financial relief to the States in Australia, Canada and the USA during the early years of their federations. Even in India it was implemented when the idea of federation was attempted to be translated into practice in 1936. As we have already mentioned earlier, the Second Finance Commission was aware of this form of providing financial relief to the States but brushed it aside on flimsy grounds. Though the Sixth Finance Commission recommended some minor adjustments, it too did not accept, in principle, debt adjustment as a form of federal fiscal transfer mainly on the ground that it will reduce funds available with the Central Government to provide future loans to the States. This reason appears to be naive because the Central Government is supreme in borrowing powers and besides, it controls most of the financial institutions in the country which supply substantial loan funds to the public sector in India. Therefore, any immediate solution to the existing burden of Central loans to the States should be sought in this policy measure of writing-off of certain unproductive loans to the States. Most of these loans were made to the States for financing expenditure on relief works necessitated by natural calamities such as droughts, floods, etc. These relief works were in the form of social security schemes which the people who faced these problems expected from the society. Though they do not occur in every State every year, from the past trend it appears that they occur cyclically in all the States over a period of time. Hence, they become a national problem which should be looked after by the Central Government, if not entirely at least partly, by assisting the States financially in the form of grants. For the present, therefore, the Finance Commission should recommend that all outstanding loans and interest payments due from the States for undertaking such relief works should be written off. And as we have already suggested earlier, the Commission should recommend that the Central Government should provide grants to the States for undertaking such works in the future. This policy measure will reduce the allocational burden[2] of Central loans on the States.

Another short-term solution which the Finance Commission may recommend is rescheduling the existing loans by extending the period of repayment from the existing fifteen years and twenty-five years for medium and long-term loans respectively to twenty and thirty years respectively. A similar recommendation has already been made by the Sixth and Seventh Finance Commissions and has been accepted by the Central Government but only in the case of some loans. However, our contention is that it should be done uniformly and be made applicable to all unproductive loans. Third, the rate of interest charged on Central loans for socially productive schemes such as health and education should not exceed the cost of borrowing by the Central Government. This may also become a long-term policy measure. Finally, the rate of interest charged by the Reserve Bank for ways and means advances should not exceed the Treasury bill rate. This again may become a long term policy also.

8.3 Long-term Measures

The Eighth Finance Commission may consider to recommend the following long-term solutions. First, all Central loans in future should be classified into the following three categories

(a) Central loans for socially productive but financially non-productive schemes involving capital expenditure included under both plan and non-plan categories such as health, educa-

2. See for details G. Thimmaiah, *op. cit.*

tion, housing for weaker sections and rural roads. Since these schemes do not yield any direct monetary returns to the State Governments as also that they have got to be undertaken by the State Governments under the present social philosophy of welfare State, the State Governments will have to assume their expenditure responsibility as far as possible from their own revenues. However, when huge funds are required for undertaking such socially productive schemes on a large scale the State Government should be assisted by the Central Government partly with grants and partly with long-term loans repayable over a period of thirty years. The grant-loan contents of Central assistance for these specific schemes should be fixed on the basis of the level of these social and economic infrastructure facilities already achieved in each State. For this purpose, the States and Union territories may be classified into two categories :

(*i*) The States and Union territories in which the level of these facilities, as determined by appropriate objective indicators are equal to or above the national average level, and (*ii*) the States and Union territories in which the level of these facilities are below the national average. We have clubbed the States and Union territories with equal to and above national average facilities to give the benefit of doubt to the marginal States when we determine the level of these facilities on the basis of indicators. The Central Government may provide 50 per cent in loans and 59 per cent in grants to the first category of States, and provide the entire Central assistance for these schemes in the form of grants to the second category of States. This method of Central assistance to certain States' plan schemes will reduce the distributive burden of Central loan on the poorer States. No doubt, the suggested method of Central assistance to certain States' plan schemes will involve some modifications in the existing formula of Central assistance to States' plans.

The repayment of this category of loans may be allowed in equal annual instalments. This method will not substantially alter the flow of funds from the State Governments to the Central Government. And the method of equal annual instalment repayment will not impose as much financial burden on the State Governments as compared with the presently operating method. Instead, their capital budgets will be eased in the long run.

(b) Central loans for financially productive schemes such as irrigation, electricity generation, lower and middle income group housing, agro-industrial undertakings, etc., may be provided on financial productivity criterion but in the form of non-repayable loans. These loans may carry interest rates equivalent to the estimated internal rate of return on each project. At the moment, the basic philosophy of perpetual loans is already in practice in India in that the State Governments have been borrowing from the Central Government partly for financing their expenditure and partly for repayment of their past borrowings is already in practice. But in this case, the financial responsibility of repayment of past loans comes up every year. Since Government is an eternal institution in a society, the idea of perpetual debt need not raise any eyebrows. However, in the suggested scheme, the liability extends only up to the period of the span of life of each project. These projects should include all those related to manufacturing activity, public transport, all public sector irrigation schemes and power generation. It is only fair that the Central Government should treat its loan to the State Governments for these projects as a form of investment which should earn some dividends. In this case the Central Government will have to fix the rate of interest equivalent to the internal rate of return. The State Governments should be free to repay the loan over a period of thirty years if they consider that the rate of interest is too disadvantageous. Further, such rate of interest should be indexed to changes in wholesale prices to compensate the loss of real revenue to the Central Government. When once this is done, there is no need for fixing variable, (*i.e.* gradually increasing) rate of interest on each and every loan.

This process will make the allocation of loan funds more efficient both economically and socially. It will also compel the State Governments to use the borrowed funds productively so as to earn annual return for repaying interest on such loans and to that extent it will reduce the development burden of Central loans on the States. However, a danger in this scheme is that the States may continue to be reckless in utilisation of loan funds and fail to raise additional tax revenue for paying interest on such Central loans. This possible budgetary substitution effect may be avoided by earmarking revenue from additional taxation towards States' contribution to determine the size of the States' plans as it is being done at present. Besides, in case of failure of any State to pay interest on such non-repayable loans, the Central Government should deduct the amount due on this account from the concerned States' annual share in the divisible pool of the yield from Union excise duties.

(c) Though the Seventh Finance Commission recommended to convert the small savings loans into loans in perpetuality, the Central Government has not accepted that recommendation. The Eight Finance Commission should recommend that 75 per cent of the small savings collections by the State Governments, should be transferred to them in the form of perpetual loans. The State Governments should be asked to pay only interest on them. This enhanced share will encourage the State Governments to mobilise more small savings.

(d) All other *ad hoc* loans (including temporary accommodations) should be dispensed with in future. In future, ways and means advances including authorized temporary overdrafts should be provided only by the Reserve Bank of India. This will not create any situation of financial stringency in view of our suggested short-term solutions. On the contrary, it will impose a necessary financial discipline on the States.

CHAPTER IX

Other Issues

9.1 Other Related Issues

We would like to raise a few related issues which are relevant to the present and future functioning of Finance Commission in India. They include: (a) the status of the Finance Commission, (b) the distribution of cost of tax collection for purpose of determining the divisible share in the net yield from income-tax, (c) use of 1971 population data for distributing tax shares, and (d) State Governments' financial autonomy.

9.2 The Status of the Finance Commission

It is now evident that the composition of the Finance Commission is becoming bureaucratic and its research cell has remained inadequate for the task. Further, the State Governments' non-plan expenditures are not reviewed annually to ensure proper financial management at the State level. The Planning Commission reviews annually their plan expenditures. To some extent this has helped proper phasing of plan expenditure and also additional resource mobilisation. Similar review is required on non-plan side. This requires a standing Finance Commission. Because of these reasons we have revised our earlier opinion on the need for a standing Finance Commission. Earlier we had argued against a permanent Finance Commission with the hope of having a well staffed research cell and permanent Planning Commission. But now, in the light of the fact that the research cell does not have even a well qualified economist and that there is urgent need for annual review of non-plan expenditure of the State Governments by an independent body like the Finance Commission, we agree with the view that the Finance Commission should be converted into a standing body. The Seventh Finance Commission which considered this issue recommened againtst making the Commission a permanent body. Since then situation has changed qualitatively particularly in regard to the growth of non-plan expenditure of the State Governments. Therefore, the Finance Commission may examine the issue afresh and recommend for making the Finance Commission a standing body.

Such a standing Finance Commission should be purely an expert body. The Chairman of the standing Finance Commission should be a judge of the High Court or Supreme Court and the members should consist of one general economist, one fiscal economist and one administrator. The Finance Commission Act of 1951 should be amended to provide for such a composition of the standing Finance Commission.

The Amended Act should also indicate the basic principles which should guide the Finance Commission in its work. This has been done in the case of Australian Commonwealth Grants Commission. There is no harm in doing it in India. Perhaps it will help the Finance Commission.

9.3 Rational Allocation of Cost of Collection of Taxes

The cost of collection of Central taxes are given combinedly for corporate tax, income-tax, tax on agricultural income, gift-tax, wealth-tax and estate duty. Up to the year 1973-74, the costs of collection in respect of all these taxes were separately accounted. But from 1974-75 the costs of collecting these major taxes have been merged for unknown reasons.

The total costs of collection of all the taxes *viz.*, corporate tax, taxes on income other than corporate tax, estate duty, wealth-tax and gift-tax if apportioned among various taxes in the following proportions :

TABLE 9.1

Allocation of Costs of Collection of Direct Taxes in India

Income-tax including corporate tax	90%
Estate Duty	2%
Wealth-tax	7%
Gift Tax	1%
Total	100%

The *inter se* allocation of costs of collection between corporate tax and income-tax is made in the ratio of 1:7 to distribute the cost of collecting corporate tax and income-tax. This distribution of cost of collection between these two taxes does not seem to be rational as may be observed from the following data relating to the yield from these taxes.

TABLE 9.2

Yield from Direct Taxes : 1981-82

(*Rs. crores*)

1. Corporate tax	19.62
2. Taxes on income other than corporate tax	15.20
3. Estate duty	17.00
4. Wealth-tax	75.00
5. Gift-tax	6.70

While the ratio between the yield from corporate tax and income-tax is 1 : 0.78, the ratio of cost of collection between these two taxes is 1:7. This apart, receipts from taxs on income, other than corporate tax, include the receipts from union emoluments, and surcharge on income-taxes which are not shared with the States. But while working out the net proceeds for sharing purposes, cost of collection due to these items are not deducted. In other words, that part of cost of collection which is due to non-shareable part of income-tax is also deduct ed from the shareable proceeds of income-tax, thus affecting the size of State Governments' share in net yield from income-tax. Therefore, before arriving at the net proceeds from income-tax for devolution purposes, it would be appropriate if that part of cost of collection which is on account of collection of income-tax on union emoluments and surcharge is not deducted from the total tax receipts. Similarly, it is necessary to distribute the costs of collection of income-tax and corporate tax on the basis of ratio of proceeds from these two taxes. This will increase though marginally the net yield from income-tax and as a result the States' share in this yield. Though, the proportion of increase may not be significantly large, we would still feel that fairness requires such a procedure.

9.3 Use of 1971 Population Data

Population as a basis of distributing federal fiscal transfers is generally justified on the ground that it represents the 'need' of the States. It is surprising to note that the Finance Commission has been asked to take into account the population of 1971, if it decides to use population as the basis of distribution of tax shares among the States. The implied assumption for inclusion of this condition in the terms of reference is that an increase in the population during the decade between 1971 and 1981 reflects the poor performance of the State Governments in the sphere of family planning and hence such a step is recommended in order to discourage high rate of growth of population.

First of all, forcing the Finance Commission to follow any criterion is against the constitutional provision relating to the powers of the Finance Commission. In an attempt to give broad guidelines and indicate important considerations which the Commission should keep in view while framing its recommendations, the Central Government has successfully imposed restriction on the scope and basis of its recommendations. Of all such restrictions, the condition imposed to use 1971 population data is certainly damaging to the power of the Finance Commission.

Increase in population does not always imply an increase due to an increase in the birth rate, as is assumed by the Central

Government. Apart from birth rate, equally important factors responsible for increase in the population are : (a) declining mortality rate due to better health conditions and improvement in economic situation prevailing in the States; and (b) immigration of population into some States and from neighbouring States owing to higher development level achieved by those States.

These factors exert greater influence on the growth of population at the State level. A State owing to positive health policies and better administration and economic development may attract outside population as it has happened in the case of the capital of Karnataka State. Population may not have increased in some other States owing to higher mortality rate, deteriorating socio-political conditions and lack of economic development efforts. Under these circumstances, it would be inadvisable to use 1971 population for distributing tax shares among the States. Because 1971 population is unrealistically low and hence fails to measure the need of State Governments. Therefore, we suggest that in case the Finance Commission has to use population criterion, it would be appropriate to consider 1981 population, which is now available for almost all the States except for Jammu and Kashmir and Assam for whom projected figures are available.

It should be remembered here that when the past Finance Commissions decided to use population as criterion for distributing tax shares, they considered it as proxy for the general financial needs of the States Governments. The Central Government has compelled the Eighth Finance Commission through the terms of reference to use 1971 census data which means that the Central Government has asked the Eighth Finance Commission to believe that the general financial needs of the State Governments have not increased between 1971 and 1981, which is most ridiculous apart from being illogical. Therefore, the Eighth Finance Commission should explore ways and means of circumventing this particular restriction imposed on its working. We know that it would conflict with the intention of the Central Government to reject this imposed condition as it has become a term of reference. But it is also true that it comes in the way of evolving a scientific methodology for distributing Central assistance among the States. Therefore, the Finance Commission may write to the President of India to free it from this restriction before finalising the report.

9.4 State Governments' Financial Autonomy

The Finance Commission should recommend to the Central Government not to interfere periodically with the financial powers of the State Governments. This suggestion may look awkward and embarrassing. But it has got a justification. The Finance Commission is going to assess the non-plan revenue gap in the current budgets of the State Governments. While so doing it has to take into account the revenue potential of the State Governments. Many State Governments in their memorandum have pointed out that their scope to raise additional revenue has come down partly because of the in-roads made by the Central Government into their taxing power and particularly in the field of sales tax. This is a true fact. The Central Government has imposed restriction on the revision of rates of sales tax on essential and declared goods. It has already taken over the power to levy sale tax on three commodities under additional union excise duty agreement. Recently the 46th Amendment to the Constitution, instead of giving the power to tax consignment transfers and sale of service contract to the State Governments, has given powers to the Central Government to determine the rate of such tax under Article 286. What is more, the Tripathi Committee was compelled to by the Union Ministry of Finance to accept their proposed scheme of expansion of sale tax to five more commodities and only asked the Committee to recommend ways and means of safeguarding a financial interests of the State Governments. All these suggest that the Central Government is crazy fore more powers. This craze may one day set-off chain reaction harming the very interest of the national integration. We are aware of the fact that the Finance Commission has been asked to look into the matter of additional union excise duty agreement. In view of the fact that the Central Government has not implemented the terms of agreement under that, the Finance Commission should resist the pressure of the Union Ministry of Finance to recommend for the expansion of the scheme to other commodities. This issue is related to the financial autonomy of the State Governments. Since the Finance Commission is provided under the Constitution to protect the financial interests of the State Governments, the Finance Commission should caution the Central Government against tampering with the financial powers of the State Governments.

CHAPTER X

Eighth Finance Commission Report : An Evaluation-I

10.1 Background

The Eighth Finance Commission set up in January 1982 under the Chairmanship of Sri Y. B. Chavan has once again kindled the interest of the economist in the issues of Centre-State relations. The Recommendations of the Eighth Finance Commission have been subjected to acrimonious comments. Financial transfers of Rs. 38,500 crores on the recommendations of this Commission is the largest amount ever recommended by the finance Commissions. The Commission has ventured to introduce some new dimensions into the federal financial system. Introduction of uniform criteria for the distribution of proceeds of income-tax and Union excise duties, distribution of additional 5% of union excise duties among the revenue deficit States and provision for an annual growth of 5 per cent in respect of the amount of grants-in-aid payable in each year of the forecast period commencing from 1984-85 in order to confer the advantage of buoyancy to the deficit States, are the most important among them. This Chapter evaluates the criteria of federal fiscal transfers and the merits and demerits of the novelties of the recommendations of EFC.

The foremost consideration for the Eighth Finance Commission in its scheme of devolution appears to be reduction of regional disparities by helping the backward States. While outlining its approach, the Commission clearly mentions that "In making the allocation between the States we had again, to balance divergent considerations. How to reconcile the need to accelerate the development of the backward States, without hindering the further development of the more advanced ones? It is true that we have leaned in favour of the former and tried to make our scheme of devolution more progressive; but we think, that this is what the national interest, at present' requires."[1] This indicates that a major objective of the Eighth Finance Commission is to reduce inter-State disparities through their scheme of devolution. There may be different views as regards to the objectives of federal fiscal transfers and one may even question the undue weightage given to the objective of equalisation in the devolution scheme. However, without going into these controversies, let us examine the Commission's recommendations to achieve this objective.

10.2 Sharing of Income-tax

The Eighth Finance Commission has recommended to retain the share of States in the proceeds of income-tax at 85% level. However, the Commission supported the long held view regarding the withdrawal of surcharge on income-tax from the financial year 1985-86 and suggested to readjust the basic rates of income-tax. This is a welcome recommendation, as it would expand the divisible pool of income tax and benefit the States. Though the Commission supports the general view that corporate tax should also be made shareable, it did not make any recommendation to this effect.

It is heartening that the Commission has recommended for reviewing the method of allocating the cost of collection between income-tax and corporate tax, by an expert committee. This is an important recommendation. Our memorandum had very clearly pointed out the arbitrator involved in the practice of the Central Government in the allocation of cost of collection

1. *The Report*, 1984, Chap. II, p. 7.

of income-tax and we are happy that the Commission has acted on our suggestion. It is expected that the Central Government will accept the recommendation of the Commission in this regard and accordingly set up an expert committee to review the matter.

10.3 Union Excise Duties

The Commission has recommended to increase the States' share of union excise duties from 40 to 45%. It may be noted that the Commission has recommended that this 5% of the net proceeds of the union excise duties (excluding that on electricity) should be set aside and distributed only among those States which have deficit after taking into account their shares from devolution of taxes and duties as proposed by them. This introduces a new principle of directly linking devolution to deficit States rather than dealing with them only through grants-in-aid under Article 275.

It is necessary to find out whether this new principle is constitutionally acceptable? The Constitution has made provision for the sharing of union excise duties with the States. It is a tax which is voluntarily shared by the Centre with the States. Once the Parliament decides to share this source with the States, all States become eligible for a share in the divisible pool on some uniform principle. To our mind splitting of the divisible pool into various portions like general purpose, and specific purpose is not justified. Article 280 of the Constitution requires the Finance Commission first to distribute the net proceeds of tax which are to be or may be divided between the Centre and the States and then to allocate between the States of the respective shares of such proceeds. There is no provision for splitting of the shareable portions of the proceeds of taxes and duties. The present splitting of divisible pool into two portions and assigning 5% of the proceeds of union excises to net revenue deficit States is against the spirit of Article 272. In fact this assignment amounts to grants-in-aid of revenue, for which Constitution has made a separate provision under Article 275. Besides this Article, there is a provision under Article 282 for giving grants for miscellaneous purposes. When there are specific provisions in the Constitution to transfer resources in the form of grants-in-aid, where is the necessity to encroach upon the scope of the various shared taxes and duties. If the Constitution had the intention of using union excise duties only for helping a few States or exclusively for equalisation purposes, the drafting of the Article 272 would have been similar to that of Article 275 which reads as follows: "... in each year as grants-in-aid of revenue of each State as Parliament may determine to be in need of assistance and different sums may be fixed for different States."

There is no such provision or even intention under Article 272. This only speaks of distributing the proceeds from union excise duties between the Centre and the States and the distribution of divisible pool among all the States. It does not say that the divisible pool itself may be split into various parts and be distributed among different types of States like revenue deficit States or famine affected States, or war affected States.

In fact, the status of Union excise duties is comparable to the status of taxes on income under Article 270 of the Constitution, and under no circumstances it should be reduced to the status of grants-in-aid of revenue. The only difference between the Articles 270 and 272 is that while the former is compulsorily shared by the States, the latter is shared at the discretion of the Parliament. However, once the Parliament agrees to share the proceeds with the States, there remains no difference in the nature of income under Article 270 and union duties under Article 272.

In fact the Eighth Finance Commission itself has expressed similar views while deliberating on the criteria of devolution of income-tax in the Report. The Commission has maintained that "It is, of course true that income-tax and Union excises are dealt with by different Articles in the Constitution and that whereas income-tax is compulsorily shared, with regard to excise duties there is a discretion. But the Constitution itself seems to attach no importance to the separation because in Article 280(3) (*a*) they are dealt with together. It refers conjointly to the allocation between the States of the respective shares in regard to both taxes which are to be or may be divided between them."[2] The Commission has also stated, "that no distinction can be drawn because of the use of the word 'manner' in Article 270 and 'principles' in Article 272. Nor does anything turn on the word 'assigned' in Article 270 and its absence in Article 272."[3]

While analysing the recommendations of any Finance Commission, we have to keep in mind their broader implications not only in the near future but also in the distant future. Our contention here is that if we accept the present splitting of divisible pool into two parts, one for all the States and 5% for revenue deficit States, nothing would prevent the future Finance Commissions:

(a) to increase the share in the net proceeds of taxes and duties of specific States from the present level of 5 per cent to any higher percentage, in fact giving larger share to the specific States than to all the States;

(b) to split the divisible pool further into two or more portions so that different types of States like, war affected, famine affected States and so on, are assisted differentially;

(c) to split the divisible pool of income-tax also on similar grounds—as in practice there is no difference between the two.

The net effect of approving of the present recommendation of the Commission would amount to reducing the status of union excise duties to the status of grants-in-aid, which in the long run goes against the interest of the States, as they would lose an assured and rightful source of divisible pool. Apart from these long term implications, the recommendation of the Commission to distribute 5% of union excise duties among the

2. *Op. cit.*, p. 44.
3. *Ibid.*

revenue deficit States will further strengthen the necessity of adopting the much criticised "gap filling" approach.

10.4 Grants-in-aid

Grants-in-aid which have been given a residuary role until recently have received greater attention of the Eighth Finance Commission. While the Commission adhered to the principles formulated by the Seventh Finance Commission, it has tried to make the grants-in-aid more flexible. In order to make the grants-in-aid buoyant the Commission has provided for an annual growth of 5 per cent in respect of the amount of grants payable in each year of the forecast period commencing from 1984-85. Though this has injected an element of growth into the amount of grant to allow for inflation, the Commission has still use grants-in-aid as a 'gap filling' factor in its system of devolution.

The recommendation for raising the grants in lieu of railway fare to Rs. 95 crores deserves praise. This was long overdue. The Government should accept this recommendation in total as it is a matter of constitutional right of the States and the Centre need not consult the Railway Convention Committee in this regard.

The recommendation to write off a substantial portion of loan amounting to Rs. 2285.39 crores is also an appropriate step towards strengthening the State finances.

10.5 Criteria for Inter Se Distribution

The Eighth Finance Commission has tried to remove the false distinction that existed so far between Article 270 and Article 272 by advocating for adoption of uniform principles of federal fiscal transfers. Income-tax was distributed among the States mainly on the basis of collection and population criteria. However, a number of criteria were used for the distribution of the States share in the net-yield from Union excise duties. The Commission has opined that "we can conceive of no reason why the Constitution makers should have wanted that only excise duties should be used for the benefit of the backward States. After all, in both cases what is transferred to the States is money. The debates in the Constituent assembly and the reports of its committee, show that no such distinction was intended to be made. Having given the matter our very careful consideration, we are of the opinion that there is nothing in the Constitution which bars the allocation of income-tax on the same criteria as excise duties."[4]

But have they really adopted a uniform basis of allocation? If we examine the recommendations, we find that for the distribution of income-tax, the Commission has adopted the following four criteria: (a) Collection of income-tax in each State, (b) population of call-State, (c) inverse of per capita income multiplied by population the highest per capita income, and (d) distance of per capita income from the highest per capita income multiplied by population. 'Collection' is given 10% weightage and the remaining 90% was recommended to be distributed *inter se* on the basis of the remaining three criteria in the following ratios respectively 25 : 25 :58.

In case of the States' share in the net yield from Union excise duties, entire 100% of is distributed *inter se* on the basis of the last three criteria as the collection has no relevance for this share. Thus the Commission cannot justifiably claim to have applied a uniform set of criteria in their scheme of federal fiscal transfers.

The Eighth Finance Commission has stated that the factor of population simplicitor has been given a predominant weightage in the distribution of income-tax share in the past and therefore, the Commission felt that more weightage should be given to the 'backwardness', and from this point of view it has the above three criteria in addition to collection. If we take the four criteria together we get the following weightages in case of income-tax.

Collection	10%
Population	22.50%,

4. *Op. cit.*, p. 44

Inverse of per capita income multiplied by population	22.50% and
Distance from highest per capita income multiplied by population	45.00%

Apparently population is given only 22.5% weightage and in distributing of the States share in the net yield from union excise duties, population gets 25% weightage. It appears as though the weightage to population factor has been reduced considerably from 80 or 90% to 22.5 or 25%, while poverty and backwardness have received greater weightage. But, are they really progressive? Has the Eighth Finance Commission really departed from its predecessors? The answer to these would be in negative. The Eighth Finance Commission with all gimmicks and formulae ultimately arrive at the same criteria as were followed by the earlier Commissions and in effect 'population' continues to hold a predominant place in the scheme of federal financial devolution recommended by the Eighth Finance Commission. The two criteria *viz*; inverse of per capita income and the distance from highest per capita income become meaningless and in fact they become in effect a representative index of population when they are multiplied by the State population. Table 10.1 presents the data relating to various criteria adopted by the Eighth Finance Commission. It should, however, be noted that the Commission did not use 1981 population figure and it did not even use the latest State income figures, and hence the percentage shares given in the Table to illustrate the futility of the round about method adopted by the Eighth Finance Commission would differ marginally from the actual percentages presented in the Finance Commission's Report. However, our purpose here is to show that the present Finance Commission has also not departed from the traditional criteria of federal fiscal transfers used by earlier Commissions.

Based on Table 10.1, a correlation matrix is worked out for the following criteria:

1. Population
2. Per capita SDP
3. Inverse of SDP

TABLE 10.1

Criteria of Federal Fiscal Transfers Used by Eighth Finance Commission

States	*Population in 1981 (lakhs)*	*Percentage Share*	*Per capita SDP 1980-81 (Rs.)*	*Percentage Share*	*Inverse of SDP*	*Percentage Share*	*Inverse of SDP Population*
	1	*2*	*3*	*4*	*5*	*6*	*7*
Andhra Pradesh	535.92	8.39	1467	5.99	.00068166	7.36	.3644256
Bihar	698.23	10.93	1870	7.63	.00053476	6.17	.3700619
Gujarat	339.62	5.32	2211	9.02	.00045228	5.21	.1528245
Haryana	128.51	2.01	2335	9.53	.00042826	4.94	.0552593
Karnataka	370.43	5.80	1458	5.95	.00068587	7.91	.2555967
Kerala	254.03	3.98	1312	5.35	.00076219	8.79	.1930628
Madhya Pradesh	521.38	8.16	1217	4.97	.00082169	9.47	.7275316
Maharashtra	627.15	9.82	2519	10.28	.00039698	4.58	.2483514
Orissa	262.72	4.11	1296	5.29	.00077160	8.89	.2022944
Punjab	166.69	2.61	3122	12.74	.00032031	3.69	.0533408
Rajasthan	341.08	5.34	1417	5.78	.00070570	8.14	.2421668
Tamil Nadu	482.97	7.57	1373	5.60	.00072833	8.40	.3525681
Uttar Pradesh	1108.85	17.37	1309	5.34	.00076394	8.81	.8427260
West Bengal	544.85	8.53	1595	6.50	.00062695	7.23	.3432555
Total (14 States)	6382.42	100.00	—	100.00	—	—	—

TABLE 10.1 (continued)

States	*Percentage share*	*Distance from highest SDP (minus)*	*Percentage share*	*Distance from highest SDP × population*	*Percentage share*	*Average percentage share as per FC criteria*	*Average Percentage share without weighing to population*
	8	*9*	*10*	*11*	*12*	*13*	*14*
Andhra Pradesh	8.88	1655	8.62	886947.60	9.90	9.06	7.67
Bihar	9.02	1252	6.52	874183.96	9.76	9.91	7.87
Gujarat	3.73	911	4.74	309384.71	3.45	3.60	5.09
Haryana	1.34	787	4.10	101137.37	1.13	1.49	3.68
Karnataka	6.23	1664	8.66	616395.52	6.88	6.30	7.45
Kerala	4.71	1810	9.42	45974.30	.51	3.07	7.39
Madhya Pradesh	10.43	1905	9.92	993228.90	11.09	9.89	9.18
Maharashtra	6.06	603	3.14	378171.45	4.22	6.70	5.84
Orissa	4.93	1826	9.51	479726.72	5.36	4.80	7.50
Punjab	1.30	000	000	000	000	1.30	2.10
Rajasthan	5.91	1705	8.88	581541.40	6.49	5.91	7.45
Tamil Nadu	8.59	1749	9.11	844714.53	9.43	8.53	8.36
Uttar Pradesh	20.55	1813	9.43	2010345.05	22.45	20.12	11.87
West Bengal	8.37	1527	7.95	831985.99	9.29	8.73	7.90
Total (14 states)	100.00	—	—	—	—	—	—

4. Inverse of SDP multiplied by population
5. Distance from highest per capita State income
6. Distance from highest per capita State income multiplied by population
7. Percentage share of States in total population
8. Average percentage share of State based on the criteria adopted by the Finance Commission

The Coefficient of Correlation are presented in Table 10.2.

The correlation matrix clearly brings out high positive correlation that exist between population and inverse of per capita income multiplied by population (+.933) and between population and distance (+.901). Further, the latter two criteria, namely inverse of per capita income multiplied by population, and distance from highest per capita income multiplied by population are also highly and positively correlated (+.933). Finally, the percentage share of States in total population and the average share of States on the basis of three criteria adopted by the Finance Commission also have very high positive correlation (+.956).

This clearly establishes the predominant place which population gets in the federal fiscal transfers recommended by the Eighth Finance Commission. Thus, the Finance Commission has failed to avoid high weightage for population. Hence, its criteria also suffer from the same shortcomings as those of the earlier Commissions. If we compare the percentage share of States the divisible pool of income-tax and Union excises as recommended by the Seventh and the Eighth Finance Commissions we hardly notice any change.

A cursory look at Table 10.3 reveals the percentage share of States in the divisible pool of income-tax and the union excise duties have remained more or less the same. The changes if there are any are negligible. Had the Eighth Finance Commission not multiplied the inverse of per capita income and the distance from highest per capita income by population, perhaps the resultant transfers would have been more equitable and helped

Table 10.2

The Coefficient of Correlation

	Variables							
	1	2	3	4	5	6	7	8
1.	1.000							
2.	–.320	1.000						
3.	.284	–.973	1.000					
4.	.933	–.551	.550	1.000				
5.	.320	–1.000	.973	,551	1.000			
6.	.901	–.548	.533	.975	.548	1.000		
7.	1.000	–.320	.284	.933	.320	.901	1.000	
8.	.956	–.501	.486	.992	.501	.9841	.956	1.000

the poor and backward States rather than helping only the populous States. To illustrate, it may be seen from Table 10.1 that UP has per capita income of Rs. 1309 in 1981-82 as per the latest figures available from the State Statistical Bureau. Kerala has Rs. 1312 per capita income. If we use Eighth Finance Commission's criteria, Kerala gets 8.79% of the share and UP gets 8.81% of the share. This is justified as the two States have more or less the same level of per capita income. However, when inverse of SDP is multiplied by population, Kerala gets 4.71% and UP gets 20.55%. Thus, two States having the same level of per capita income get substantially varying percentage of share in the divisible pool. Infact, there are cases where States with lower per capita income get lower share, if they are less populated. This clearly shows that though the Eighth Finance Commission did not accept the practice of giving greater weightage to population and refused to accept population as the sole index of general need, in their actual scheme of federal fiscal transfers, they have finally resorted to population criterion. At least the earlier Finance Commissions frankly admitted that population is an important criterion, the Eighth Finance Commission after rejecting population criterion on theoretical ground, in effect it uses population though through a round about method. Therefore, the recommendations of the Eighth Finance Commission generate a mixed feeling. While the substantial amount of devolution recommended to be transferred by the Centre to States strengthen the State finances, the methodology adopted by them for determining the fiscal needs and criteria used for *inter se* distribution disappoints a number of States.

Finally, we would like to add that there is need for setting up Centre-State financial cells at the State levels in order to enable the future Finance Commissions to protect the State's fiscal needs more realistically and enable them to submit their report in time by avoiding undue delay in supplying essential statistics and information. One of the reasons for the delayed submission of the Eighth Finance Commission's Report is the lack of timely supply of data by various States. As a result, they had to make some interim recommendations. As the budget and the plans for the year 1984-85 were finalised on the basis of interim report of the Finance Commission, the Centre

TABLE 10.3

Percentage Share of States with Sikkim, as Per Seventh and the Eighth Finance Commissions.

Sl. No.	*States*	*Income-tax Share*		*Union excise duty (40%) share*	
		7th F.C.	*8th F.C.*	*7th F.C.*	*8th F.C.*
1.	Andhra Pradesh	8,021	8,187	7,691	8,587
2.	Assam	2,521	2,789	2,793	2,977
3.	Bihar	9,536	12,060	13,021	13,202
4.	Gujarat	5,957	4,409	4,101	3,506
5.	Haryana	1,819	1,074	1,177	1,017
6.	Himachal Pradesh	595	555	521	587
7.	Jammu & Kashmir	818	838	839	856
8.	Karnataka	5,440	4,979	4,876	5,077
9.	Kerala	3,948	3,760	4,035	3,800
10.	Madhya Pradesh	7,354	8,376	8,725	8,852
11.	Maharashtra	10,949	8,392	6,632	6,216
12.	Manipur	188	220	218	213
13.	Meghalaya	178	184	200	194
14.	Nagaland	085	088	097	096
15.	Orissa	3,738	4,202	4,682	4,596
16.	Punjab	2,713	1,744	1,226	1,317
17.	Rajasthan	4,362	4,545	4,813	4,695
18.	Sikkim	035	0.35	028	039
19.	Tamil Nadu	8,048	7,565	7,637	7,317
20.	Tripura	258	269	373	292
21.	Uttar Pradesh	15,422	17,907	18,290	19,097
22.	West Bengal	6,015	7,800	8,025	7,449
	Total	100	100	100	100

had to resort to unilateral decision to implement the main recommendations of the Commission only from the year 1985-86. Thus the Eighth Finance Commission's recommendations are valid only for four years. As a result, the States have lost the share that they would have got during 1984-85 as per the main recommendations. In order to avoid such recurrences in future and to estimate the fiscal needs of the States in a realistic manner, it is important to set up 'Research Cells' at the State level.

CHAPTER XI

Eighth Finance Commission Report : An Evaluation-II

The report of the Eighth Finance Commission, which has been accepted by the Government of India, has received mixed reactions from the States. Now the report has been circulated to all concerned, it is time that we start assessing the implications of the Commission's recommendations and of the action taken by the Government of India.

11.1 Disappointing Approach

We have to evaluate first the methodology and the approach used by the Commission to formulate its recommendations. It may be recalled that in the past the Finance Commissions did not explicitly outline their methodology, assumptions and calculations which they used for formulating their recommendations. This prevented the researchers from evaluating objectively the methodology of the Commissions. However, the Seventh Finance Commission for the first time explained certain details about its methodology, The Eighth Finance Com is-sion has gone a step further in placing before the public their assumptions and judgment along with the views of the States. It has also continued the Seventh Finance Commission's practice of assessing the financial position of the Central Government.

Constitutionally provided Finance Commission was expected to place before the public all its home work for the evaluation of the experts. The Eighth Finance Commission has tried to meet this demand to a considerable extent. In Chapter III it has presented the details about the way it has reassessed the projections of the revenues and expenditures of the State Governments on non-plan revenue account. In Chapter VIII, it has gone into the details about the standards of administrative services achieved in different States and in Chapter XIV it has assessed the non-plan capital gaps of the States. For the purpose of evaluating the methodology and approach of the Eighth Finance Commission we have to take into account the contents of Chapters III, VIII and XIV together.

The Eighth Finance Commission has tried to answer, though unconvincingly, the charges levelled against the traditional 'gap filling' approach which was followed by the earlier Finance Commissions. The Eighth Finance Commission has observed that "Most of the earlier Finance Commissions have been castigated for adopting what has been called a 'gap filling' approach. And, it will be said that we have done the same. The two main objections raised against this approach are : firstly, it encourages the less well-managed States to squander resources, knowing that their deficits will be made up by the Finance Commissions and secondly, that a revenue deficit is not a complete indication of the needs of a State."[1]

The Commission has gone on to answer these criticisms in the following way: "As regards the first objection, we need only say that it is not as if the Finance Commissions accept the forecasts sent by the States at their face value. We, like all previous Finance Commissions, have realistically reassessed the

1. *Report of the Eighth Finance Commission*, New Delhi, 1984, p. 8.

forecasts and applied certain norms. Our approach has been objective both on the revenue and expenditure sides."[2]

"As regards the second point, we think, that the requirements of the States on account of developmental needs should, according to the existing practice, be estimated and generally met by the Planning Commission. Consequently, even if fiscal needs are taken into account, they would have to be limited to the needs on non-plan account for which we have made appropriate provisions."[3]

While appreciating the frankness of the Eighth Finance Commission in acknowledging the criticisms against the 'gap filling' approach of the past Finance Commissions, we wish to reiterate that it has not done any objective assessment of the fiscal needs of the States even on non-plan revenue account. The reassessment of the forecasts made by the Commission by applying certain norms is only a continuation of the old practice. The only novelty here is that the Commission has made known its assumptions to the public particularly relating to the rates of growth of revenue and expenditure assumed for reassessing the forecasts of the State Governments on their non-plan revenue account. Secondly the Eighth Finance Commission has openly passed the buck on to the Planning Commission to take care of the financial needs of the States in the development sphere. It is a well known fact that in India it is very difficult to demarcate clearly development from non-development spheres expenditure particularly in a context where maintenance of law and order becomes a precondition for undertaking development programmes in the short run at least. Further, the plan and non-plan classification of expenditure overlaps with both development and non-development expenditure. What is more, even revenue and capital accounts of the Government budget do not clearly demarcate consumption and investment expenditure of the Government. Under these circumstances, the Commission's assessment of the fiscal needs of the States on non-plan account does not convince that it has excluded financial needs of the States for plan purpose. Furthermore, the Commission

2. Report of the Eighth Finance Commission, New Delhi. 1984, p. 8.
3. *Ibid.*

TABLE 11.1

Rates of Growth of Revenue from Major Sources as Estimated by NIPFP for the Period 1970-82 and Assumed by the Eighth Finance Commission for the Period 1984-89.

States	Stamps and Registration		State Excise		Sales Tax		Vehicle Taxes		Electricity Duty		Entertainment Tax	
	Esti-mated by NIPFP	*Assumed by the Commn.*	*Esti-mated by NIPFP*	*Assum-ed by the Commn.*	*Esti-mated by NIPFP*	*Assum-ed by the Commn.*	*Esti-mated by NIPFP*	*Assum-ed by the Commn.*	*Esti-mated by NIPFP*	*Assum-ed by the Commn.*	*Esti-mated by NIPFP*	*Assumed by the Commn.*
I. Non-Hill States												
1. Andhra Pradesh	13.18	9.5	13.43	10.0	17.87	10.5	11.56	7.0	—	12.23	8.0	
2. Assam	7.00	5.0	7.17	7.9	12.47	7.0	10.73	6.0	12.96	13.49	7.0	
3. Bihar	4.68	5.0	9.50	7.0	16.67	9.5	13.10	8.0	5.82	4.58	8.0	
4. Gujarat	12.60	8.5	18.42	7.0	16.58	9.5	8.83	7.0	21.10	15.13	10.0	
5. Haryana	12.37	8.0	16.03	10.0	18.23	10.5	18.88	11.0	23.51	13.12	8.0	
6. Karnataka	10.34	6.0	13.54	10.0	15.35	8.5	11.92	7.0	6.71	13.94	9.0	
7. Kerala	15.41	10.0	20.95	7.0	14.53	8.0	8.29	7.0	10.57	—	—	
8. Madhya Pradesh	11.30	6.5	12.19	7.0	14.66	8.0	18.42	10.0	193.30	12.12	8.0	
9. Maharashtra	6.78	7.0	18.88	10.0	15.89	9.5	8.92	7.0	13.09	11.28	8.0	
10. Orissa	11.52	7.0	5.59	7.0	16.72	9.0	9.14	7.0	22.31	17.01	8.0	
11. Punjab	9.90	7.0	13.54	10.0	12.99	10.0	13.26	8.0	18.76	9.34	8.0	
12. Rajasthan	7.95	5.0	4.04	7.0	16.74	9.0	14.32	9.0	18.65	12.67	8.0	
13. Tamil Nadu	9.24	5.5	—	10.0	16.61	10.9	6.95	7.0	—	11.94	8.0	
14. Uttar Pradesh	15.15	10.0	9.61	7.0	17.35	9.0	11.87	7.0	13.50	13.38	8.0	
15. West Bengal	7.49	5.0	8.18	7.0	13.99	8.0	13.69	8.5	6.69	11.79	8.0	

II. Hill States											
1. Himachal Pradesh	7.31	4.0	10.87	7.0	16.04	—	7.62	6.0	24.76	1.05	6.0
2. Jammu & Kashmir	10.91	5.5	4.04	10.0	18.11	—	22.04	11.0	21.64	11.27	6.0
3. Manipur	3.12	4.0	15.20	7.0	10.66	—	12.57	6.0	NA	10.32	6.0
4. Meghalaya	7.92	4.0	18.15	7.0	15.24	—	15.62	6.0	16.03	5.40	6.0
5. Nagaland	21.43	5.0	11.78	7.0	19.34	—	15.20	6.0	NA	18.56	6.0
6. Sikkim	5.00	4.0	18.71	7.0	15.86	—	15.09	6.0	NA	16.77	6.0
7. Tripura	8.72	5.0	9.42	7.0	33.00	—	5.74	6.0	NA	13.87	7.0

Source: Report of the Eighth Finance Commission, 1984.

has claimed that it has tried to reduce the inter-State regional imbalances in addition to covering the revenue gaps of the States. But what it has attempted to is to reduce inter-State inequality in revenue raising capacity and regional imbalances in the standards of administrative services. Since it has tried to do this within the framework of the "gap filling" approach, its recommendations have produced revenue surpluses to some States which can be used for development purpose. This would mean that the Commission has stepped unknowingly into the shoes of the Planning Commission. Our contention is that the methodology used by the Eighth Finance Commission has led to such surpluses being accumulated by some better-off States and some of the marginally better-off States joining the ranks of less developed States as it has happened in the case of West Bengal. Therefore, the Eighth Finance Commission cannot escape from the charge of perpetuating the 'gap filling' approach notwithstanding their explanation to the contrary.

The Eighth Finance Commission has given more details about their reassessment of the States' forecasts of revenue and expenditures in Chapter III. From this it becomes clear that it has not accepted the historical growth rates worked out by a research institution. It has tried to adjust them according to its 'best judgment'. But this 'best judgment' appears to have created an element of bias either in favour or against some States in the growth rates of each of the six tax revenue and seven non-tax revenue items which the Commission has considered. The Commission has applied different growth rates for each source of revenue for different States. The Commission has assumed a minimum of 7 per cent of annual growth rate and a maximum of 10.5 per cent for the yield from sales tax and excise duty. In the case of stamps and registration a minimum of 4% and a maximum of 10% have been assumed. The Commission has been a bit lenient in regard to the irrigation receipts, dividends and receipts from departmental schemes. However, for receipts from mines and minerals, they have assumed a minimum of 5% and maximum of 10% growth rates. They have assumed 7% net return on investment in power projects.

In this sort of exercise a question arises as to the objective criterion used to apply minimum or maximum rate of growth of yield from specific sources to a particular State. If the historical rate of growth of revenue from a particular source of a State is in the neighbourhood of either the minimum or maximum rate, use of such minimum or maximum rate is justified. On the contrary, the Commission has applied different growth rates for the same revenue source for different States notwithstanding uniform historical growth rates The historical growth rates estimated by a research Institute and the actual growth rates assumed by the Commission for each source of revenue are presented in Table 11.1. It is evident that no uniform principle is followed by the Commission for applying growth rates for different source of revenue. If the purpose was to use the past growth rates, then the Commission should have asked for the estimates of historical growth rates for only five years immediately preceding, 1984-85, instead of obtaining the growth rates for a period of 12 years. Apart from this, there is no uniform relation between the estimated historical growth rates and the assumed growth rates except that the assumed growth rates are consistently lower than the estimated growth rates except in the case of State excise. Then what is the justification for getting the historical growth estimated by research institution? In the case of expenditure forecasts, the Commission has assumed 7% growth rate for education expenditure, and 6.5% expenditure for police expenditure and it has tried to include the expenditure on account of emoluments, terminal benefits, if they were implemented before 1983-84. It has also made some provision for maintenance of buildings, capital assets, irrigation works, flood control works, etc.

Further, from the data presented in Table 11.1 it becomes clear that the Commission has assumed relatively lower rates of growth of revenue as compared to the estimated historical growth rates. Though this may appear a favour shown to the States, if we closely examine these growth rates, it becomes clear that the difference between the historical growth rates and the assumed growth rates vary from State to State. In other words, wherever historical growth rates have been higher the assumed growth rates are not uniform for different States. For example, for Kerala, Gujarat and Maharashtra, the assumed growth rates for State excise revenue are lower than the assumed growth rates for other States even though their historical growth rates were very high. Such discrepancies have injected an element of subjective value judgment into the determination of the fiscal needs of the State Governments.

Similarly, while training of the administrative people who are in service has been identified as a special expenditure need the request of Maharashtra, West Bengal and Tamil Nadu for upgrading the municipal services of urban local bodies has been turned down. Thus the Commission has not used any clear cut uniform objective criterion for estimating the resource gap of the State Governments. Therefore, the philosophy which is involved in the fiscal needs approach has not been followed even while estimating the financial gaps of the State Governments under the traditional gap filling approach.

Coming to the upgradation of standards of administrative services, the Commission has selected police, education, jail administration, tribal administration, health, judicial administration and treasury and accounts administration and training. Of all these, except health and education, the rest of them are police State functions, and one new addition which the Commission has made is the training of the administrative staff. Education and health which were taken into account by the Sixth Finance Commission were made to be excluded by the Seventh Finance Commission through their terms of reference and it is heartening to note that the Eighth Finance Commission has brought them back for the purpose of upgradation of these services. The Commission has taken into account all-States' average norm and have tried to provide the required expenditure to bring the standards of those States whose services fell below all-States' average level up to that level. In most of the cases, the Commission has given importance to providing housing facilities, office buildings and in a few cases appointment of personnel like additional teachers to convert single teacher schools into double teacher schools and to provide extra staff to police department and the like. One noteworthy feature of this exercise is the Commission's clear indication of providing extra expenditure requirements for school buildings and additional teachers. But it is surprising that the Commission has not bothered to pay attention to the findings of All India Education.

Survey for 1982 which reveals that 53 per cent of the primary schools and 31 per cent of the middle schools lack pucca buildings; 34 per cent of the primary schools and 23.4 per cent of the middle schools do not have mats, benches or chairs for the children to sit on; 29.7 per cent of the primary schools and 29.6 per cent of the middle schools do not have black boards. Most of these schools do not have urinals. How did the Commission ignore these basic needs under education?

Under health services the financial needs of the States for improving facilities like staff quarters and allowances and equipment for doctors posted to rural areas are taken into account. But the Commission has turned deaf ears to the expenditure incurred on medicines. Apart from such arbitrary consideration of the fiscal needs of the States, the Commission has used all States' average as the norm for the upgradation of the standards of these services. As a result many States are not made eligible for any special assistance under the scheme. Probably, if the Commission had used the highest State's standard as the norm, it would have helped many States, though it would have involved substantial amount of financial transfers from the Centre.

The Commission has taken into account some special problems of different States. But here again an element of bias has been introduced by taking into account the expenditure required for developing the necessary infra-structure facilities in Bastar district of Madhya Pradesh and excluding the requests of Maharashtra, Tamil Nadu and West Bengal for assistance for solving the problems of urban congestion in cities of Bombay, Calcutta and Madras. Thus while the infrastructure facilities for tribal area like Bastar district is appreciated, the requests for the funds required for improving urban civic services has been ignored. Thus the claim of the Eighth Finance Commission that they have made an objective assessment of the fiscal needs of the States by reassessing the forecasts on an uniform basis against some norms is not borne out by the exercises of the Eighth Finance Commission which are made explicit in its report.

The Eighth Finance Commission has, no doubt, taken a realistic view of Central Government's financial requirement over the next five years and also the growth of its revenue. They have tried to reduce the projected amount of food subsidy from the suggested amount of Rs. 4884 crores to Rs. 4433 crores. Similarly they have reduced the fertilizer subsidy from the suggested amount of Rs. 10197 crores to Rs. 6581 crores. But they have assumed very low rate of dividends of zero per cent, 3% and 5% respectively on investment in public sector undertakings classified as promotional, financial and commercial undertakings. These rates are far lower than those assumed by the Seventh Finance Commission and even by the Planning Commission. Notwithstanding this, the Eighth Finance Commission has made realistic estimate of the surplus revenue which the Central Government will be able to transfer to the States over the next five years.

11.2 Illusion of Equity

The Eighth Finance Commission has claimed that it has tried to achieve equity in the distribution of divisible pool of Central taxes. It is true that it has attempted to reduce inequalities in the revenue raising capacity of the States. But the out-moded 'gap filling' approach used to determine the shares of individual States in the divisible pool of Central taxes has off-set whatever equalisation they have tried to achieve by devising some criteria for *inter se* distribution of divisible pool of Central taxes. This is evident from Table 11.2. We have presented in Table 11.2 the per capita and percentage shares of individual States recommended by the Seventh and Eighth Finance Commissions. It may be observed that per capita shares of individual States have increased under the recommendation of Eighth Finance Commission as compared to the per capita shares recommended by the Seventh Finance Commission. This is mainly because, in absolute terms, the Eighth Finance Commission has recommended Rs. 18609.04 crores more than the total amount recommended by the Seventh Finance Commission. This would suggest that the Eighth Finance Commission, like all the earlier Commissions, has tried to reduce vertical federal fiscal imbalance. Though this is necessary, the way it is done has distorted the equity effect in the *inter se* distribution of federal financial transfers. Normally, in order to achieve equity in the distribution of federal financial transfers, it is necessary first to reduce horizontal federal fiscal imbalance. Once this is achieved, vertical federal fiscal imbalance will automatically be reduced. In other words, equity in the federal financial transfers can be consistently achieved only by reducing horizontal federal fiscal imbalance first. This will automatically reduce the vertical federal fiscal imbalance. But the Eighth Finance Commission, like all the previous Commissions, has tried to reduce horizontal federal fiscal imbalance through reducing the vertical federal fiscal imbalance. Thus the Commission has made equity objective to stand on its head.

This becomes clear if we examine the percentage shares of individual States in the devolution of financial transfers. In Table 11.2 it may be observed that the share of relatively better-off States like Gujarat, Maharashtra and Punjab are reduced substantially but the share of Haryana, which is equally a better-off State, is reduced only marginally. Further, while the share of West Bengal, which has been a better-off State until recently and now which can be reasonably considered as a middle income State, is substantially increased, the share of Tamil Nadu which is another middle income State is substantially reduced. What is more, the share of Madhya Pradesh, which is relatively a poorer State with substantial tribal population, has gone down. Such distortions have crept in mainly because of the outmoded 'gap filling' approach adopted by the Commission.

Since the tax shares and grants-in-aid are distributed on the basis of different criteria, such conflicting results are bound to emerge. This becomes evident if we examine the shares of individual States in the net yield from the income-tax and union excise duties. It may be observed from Table 11.3 that the shares of Gujarat, Haryana, Karnataka, Maharashtra, Punjab,

TABLE 11.2

Per Capita Resource Transfers from Centre to the States by Seventh and Eighth Finance Commissions

States	*Per capita tax shares recommended by*		*Per capita grants recommended by*		*Total per capita financial transfers recommended by*		*Percentage shares in the Devolution under*	
	Seventh Finance Commn.	*Eighth Finance Commn.*	*Seventh Finance Commn.*	*Eighth Finance Commn.**	*Seventh Finance Commn.*	*Eighth Finance Commn.*	*Seventh Finance Commn.*	*Eighth Finance Commn.*
1 Andhra Pradesh	281	515	4	26	285	541	7.31	7.34
2. Assam	250	629	11	179	261	808	2.49	10.70
3. Bihar	307	573	9	31	317	604	10.62	10.70
4. Gujarat	283	416	—	21	283	436	4.63	3.77
5. Haryana	239	331	—	9	239	340	1.48	1.11
6. Himachal Pradesh	262	1263	499	567	797	1843	1.56	1.96
7. Jammu & Kashmir	365	1230	363	636	628	1866	1.81	2.84
8. Karnataka	270	461	—	4	270	465	4.82	4.38
9. Kerala	300	490	2	11	302	585	3.70	3.27
10. Madhya Pradesh	293	534	12	32	306	375	7.67	7.50
11. Maharashtra	272	257	—	3	272	419	8.22	6.68
12. Manipur	269	2137	1116	1211	1385	3350	0.93	1.19
13. Meghalaya	282	1868	750	1069	1031	2937	0.64	0.97
14. Nagaland	223	4068	2783	2885	3007	2592	1.15	1.34
15. Orissa	308	591	64	132	372	723	4.72	4.84
16. Punjab	249	363	—	21	249	384	2.01	1.64

17. Rajasthan	257	448	6	40	263	488	4.33	4.25
18. Sikkim	16	2117	1212	1364	1228	3481	0.18	0.27
19. Tamil Nadu	305	504	7	5	310	509	7.21	6.25
20. Tripura	284	1703	700	1018	951	2672	0.96	1.42
21. Uttar Pradesh	288	533	10	17	298	550	15.90	15.47
22. West Bengal	288	516	4	115	292	631	7.66	8.74
Total	285	528	24	56	308	584	100.0	100.0

Note: 1.* Inclusive of Margin Money Grants.
2. 1981 Census population has been used for estimating per capita figures.

Tamil Nadu and West Bengal in the net yield from income-tax have declined and the shares of Bihar, Madhya Pradesh, Orissa, and Uttar Pradesh have increased. Here, West Bengal, Karnataka and Tamil Nadu which are middle income States have also faced the fate of high income States. As against this, if we examine Table 4, we find that the shares of Andhra Pradesh, Karnatka and Punjab have increased, whereas the shares of West Bengal, Tamil Nadu, Orissa, Kerala, Haryana and Gujarat have declined. In other words, the shares of some of the middle income and even poorer States have declined in the elastic source of tax share, *i.e.*, net yield from the union excise duties.

11.3 Income-tax Share

Under the Constitution, Article 270 compels the Central Government to share the net yield from income-tax with the State Governments. This is actually a continuation of the financial provision of 1935 Act. Now the divisible pool of income-tax has been narrowed down by not merely excluding the yield from corporate tax and surcharge from income-tax but also by certain policy changes introduced by the Union Finance Minister in the budgets over the past years. They include raising of the exemption limit of the income-tax, reduction of rates of income-tax and raising of various allowances under income-tax. These have adversely affected the overall yield of income-tax. This fact has not been taken into account explicitly by the Eighth Finance Commission. However, the Commission has conceded the request of the State Governments to merge the surcharge on income-tax in the income-tax rate or in the absence they have recommended for its abolition. Thus the Central Government has been made to agree for considering the yield from surcharge also as a part of the divisible pool. Even on the question of including the yield from corporate tax, the Commission have recommended that the Government of India may examine it independently. Further the Commission has paid attention to the disproportionately unequal allocation of the cost of collection (7:1), between income-tax and corporation tax and has advised the Central Government to constitute

TABLE 11.3

Shares of Individual States in the Net Yield from Income-tax

States	*As per the recommendations of*	
	Seventh Finance Commission (1979-84)*	*Eighth Finance Commission* (1984-89)*
Non-Hill States		
Andhra Pradesh	8.021	8.187
Assam	2.521	2.789
Bihar	9.536	12.080
Gujarat	5.957	4.409
Haryana	1.819	1.074
Karnataka	5.440	4.979
Kerala	3.948	3.760
Madhya Pradesh	7.354	8.374
Maharashtra	10.949	8.392
Orissa	3.738	4.202
Punjab	2.713	1.744
Rajasthan	4.362	4.545
Tamil Nadu	8.048	7.565
Uttar Pradesh	15.422	17.907
West Bengal	8.015	7.800
Hill States		
Himachal Pradesh	0.595	0.555
Jammu & Kashmir	0.818	0.838
Manipur	0.188	0.220
Meghalaya	0.178	0.184
Nagaland	0.085	0.088
Sikkim	0.035	0.035
Tripura	0.258	0.269
Total	100.00	100.00

Note : *Percentage with Sikkim

an expert committee to set right this lacuna. The Commission has also included 'interest recoveries' as part of the divisible pool under income-tax. Thus without affecting major changes, the Commission has shown small mercies to the State Governments.

TABLE 11.4
Shares of Individual States in Forty Per cent of the Net Yield from Union Excise Duties

States	As per the recommendations of	
	Seventh Finance Commission (1979-84)*	*Eighth Finance Commission* (1984-89)*
Non-Hill States		
Andhra Pradesh	7.691	8.587
Assam	2.793	2.977
Bihar	13.021	13.202
Gujarat	4.101	3.506
Haryana	1.177	1.017
Karnataka	4.876	5.077
Kerala	4.035	3.800
Madhya Pradesh	8.725	8.852
Maharashtra	6.632	6.216
Orissa	4.682	4.592
Punjab	1.226	1.317
Rajasthan	4.813	4.695
Tamil Nadu	7.637	7.317
Uttar Pradesh	18.290	19.097
West Bengal	8.025	7.449
Hill States		
Himachal Pradesh	0.521	0.589
Jammu & Kashmir	0.839	0.856
Manipur	0.218	0.233
Meghalaya	0.200	0.194
Nagaland	0.097	0.096
Sikkim	0.028	0.39
Tripura	0.373	0.292
Total	100.00	100.00

*Excludes the excise duty on electricity.

As regards the shares of the States, the Commission has retained the States, shares at 85% on the ground that it has recommended for the inclusion of the net yield from surcharge. This is not convincing because the yield from surchage does not amount to more than 15% of the net yield from income tax which has not been conceded by the Commission.

In regard to the *inter se* distribution of this yield, the Commission has continued to distribute 10% of the net yield from income-tax on the basis of 'assessment' (as proxy for contribution), and the remaining 90% on the basis of three-factor formula namely 25% in proportion to population of each State, 25% on inverse proportion to population of each State, 25% on inverse proportion to per capita income multiplied by population of the concerned State and 50% on the distance from highest per capita State, income multiplied by concerned State's population. It may be noticed that though this three factor formula gives an illusion of equity, in effect the use of per capita income twice gives indirectly more weight to population. Quite apart from this, the formula is complex for working out the States' share and statistical rounding off of the percentage itself may deprive some States of some amount. Further, the Commission after facing the usual problem of the highest per capita income State (Punjab), losing a portion of the share, assumed its distance as equivalent to that of the next highest per capita income State (Haryana). This awkward situation has diluted the objectivity of the formula. Furthermore, while the Commission has repeatedly maintained that the developmental needs of the States will be taken care of by the Planning Commission, it has used the criterion used by the Planning Commission (distance from highest per capita income multiplied by population of the concerned State) for distribution of plan grants for distribution of tax shares. The contradiction between precept and practice is evident. Thus even in the determination of the size of the divisible pool of income-tax, though the Eighth Finance Commission has tried to defend the States' cause, it has only thrown some crumble to the States in the form of inclusion of surcharge, and 'interest recoveries', and proper allocation of costs of collection, without asking the Central Government to allow the States to share the net yield from corporation tax. What is more, the *inter se* distribution of the States' share has been made complicated. The promised equity of the three factor formula has been diluted by the continuation of the distribution of 10 per cent of the yield on the basis of 'contribution'.

11.4 Union Excise Duties

In regard to the share in the net yield from union excise duties, the Commission has continued the error committed by the earlier Commissions by recommending to increase it from 40% to 45% which is unjustified. But at the same time, it has tried to distribute the additional 5% only among the net deficit States. This has, no doubt, injected an element of need based distribution but the whole purpose is diluted by increasing the overall share to 45%. What is more, the distribution of the States' share in the net yield from union excise duty is also made on the basis of the three factor formula mentioned earlier. The Eighth Finance Commission have made a beginning by using one unified formula to distribute the net yield from Union excise duties and 90% of the share of income-tax. Though this method has got its own merit, it is not an integral part of fiscal needs approach and hence it cannot reduce horizontal federal fiscal imbalance substantially. This is evident from Table 11.4 which shows that the share of Rajasthan has come down whereas the shares of middle level States like Karnataka and Andhra Pradesh have increased. What is worse the share of Punjab has increased.

11.5 Additional Excise Duties

Regarding the distribution of the net yield from additional duties of excise duties, the Commission has rightly reviewed and reassessed the criteria used by the Seventh Finance Commission for distributing this yield. It may be recalled that the Seventh Finance Commission had recommended the distribution of the yield from additional union excise duties on the basis of despatch of sugar to different States. As regards textiles and tobacco, the Seventh Finance Commission determined the States' share on the basis of share of each State in the total SDP of all States. The Eighth Finance Commission has revised these criteria and in view of the fact that there is positive relationship between State domestic product and consumption of the commodities on which the additional duties of excise duties are levied, they have distributed the net yield among the States 50 per cent on the basis of the share of each State in the average State domestic product of all the States for the years from 1976-77 to 1978-79, and 50 per cent on the basis of population figures as given in 1971 census.

It may be observed here that the yield from additional Union excise duties is in the nature of tax rental share. Hence, the entire yield should be distributed among the States on the basis of compensation principle. Since the yield has grown beyond the original amount to be compensated, the Finance Commissions of has started using equalisation criteria also for the distribution this yield. While this may be defended from the point of view of achieving fiscal capacity equalisation, it is wrong in principle because the entire yield should be distributed on the basis of either derivation principle or in proportion to the consumption of these commodities. Since SDP is a reasonable proxy for consumption, the Eighth Finance Commission should have distributed the entire yield in proportion to SDP of each State to the total SDP of all the States.

The Eighth Finance Commission has also looked into the failure of Central Government to fulfil the assurances given to the States from time to time after the agreement was reached in the National Development Council in December 1956. The first assurance was that the proceeds from the additional duties of excise will attain at least 1008 per cent of the value of clearances and the second assurance was that the ratio between basic duties of excise and additional duties of excise on these three commodities would not be greater than 2 : 1. Both these assurances have not been fulfilled by the Central Government. However, the Commissions were informed that a Standing Review Committee for additional excise duties was set up with Secretary, Planning Commission as Chairman and Finance Secretaries of all the States as members. The Committee has recommended that the first assurance may be achieved in three stages, 8.5% by 1984-85, 9.75% by 1987-88 and 10.8% by 1989-90 and the Commission has given time for the Central Government to ultimately fulfil these assurances.

The Eighth Finance Commission has continued, on the

request of the State Governments, the distribution of estate duty in respect of property other than on agricultural land, on the criteria which was used by the Seventh Finance Commission. They have also continued the criteria for the distribution of grants on account of wealth-tax on agricultural property since the yield from these two taxes are not substantial, the Commission has not taken into account the yield from these two taxes for the purpose of estimating the budgetary gaps of the States. The Commission has recommended that the States may be allowed to use these transfers for their plan purpose. This recommendation once again supports our view that the Eighth Finance Commission have violated their own demarcation of the responsibilities of the Planning Commission and the Finance Commission.

11.6 Grants in lieu of Tax on Railway Fare

The Eighth Finance Commission has boldly defended the case of the State Governments in regard to their claim on the tax on railway fare. The Constitution very clearly guarantees this tax under Article 269 for the benefit of the States and accordingly it was levied until 1961. But because the operation of the tax created some administrative problems, it was abolished unilaterally and was replaced by a compensatory grant. What is more, this compensatory grant stagnated at low level even though railway passenger and goods traffic as also the fares and freights have been increasing virtually every year. Consequently the State Governments have been pleading for either upward revision of the compensatory grant or reintroduction of tax on railway fare and freight. The Eighth Finance Commission has done justice to the interests of the States by substantially increasing the compensetory grants to Rs. 95 crores. But it is surprising that the Central Government's memorandum accepting the recommendations of the Eighth Finance Commission indicates that the Government of India has accepted it only in principle subject to its approval by the Railway Convention Committee. The Railway Convention Committee has no business to interfere in the constitutional rights of the State Governments to have their share from this tax. Therefore, the Central Government should view the problem more realistically and honour the recommendations of the Eighth Finance Commission by asking the Railways to pay the recommended amount of grant.

11.7 Grants-in-aid

The Eighth Finance Commission has attempted to introduce some novelties into the grants-in-aid under Article 275. But in effect these novelties have introduced distortions into the system of federal financial transfers. After referring to the principles of grants-in-aid enunciated by the Seventh Finance Commission, the Eighth Finance Commission has formulated its recommendations on grants-in-aid mainly on functional basis. The Commission has made recommendation in four parts. In the first part, the Commission has recommended grants-in-aid to eleven States for filling the revenue deficits as reassessed by the Commission. The Commission has for the first time allowed the revenue gap grants fixed for each of the five years from 1984-85 to grow at an average rate of 5 per cent. As a result of this 5 per cent growth factor, the Central Government will be required to transfer Rs. 1690.93 crores as against the nominal deficit of Rs. 1513.12 crores, as the reassessed deficits of the States. In the second part, they have distributed 5 per cent of the net yield from Union excise duties among eleven net deficit States as additional grant. In the third part the Commission has provided additional grants for special problems for only ten States. This part of the grant is given irrespective of whether any of these States has experienced revenue surplus or not after the devolution of tax shares. This would suggest that the fiscal need is not the criterion on the basis of which grants-in-aid is determined for meeting expenditure arising out of special problems because the revenue surplus States will not be entitled for these grants under fiscal needs approach. Once again this recommendation goes to prove our contention that the Eighth Finance Commission has not used fiscal needs' approach to formulate their recommendations. Finally, additional grants-in-aid are recommended to all States for meeting additional expenditure on account of sanction of three instalments of Dearness Allowance to State Government employees.

All these grants are recommended over and above the earmarked grants made for assisting the States to undertake relief works. The Commission has also recommended additional grants for meeting the non-plan current expenditure on account of interest burden on public debt and committed expenditure during the Seventh Plan period.

11.8 Financing Relief Expenditure

The Commission has continued the old practice of giving 5 per cent of the plan grant in the form of advance grant and have doubled the margin money required for financing relief expenditure. The earlier Commissions determined the probable expenditure on relief works on the basis of the past expenditure incurred by the State Governments on that item and determined the probable expenditure on relief works which might become necessary in the next five years. They determined the budgetary gaps of the States by adding this amount to the reassessed growth of expenditure of the States. The Eighth Finance Commission have alomst doubled the margin money which was recommended by the Seventh Finance Commission. Besides, the Eighth Finance Commission has made one departure from the recommendations of the previous Commissions in the manner of funding the margin money. The earlier Commissions made a provision equivalent to the margin money in the expenditure forecasts of each State. The Eighth Finance Commission has recommended that the Central Government should contribute 50 per cent of the margin money every year. And this Central share of the margin money need not be released to the States which do not face natural calamities. The amount may be accumulated showing it to the credit of the State Governments and should be available to the States whenever they face drought and such other distress situations. The unclaimed amount of Rs. 50 per cent of the Central shares should be carried forward to the next year so that the accumulated fund will be available for the State Governments whenever they need. This recommendation has tried to introduce some elements of the earlier proposal to create Famine Relief Fund, without allowing the fund to be invested in any income earning assets. However, this recommendation suggests that in effect the eighth Finance Commission have allowed in the revenue expenditure forecasts of the States only 50 per cent of the recommendied amount of margin money and have left the remaining 50 per cent with the Central Government for drawal whenever need arises. This is a naval feature of the Eighth Finance Commission's recommendation for financing relief expenditure.

The Commission has also recommended to the Central Government to remove administrative hurdles which are presently operating in sending Central teams to the States for making on-the-spot-study, for releasing the funds after the teams return and for extending the financial assistance beyond 31st March. The Commission has fixed the time limit for the first two procedures. The Central Government should send teams within 15 days of receipt of the report from the States giving a broad assessment of the damage caused by the calamity and assistance required and also that the Central Government should sanction the assistance and release it within 15 days of the return of Central team. These recommendations will go in a long way in removing unnecessary misunderstandings between the Central and the State Governments in managing relief works.

11.9 Non-Plan Capital Assistance

In their assessment of the non-plan capital gaps of the States, the Eighth Finance Commission has used the following methodology. The capital expenditure outside the revenue account including outlays required for administrative buildings are kept outside the non-plan capital expenditure. Similarly the net receipt from fresh market loans are treated as plan resources. Therefore, repayments of such loans have been ignored for the purpose of working out non-plan capital gaps. However, repayment of loans to the LIC and other financial institutions has been treated as non-plan liability and taken into account for working out the non-plan capital gaps. Third, while no recoveries of loans have been assumed from the State Electricity Boards, recoveries of other loans have been taken into account on a normative basis. Fourth, repayment of all outstanding Central loans including small savings loans, and overdraft loans are treated as non-plan liability for the purpose of working out non-plan capital gaps. Finally, transactions under cash balance investment account have been kept out of their assessment of non-plan capital gaps.

It may be observed here that the capital expenditure outside the revenue account is treated as plan expenditure and repayment of market loans are considered as plan disbursement. Only institutional finance is treated as non-plan capital liability. To this extent, the non-plan capital gaps of the State as assessed by the Eighth Finance Commission is an underestimation.

The Commission has recommended writing-off of loans made for non-productive relief and rehabilitation works and have rescheduled the repayment and payment of interest on other loans by consolidating them. Though this is a long-standing demand of economists, the Eighth Finance Commission has not provided much relief to the State Governments in terms of write-off of unproductive loans. The States will benefit only to the extent of Rs. 405.20 crores. But consolidation of loans and interest on them and rescheduling of their repayment will benefit the States to the tune of Rs. 1880.19 crores.

11.10 Revenue Potential under Articles 268 and 269

In regard to the scope for revising rates of taxes levied under Article 26, the Commission has even ruled out revision of rates on stamp duties on certain receipts, proxies, debentures, transfer of shares, insurance policies. The Commission has observed that stock exchange is in the formative stage of development in the country and no tax be levied on transactions in stock exchanges. Similarly it has not recommended taxes on the transaction in future markets on the lame excuse of administration problems.

They have ruled out the scope for levying tax under Article 269 on sale or purchase of newspapers on the ground that it will curb newspaper reading by pushing up prices. It is surprising that the Commission has ignored the recommendation of an NCAER study to levy tax on elite magazines and journals and their like. The Commission has, however, recommended a tax only on advertisement published in newspapers, by exempting the small newspapers particularly in regional languages. Though the Commission has held the view that there is scope for levying tax on railway passenger fares, no taxes has been levied so far as the present arrangement of grants in lieu of railway fares continues.

Thus the Eighth Finance Commission for the second time have ruled out the case for Central Government's initiative to exploit taxes mentioned and Articles 268 and 269 for the benefit of the State Governments. This would suggest that the State Governments should not depend upon the mercy of even the Finance Commission for forcing the Central Government to use the constitutional sources of revenue for the benefit of the States.

11.11 **Other Recommendations**

At the end, the Commission has made certain general recommendations (*a*) synchronise the operation of the recommendations of the Finance Commission with the operation of the Five-Year Plans, (*b*) create a strong permanent cell in the Union Ministry of Finance for monitoring the recommendations of the Commissions and also for preparing necessary data and other information required for the benefit of the next Commission. It has also recommended similar cells in the Finance Departments of the State Governments. Consequently, it has ruled out the need for a permanent Finance Commission. It has also recommended for giving enough power to the

Commission through the Members-Secretary to incur expenditure and make recruitment of the personnel required by the next Commissions.

Finally, the Eighth Finance Commission has produced largest number of dissenting notes and for the first time the Chairman has also coauthored a dissenting note. This was expected from the background of the members of the Commission. The Commission did not have an economist as a full time member. A member of the Planning Commission served on the Finance Commission on part-time basis and through him the Planning Commission's criterion for distributing a part of the Central assistance has been injected into the three factor formula for distributing the income-tax and union excise duty shares. Other members were mostly general or specialist bureaucrats. The fears expressed by some of us about the possible consequences of such a composition have come true. The only redeeming feature of this confusion is that the Central Government has accepted the majority of report ignoring the dissenting notes.

The Government of India has accepted most of the majority recommendations. But they have implemented the final report for four years from 1985-86 to 1988-89 and for 1984-85, interim recommendations are applied. This was partly the creation of the Commission itself who could not complete their work within the original period given. At least the Commission could have recommended a devolution of a sum equivalent to the difference between their final and interim recommendations. Failure to do it has created bitter controversy over the true intentions of the Central Government. Even now, the Central Government with a view to synchronising the period of the Seventh Plan with the period covered by the recommendations of the Eighth Finance Commission, may extend the recommendations of the Commission to 1989-90. But the State Governments may feel that the Ninth Finance Commission may take a different view and possibly increase the extent of financial ransfers to the States for 1989-90.

Index